GREEN GOLD

A TALE OF BOATS, GIRLS, CUNNING PLOTS AND RETRIBUTION

BOOK 4 IN THE FIREBIRD SERIES

IAN DOLBY

DISCLAIMER:

This is a work of fiction. While names, characters, businesses, events and incidents are the products of the author's warped imagination, places and locales are as correct as possible, but are used in an entirely fictitious manner. Some characters are a composite of several personalities the author has encountered in his travels across Australia as such richness of true-life character could not be ignored. However, any resemblance to actual persons, living or dead, or actual events is unintended, accidental and purely coincidental.

The opinions expressed by the various characters in this story are deemed appropriate for their role and should not be assumed to be those of the author. I ride bikes and embrace the right to freedom of the open road on two wheels for everybody.

Published in Australia by Silverbird Publishing

First published in Australia 2019
This edition published 2021
Copyright © Ian Dolby 2019
Cover design, typesetting: WorkingType (www.workingtype.com.au)

The right of Ian Dolby to be identified as the Author of the Work has been asserted in accordance with the Copyright, Designs and Patents Act 1988.

Dolby, Ian
Green Gold — Book 4 of the Firebird Series
ISBN: 978-0-6487179-1-1
pp442

ABOUT THE AUTHOR

I was born and raised on the Gold Coast, Queensland where my extended family always had boats. My love of sailing came from this background and developed through a series of racing catamarans that in turn led to the purchase of an old 47-foot wooden, engine-less, monohull yacht that had been built in Ireland in 1905 and had taken part in the Dunkirk evacuation. I lived on this boat at a marina in Rushcutters Bay, Sydney Harbour for several years and my engine-free adventures on this wonderful old boat may one day appear in writing.

The love of flying dragged me away from the boating scene, and after 38 years of glider, aeroplane and helicopter flying, I have retired to live in country New South Wales with my partner, who is my Chief Editor, and our two cats. While my writing has evolved from a part-time hobby to become a full-time occupation, it is no less enjoyable while the story lines keep coming to mind.

Thank you Jenny, for the brainstorming sessions
when the plot grew foggy

Thank you Wayne and Lyn for
your invaluable input as beta readers

Welcome to the Krazy kitten,
whose carefree antics are a joy to behold

And always The Bandit...never forgotten.

CONTENTS

PROLOGUE: ANNA'S STORY
18 MONTHS EARLIER

Anna walked quietly along the jungle path, sweating freely in the stifling humidity, while trying desperately to avoid the probing tendrils of vines and creepers intruding on the well-worn path.

She was a tall girl, just over 6 feet, but being big-framed, her wide swimmer's shoulders and long legs were in proportion, while her athletic training let her move easily and gracefully. Her long, white-blonde hair was pulled loosely back into a ponytail which at least kept the flies and other bugs off her back as it swished back and forth.

'Focus and think!' She told herself for the twentieth time. *'Or this is going pear-shaped very quickly.'*

She had lost touch with her tour group about half an hour ago and suspected she'd strayed over an invisible border into what was considered hostile Rebel territory. Unfortunately, she had no hope of identifying the correct path they had taken on their earlier outbound journey, so basically, she was lost!

The warnings she and the others had received only that morning rang in her ears as she tried to hurry quietly, fighting the rising sense of panic.

'No matter what, don't separate from the main group! Rebel groups frequent the disputed border area and although they generally won't hassle a large group of tourists, stragglers are considered fair game!'

'Stupid bitch!'

For the tenth time, she cursed herself for the impulse which had made her detour off the trail to photograph the moss and jungle covered stone ruins she'd spotted. But then she stopped sharply as she came upon a small clearing, sun-bright after the dim, diffused

1

green light of the jungle. Only about the size of a large domestic lounge room, she still paused to look carefully about and listen before darting quickly across.

Except that she didn't quite make it!

There was a painful grabbing sensation at her ankle, a moment of vertigo when she had a sudden, soaring impression of the ground falling away under her as she was swept high above the jungle floor, to dangle helplessly, suspended painfully by one ankle. She bounced up and down a few times as the tree branch bowed under her weight, coming to rest with her head three or four feet above the leaf-litter covering the jungle floor.

When her senses settled down, she realised she was dangling upside down, held by a thick rope of twisted vines which gripped her left ankle rather tightly. Already moderately painful, she suspected it would soon hurt even more, unless she could get down in a hurry.

As one part of her mind ran through possible escape plans, she realised the reason she couldn't see too well was her loose shirt hanging over her face and head! Awkwardly, she tugged it off, blinking in the bright light as it fell away.

It was about then, that the individuals who had apparently set the trap, silently appeared out of the surrounding bush and encircled their inverted captive.

She noted vaguely, there were seven or eight short, slim, brown men dressed in a motley collection of rags, but well armed with what looked like semi-automatic rifles and long-bladed machetes tucked in their waistbands.

She barely had time to register the details before the rope jerked a couple of times, then she found herself dumped unceremoniously in a tangle of limbs at the feet of a bigger man. She supposed he was the leader of the rag-tag bunch of what she supposed were the dreaded rebels. As her vision blurred with the shock of landing on her head, suddenly they didn't look quite so short! In rough pidgin English which was difficult to understand, he asked, 'You with tourist group? You look at old house?'

She nodded, 'Yes. I'm an Australian.'

He nodded impatiently then listened as one of his men trotted up and said something rapid-fire in the local dialect. He rattled off a string of instructions to his men, before turning back to Anna. 'We go now, must hurry. Other men come. We not go, we fight. You walk OK?'

Anna shook her head, 'No. My ankle is hurt. I can only walk slowly.'

He knelt and felt the foot which had been caught in the rope snare with surprisingly gentle hands, shaking his head when she yelped as he squeezed the swollen mass around her ankle. 'No good walk! Small damage only. Hurry. We carry. Must go now.'

Anna translated that to mean she only had a bad sprain and nothing was broken. She was appalled however, when two men produced a long bamboo pole, laid it beside her and trussed her to it with many windings of the plaited vine rope. They avoided her damaged ankle, but wrapped her legs from the knees down to just above her ankles and lashed her wrists together with a much softer rope made of woven grass. Another band of the soft rope was passed several times around her waist and up to the pole.

Any protests she made were either ignored or the leader made the universal silence gesture with the back of his hand drawn across his throat. It took only minutes before they were ready and four of the men picked up the pole, two at each end, leaving her suspended beneath it. It was when they set off at an economical trotting pace along another well-used narrow track, she realised she was still topless, her rather full, but firm breasts standing up on display.

Despite her trussed condition, the ride wasn't too bad as the bamboo pole was quite flexible and absorbed most of the jolts, although her legs and wrists were going numb. The men trotted in single file on the narrow track and seemed tireless, but after about thirty minutes, the four carrying her changed over, the changeover being made literally on the run. Another twenty minutes passed, before they entered a clearing where a small native village stood.

It consisted of several shabby-looking woven grass huts with bamboo poles crudely placed to keep them from falling over, scattered around the bare clearing.

A few ragged children chased some scrawny chickens around the cleared dirt area between the huts as Anna was dumped unceremoniously in front of what at a stretch could be called the main hut, since it was a little bit longer than the others. Although she hadn't been touched by any of the men, she was uncomfortable with the way they were looking at her bare upper body and her brief shorts.

A tall man of mixed ancestry finally came out of the main hut and conferred briefly with the leader of the patrol that had grabbed her. There was much discussion, before she was untied from the pole, but with her wrists and ankles still tied, she was pushed into a tiny hut, given a bottle of dirty water and left alone to contemplate her fate.

Later that day, a filthy bowl of sticky rice was dumped on the floor. To eat it, she had no choice but to kneel in front of it, scooping bits up with her bound hands. The hut door was left open and several men gathered around to point and laugh at her, until chased away by the main man. After darkness fell, the drinking started and she expected the worst was about to happen and was almost relieved when the boss staggered over to her prison, unbuttoning his fly as he approached.

She'd been sitting against one of the bamboo support poles, her shorts and legs filthy from the bare dirt floor, so when he came in and closed the door, she drew her legs up in an automatic defensive posture, but he just grabbed her sore foot and painfully pulled her legs out straight.

There was plenty of firelight shining through the gaps in the rotten woven matting which comprised the walls, as he looked her over, swaying drunkenly on his feet. He then grunted something and pulled a knife from his waist, carelessly slicing through his pant's waistband at the same time and dropping them around his ankles. He looked puzzled for a few moments, then shuffled forward, bent over and cut the grass ropes that bound her ankles. The problem came when he stood up too quickly and his alcohol-fogged brain couldn't keep up with the motion and pitched him over backwards. With his feet tangled in his pants, he landed hard, banging his head on the packed dirt floor and driving all the air out of his lungs.

He let out a loud grunt then a series of shallow gasps as he vainly tried to draw air into his lungs, managing to sound like he was getting on with business. If one were drunk enough, that is, which seemed to be the case as several of his men cheered loudly, apparently to encourage him to greater efforts. Anna thought that she'd better chuck in a few screams and protests to add to the impression of rape in progress.

That must have worked since there was a general round of laughter following each one she uttered. About then, the leader started to make noises like he might be coming around, so Anna gritted her teeth and kicked him hard in the head with her expensive hiking boots. He grunted so she did it again, then several more times, a lot harder. When he stopped grunting she scooped up the fallen knife, and awkwardly cut the ropes on her wrists. Although she didn't have a shirt, that wasn't going to stop her. She could have taken the smelly rag her would-be rapist was wearing, but felt cleaner without having to touch him.

Finding the largest gap in the woven wall, she peered through to see the rebels sitting around the fire, passing a bottle in endless circles while calling out toward her prison hut as if asking when it was going to be their turn.

'*That's never going to happen, you diseased pricks!*' she thought to herself as she moved around the hut peering through more gaps to see if there was a guard of any description, but they were all either passed out or well on the way to being so. She was reluctant to touch the barely breathing rebel, but thought she should check him for anything useful for her to make good her escape, but there was nothing apart from the knife, which was at least razor-sharp.

It was the work of moments to slice down through the semi-rotted matting and make a gap big enough to slip through. Her bare chest copped a fair bit of scraping on the way through, but she hardly noticed. There was just one hut between her and the jungle and no one in sight, so keeping the prison hut between her and the fire, she calmly walked past the last hut. Skirting the ragged edge of the jungle within a few paces she came to a narrow trail that looked well-used, and followed it.

Within moments, the dense jungle swallowed her and the faint trace of firelight disappeared. Another three paces and she walked into a bush, which forced the realisation that she really wasn't going to make much of an escape that night and the idea of being so close to the camp was terrifying. Especially when the rebels found their beloved leader was probably brain dead!

She'd just sunk to the floor of the trail in despair when a sweaty hand was silently clapped over her mouth, and a sinewy arm clamped her upper body tightly back against a hard-muscled chest, preventing any movement. She did manage one kick backwards, connecting with the man's shin and drawing a sharp hiss of pain. A heavily accented voice whispered in English, 'Stop, please Missy! We try to help. No noise, please.'

Anna couldn't do much more anyway, so she relaxed and nodded against the clamping hand, which was cautiously withdrawn. 'OK. I'll behave,' she whispered, 'who are you?'

'No talk, you follow. Hold this.' The same sweaty hand passed her a length of the ubiquitous plaited grass rope, then a moment later, it tugged slightly to the left and she obediently followed, stumbling slightly until her feet found the more level track again. Then it was just a case of following the direction of the rope. Several times it went slack and she quickly learned; it meant bad guys were close and to take just one step sideways off the trail. She didn't realise just how close they were until a foot stepped on her boot, cursing softly as it skidded off and the owner regained his balance and continued down the trail.

After what seemed an interminable time groping through the

blackness, the guide rope bore left sharply and she panicked for a moment until she found the trail centre again, reasoning they must have turned off the main trail. If it meant they were leaving the rebel troops behind, she was very happy. A short time later, she abruptly stumbled out of the all-enveloping jungle onto a narrow, sandy beach with an almost glassy-calm sea lapping quietly at its edges. Starlight gave enough illumination to see a long, open boat pulled up on the shore, a modern outboard motor clamped to the stern.

She also saw that her rescuers were more dark-skinned natives, but these were dressed rather incongruously in tidy jeans or neat shorts and T-shirts with fancy logos front and back. They wore what looked like designer-brand joggers on their feet and all wore new baseball caps.

They stopped as a tall, handsome Eurasian man returned from up the beach, allowing Anna time to get her bearings. He held out his hand to her, shook it with a firm grasp. One of the other men who obviously had a small amount of English said, 'Him Gilbert. No can speak, but hear good.'

'Ahh...I'm Anna and thanks for the rescue. I had just run out of ideas when you found me.'

Gilbert nodded and Anna's mind was spun out by this additional piece of strangeness. The short native man spoke again, 'In boat please Missy. Go to home island away from bad pirate mens.'

Now she could see, Anna climbed easily into the boat and the others in the squad followed. Happily, the engine which looked nearly new, started first try and ran quietly and smoothly as they motored at a steady speed less than two kilometres to another island which looked depressingly similar to the one she'd escaped from.

'King meet you,' volunteered her interpreter.

'King who? And what's he king of?'

'King Mikhail. You see, very soon.' was the enigmatic reply.

'Any chance of getting a shirt?'

The man shook his head. 'No shirt.' He pointed, 'no pants either. King want you that way.'

Anna started to bristle at that piece of information. 'I certainly will not take anything else off! He can't order me around!'

The little man shook his head, then nodded past her shoulder, and a set of immensely strong arms pinned her arms by her side as another little brown man quickly bound her ankles together again, then her wrists suffered the same fate.

Anna started sounding off like a ship's siren, so a pad was slapped over her mouth and bound with a strip of grass cloth.

'King is King, 'an can do anyt'ing! King good to my peoples. Missy no say 'no' to King! Missy go back to pirates if no agree.'

Anna could only glare at him in silence. About five minutes later the boat turned into a small bay, really not much more than just a gap between two rocky arms that thrust out into the calm sea, before it pulled into a narrow, slowly flowing creek, virtually concealed by tightly clustered palm trees growing right to the water's edge. In the dimness, the village appeared to be equally well concealed by the dense, uncleared growth of palm trees that extended a long way back from the beach. The sight of the clear water, with the sandy bottom visible even in just starlight was cool and inviting, and set up a raging thirst that stuck her tongue to the roof of her mouth. Her ankles were numb and she dreaded the agony of returning circulation when finally cut free.

She wasn't given any chance to run as, despite her size, she was picked up easily by Gilbert and carted to a bizarre structure that couldn't have looked more out of place.

It was a large, garish tent, apparently made of panels of silk of many different colours and designs, but with a far more practical, heavy vinyl roof, coloured in some sort of a camouflage pattern. A kerosene lamp hung over the entrance and a soft warm glow from within what looked like a small circus tent, suggested more were inside.

Gilbert gently placed her on a large, ornate carpet laid on the soft, white sand at the entrance to the tent and went inside, leaving her on her back with two of her former rescuers watching her.

There was nobody else wandering around and she supposed as was normal practice, the locals rose with the sun and went to bed when it set.

After a while, there was a command issued from inside the tent and two different guards came out to stand over her prone form. One carried a long, thin filleting knife with a slightly curved blade. Anna tensed up when she saw it, so the man smiled awkwardly as he bent down and carefully and gently slipped one finger into the leg of her shorts, before he slowly ran the edge of the razor-sharp blade up to her waistband, the heavy denim material peeling back like he was cutting wet newspaper. He gave her another apologetic smile then repeated the action on the other leg, then almost delicately laid the remains of her shorts out from either side and down from her crutch.

The action was repeated on her pink panties until she lay bare. At that point, the rope around her ankles was cut after one of the guards tied a rope to her bound wrists first. He then helped her upright and led her into the house-tent. The first room was a small antechamber with a sand floor covered with exotic, colourful rugs.

They passed through a silk curtain into a larger space dominated by a long, solid-wood table, the sand floor completely covered by more ornate rugs in a bewildering display of colours and patterns. Several elaborately carved chairs were fitted into the remaining space.

In one of these sat a large, overweight white man, sweating profusely and clad in a bright red silk caftan, dotted with beautifully embroidered yellow flowers. At her appearance, he clapped his hands in pleasure and spoke to Anna in excellent, but slightly accented English, in a soft, melodious voice.

'Welcome to my humble abode, my dear. I do hope your journey was not too distressing or uncomfortable, but time was of the essence. And I apologise in advance for the necessity to have you naked, but the reason will be revealed...ha, ha, very shortly.'

Anna tried to grunt through the gag, but the guard at her side growled something she didn't understand, although she got the intention!

'Please let me finish before you berate my men and me for your abduction. You had wandered into dangerous territory and I must presume you were attached to that group of Australian archaeological students.'

Anna nodded slightly, still held in the grip of her guard.

'Good. Now, the trap that caught you was set by a group of rebels who live in the surrounding hills. Although I sometimes trade with them, they are not very civilized and it was one of their hunting parties who found you.

The last white woman who fell into their hands was made available to all the males in the camp. They serviced her repeatedly, day and night, for three days. After that, she was deemed to be of no further use and her head was delivered to her friends who were still looking for her. Her body was fed to their pigs so there were no remains.'

Anna looked horrified at this and the man indicated her guard could remove her gag. She spoke in a trembling voice.

'I suppose I should say thank you for saving me, but where are we, who are you, why am I still tied up, why am I naked and what do you want with me?'

The man looked at her for a long moment.

'All these questions, and good ones too! My name is Mikhail. Where we are will remain secret for now, as I don't want you running away until I've had time to assess your usefulness to my plans.'

'So I'm still a captive!' she said bitterly.

He shrugged and his whole body wobbled.

'At this time and for the moment? Yes!' he replied. 'Depending on your answers to my questions and how you behave, I may have something to show you; a demonstration if you like, which could make us both a lot of money. Tell me, what is your job in Australia?'

'I'm an Account Manager with a small advertising agency. The archaeology thing is just my hobby.' Anna replied, wondering what the hell that had to do with being kidnapped in the jungle.

Mikhail clapped his hands together. 'Excellent! This could be very, very good! But for now, I forget my manners. You are dirty, uncomfortable and probably need to relieve yourself. My man Gilbert, will show you the bathroom and find you some clean clothes.'

Anna hadn't wanted to admit it, but her bladder was so full, she was about to pee where she stood and she did feel very dirty.

He lifted his voice slightly. 'Gilbert. Would you oblige me and look after our guest?'

A few moments later, a curtain parted behind him and Gilbert stepped through.

'Ah, there you are,' Mikhail said, 'and what is your full name, my dear?'

'Anna Copeland.' Anna supplied.

'Miss Copeland,' Mikhail said smoothly, 'you've already met Gilbert, however I must add that while he is unfortunately a mute, he is highly intelligent and fluent in six languages.'

'Gilbert, please show her the bathroom and find some clean clothes. And do keep an eye on her for the moment until we've talked further.'

Gilbert nodded, a gleam in his eye as he motioned to Anna to follow him. The guards were dismissed as Anna shuffled past Mikhail and followed Gilbert.

He led the way along a hallway with fabric walls and stepped up into a small room built of bamboo like a cage. The poles were arranged vertically with arm-width gaps between each that let in light and air, that is, if it were daylight outside. The floor was built the same, but the poles were close together.

A hole-in-the-floor toilet was to one side, with the unusual addition of two parallel pieces of bamboo, mounted above the floor either side of the hole to provide a rudimentary seat. Above head-height. a bamboo pole protruded into the room from the outside wall with a tapered wooden plug in the end of it apparently a crude shower. The various gaps in the floor provided natural drainage.

As Anna took in the facilities, Gilbert bent and untied her ankle restraints, then removed her wrist bindings.

'Thank you,' she said.

He nodded and made a soft grunt.

'So you trust me now, do you?'

Gilbert smiled and shook his head. Anna had noticed that there was no door or curtain.

'Come on! I need a bit of privacy.'

Gilbert just smiled again, pointing first to his chest and then to the floor where he was standing.

'Terrific!' Anna muttered and shrugged. At this stage, she couldn't really care less who watched what. Her bladder was busting, so she squatted over the toilet hole and couldn't help a groan of relief.

She felt Gilbert's eyes on her, but for some reason, didn't feel threatened or bothered.

Finally finished, she stood and wiped herself on some sort of soft leaf from a box hung on the wall.

Stepping over to the shower outlet she noticed soap, shampoo and clean towels were laid out on a bench. Removing the wooden plug released a stream of water that was gloriously clean, cool and contained tiny bubbles which made it strangely invigorating. She drank deeply as she scrubbed herself repeatedly with the fragrant soap and shampooed her ratty, tangled hair. The thought crossed her mind that the tiny bubbles in the water made it look like fine champagne, which might explain the lovely feeling of it sliding across her skin.

'I must be tired,' she berated herself, *'so focus and maybe you can get away!'*

She ignored Gilbert's watchful gaze and concentrated on the delightful feeling she got from drinking the water which seemed to have a better effect on her than champagne.

'It can't be poisonous, but it's giving me a lovely feeling and all my aches and pains have just washed away! So it's not only good outside, but inside as well. I really need to find out more about this place!'

Gilbert made no move to hurry her along and although she'd never been an exhibitionist, she felt curiously at ease with his presence, to the extent she made no real effort to be modest while washing herself.

When she'd finished and had drunk some more of the highly invigorating water, she plugged the flow and dried herself under Gilbert's impassive gaze. When done, he handed her a clean, but well-worn pair of shorts. She wasn't bothered by the lack of undergarments.

'Can I have a shirt, please?' she asked.

He shook his head as he tied her wrists across each other again with the soft cotton rope and led her back to the living room where Mikhail waited.

Gilbert indicated that she should sit on one of the wood chairs in front of Mikhail's.

'How do you feel now, my dear,' he inquired.

'Much more comfortable, thank you,' she replied, holding her bound hands up, 'but I'm still restrained and half-naked.'

He chuckled, then made a sign to Gilbert who turned to a chest of drawers and removed an object and held it out to show Anna.

It was a small green glass cosmetic jar of about 1.5oz or 45 ml capacity, with a plain plastic screw top that Gilbert removed before passing the jar to her. Anna grasped it awkwardly in one hand and peered inside. It held a semi-translucent, pale green gel, looking like Aloe-Vera extract, and which gave off a strong, leafy odour which was strangely pleasant.

'Hold it to your nose and breathe deeply, please Anna,' Mikhail asked quietly.

Anna did as asked and suddenly felt light-headed for a few moments, which she put down to the events of the morning.

'Do that again,' Mikhail instructed. Anna shrugged, but

complied and again felt pleasantly lightheaded for a few moments.

'Do you find that pleasant?' Mikhail asked.

'Yeah! It's not too bad at all,' Anna cautiously replied. 'It's a strong smell and just made me feel light-headed for a few moments, but I am very tired. So, what is it?'

'It's an extract of local herbs, and is based on a recipe for a paste the local medicine man has been using for hundreds of years,' he replied. 'It has some interesting properties.'

'Oh yeah! What?' Anna asked, cynically.

'There are several, in fact, but there is one I would prefer you to experience directly. If you will just hold still, Gilbert is going to rub some behind your ears where it will be rapidly absorbed through your skin. I guarantee it is not toxic, nor harmful in any way.'

Anna felt nervous as Gilbert took the jar, scooped a small amount out on his fingertip and with a gentle touch, he dabbed some behind each ear, then carefully rubbed it in.

'Now what?' asked Anna.

'Just wait a few more minutes and tell me what you feel,' Mikhail instructed.

At first Anna noticed nothing, except for the scent of the natural perfume which seemed to be growing stronger than before. Then she felt the skin where it was rubbed in becoming warm and tingly. The tingling sensation spread slowly down her neck to her shoulders. It felt pleasant and she said so.

'Good, good!' said Mikhail, rubbing his hands together and beaming.

A further minute or two later, she felt even better, quite euphoric even, as well as somewhat warm all over. With a start, she realised, despite the weird circumstances, the tingling was spreading all the way down her body and she felt quite aroused.

She didn't report *that* to Mikhail, but was betrayed by her bare nipples, which had become swollen.

'And how do you feel now, my dear,' he asked, smiling at her obvious reaction.

'Really good!' Anna replied, cheerfully, 'I feel warm and tingly all over.'

'Excellent!' he replied. 'This is sort of the first stage of this particular effect. To move on to the second stage, would you care to rub a small amount of the gel onto each your breasts; just around the nipples will do nicely, but perhaps not on them?'

It was a most curious request and Anna looked at him for a moment as though she might refuse, but then just shrugged. The way she felt, it seemed a reasonable request, particularly as it meant Gilbert had to untie her wrists.

Her breasts were medium-sized, but full and up-tilted, the nipples still swollen. She spread some gel as he suggested and rubbed it in. The pale green colour disappeared quickly, leaving no trace on the surface.

'That feels nice,' Anna said, moments later, looking carefully down at her breasts with a goofy grin on her face, 'still warm and even more tingly!'

Then moments later, 'Wow! Like really good!'

In fact, not only was she feeling really good, but she could feel she was becoming more aroused.

'Bloody hell!' she thought to herself. 'What is this stuff? Some sort of local aphrodisiac? It's stunningly effective! I feel like grabbing the nearest halfway decent guy and pulling him on!'

She could see Mikhail and Gilbert watching her reactions closely.

'This is very powerful stuff!' she said, having trouble getting her tongue properly around the words, as her head had started buzzing as though she were slightly drunk. 'What is it? It can't just be herbs!'

Mikhail ignored her question as he purred, 'Excellent! Now, how do you feel about taking your pants off?'

Anna looked down, and seemed surprised to see that she was wearing any then shrugged, 'Yeah, sure!' Anna said. 'It's really hot anyway. Is boyfriend here going to take his off as well? He's already watched me pee and take a shower and I'd like to see what he's got.'

'He would be happy to do that,' Mikhail replied, 'but perhaps not really necessary at the moment!' He looked like he'd been using the stuff himself since beads of sweat were popping out over his gleaming bald head.

'Oh well, if he won't, then I will." said Anna, standing, before reaching down to fumble with her shorts, which moments later dropped to the ground leaving her naked again.

'Thank you my dear. If you would just remain standing by your chair for a moment, I think it fair to say your actions have just demonstrated some of the effects of the gel I have named 'Green Gold', but there is yet another property which makes this substance valuable.'

'What would that be?' Anna mumbled distractedly, rubbing both hands up and down her bare thighs as if scratching an itch.

'Do you still have any bruises left over from your encounter with the pirates?' Mikhail asked, scanning her tall, finely-muscled body yet again.

Anna thought a moment, 'Not as many as I had,' she reported, 'and that's another thing I wanted to ask you about. What's with the water? When I started my shower, I was covered in bruises and was sore and aching all over. Between that bloody rope trap and being slung under a pole like something out of a cartoon, had knocked me about. But then within minutes of washing in the water and drinking a lot of it, I felt so much better it was amazing!'

'Ah...yes, the water. I can't claim to have helped create that since it's always been here, but that particular spring flows over an odd set of rocks and mineral deposits up in the hills behind this village and from the limited analysis I've had done, it contains some type of magnesium compound, among many other minerals. The Islanders have known for generations it has extremely beneficial effects on the human system, and they actually worship it for its health-enhancing properties. There are some stories about age-slowing properties, but that has been difficult to verify as the locals are reluctant to talk about their divine gift and it's quite impossible to find out anyone's age.

But I was asking you about a bruise which was still sore. I can't readily see one and I have been looking.'

She surprised herself by giggling, 'I know you're been studying me because I could almost feel your stare! But yes, there is a bruise on my bum where I kept hitting exposed tree roots when they carried me. I don't know if it's faded yet, but it's still sore.'

'Good! For my final demonstration, I'd like you to let Gilbert rub some of the gel on the sore parts, if you'd just tell him where.'

So, Anna happily indicated the sore bits on her bum and Gilbert tenderly rubbed a small portion of the gel into each spot. There was the now familiar feeling of pleasure and a tingling sensation that radiated out from the spot where it was applied, but the twist was that the pain faded within seconds, yet the site wasn't left numb like with normal pain blockers.

'Fantastic!' she exclaimed. 'So that's the other thing that this stuff does?'

He nodded. 'The point of my demonstrations of the gel's properties are to prove that as an aphrodisiac, it is easily capable of suppressing your normal female inhibitions sufficiently so you were quite happy to take your pants off and walk around naked in front of two strange men, without being otherwise coerced.

The other part of its almost magical properties is the powerful analgesic effect. It has equally powerful healing properties, but they cannot be easily demonstrated in the short term.'

Anna was both highly impressed by the properties of the gel and intrigued as to what sort of proposition the fat Mikhail might have to put to her.

'OK Mikhail, let's assume that I'm highly impressed by your unorthodox demonstrations but why don't we cut to the bottom line. Where do I come in and why are you so pleased with my background?'

He looked appraisingly at her again, although it was more like someone considering what price she'd fetch on the open market, rather than a potential rapist.

17

'I've been selling small batches of the gel into China as both an aphrodisiac and for pain relief to traditional medical practitioners, but as the quantities were limited, the prices have been very high, which in turn restricts the market. For instance, the small jar Gilbert has been using on you holds just 45 millilitres, yet sells for US$500 in Shanghai, so the return on the product is excellent. As you can imagine, production costs are minimal and the cost of shipping small batches is low. Therefore, the profit margin is huge although the overall income isn't great because of the small quantities involved. I retain a percentage and use the remainder to improve the Islander's quality of life, trying not to spoil them in the process.'

'You will see tomorrow they are a happy, unspoiled people, still living as their ancestors did, but with schooling and much better health care. No TV satellite dishes for this island! Also, I don't play missionary by messing with their minds and traditional beliefs in any way.' He chuckled, setting up dangerous-looking waves and jiggles of fat at several levels throughout his huge body.

'Much of the island is covered in the bush which supplies the leaves as raw material for the gel, so there is no shortage of it. We just need to get the new production line, Gilbert and I have designed, working properly. When we achieve that, production will increase five or six times over what it is now.'

Anna shivered and decided to pull her shorts up. 'Could I have a shirt of some sort please? I'm feeling a bit cool.'

'Of course, my dear. Now that both my demonstrations are over, I expect the arousal effects of the gel are diminishing slightly, although they will persist for many hours to come. However, I think you'll find that the aches and pains will stay away as the water contributes as well. Gilbert, please fetch the lady a shirt.'

He nodded, went through a curtained doorway and returned moments later with a Western-style, button-up shirt made from a soft fabric with an attractive pattern in beautiful shades of blue and grey.

She slipped it on, marvelling at the silky soft feel of the super-fine fabric and loving the pattern and colours. 'This is a terrific shirt, it feels like silk!' she told Mikhail. 'I have a friend with a clothing store in Double Bay who could sell heaps of these.'

'Good, very good! The fabric is also a local speciality and is made partly from the same bush that produces the leaves and from bamboo. I do believe that as this is working out so well, the time is correct to reveal the plan I have to offer you. If you accept my idea, it will mean a chance for you to return to civilisation, as well as earn a lot of money. Unfortunately, refusal will probably mean return to the pirates who will not treat you so well.'

'I certainly wouldn't like that option,' she said, 'but I have a feeling there's going to be a price I've got to pay sooner or later.'

Mikhail clapped his chubby little paws with glee, 'Oh how precious! Beautiful and smart! This is wonderful Gilbert, is it not?'

Standing to one side, Gilbert gave an enigmatic smile, leading Anna to think that Gilbert wasn't as dumb as he tried to act and making her feel uneasy.

Mikhail ignored her as he opened a large writing pad and scribbled away making notes.

'Look. Don't worry about any propositions. Just let me go and I'll tell my friends I got lost, the locals found me and looked after me.'

He distractedly waved her protest aside, 'No, no. Not just yet. Before you think about running away, which is something we cannot allow, I need to lay out my proposal. But first, I believe it is time for some refreshments.'

He called out in what she took to be the native tongue and within a minute or two, a small, slim girl, wearing a beautifully-patterned long skirt but no top, appeared through a beaded curtain with a tray holding steaming mugs of a fragrant tea and a platter of succulent fruit. She was pretty, had small breasts, a lovely smile and what looked like in the dim light, a dusky colouring.

'Please sit and have some tea and fruit,' he invited.

Anna sat and helped herself to the fruit and tea and waited to hear what Mikhail had to say.

19

'I needed you to experience first-hand the powerful effect this substance has on anyone's normal inhibitions. For a hundred years or more, the locals have been producing this stuff to trade with other tribes for food and goods they need, but I want to market it to Western society in decent quantities. The small amount I've been selling to Oriental society can be expanded considerably.'

'So? What's this got to do with me?'

'Quite simply, now you know what it can do, you will be ideal as my traveling salesman and distribution outlet. You see, for various reasons, I'm unable to travel to other countries. Heh, heh, heh!'

'Gee, that's surprising. But really, you've got to be kidding, Mikhail! Me work for you?'

'Now, now my dear. Sarcasm doesn't become you. But you would, in fact, be working for yourself, since we would be partners. I look after the manufacturing and supply, while you put your marketing skills to more profitable use than working for somebody else.

Despite selling the gel for US$500 up to now, I have decided under the new arrangement, one jar should sell for AU$500. For every jar you sell, you keep $200, which means that $300 gets returned to me. I think you will agree that I am being most generous, although you will have the expense of import duty and distribution.'

Anna just nodded.

'I already have a bank account set up in Port Vila, Vanuatu, where there is no income tax and total customer confidentiality.'

Anna squirmed into a more comfortable position on the hard chair as her mind raced. Although she was desperate for a chance to get away, she was surprised she was genuinely considering the deal!

'If I agree, how would it work?'

Mikhail clapped his hands in delight. 'I knew that you were the right one!'

'Don't get too carried away, Mikhail. I haven't agreed yet.'

'OK then, it will be like this. The gel will be packaged in the same small glass jars you see here, labelled as liniment. It will have a list of natural ingredients and is therefore quite legal for import and doesn't need approval from the Australian authorities to sell. You will take a supply of liniment with you, and perhaps use one jar to offer free trials. I think you'll agree that once your customers experience the potent effects of the substance, little salesmanship will be required!'

Against her instincts, she found herself sharing a conspiratorial grin.

'Yes, I think that would be fairly safe to assume.'

'So when you make sales, you transfer my share to the account in Port Vila and enjoy your share. I'll send fresh supplies by airmail as required. Just fax or email your requirements to my Singapore contact.'

Anna looked thoughtful for a moment. 'But I still don't understand why it has to be me? Why can't you get someone else to do this? Maybe your Singapore contact, for instance.'

He sighed theatrically, 'Because, dear lady, you are the perfect person to vouch personally for the performance of this liniment or gel if you want to call it something different. And,' he said, waving his hands around in a sweeping gesture, 'there aren't too many Caucasian females passing through here to choose from!'

As a marketing person, you should understand when I say an attractive, well-spoken, intelligent young lady vouching for the aphrodisiac effects, along with its powerful medicinal properties, makes for a terribly potent salesperson! So much better than a male trying to say the same thing. He'd just be regarded as a pervert by most potential customers.'

'So that's it? No other strings?'

Mikhail smiled. 'Just the one. To keep an eye on things at first and help you, Gilbert will travel with you. I would be obliged if you can accommodate him for the duration, perhaps a couple of months. He will, of course, have money to pay his way and he will be happy to be your manservant.'

She shook her head. 'Why would he do that Mikhail? Come on!

I've been conned by experts and this smells of a con with hidden strings!'

He shook his head. 'You're reading too much into this, Anna,' he protested gently. 'Gilbert is being mentally stifled here on the island and needs to get out into Western society where his fertile mind can be stimulated. Society is also a place where it is difficult for him to go alone, being mute. But as your manservant, he will have the perfect introduction and exposure to people who can assess and hopefully accept him in his own right without the stigma of being a mute. Under such conditions he will blossom and be a perfect companion to you and a marvellous assistant in the growth of the business.'

Anna was silent a moment. 'I can't see how that's going to work out! How can I turn up at Immigration with Gilbert in tow? He'll need a visa and passport. And even acting as my manservant, how is he going to fit in to civilisation in a big city like Sydney?'

Mikhail chuckled. 'Don't worry, my dear. Gilbert has all the paperwork required and already has briefly visited big cities before. I think you'll find he can clean up quite well! He just needs a mentor and some support.'

Anna couldn't think of any more objections for the moment, so she said, 'I need to consider this very carefully. It's really been a bit too much to take in all at once, so let me think about it for a few days.'

Mikhail beamed, 'Of course, my dear. Please forgive me. I have pushed you much too hard straight after your rather arduous rescue. I apologise and can only say I have been so excited to find someone who could help both my business and Gilbert. But please accept my hospitality and think my proposition over carefully. Ask anything you want to know. Nothing will be kept hidden from you! And tomorrow when you are more rested, I will have you escorted around the village to see the rather basic production facilities for yourself. Gilbert will look after you.'

As an end to their discussion, Mikhail said, 'You are now free to roam the camp, but I would caution you against straying into the jungle alone. Remember the rebels visit this island sometimes and if you stray away from the protection of the camp, you could be seen as an easy target again. I will however, send a message to your associates that you are safe and resting after your ordeal. Unfortunately, you will inform them, you will be staying here a while longer, so they should proceed back to their homes without you.

Gilbert will now show you to your sleeping space. Regrettably, we have no suitable underclothes, so you will have to do without.'

Gilbert showed her a small, spartan cubicle near the bathroom, with a double-sized bed of bamboo slats covered with a foam mattress which proved comfortable. He was deferential and solicitous, and she found his change of attitude odd, but once again, strangely comforting. Left alone, she used the facilities next door, realised she was quite exhausted from the day's activities and excitements, as well as the after-effects of the stimulating green paste, and was asleep ten seconds after her head hit the pillow.

DAY TWO

She slept as though dead and wasn't aware of the shadowy figure who soundlessly appeared in her doorway at odd intervals throughout the night, observed her for a few moments, then faded away again.

Shortly after dawn, she woke to the sound of two birds trying out for a song contest, or that's what it seemed like, so she lay in the cool comfort of the early morning air, savouring the feel of her ache-free body which should have been wracked with pain and muscle cramps. She also used the time to review all that Mikhail had presented to her the previous night, and although tempted to accept his deal, she decided to make her escape at the earliest opportunity.

It wasn't long before bladder pressure made a visit to the bathroom a necessity so without bothering to dress, she used the toilet, then took another reviving shower in the champagne-bubbling water. Tiredness slipped from her like the soap suds which ran down through the gaps in the floor. She also found it strangely liberating to be showering in a small room where the gaps between the bamboo poles forming the walls were wide enough that she could slip her hands through and could see locals walking past outside, although they paid little attention to the naked white girl in the bamboo cage.

Refreshed, she had just dressed, when the small girl who'd served the tea and fruit the night before appeared, made a small bow, then said, 'Good Morning Missy. I am Mai-ling. May I bring you some breakfast?'

She was dressed the same as last night with a colourful wrap tied around her slim waist and nothing else, her small, bare breasts bobbing delightfully as she moved, making Anna realise she must still be affected by the green gel. She couldn't remember being aroused by the sight of another girl's bare breasts, before this.

As Mai-ling went to organise some food, Anna finished dressing, glad that her stout and comfortable walking boots and socks were intact, cleaned and sitting beside her bed.

After a breakfast of more fresh fruit and a strange but tasty nut, she decided to take Mikhail at his word and wandered out into the village which was like a small military base with some armed men moving about. Gilbert appeared silently and accompanied her, letting Anna go where she wanted, and she soon discovered the long, open-sided hut which was the production facility for the green paste, with long tables covered in a variety of bushes and branches being stripped of their leaves by several slim, native girls. They were dressed like Mai-ling with a short wrap of coloured cloth around their waists, the rest of their bodies bare and gleaming with sweat in the oppressive heat.

They smiled and giggled at Anna as their slim hands rapidly stripped the leaves, which were fed into large pots heated by small fires, at the other end of the hut.

A thick, green soup steamed gently in the pots, stirred by a wizened old man with grey, wispy hair and beard, the now-familiar pungent aroma rising from the surface, giving Anna another surge of the light-headedness she'd felt the night before, along with more of the same delightful tingles running through her body. The old man grinned toothlessly at her as he leaned on his long wood pole and chattered something unintelligible in the local dialect.

She idly wondered how he remained unaffected by the brew, but maybe that was why an old man was in charge of the brew pot!

Feeling tired, Anna found her room again and slept for a while, lulled to sleep by the musical lilt of the native voices outside the thin, fabric walls.

When she awoke, it was late afternoon and she felt hot and sticky. Venturing outside, she wandered down to the small, flowing creek where the water looked cool and inviting.

She walked along the banks away from the village, but noticed Gilbert was keeping her silent company at a distance. No longer intimidated by his presence, she waved him closer and pointing to the water and herself, made swimming motions.

Gilbert nodded and smiled and as he sat under a tree to keep watch, she undressed and slid quietly into the cool water. It was refreshing and washed the sweat off.

Not wanting to push her luck, she didn't stay long. Leaving the water, she used her hands to brush most of the water off her body before dressing. Gilbert watched her carefully throughout, before escorting her back to the camp as darkness fell.

Later, after a tasty meal and a surprisingly intellectual discussion with Mikhail about the economics of trade, she retired and slept deeply until awakened at dawn by a pretty, half-naked house girl with a mug of steaming tea.

She was allowed to stay in bed and appreciated the rest.

Getting up around midday with a rumbling stomach, she found a plate of chopped fresh fruit on the main table. As she started eating, the same house girl silently appeared and asked in broken

English if she wanted more tea. It was quickly produced, but Anna refrained from questioning her.

She spent the rest of the day wandering the camp, noting with amusement, that the men all treated her with respect and she got the impression it wasn't just due to Gilbert's occasional, distant presence.

That evening, after an excellent dinner of spicy pork, savoury rice and more intellectual discussion, Mikhail retired early. Anna and Gilbert sat around the table drinking tea as the house girl cleared up around them. She was tiny and pretty, still just wearing a short sarong with gaping sides wrapped around her impossibly small waist. Anna could see she was naked under it. Her tiny breasts were perfectly formed and she flirted with Gilbert, sliding her breasts against him as often as possible and in return he gave her many pats and caresses to her little bum.

'Is she your girlfriend?' Anna asked, after observing this by-play.

He shook his head, perhaps looking a little disappointed.

'Perhaps she's too small for you?' Anna said with a cheeky grin.

Gilbert nodded and grunted, but that was the end of any worthwhile discussion with Gilbert that evening.

As Mai-ling served her breakfast the next morning, she asked Anna if she'd enjoyed the swim yesterday.

'Oh yes! It was beautiful. That water is so invigorating!'

'Yes, it is special and I'm glad you enjoy it so much,' said Mai-ling, 'perhaps I can come swimming with you later this morning when I have finished my housework?'

Anna smiled. 'Sure. That'd be fun. Let me know when you're free.'

She smiled, bobbed her head and left.

Mid-morning, Mai-Ling returned and produced a piece of the impossibly soft, colourful cloth for Anna which turned out to be a short wrap, the same as she and the other girls wore. The colours were bright, in a pretty pattern, and Anna was delighted to slip her shorts and shirt off and just wrap the short sarong around her hips. Mai-ling also produced the small jar of the magic gel.

'King asked if you would please try more of the gel. The Medicine Man has diluted the mix slightly, based upon your report yesterday that you were still feeling the effects.'

Anna shrugged, 'Sure, I don't mind. We're only going for a swim.' Anna let her rub the gel behind each ear and delighted in the tingling rush that rapidly spread downwards from there.

Mai-ling giggled as she looked at Anna's jutting breasts with their hard nipples and when she stroked them gently, Anna felt a strong tingle in her loins.

Mai-ling took her hand and they strolled up-stream beside the creek until they were well clear of the camp where they came upon a small rock pool. Anna attracted many admiring looks from the menfolk as she passed through the camp, but once again, it was with respect, not lust. As usual, Gilbert followed at a distance.

The water looked inviting and in moments, they had shed their wraps and dived in. Mai-ling was like a slippery seal in the water, diving around Anna and sliding her tiny hands over her body. Despite Gilbert's distant presence, they enjoyed a bit of a fool around, but soon after they dressed and returned to the home tent.

At dinner, Mikhail smiled at Anna's new outfit with just the short sarong around her hips and questioned her about the effects of the weakened gel.

'It still seems strong to me,' she said frankly and with no feeling of shame or awkwardness, 'but perhaps it's because I've not used it before. The effect seems to last over 12 hours.'

She glanced down at her erect nipples which reinforced the point without further words.

Mikhail smiled as he looked. 'Yes. I can see that,' he chuckled appreciatively. 'It has been diluted a little already, but I have instructed the Medicine Man who does all the mixing to increase the quantity of the oil which carries the herbs through the skin so quickly. This will dilute the effect a bit more and also increase the amount of liniment we can produce.'

'More profit for you and me! Provided you accept my offer soon, that is.' he added with a serious look.

'So what other businesses do you run from here?' she asked, sipping an excellent coffee while distracting him from demanding her acceptance of his offer. 'This little enterprise could be a nice earner, but hardly earth-shaking!'

'Basic trading in things like coffee and medicines,' he replied honestly, 'but also guns and other armaments as required.'

At Anna's frown, he added. 'People always want to hurt each other and I'm not about to take a strong moral stand when there's a nice profit to be made. But I don't deal in drugs of any description! Never have and never will!'

Anna was somewhat mollified by his strong reaction to drugs and decided she probably shouldn't press for any more information, but decided on the spot that she should make a break for freedom that night. Accordingly, after the meal and as it was still light Anna wandered down to the beach which formed the shore of the beautiful blue bay.

The water was warm and small waves lapped quietly at the white sand. She passed many locals as well as several armed men, all of whom smiled and waved a greeting.

She became aware of one man however, with the ubiquitous AK-47 over his shoulder who kept a constant 20-meters from her, staying up in the tree-line and she guessed he was standing in for Gilbert.

Trying to just move casually and not stare at anything in particular, she strolled past the usual line-up of canoes drawn up on the sand, noting they all had their paddles resting inside.

Most paddles were of the single-blade type, but there were two one-person canoes where the owners had been experimenting with home-made versions of the double-bladed type she was more used to and which was far more efficient for one person to use.

Much of her training for competition swimming involved paddling canoes, so she was confident she was both fit enough and capable of paddling a one-person canoe a long distance.

Back in her room, she finished her ablutions and made quiet preparations for her unscheduled departure. She'd saved a small amount of dried food and had managed to build up a supply of water in small jars and other containers. Mai-ling had given her a finely crafted shoulder bag that would hold all her supplies and as an afterthought, she took two boxes of the gel, each holding ten jars of the precious stuff. With the shoulder bag bulging, she stowed it carefully under her bed and slipped beneath the top sheet.

Despite her best efforts, she drifted off to sleep, but awoke with a start at 11 o'clock. Cursing softly, she silently swung out of bed, dressed in normal clothes and grabbed the two wrap-skirts for sun protection. The soft rugs everywhere made her exit from the tent quite silent and with no guards visible, she stayed close to the trees until she was above the one-person canoes with the double-paddles. The moon phase was helpful by being both just a sliver, and at the moment, hadn't risen yet.

No guards were in sight, so taking a deep breath, she moved quickly and quietly down to the selected canoe, loaded her bag and slid it into the water. With a final glance around at the peaceful, darkened village, she pushed off and set a steady paddling stroke she knew from long experience was sustainable for a long time.

DAY 5

She'd already considered the best way to head, and with the adjacent island the rebels seemed to favour off to the west, she headed south, where a series of small islands stretched into the distance. She hoped there was decent land beyond them, as her supplies and her endurance would only be good for three or four days.

To make good her getaway, she pushed hard for the first few hours and was rewarded with no sign of pursuit as the next little island in the chain was passed, deliberately keeping well off-shore to avoid being spotted by an insomniac villager.

While not as light as her training kayak back home, she found the little native canoe was nicely made, tracked straight and needed little effort to maintain a good pace.

Around dawn, she was really feeling the pace and decided to get into endurance mode before she burned out. By paddling for 30-minutes, resting for 5, then 30-minutes paddling again, she was able to conserve her energy, while keeping the kilometres slipping astern.

DAY 6 & 7

The chain of little islands had long been passed and she crossed into a long stretch of open water where she felt sufficiently safe from discovery to stretch out in the small canoe to sleep. Her supplies were almost exhausted, but she hadn't dared to put in at any of the islands she'd passed in case they were inhabited and not friendly to an Australian female in a stolen canoe.

DAY 8

Desperation was now setting in as there was no sign of land in any direction. She even chanced standing up, using the long paddle to help keep balance, so as to see a little further, but the horizon remained stubbornly clear. She finished the last of her water around midday and slowed her pace to conserve her fast-dwindling reserves of energy. Inevitably, dehydration caused all sorts of hallucinations and it was late afternoon when she lay down to have a rest, with the intent of paddling in the cool of the night. Her thirst had become like a raging monster, but so far, she had avoided the twin traps of drinking seawater or urine, both of which were high in salt and only made things worse.

She'd slipped into a mild delirium, when she felt the scorching rays of the sun suddenly eclipsed and spent a pleasant few moments thinking about the huge, black rain cloud which must have cast the shadow and was about to dump its life-saving load of cool, fresh water on her.

She was quite annoyed when the black cloud spoke in an Australian accent and with a thick, furred tongue, she gasped, 'Black clouds don't speak. Fuck off and let the real one dump its load on me!'

'Definitely delirious!' the fake cloud replied. 'We'd better be careful giving her water.'

'Didn't I tell you to fuck off. You're not the real black cloud. You're going to stop the rain.'

She felt the canoe wobble violently and tip up on end, as hands grasped her under the arms and dragged her out of the tiny craft.

'Get her bag and the fabric, please Roger,' a female voice said, 'while I hold her here. We'll need the topping lift to hoist her into the cockpit. She won't be able to stand. And we're probably going to have to let the canoe go. We'll never get it on deck.'

'Yeah, you're right, hang on a moment 'til I get the topping lift unshackled.'

Anna woke to a dim light overhead and a cool cloth draped over her forehead. She felt light-headed, but her thoughts were lucid as she noted she was naked again, although this time the bed was tilted at a slight angle and there was the sound of water gurgling nearby. Her first efforts to speak produced a dry croak, but after some water was dribbled into her mouth, she was able to make intelligible sounds.

'Where am I?'

A girl's cheerful face swam into rough focus. 'Welcome back, sweetheart. Don't try to talk too much, but I'll let you have a bit more water. My name is Jill, my friend is Roger and you're on a yacht we've chartered. You're dehydrated and a bit malnourished, but otherwise in good shape. I'm a nurse and Roger's a doctor, so you're in good hands. When you feel a bit better, you can tell us about your adventure. I'm sure you've had one!'

Anna managed to croak, 'Don't go north, please! They'll be chasing me,' before she drifted back to sleep.

Jill wiped her face gently with the wet cloth again as she murmured to the sleeping girl, 'No problem there, dear girl, since we're heading southwest, but I can't wait to hear what's behind that request. And two boxes of small bottles of green liniment are a strange thing to be carrying in a native canoe fifty miles from the nearest land. Still, you're in generally good condition and should recover without any problem.'

PART 1: RETRIBUTION

CHAPTER 1

FIREBIRD, PRESENT DAY, SATURDAY

I'm Harry Stevens and for a change, there was a strong southwest-erly breeze coming over the port quarter of my 60-foot sailing catamaran *Firebird*, pushing it along at a steady 19 knots. We really needed this favourable breeze to conserve our dwindling fuel stocks. My companion boat, the long and sleek AB100 Italian super-cruiser *Seeker*, owned and crewed by David Robson and Corrine Johns, was maintaining an effortless position 50 metres off our stern quarter, idling along on just one of its three massive engines to also conserve fuel. We'd not long left Broome and were heading for Bali on the trail of Terry Williams and a monstrously evil bitch called Paula Henderson; the two principals who were responsible for setting up a home-grown eco-terrorist mob that tried to destroy the Austra-lian oil and gas industry.

With all Eco-terrorists eliminated except for these two mongrels who fled the carnage of their collapsed dreams, the new mission we'd been encouraged to accept, was to find and eliminate the mur-derous pair in their hide-out in the north of Bali, before they caused more trouble. Unfortunately, there could be no openly-official sanc-tion for the mission, as were we heading for a foreign country. We were also using the dubious cover of being wealthy layabouts on permanent holiday, looking for good dive sites.

A personal side mission was to look for an island which grew a strange and almost magical herb, both to help our friends, Jill and Roger, and hopefully boost our income stream,.

Our combat effectiveness was further hampered by the fact that five of our well-trained regular crew had already returned to their daytime jobs as serving Queensland Police officers at Southport.

Two places were taken by Roger and Jill, the doctor and nurse from the now defunct EarthCare organisation that we'd helped pull apart, but they were effectively non-combatants although they knew where the magic herb island was located, as well as where Terry and Paula had gone to ground.

We also had two converts from the bad guys in the last operation; Brianna, who at least had rudimentary training as a soldier, and a giant of a man Alex, who was proving extremely useful and competent both with weapons and boat-handling.

Additional new crew were gained in most peculiar circumstances and comprised four sailors from the Royal Australian Navy patrol boat, *HMAS Glenelg*. They had assisted us in Western Australia, so we knew they were reliable and wouldn't flinch from inevitable violence.

I stupidly got myself shot in the last operation, but that was healing nicely thanks to quick action by one of my crew and by some mysterious process set in place by my over-grown and mystical cat, Jasper. I can't explain half the weird things he does, but I can say he eliminated most of the pain almost immediately and started a healing process which saw my arm and shoulder almost fully functional after just a week.

Our plan was to kill two birds with one stone, literally, by heading up into the Indonesian Archipelago via the north side of Bali, to firstly, find and hopefully deal with Terry and Paula, then find the mysterious Herb Island and do a deal with the so-called 'Weird Harold' Mikhail who ran the place to distribute the magical, mystical green gel that'd been dubbed 'Green Gold'. Just your normal, everyday, family-holiday fun stuff!

Still, since just 45 mls of the green stuff sold for US$500 or AU$705, the name was fitting as was the incentive to do a deal.

Even though Sandy (my long-term girlfriend and stalwart partner), Dave, Corrine or myself were hurting for a dollar, but with inflation and all, one shouldn't pass up the chance for a decent earn!

Roger and Jill had told us about this magic gel and Corrine

already had some interesting first-hand experiences of its effects, but I'd yet to try it myself. Both Sandy and I were looking forward to having some fun exploring some of its sexually-oriented benefits, my darling girl proving to be almost as much a deviant as I was — if not a tad more!

When we were in long-range cruise mode, *Firebird* was the slower of the two, so I did my best to maintain a minimum of 14 knots, on engines if necessary. *Seeker* on the other hand, due to an insane amount of diesel and turbine horsepower, was capable of around 80 knots.

On a day like this, however, with the wind doing all the work, the steady 18 to 19 knots under sail alone was a silent treat. It also delighted Jane, our loaned Navy Petty Officer, who was a self-confessed sailing nut and insisted on turning the autopilot off and taking the wheel herself.

Our other Navy crewmember, the short, but muscular and cheerful Rick, was also shaping up to be a handy and enthusiastic crewie.

Before we'd left Broome and after picking up Roger and Jill, we'd had a round table conference where everyone was encouraged to chip in ideas. There was only one Captain on each boat, but on operational planning sessions, anybody could speak up.

I told them of the new arrangement for entry into Indonesian waters where we were to go to the Marina Del Ray on Lombok, an island east of Bali, who were approved to handle all the paperwork associated with our official entry into Indonesia, including the physical inspections. I'd been assured that our cats, Jasper and Krazy, wouldn't be a problem so long as they stayed aboard.

That led to discussion on how to hide the pieces of the big weapons, the two machine guns and the boxy little MK 47 grenade launcher. Our Navy crew said they would handle stripping all three weapons down to unidentifiable parts which we could pass off as engine spares or be hidden in plain sight. The collection of smaller weapons on each boat would remain hidden in the cleverly designed lockers and spaces already made for them.

I didn't discuss my more detailed plans to look after Terry and Paula, as I needed to develop them further before airing them for debate. I did, however, speak privately to Corrine to see how much C4 she had left after the bikie operation. 14.5 kilos of C-4 and a roll of Det. cord was much more than I needed for my plan, where two or three kilos would be enough

The new crew had settled in well and frequent chats with Dave via radio or SatPhone indicated he was well pleased with his crowd. So we sailed on, enjoying the steady breeze, clear weather and the rising air temperature, although the higher humidity levels that went with it weren't so welcome and the air-con was used more often.

SUNDAY

Dawn saw the rugged, green hills of southern Lombok poking above the northern horizon. Watch-keeping had reverted to daytime mode where just one person was the designated lookout, but with land in sight and our marina just 1.5 hours away on the other side of the stubby peninsula, I kept the duty and badgered the girls into whipping up some breakfast.

As we tracked clockwise around the landmass of Lombok, I made a last-minute check of the weapons hiding places. Some, like the barrel of the MK47 grenade launcher were hidden in plain sight. Since it didn't have cooling holes or fins, it had been converted into an antenna base, with a standard VHF whip antenna apparently screwed to the top of it and mounted on the Targa Bar on *Firebird*. A coat of white enamel completed the disguise.

The two Browning .50 cal barrels presented more of a challenge to the ingenuity of Terry and Gillian, but they came good by creating what looked like a gym in the small vestibule outside the crew cabins on *Seeker*. The two quick change barrels with the handles sticking out, had their ends capped with plastic bottle tops and were painted a bright pink then clamped to the overhead panelling to look like chin-up handles.

Dave contributed two sets of small dumbbells, a stack of weights and two pair of boxing gloves to add to the illusion that the small area was a gym.

As soon as we were in radio range I called the marina to announce our arrival and was given directions to the Quarantine Buoy, where we were met by two cheerful marina staff who announced they would escort Dave and me, as the Captains, to the Port Clearance Office where a Customs and Immigration Official would inspect our papers. As the applications with boat and crew details had been emailed three days ago, we were effectively carrying duplicates and in fact, the interview went very smoothly. There were no anomalies noted, apart from the cats who seemed to be cause for hesitation, regardless of having vaccinations, micro-chipping and rabies shots.

To break the impasse, I made the suggestion to both our marina representative and the Customs official, 'Perhaps a certificate could be written out to allow the cats entry on the proviso that they are to remain aboard at all times and that *Firebird* is to use a mooring for the duration and not a marina berth. Perhaps the cost of such a certificate would be better paid in cash as there is no such certificate amongst all the others.'

Having said that, I laid two $100 Aussie banknotes on the table and was pleased when they disappeared almost immediately.

'That is a most sensible suggestion sir,' the Customs chappie said, 'if the marina staff can raise a document saying so, then I will be pleased to sign it.' The marina rep smiled and trotted off to organise the certificate, while Dave and I exchanged pleasantries with the official. After some trivial questions, the one I was hoping for came up.

'Where will you be travelling to, Captain?'

'We are keen to visit some of your most excellent diving spots which are reported as being the best in the world,' I stated, 'as well as discovering some of the cultural diversity your vast country is renowned for. This is our first visit to the Archipelago and it seems to have a great deal to offer visiting yachtsmen.'

He beamed and agreed wholeheartedly with that plan. 'You have 60-day visas, so I hope that will be sufficient time for you to see some of my wonderful country, but if it is not, then you may return at any time and be most welcome.'

I nodded gently. 'That is good to hear, sir, and if this visit is as good as planned, we shall certainly be returning.'

We exchanged beaming smiles until the marina dude, whose name I had no hope of pronouncing, returned waving a piece of paper. He placed it in front of me to sign and then had the Customs official do the same. Armed with a copy of that, we stood and prepared to return to the boats with our Customs friend in tow.

The inspection was quite quick and amicable, with the false antenna and gym set not receiving more than a cursory glance.

As he left, I slipped another $100 note to him. 'This is just to show my appreciation of your helpfulness and advice, Sir, and I hope we have the chance to renew our friendship in the future.'

He took the note gratefully and favoured us with a big smile and a firm handshake, so it would appear that I did the right thing. The marina chappie directed *Seeker* to a berth at the main wharf and *Firebird* to a mooring buoy that was as close as possible to the wharf. I was quite happy with the arrangement especially as this was the dry month. I'd also been assured that security in the bay was good and no one would try to rob the boat or us.

As usual, I wasn't going to rely on an assurance and planned to use *Firebird's* built-in intruder deterrent system as our own protection strategy!

With the formalities of our arrival in Indonesia out of the way, we cleaned up the boat, hosed the salt off the upper decks and changed into better casual gear. Joining *Seeker's* crew at their berth, we all traipsed up the long jetty to the main building where the bar and restaurant were located and proceeded to celebrate our first international voyage. It was a happy time, but I mentioned to Sandy,

Dave and Corrine that we needed to plan the serious business; the take-down of Terry and Paula, very soon.

'Perhaps we should just stay here for a few days to look as though we're settling in for a while,' Sandy suggested. 'It is a lovely place and much better than what the Bali waterfront looks like.'

There was general agreement to that suggestion, our four Navy crew looking slightly bug-eyed at living, even temporarily, the life-style of the rich and famous as they slurped down their drinks!

'OK. That might work with my rough plan,' I said, provoking Sandy to backhand my arm.

'C'mon Harry. We're all here and relaxing, but we're not too pissed yet, so let's talk!'

'Yeah, OK already! I think for the sake of cover, we need to be seen doing normal touristy things, so perhaps Corrine, Dave, Sandy and I might head over to Bali on the ferry, hire some scooters and whizz up to that Lake Batur place on a bit of a scouting run. The rest of you should stay here and get stuck into the various activities they offer.'

That idea created a round of disagreement from Roger and Jill.

'C'mon guys. We can't all go!'

'Why not?' Jill demanded. 'We've got almost as much interest in this as you have.'

Discussion was animated and various reasoning flew back and forth, but Sandy picked up on what I was thinking and that was that we couldn't all go, and equally, we couldn't leave only our new crew in charge, so she cut in on the talk.

'We need to act as normally as possible and not attract attention any more than we already have. Coming here was a good idea, as already we're physically separated from anything that happens on Bali, but if we try to move around as a group, we're too noticeable so we need to break up into smaller parties. We must make sure nothing we do can connect us with anything going wrong in the north of Bali.'

'As much as I hate to say it, I think that Harry, Corrine, Roger,

Jill, Jane and Rick should go to Bali, leaving myself, Dave, Terry, Gillian, Alex and Bree to look after the boats and play at being degenerate yacht people. That way, it will look like we decided to do different activities which would be normal behaviour for a diverse group.'

Sandy stood up, 'Just chat amongst yourselves a moment. I'm going to ask Reception about a few things.' It was an Assistant Manager who looked after her enquiries and she returned armed with a handful of brochures and assorted pieces of paper.

'Right,' she resumed, 'a few details to help planning. The marina ferry to Bali leaves at 08:00 and does a return run at 17:00 daily. Car hire is not recommended due to traffic behaviour and the narrow roads, which is why everyone uses scooters and all reputable hire companies have a two-day minimum hire period. And you don't want to hire from the disreputable ones!'

She tossed a handful of colourful flyers on the table. 'For those of us who must remain behind, there are a heap of activities and things to see and do, either based here or nearby, so we can be kept busy.'

'It is entirely natural that some of us would want to visit Bali, and others will be happy staying here.'

Terry and Gillian nodded enthusiastically, 'That's us,' Terry said, as he and Gillian sorted through the activity's brochures, 'although we don't have much money and some of these things are a bit pricey.'

'Don't worry about money,' I chipped in. 'Book all the activities or excursions you want through Reception here and put it on the boat account. It'd look odd if we didn't spend up big, so do as much as you can!'

There was a round of 'Thanks Harry', from the new crew, so I moved onto the next phase of my cunning plan. 'Based on that,' I said, ideas still popping up in my brain, 'I think that the Bali group should perhaps rent accommodation in Bali for a few days to maintain appearances. Trying to move without being seen is impossible and dangerous, but if we blend in and behave as expected, we're just another group of tourists.'

That sparked a round of discussion until Sandy, as organiser, said, 'I'm afraid it is going to be the best way. The question now is where do you stay?'

She found a detailed map of Bali amongst all the other bits of paper and opened it out.

I looked at Jill and Roger. 'Can you find where their house is on this map?'

They leant over it looking carefully. After some muttered discussion, Jill put her finger on a spot on the caldera rim, directly south of the crater lake. 'It's here, alongside this hotel. As we said, it used to be a hotel annex, but business dropped off and the annex was sold. Paula bought it cheaply, but spent a lot of money tarting up the interior. One of the Admin girls who handled the work invoices said all the work was internal and nothing was spent on the roof or outside.

She heard Terry and Paula arguing about fixing up the outside, but Paula said it could wait because the inside was more important. Didn't make sense to her.'

I was getting excited again, 'No, but it suits my plans. Just hang on a minute.'

CHAPTER 2

MARINA DEL RAY, LOMBOK, SUNDAY

I went over to the Assistant Manager who was still hanging around chatting to the Receptionist and asked him to check for rooms in the aptly named Crater Hotel.

'Oh, that is a very good hotel sir,' he said, as he looked up their phone number, 'with an excellent restaurant. We often have our guests visit there and they are most generous with their praise. The view of the volcano and the lake is spectacular and being high, the air is cool, so many like to walk the bush trails.'

He called the hotel, speaking in rapid-fire Bahasa I presumed, not understanding a word of it.

Pausing mid-speech, he said, 'They have only three rooms available sir, from tomorrow night, but they will have more rooms next weekend.'

I thought rapidly, and then made a command-level decision, 'We don't want to wait when there's so much we want to do and see, so we'll take those three rooms for three nights from tomorrow night, Monday, if that's OK?'

He went back to the phone and when he'd finished, hung up and said, 'All arranged, sir. I have booked three balcony rooms, all adjoining with en-suite facilities for three nights commencing tomorrow night, Monday. I made the presumption you would want to travel to Bali on our ferry as safe mooring for your boats is not readily available. Therefore, the hotel is sending a mini-bus to collect you from our terminal.

They will also bring you back to us on Thursday, and for a small consideration, the driver will make a tour of the coastal road if you wish.'

I was overwhelmed by the standard of service and said so, making him smile with pleasure.

'It is our happiness sir, to make your stay with us as pleasant as possible.'

'Excellent. The rest of our group will be staying here and wanting to indulge in several of the activities that you have advertised. I have suggested they book everything through you. Could you please charge all fees to the boat account?'

'Certainly sir. The deposit you made when you checked in will be quite sufficient for now.'

I thanked him again and returned to the others who were debating who'd do what and how often, but I had their attention when I sat down.

'OK. Here's the go. There are only three rooms available at the Crater Hotel from tomorrow. That's all they had at short notice and since we don't want to hang around too long, I've booked them.'

I grinned at my other five travellers, 'I'm sorry about the room arrangement, but we'll have to share as three couples. It'll attract too much attention if we try any other combination and I don't think we should do anything odd to attract attention. Can we all work with that?'

Dave and Sandy nodded agreement with my reasoning and looked philosophical, Corrine shrugged, smiled and said, 'No problem for me,' while Jane and Rick exchanged a look and also shrugged. 'We'll work with it,' said Jane.

'OK. We take the 08:00 ferry across tomorrow morning and the hotel picks us up from there. We'll be back on Thursday.' I looked at Corrine and said, 'In case our targets are in residence, we'll take the C-4, detonators and the Det Cord and would you prefer two PMR 30s with suppressors as well?'

She nodded. 'Yeah. That's a good choice. Even with the magnum round, it still doesn't sound like a gunshot if there aren't too many in a row.'

'Should we take any weapons?' Jane asked.

'No more guns,' I said, 'but perhaps a knife each would be useful. Sandy has two or three Gerber Mk II fighting knives tucked away. And gloves for all of us. No fingerprints.'

I left the detailed briefing for when I'd worked it out more thoroughly myself, and with that planning session out of the way, a fairly serious party developed. We even joined in with a few other couples in the lounge who seemed to be in a similar frame of mind.

When eating time came around, we ate where we were by ordering a series of dishes that could be eaten as finger-foods, and the cooks had fun trying different dishes on the 'crazy Aussies' as we'd been dubbed.

It's been said the best way to see what people are really like is to observe how they behave when pissed, so by that benchmark we had a bloody good crew since all the newcomers stayed happy and mixed in well! Even the younger Rick and Gillian, who'd been so overawed by their luxurious surrounding just hours earlier, lost most of their reserve and had a ball!

The wobbly-boot walk back to *Seeker* was funny, but the dinghy ride out to *Firebird* was hilarious! Somehow, we managed not to get too wet. The four pissed possums who lurched up the transom steps were greeted by two starving pussies, demanding food, attention, pats, food, attention and a bit more attention.

MONDAY

It was a rough awakening early next morning as I had some clothes packing to do, some hardware to be found and Jane and Rick to be stirred into action. I was pleasantly surprised to find they were way ahead of me and were waiting in the cockpit, dressed, packed and ready to roll. We had an early breakfast on *Seeker* and were ready on the wharf beside the 14-metre fast ferry by 08:00 where three other passengers, the Skipper and a crew-girl joined us.

I found the trip interesting in the way that the Skipper tracked north about the top of the two islands of Nusa Penida and Nusa Lembongan to avoid the worst of the tidal overfalls caused by an ocean floor covered in large peaks and troughs. The boat traffic approaching the Bali ferry terminal was rather intense and I was glad we didn't make the trip in *Seeker or Firebird* as I'd first intended.

I again mentally thanked the marina Assistant Manager who organised the trip, when I spotted a young local holding a hand printed sign that said 'Stevens' standing in a prominent place as we left the ferry and wandered up the wharf.

'Mr Stevens? I am from Crater Hotel. Welcome to Bali. This way please sir.'

Our transport was a battered, eight-seater people mover that lacked any semblance of creature comforts except for a radio tuned to a non-stop heavy-metal station with the volume gain set at 105db! Windows jammed open took care of ventilation, and seats were secured to the floor by a minimum of bolts, adding to the lurching motion the stuffed dampers could do nothing to suppress. Although vehicles officially kept to the left as in Australia, it seemed that any gap, whether to the left or right was fair game and it was more like being a passenger in a dodgem car at an outback show, than a safe, sane drive to our hotel in the mountains!

Clearing the port area was exciting enough, but after a brief drive on a nice stretch of four-lane divided highway, we plunged back into the total traffic chaos that passes for standard Bali driving. The only rule seemed to be to dodge anything bigger than what you're driving, and demand right of way from everything smaller!

Scooters were in their teeming thousands, darting in and out of the cars and trucks, often with weird loads balanced precariously on the rider's head or back, or strapped to the handlebars, like a half-grown pig I saw. There was also the local habit of transporting the entire family on one scooter and the frightening sight of three adults, three children and two babies wobbling along on a groaning little Honda 90 step-through will stay in my mind forever!

The experience reinforced what people had said in their blogs about Bali. Either get a scooter and a good helmet or hire a car with a local driver. The trip through the sprawling suburbs on the narrow roads populated mainly by scooters was eye-opening and it seemed that every hundred metres or so was either a scooter hire shop or a scooter repair shop. Small roadside stalls frequently had a person selling one litre bottles of petrol. I'd been told the quality was often dubious, although the price at about 0.80 cents per litre was very cheap.

After about an hour of dodging other maniac drivers, we noticed the road was starting to climb and the driver politely informed us that we were now out in the country. The only difference we could see was that sometimes there was bush and trees on one side of the road, but never on both sides!

It seemed that on Bali at least, if there was space, someone would build something.

As the road continued to climb, the map indicated we were on the ascent of the side of the old volcano, whose glorified and petrified guts we were shortly going to see from the comfort of our hotel room balconies. The other positive thing we noticed was the air becoming cooler and less humid; a welcome change, although the smells that often blew in through the 8/40 cooling system were undiminished, as was the volume of traffic.

'Where the hell are they all going?' Corrine demanded, but nobody had an answer, least of all the driver. Finally, we crested a rise where the road turned sharply left, but we wheeled to the right, straight into a small courtyard surrounded by ramshackle shops and empty buildings, but a tidy building at the end with a sign announced that it was the Crater Hotel complete with Bar and Restaurant. If the others felt like I did after that trip, the Bar would be our first stop.

Our driver, however was all smiles, especially when he was generously tipped for delivering us in one piece and helped unload our bags and carry them through to Reception. The interior was in stark contrast to the exterior, being all polished wood, with many ornate carvings. Soft, normal music played in the background and any comparison to the Eagle's song quickly faded. The Receptionist was an attractive young lady who spoke excellent English and had three balcony rooms ready for us.

In answer to the most important question, she replied,

'Your rooms all have a mini bar, although the main bar is just behind here in the dining room. It is always open. If you care to follow me, I will show you to your rooms.'

She led the way past the dining room which had stunning views out over the deep volcanic crater literally right at our feet, to the towering spire of the volcanic core itself. The sheer size of the thing viewed from so close was amazing, particularly when it was realised the spire was worn down to about one quarter the size of the original.

A long corridor floored with polished boards, had numbered doors opening left and right with the left side being the balcony ones with the great view. Half-way down, she stopped and unlocked the first of three doors in a row, so Corrine and I took that one, with Jane and Rick next door and Jill and Roger beyond that.

'All rooms have connecting doors if you wish to join them together,' our charming hostess said, handing the keys over. 'The evening meal is at 6 pm and a gong will be sounded at that time. Breakfast is from 7 am, although we do not sound the gong for that!' she added with a smile, before graciously making a small curtsey and returning to her station.

The rooms were beautiful. Immaculately clean with a normal western-type bathroom and the promised stunning view of the volcanic spire which seemed close enough to touch. There was also just one king-sized bed.

'Ah well, Mouse. I guess we'd better behave ourselves. Do you want the left or the right?'

She giggled. 'Right for me, thanks Harry, if that suits you.'

'Well, if we're not fooling around, it doesn't matter too much, now does it?'

By answer, she giggled again and visited the bathroom, while I stowed our special hardware bag in the back of the wardrobe and went to find the bar. Jane and Rick had beaten me to it and were seated so they could take best advantage of the view, which was just as spectacular from there as from our balconies. I quickly discovered it was even better viewed over the top of a tall, frosty glass of Bintang beer off the tap, served by a delightful young lady who was quite happy to book everything to my room and looked to be related to the pretty receptionist.

There were just two other couples in the room, but they were well away from us.

'Happy with your room?' I asked, 'and sorry about having to share. I think appearances are important at the moment.'

Jane grinned, 'We'll sort it out and we certainly understand the need to look as normal as possible.'

Rick gave a cheeky grin, 'Yeah. It's not often a Leading Seaman gets told to share a bed with a Petty Officer in the line of duty!'

Jane and I laughed and she playfully kicked him in the shins. 'Smart arse! Remember the rule; what happens off the boat stays off the boat!'

'I know what you mean,' I smiled. 'I'm a Commander sharing a bed with a the equivalent of a Petty Officer!' I sighed theatrically. 'The things we have to do in the name of the job!'

'Speaking of Petty Officers, where is Corrine?' Jane asked.

'I think she might be having a look for alternate exits from this place,' I said quietly. 'There's a security guard stationed out the front of the courtyard, so we don't want him remembering that two or three tourists went for a midnight walk on the night that bad things happened nearby.'

'Oh. I didn't notice or think of that,' Jane said, frowning. 'We don't get to play at this James Bond-type stuff in the Navy. For us, it's relatively clear who the bad guys are and what we can do to stop them, but this is a whole different level of thinking.'

I nodded at her assessment. 'I had similar trouble when I left the

SAS and got talked into doing this stuff. But once you adjust your thinking, it comes way too easily after a while!'

'If you don't mind my asking, what do you do when you're not chasing bad guys? I mean, you don't do this stuff all the time, surely?'

I laughed, 'Hell no! And thank goodness I don't! Operations suiting our special undercover unit only come along once or twice a year perhaps, so the rest of the time, I live on my boat with Sandy and the pussies. We hang out, sail for pleasure and just generally have some fun.'

She sighed and smiled at my description. 'That sounds idyllic. Already I love your boat and the two pussies and I love sailing *Firebird*. But that Jasper really is something else. He's not just a cat, is he?'

I smiled gently. 'No, he's not. I can't explain a fraction of what I've seen him do and you saw what he did to my shoulder when I was shot.'

'Oh shit! I'd forgotten all about that! How is it?'

By way of answer, I undid two more buttons on my shirt and pulled the cloth off my shoulder, showing her the puckered, pink, star-shaped scar just under my shoulder bone.

She looked astonished, 'But that was less than ten days ago! How can you heal so quickly?'

I shrugged, 'You were there. Melissa cleaned and dusted the hole, then bandaged me up. The only other treatment was when Jasper clamped his jaws around it and soaked the bandages in his saliva. He repeated the treatment a couple of hours later and refused to let Melissa or Sandy change the dressing for days. They were afraid it was going to fester, but I wasn't in pain and the next day I had reasonable use of the arm. When Jasper finally did let them take the bandages off, this is how it looked.'

She shook her head. 'Amazing. I hope someone took photos of the whole thing!'

'Yeah. Melissa did before she went back to Southport and Sandy took more after that.'

'I'll bet Roger will be interested to hear that story.'

'Yeah, he probably will, although the green paste he's got is supposed to be rather amazing too, according to Corrine.'

Just then, the lady herself padded into the room, smiling at the sight of me with my shirt half off.

'Bloody hell, Harry! I leave you alone for five minutes and you're taking your clothes off for a pretty girl! You're hopeless!'

I grinned at her, straightening my shirt, 'Sorry Mouse. Jane was talking about Jasper's mystical qualities and I showed her the progress of my wound.'

She laughed, 'Yeah, that's quite a good one, but I reckon you should tell them the 'Jasper and the Giant Croc' story!

CHAPTER 3

Rick jumped to his feet, 'I'll get another round, but don't start without me. This is good stuff!'

He was still ordering when Jill and Roger walked in and joined us. After shuffling chairs around, Rick completed the resupply run, so I told the story of Jasper and the giant crocodile to a rapt audience.

'So it was like he was in mental communication with the beast?' Jill asked, leaning forward in excitement.

Corrine took over by replying, 'Definitely. The croc wanted to rest peacefully for some reason. Maybe he was chased by an even bigger one or a younger male, and Jasper seemed to tell him he could sleep on the stern board without fear of being attacked by animal or man. Jasper wasn't happy when Dave had a gun in his hand and was ready to shoot the croc. That's when he actively defended the croc.'

'But how do you account for him dragging Harry over to sit with the croc while he went to pee?'

'All we know is, we saw him take Harry's hand and pull him over to just in front of the croc's nose and made him sit. If you look at the video you can see his actions clearly and they can't be confused with anything else. Jasper wanted Harry to sit with the croc while he, Jasper, went to pee, have a drink and a feed.'

'It was just as well the croc didn't wake up while Harry was sitting there,' Roger remarked dryly looking at me, 'or it would have been 'Good night Harry'!'

'But that's the thing! He did wake up!' Corrine said. 'It was so weird! The croc eyeballs Harry sitting there, just a couple of centimetres in front of his snout, grunts, then goes back to sleep as if he's happy he's still being looked after and can continue resting!'

'And you've got all this on video?' Roger asked, disbelievingly.

'Yep. Tracy got it all on a UHD handy-cam, plus I had the mast-head camera in motion-detect mode, so we have the whole sequence from when the croc first climbed up on the stern board to when he left.'

'Fantastic! I've got a couple of friends who would love to see the video. They're researchers looking at animal to human interaction and communication, and are trying to prove a form of telepathy is the way to actually communicate, rather than using words or pictures. They'll go nuts over Jasper and the videos. Even just the fact you can talk to him and he obeys accurately, is enough for a white paper. But you'll have to agree to it and put up with the barrage of questions they'll fire at you.'

I laughed, 'Yeah, OK. When this is over, let them know and we'll see if they'll want to do some interviews. But under no circumstances will I let him be probed, prodded or tested in a laboratory! Jasper stays in his environment at all times. They come to him. Barbara from *Glenelg* fully understood that when she did some interviews with Jasper and me. She also has a copy of the croc encounter!'

'OK. That's certainly fair enough. I talk to them often, so I'll pass this stuff on. But don't be surprised if they turn up on your doorstep one morning. These folks have some serious funding!'

I looked around to make sure we were still well out of hearing range of the other two couples, who'd just been joined by two young, good-looking guys who looked very fit. Although the two women looked excited to see them and their husbands less so, I didn't get the feeling that they could have anything to do with our business.

I looked questioningly at Corrine who said, 'No, I don't think so either. I did find a back way out, though. The accommodation corridor has an emergency exit door at the end which leads down under the building to a service area where old junk is stored. That opens onto an overgrown area with a gate in the fence, giving access to what looks like a disused lane for construction vehicles. It follows the hill contour and should run right below T & P's place.'

'Hold that thought, Mouse.' I went to Reception and asked the girl for a local map showing the walking trails in detail. She pulled a sheet off a stack sitting on the counter and handed it over.

'We printed these which shows the trails, and most walkers find that's all they need.'

'Do you have a more detailed one?'

She thought a moment, then said, 'Yes. I do have a much more detailed map but most hikers don't want all the detail. Just a moment, please.'

She scratched through a file cabinet, finally producing a 1:25,000 topographical survey map and which covered the local area. 'Would this be what you are thinking of?'

'Perfect! May we borrow it for a short time?'

'No problem sir. It's the only one we have, but you can keep it for the duration of your stay and return it when you check out.'

Returning to our extended table and five expectant faces, I folded the map carefully so the local area was showing and laid it on the table. 'This should help pinpoint their house,' I said to Jill and Roger, 'if you can think clearly about what you've heard.'

We all looked carefully and Corrine traced a small finger along the contour lines.

'Here's the service track I found and it curves around the other hotel that's almost next door and looks like a haunted mansion.'

Jill suddenly got excited, almost bouncing up and down in her chair. 'That's the one! That's it! I recognised the weird carvings and sculpture on the hotel from a photo she showed us. The place they brought isn't directly attached to the main hotel. But because flat land up here on the rim is rare and costs heaps, they built the annex out over the crater drop-off. It scared the shit out of guests, so no one wanted to stay there.

It wouldn't pass building regulations now, but back then, no one cared. It's supported by a bunch of bamboo poles. Paula joked that when a strong wind blows up out of the crater, the whole house moves and sways and it always creaks and groans. She boasted that's how she bought it for peanuts.'

Corrine dragged the map back. 'So this small building just past the hotel is it?'

'Yeah. You can see where there's a driveway coming off the hotel access when it was part of the hotel, but Paula wanted some privacy, so she had a tall fence built to enclose the driveway. There's a small parking area out front of the house itself.'

I had a look and checked the contour lines. 'These contour lines are very close, Mouse. How steep did it look when you went down there?'

'I didn't go right down because the rear access is right under the end few balconies, but it got a lot steeper behind where the hotel would be. Almost vertical in fact, with the heavily overgrown track carved out of the slope. There doesn't look like there's much below it apart from a few small industrial buildings.'

I measured a few things, then outlined a plan for the group. Typically, there were some arguments and some good suggestions for changes to be taken into account. The plan was polished a bit more as the afternoon slid quietly into evening. Our group became more relaxed as the sun disappeared behind the hills to the west, leaving the tip of the old volcanic plug bathed in a golden glow which slowly retreated until it disappeared, leaving the whole crater in darkness.

We didn't have to move far to a dining table and enjoyed another feed of tasty Indonesian dishes washed down with yet more of the delightful, sparkling Bintang beer and white wine. After dinner, Corrine, Jill and I left Roger, Jane and Rick sampling a few more beers and chatting with the other group of two couples and two young guys, while we went for a casual stroll. The evening air was cool enough so the hoodies Corrine and Jill wore didn't look out of place. They both wore baseball caps as well and pulled the hood in tightly around their faces on the off chance we ran into Terry and or Paula.

We strolled firstly to the west where the right side of the road ran along the very steep cliff top. There were various unidentifiable shops, some empty, and other business enterprises on the other side of the road. Despite the darkness, traffic was just as heavy, most of it two wheeled and I shuddered to imagine riding a scooter with pathetic lighting on such narrow roads and in heavy traffic at night. After a hundred metres, we turned and wandered back the other way, passed our Crater Hotel entrance and down the hill, also passing the entrance to the other weird-looking hotel.

'Up that driveway,' Jill said, 'there's the hotel carpark and another driveway heading off the rear of the area that leads to Paula and Terry.'

'Can we walk up there?' I asked.

'Sure, we're Westerners. We can do most anything. I should tell you though, that there's a Police Post on the opposite side of the road.'

'Yes, I know. I also found out that it becomes an un-manned post anytime now and stays that way all night.'

We wandered up the driveway and as Jill said, the carpark occupied most of the side of the hotel, which was probably the most architecturally bizarre construction I'd ever seen. It had turrets, gargoyles, little spires, big spires and ornate cornices and window frames with curlicues. The best one could say was at least the design was consistent — consistently bizarre! We got to see the private driveway heading down into the gloom from the rear corner of the carpark and on the way out, I asked the girls to wait while I ducked into Hotel 'Bizarre' for a moment.

'OK. That'll do us for tonight,' I said when I came out, 'let's go join the others. They're probably pretty much pissed possums by now!'

They weren't too pissy, but all three had a glow on. I was surprised Roger seemed to enjoy putting a few beers away, but if it made him relaxed and happy then that was a good thing.

We grabbed drinks too and settled down to tell them of the small changes to my cunning plan.

Heading back to our room an hour later, Corrine remarked, 'It looked to me as if our two Navy dudes might be feeling like a bit of fooling around tonight. They've become quite close.'

I smiled at her. 'Ah, good luck to them. Rank keeps them separated on the patrol boat, so here they can do what they want.'

She gave me a meaningful look. 'We are behaving ourselves tonight, aren't we?'

'I guess so. We did say we would.'

'Yeah. We did say that, so I suppose we should.'

'Well, at least let's think about it!'

She gave a delighted grin, 'Good man. Thinking about it is good.'

In the desert, Corrine and I had shared a strong mutual attraction, but rank reared its ugly head and kept us physically apart since Majors weren't allowed to fool around with Sergeants, however consenting both might be. When we were invalided out of the SAS, we lost touch almost immediately until we ran into each other in bizarre circumstances on the Gippsland Lakes in the middle of an operation, so we had never found the opportunity to scratch that particular itch.

Once in the room, we went straight out on the balcony where Corrine pointed out the gate in the back fence and the faint track which barely showed in the weak light. Giggles from the next room were a cue for us to go inside, close the door and turn the air-con on.

By the time we'd both had a shower, there were definite sounds of passion coming from next door, so I turned the radio on low and found a western music station.

I had the last shower, so Corrine was already in bed when I emerged, a towel wrapped strategically around my waist. I went around doing the usual manly thing by checking doors and windows, then without trying to be silly, went to the vacant side of the bed and dropped the towel and climbed between the sheets.

I'd really been trying to be nonchalant about the fact I never wore pyjamas and didn't even own any, but as I slid into bed, Corrine giggled.

'Holy crap, Harry! You must have washed everything way too much! I think you've got your tail on backwards!'

I tried to sound offended, 'I have absolutely no idea what you're talking about, young Miss!'

'No idea my arse,' she cackled, 'I'm referring to the part of your anatomy that's a lot bigger than it was the last time it was on display!'

'I'll have you know that I don't just put it on display! But on this occasion, if you just ignore it maybe it'll go away.'

'Just ignore it, huh? OK, if you say so, but try to keep it over your side of the bed if you can.'

'Yes, dear. I'm going to study this map for a short time, then I'm turning my light out and going to sleep.'

'Bravo, Harry. That's what I like to hear. Mind over matter. If I don't mind, then sharing the bed with that thing won't matter!'

She giggled again and lifted the bedclothes to take another look. 'Oh dear, he's grew some! Can't you keep control of your organs?'

I frowned at her mirth and yanked the bedclothes down, 'I'm trying to, bugger it! Give me a break. It'll go away in a minute or two.'

'There's only one thing that will make it go away, and we said we weren't going to do that!'

'Actually, what I thought we agreed, was we were going to *think* about behaving ourselves.'

'Oh, yes. How silly of me to forget. In that case, I've just done all the thinking I'm capable of doing tonight, so I'll just scoot down and inspect this thing, shall I?'

I growled, she giggled, and while I did look at the map for a very short time, Corrine was way too busy to ignore, so I dumped the map and proceeded to do what had been almost started years earlier and half a world away. With the first round a great success, we compared bullet scars while we rested. She was fit, athletic and delightful to be with. Perhaps the wait was worthwhile as the next two rounds proved.

I woke the next morning when Corrine got up and went to the bathroom and still had my eyes open when she came back out, grabbed some clothes off a chair and started getting dressed.

She grinned at me as she dressed, not trying to be overtly sexy, but managing to anyway.

'C'mon big boy. Time is a 'wasting and so's breakfast.'

She watched carefully as I threw the covers back and swung out of bed, but made no further comment, apart from flashing a cheeky grin as I brushed past on my way to the bathroom where I emptied a full bladder.

Corrine called through the door, trying unsuccessfully to stifle a fit of the giggles. 'That's why it's called a piss-horn Harry, although on you it's more like the 'might or might not Matterhorn!'

Sometimes I don't like that girl!

Roger and Jill were ahead of us and Jane and Rick wandered in last, looking a bit sheepish, although Jane couldn't suppress a satisfied grin.

'What's the go for today, Harry?' Roger asked.

'We're tourists today,' I replied after swallowing a tasty morsel of bacon. 'Have a look at the tours, walks or other activities they've got brochures for at Reception and choose one or two.

Tonight, we do the job.'

That grabbed their interest, so Jane went to Reception and collected a handful of things-to-do sheets. When she came back, Roger asked, 'Shouldn't we wait until tomorrow night so we will be leaving the next morning?'

I looked around, but apart from the two couples from the night before, all looking tired, hung over and minus the two young dudes, we had the place to ourselves, although the Receptionist had told me that a large tour group was booked in from today for three nights.

Lowering my voice, I answered, 'Last night, I checked with one of the owners of Hotel 'Bizarre' next door to see if he would talk about the two ex-pats who bought their annex and he was quite chatty. Definitely an odd-ball, but helpful. Anyway, he said, that because Paula and Terry have an arrangement for the hotel staff to do their cleaning, he knew they are there at the moment, but had mentioned they were going down the coast tomorrow to Atlas Pearl Farms where they were looking to buy into a "business enterprise".'

'He certainly was chatty, to reveal that much,' Roger observed dryly.

I shrugged, 'Yes, well. He was gay, so I had to pretend my two mates and I were looking for some fun. He was keen to see us, so I had to say we already had appointments with others, but there were several other guests staying next door who might be interested. He also said the couple who owned the house were often looking for 'interesting sexual partners'!'

'I asked him to keep my enquiry quiet, but that wasn't a problem. Since the government has been cracking down on gays, they've all had to go under-cover.'

'Anyway. The upshot of it all is; we act tonight. There's a big group checking in today and with all the coming and going, our movements shouldn't be noticed.'

So we bushwalked along the crater rim, then were driven down to the main town beside Lake Batur where we could at least look at a bewildering variety of shops and tried a couple of bars, but we restricted drinking to sealed, bottled fruit juice. We were back in the hotel by mid-afternoon, with everyone getting edgy and endlessly reviewing his or her part in the operation. Corrine and I were the only ones used to this sort of mission, although that didn't make us immune from the pre-attack nerves.

CHAPTER 4

CRATER HOTEL, LAKE BATUR, BALI, TUESDAY

Dinner that evening was a subdued affair around our table, although the restaurant was fairly jumping with the new tour group just checked in. They were a mixed bag of ages, but none were over forty. Some were Aussies, with the rest being Poms and Yanks. There was a group of four girls who sounded like Swedish back-packers and they were pretty and frisky, as were most of the others with loud talk, laughter and endless traffic to and from the rooms.

As cover, we couldn't have asked for a better situation.

Even with the noise as cover, it was still too crowded to talk about nefarious activities in the dining room and bar, so we retired early to our room where everyone sat where they could and demanded I go over our plan again. I did and after the third repeat, had to call a halt to any more discussion. We tested our comms equipment, which consisted of the mini radios headsets we'd brought with us, courtesy of the Queensland Police and the last operation.

The other four grew even more solemn when Corrine and I stripped and cleaned the two PMR-30 .22 magnum pistols, Corrine's with a long, tubular suppressor screwed to the barrel and even though the magnum round was supersonic, the capable Isis 22 muffler did a decent job of taking the crack out of the sound of the shot.

She also carefully sharpened her favourite knife, the Gerber MK II, to a razor edge.

To soothe the nerves a bit, I discussed our exit strategy in case of a glitch in the plan, but it was still a long wait. One o'clock was to be show time, and although no one wanted to even try to sleep, Jane and Rick excused themselves for a while. It quickly became obvious what their choice of stress-relief was, and I certainly wouldn't have

62

minded indulging in some more myself. I wasn't sure if Corrine still felt the same before a mission, but as a mental diversion, I asked Jill and Roger about the green paste project and I got some more good information.

'As you've seen, we've loaded the boats with weapons just in case, but do you know what the current situation with pirates is?' I asked.

'Not good, really,' Roger admitted, 'despite what the Government tries to tell tourists. There are some areas which are real hotbeds of activity, usually on shipping crossroads and although small boats aren't usually targeted because they have little real value apart from the boat itself, sometimes a kidnap is planned and that's when things get really nasty. Mainly because it often degenerates to a stage where the males are killed immediately and the females cop a rape-fest! That's why most yachties I know, prefer to be as heavily armed as they can get away with.

Therefore, I'm very happy you're got some heavy firepower, since both boats are big enough and expensive-looking enough to be attractive.'

'This area where the island is. Is that in a pirate area?'

He grinned, 'You betcha! Right in the middle of one. The next island has a rebel group based there and their main source of funding and entertainment is piracy. The whole region has numerous groups, some more organised than others, but they're all dangerous. I'd like to slip in, do our business and slip out again before we attract too much attention.'

'But you haven't made any sort of approach to this self-styled King before, have you?'

'No, I'm afraid not. All we were hoping to do was to try to pick up from where Anna left off if he hasn't already replaced her with somebody else.'

I nodded, 'Don't feel bad if it doesn't work out. It'd be nice to get some samples of the stuff at least, but our primary objective was to tidy up this nasty loose end. The green paste was a bonus and an excuse to cruise through some magnificent islands. The dive sites alone are worth the visit.'

'But we wanted to be able to pay our way,' Jill protested.

Corrine looked up from stropping her knife, 'Don't worry about that. The money is not an issue and I appreciate what you did for me at EarthCare. I haven't used any of that sample jar you gave me yet, but I can still remember the effects of the treatment I had!'

That raised a rare laugh and made me really keen to try it.

Jane and Rick weren't the only noises happening around as there was a constant parade of persons up and down the corridor, with doors banging and happy voices chatting, but by midnight, things had settled considerably and our crew were all back in our room, dressed for their part. Corrine fitted each person with the mini radio headsets which had a tiny boom mike and transmitted by a press on the ear piece. The batteries were fully charged, all were tested, and worked perfectly.

By 01:00 the other guests had mostly settled down, although there were a few diehards keeping the bar open and provided enough movement that two more wouldn't attract undue attention.

As per the plan, Jane and Rick left via the front door and went out into the street where they were to go into the parking lot of what we'd dubbed the 'Hotel Bizarre' and to hang around as best they could without getting arrested. Their job was to alert Corrine and me if anyone left the target house, or if any police or security personnel approached the house.

Roger and Jill went to sit on their balcony with their room lights out, covering our escape route by watching the rear access for anybody else wandering around who might see us entering or leaving.

Lastly, Corrine and I made our way along the corridor to the back door without meeting any other guests and went down via the back stairs. We both wore tight-fitting dark clothes that look less suspicious than an all-black outfit. We rolled the balaclavas up on our heads like caps and wore loose jackets over the top in case we bumped into someone before we left the building, but all was quiet, so we left the jackets at the foot of the stairs.

We tried to move as quietly as possible through the long, un-mown grass, but with the traffic on the road above and the few drinkers still in the bar, we could have had a marching band leading us and not been noticed.

The hillside was steep, but the old service track wasn't too overgrown and it was fairly easy to walk along. It was only about 100 metres across a hillside which became much steeper, before we could look up a slope at a web of bamboo scaffolding supporting a house that had most of its bulk hanging precariously out over the cliff. It was hard going to get up to the first of the support poles and we had to be careful as the noises that covered our exit from the hotel were absent now that we were underneath Paula's house. We couldn't see any lights on above us, which was a blessing.

In her element, Corrine slipped away as quietly as a shadow to recce the area, so I stood still and listened but all was quiet — so much so that when she touched my arm five minutes later, my heart skipped a beat or two in fright!

She didn't use the radio, just murmured, 'We can climb up the bamboo supports and gain access to the veranda, but we'll have to be quiet as the best access point is their open bedroom window.'

She might have found it easy to climb the slippery bamboo poles, but I didn't, although I thought I was quiet. That was until Corrine re-appeared beside me and murmured, 'Stop shaking the house, Harry. We don't want to be under the fucking thing when it gets re-located downhill.'

'Sorry! I didn't think I was.'

She patted my arm and disappeared upwards again, luckily in place to help haul me over the edge of the veranda after I'd negoti-ated the last of the bamboo gym set. She showed me the clenched fist signal that means 'freeze' before soundlessly flowing into the house through the open window just in front of me. Snores and heavy breathing indicated that hopefully it was Terry and Paula making the noise and not some hapless sleepover victim.

I knew better than to move before being told and heard one set of soft snores change followed by a slight grunt, a rustle of bedclothes then deep breathing resumed.

The dark rectangle of the open window deepened and an arm appeared, the fingers beckoning. Two paces and I was able to slide carefully inside, Corrine steadying me as I stood beside the bed. A faint wash of light came in through the open bedroom door, perhaps from several LED displays, but enough to show a woman who I presumed was Paula laying on her back doing the deep breathing I'd heard. The man beside her matched Terry's description and he was also doing deep breathing exercises.

Beside me, Corrine was tucking a small roll of thin leather away in her bum bag, which told me that she'd probably injected both with one of her special sleeping drugs.

I keyed my radio. 'Yo, team. Any activity?'

'Negative one,' that was Jane and Rick.

'Negative two,' for Jill and Roger.

'Roger that. Inside and all good.'

Corrine spoke quietly, but normally. 'There's no one else in the house, but we have to be careful about lights. Just use the red lens on your mini torch. There's a study or office over the other side of the lounge room that should be the best place for papers. You look and I'll watch the sleeping beauties.'

I had a quick scout through the other rooms, pausing briefly in one room that on first glance was a home gym, but a second, longer look showed that it was a combination torture chamber and S & M room. The stack of folded plastic sheets in one corner was a dead giveaway, pun intended. An assortment of nasty dark stains on the various metal fittings, including some splashes on the walls told another story and helped strengthen my resolve that these mongrels had to be eliminated.

In the office I found a collection of files, most of which were just the normal household record keeping, but there were several others that were all about EarthCare, EarthSquad and the planned operation against the natural gas plant.

Searching further, I found a locked cupboard in the bottom of a floor-to-ceiling stack of shelves, but which yielded in seconds to a letter-opener. I was expecting a safe with dual combination locks, but was amazed to find that Paula and Terry had trusted much of their ill-gotten gains to a $5 lock fitted to a flimsy wooden cupboard door.

Two fat pilot's bags stood side by side in the space with a much smaller soft case, like a small leather tool roll, sitting on top. The small roll looked dirty and stained, but it was tossed in my backpack with the files, while the pilot bags went with me. An exhaustive search didn't reveal anything else of interest in the room, so I returned to Corrine in the master bedroom, detouring via the torture chamber to cut off a length of rope.

'Took your bloody time Harry,' she grinned, 'find anything?'

'Yeah. Got some EarthCare papers and a couple of bags from a locked cupboard, but I couldn't find a safe.'

She chuckled, 'The idiots don't have one. The floor isn't strong enough. I asked his Lordship.'

I looked over and saw Terry was awake, his eyes wide and staring at Corrine with a terrified expression, his mouth straining against a gag consisting of a pair of Paula's panties by the look of them. The pillow was saturated with blood and a chunk of flesh lying on it proved to be his left ear, neatly sliced off flush with his skull.

His feet were secured with nylon cable ties and his wrists were cable tied to the bedhead.

I jerked a thumb at Paula, lying on her back with her mouth open in a most un-lady-like pose.

'I shot her up with my instant knock-out cocktail. She thought it was a mosquito biting her, but by the time her hand reached out, she was under!'

I nodded my head admiringly, 'Nice work, Mouse! So she should behave herself for a while?'

'Yep. At least another couple of hours, or until I hit her with the antidote like I did with his Lordship here.'

With Terry listening, and playing 'good cop, bad cop', I asked. 'OK, is there anything we need to ask these pieces of crap which might convince me to go easy on them?'

Corrine caught on. 'We know everything else about them, but maybe if we got their bank account access details, would that be enough?'

I pretended to think a few moments, then reluctantly said, 'Maybe. But we need to verify that they are legitimate before we let them go.'

Terry started making noises behind the gag, so Corrine pulled her Gerber MK II knife, stepped up to the bed and spoke to him. 'If I loosen this gag, you will not scream or yell. You will tell us where we can find your bank access details and the computer log-in details. For every piece of incorrect information, I will slice off another non-vital portion of your anatomy! You've lost one ear, but next time I'll be starting with your miserable little cock, then one ball at a time, so that's three lies you can tell before you're even less of a man than you are now! Is that clear?'

Tears streamed down his face as she delivered the words calmly and quietly that left no doubt in his addled mind that she would do what she said. I knew that she would too and that I'd happily hold the arsehole down while she did it!

He nodded frantically, so she gently pulled the wadded panties out of his mouth. His first few attempts to speak just produced croaks.

'Ah, c'mon Mr Williams, you going to have to do better than that! How can I get bank access when you won't speak a language I can understand?'

He rocked his head violently sideways toward the small bedside table where a glass of water rested.

'Ahh. You want some water? OK. This is good. Now we're communicating!'

I held the glass up to his parched lips and let him have a good suck. 'Now. Let's try again,' Corrine said.

He gasped, 'There's a small notebook in the bedside table drawer. It has the bank account details and the log-in ID and password for the Internet Banking. There's no password for the computer. Please don't cut me up any more. I'll do whatever you want, but just let me go. You can do what you like with Paula. She's one crazy bitch!'

I looked at Corrine as I passed the notebook over. 'Gee. There's a declaration of true love if ever I heard one! What a dipstick you are Mr Williams. You two make a really good pair!'

Corrine laughed as she padded through to the office where the Dell PC sat. I stayed supervising things in the bedroom, but shoved the panties back into his gob first. He nearly choked on them, but got the hang of breathing again and carried on, his eyes spinning like a pokie machine's reels.

I made another check-in with the lookouts, but all was still quiet out front and back, so I sat in a chair and contemplated my navel until Corrine came back and beckoned me out into the hallway.

'There were four accounts, all in Vanuatu and in US$, two of which looked more like day to day operating accounts, one for each of them. They had around $25,000 in each, but the other two were called Investment Accounts. They had US$4 million in each, with weekly deposits of $250,000 going into each one, regular as clockwork!'

'Bloody hell! That's some money trail! How easy will that be to trace?'

She shook her head. 'I already took a bit of a look and it's next to impossible. It's been bounced around the world multiple times; in and out of dummy corporations or shell companies, using all the tax havens and those countries whose banking laws make the Swiss laws look like their famous cheese!'

'So, what's the go with the money and the accounts?'

She had the grace to blush slightly, although in the dim light it was hard to tell.

'Seeing as how the money is untraceable, I decided that not all pirates should live north of here. I took the liberty of creating two new accounts in the National Bank of Vanuatu, one for you and Sandy and one for Dave and me. They're Username and numbered accounts to preserve anonymity and can be accessed from anywhere in the world via the Internet. You can move funds around to other accounts if you want, or just leave them there as you see fit. Just remember no one will be tapping on your door wanting them back! Ever!'

She passed a slip of paper across, 'Don't lose that. Your username is Firebird@38, the account number is the Bank's number and I transferred US$4,027,000.00 into your account and a similar amount into ours.'

While my head was reeling with this info, she went on, 'I also set up transfer instructions to empty their accounts into ours weekly. That will only last as long as it takes for word to filter through to the money source that the recipients have carked it! Still, with the secrecy surrounding this operation, it could take a while and we might do some good with it in the meantime. You really do have to think about your retirement, my dear man. It's no good scraping along on your last couple of million, you know! Very bad for the playboy image.'

Finally, I laughed with her and gave her a big hug and kiss. 'You're right! Stuffed if I want a greedy Government grabbing it. I must confess I really don't mind having a few extra bob to rub together. It's become quite addictive! But back to reality, what do you want to do with these turkeys? Do you think we've bled them dry?'

'Yeah, I reckon so. The only question is, do we wake Paula up and let her see that she's going down?'

'We have to make sure they don't survive the house collapse. Can we be sure of that?'

By way of answer, out of an inner pocket, she pulled a wicked little tear-drop shaped leather bag with a stout leather strap attached. 'This, my darling man will make sure they don't survive, and any investigation won't reveal anything suspicious. That, plus another little surprise I've planned. All you have to do is get your papers and bags back down the scaffolding and safely down onto the service road. I'll be a quick as I can, but just be ready to move fast when I do come down, because things will be happening quite quickly after that and I'd like to be back in our room before the first pop.'

She was being mysterious, especially when she dug Terry's mobile out of the bedside table drawer and slipped it in a side pocket. I checked in with the lookouts and received the 'all-clear' from each, then I glared at Terry who was looking wildly around, but unable to move, a situation I was sure he had been in many times since he met Paula!

I ducked out through the window, retrieved the two heavy pilot bags, now joined by the length of rope tied to the handles so I could lower them to the ground, and strapped on the backpack full of papers. The climb back down the support structure was more difficult than coming up, but finally I was clear of the underside of the house, stumbling under the weight of the extra items. I also noticed several critical bamboo braces and major structural intersections were already wrapped in yellow Det cord.

CHAPTER 5

CRATER HOTEL, LAKE BATUR, BALI, WEDNESDAY AM

It was extremely awkward stumbling down the very steep slope with the two heavy bags and the paper-filled backpack, but I made the service track safely.

About five minutes later, there was a soft rustle in the long grass and Corrine trotted up to me, hardly breathing fast. She grabbed up the cases and urged me along to the back corner of the Crater Hotel property. It didn't take long to get through the gate, up the slope and the back stairs.

On the way, she recalled Jane and Rick from the Bizarre Hotel grounds, telling them to move as quickly as they could. We were both sweating heavily when we slipped in through the hotel back door and along to our room. We'd just got inside when we heard Jane and Rick enter their room safely.

Dumping the bags, and at Corrine's insistence, we turned all the lights out, then went out onto the balcony where we could talk to Roger and Jill two rooms along, and then Jane and Rick came out too.

'What's going to happen,' Jane asked, 'are you guys OK?'

I chuckled, 'Yeah. We're fine thanks, and that was a good job out front. But I'm glad you're back safely.'

'OK, get ready to duck! It's showtime!' Corrine said, excitement in her voice, as she angled her mobile up to the light and dialled a number from memory. We could hear the ring tone for a few seconds, before there was a bright, white flash from a hundred metres away which lit up the whole side of the crater. It was followed by a huge cloud of glass and shattered wood that sprayed out and up for a hundred metres, propelled by a huge explosion which shattered the peace of the night with a thunderous roar that battered the senses.

We just had time to drop behind the fascia boarding as pieces of debris splattered the hotel front and blew out most the windows on the open side. As the rolling clap of thunder slowly spread out over the vast expanse of the crater, screams erupted on all sides with panicked guests rushing around like headless chooks. Then came a sharp crack from the underside of the largely decapitated house and in exquisite slow motion, the remains settled down onto the hillside like a kneeling camel, before commencing a slow tumble down the steep slope.

Pieces of house showered in all directions and the destruction was so rapid and complete that few bits even reached the factory building far below. It left a trail of burning debris behind like a long, yellow finger pointing back up the hill where there was a gaping hole in the row of buildings like a missing tooth in a small child's smile.

While Corrine and I grinned at each other like naughty kids who'd just played a joke on Mum and Dad, pandemonium seemed to be erupting within the hotel as someone went from room to room banging on doors to make sure no one was hurt. We quickly stripped our dark clothing off and went to the door just clad in jocks and panties, pretending we'd been in bed.

The Night Manager was most distraught. 'Forgive me Sir and Madam, but are you not hurt? I am most dreadfully sorry for this terrible thing. This has never happened before. Terrible! Just terrible!'

'We're fine,' I reassured him, as the sight of Corrine's bare chest served to temporarily distract him from his distress, while behind him in the corridor, guests rushed to and fro, seemingly without purpose, although an increasing few were gathering around the Manager to hear his words.

'Do you know what's happened?' Corrine asked, managing to stifle a yawn. 'It all seems terribly exciting!'

'Oh, no! It is a terrible thing missus! But I don't know what has happened except there was the most terrible explosion and most of the hotel windows on this side of the building have been broken.

We shall have to put mattresses in the bar and dining room until we can clear up the broken glass. I must ask you to please pack your baggage and move to the dining room where the Receptionist will check off your names. Only those facing the crater are affected by this terrible thing.'

He turned to address the group gathered around. 'All those with rooms facing the road may stay in their rooms, but all others please pack your baggage and move to the dining room. Please, please be careful of all the broken glass!'

Before he left, I said, 'Our room was somehow spared any damage. We would appreciate being allowed to stay in it.' After asking permission, he took a quick look and agreed, so that spared us the bother of shifting.

Now that he'd calmed down, that effect spread to the other guests and the noise level dropped considerably as by twos and threes, they drifted off to either pack their gear or to return to bed. Several guests had been outside and found their way into the carpark of the Hotel Bizarre, but there was little to see apart from a missing house and more of the debris field. The Police belatedly turned up and chased everyone out of the carpark so with little to look at, the lookers and peepers came back to the hotel. I overheard the Manager telling the Receptionist there had been a lot of damage done to the Hotel Bizarre although no one was injured as they had very few guests.

Jane, Rick, Jill and Roger had to move out of their rooms, so I got them to bring their bags into our room for security. I also collected the mini radios and put them in the special gear bag along with the balaclavas, weapons, ammunition and the left-over Det cord and unused C-4 and detonators. We had a debrief in our room where we ran over the highlights of the operation. Corrine glossed over the details of taking out Terry and Paula, but she was able to assure the group they weren't able to cause any further trouble.

We hadn't had a chance in all the excitement to look at the files I'd grabbed, nor to look in the two heavy pilot bags so I didn't mention them, nor did we mention ratting the bank accounts, figuring that was private business.

The Manager came to the door while we were still talking, 'My wonderful staff have managed to clear your two rooms of glass so I am pleased to say that you may return to them, although there will not be glass in the windows and the air will be quite chill in the morning.'

Roger chuckled and looked at his watch, 'Well, I guess that would be about now!'

The little man looked concerned all over again. 'Oh dear. It's half past three already. Your night's rest has been ruined!'

'Not your fault, sport!' Roger suggested. 'Unless you planted a bomb or started a gas leak.'

'Oh, don't say such things. Bombs, gas leaks! Who knows?'

We thanked him profusely and offered some cash for the staff for doing a great job. He was most happy with that and trotted off to find them, while Roger, Jill, Jane and Rick collected their bags again and returned to their rooms. It was only then I realised that Corrine was still just wearing panties and I was in jocks, but nobody had seemed to notice or mind. I guess that it was that sort of night.

Now we were alone again, I decided to check out the contents of the pilot's bags. They were locked, but setting the combination locks to the default 0000 allowed the latches to pop.

I looked in the first one, then opened the second and checked its contents before looking around. Corrine was just coming out of the bathroom, so I called her over.

'Yep. What's up, Doc?' She said in her cheekiest Bugs Bunny voice.

'You remember that these bags were very heavy?'

'Yep. Remember that. So — what's the problem?'

'There could be a problem if there was such a thing as having too much money.'

'What are you talking about, Harry. You're not making much sense. Are you having an adrenaline low? Or just need another round of nooky.'

'OK, smart arse. Take a look in those two bags.'

She squatted down in front of them, striking an interesting pose from my perspective and opened the first to see it was packed tightly, right to the top with fairly new $100-dollar Australian banknotes all done up in bundles with paper straps marked $100,000 around them.

'Oh! Wow! Now I see what you mean. This really is something else! Did you know they were full of cash when you grabbed them?'

'No way! I thought they were more files they'd accumulated. I never thought about money.'

'OK. So how much is here?'

I reached out and lifted the top bundle, revealing it was made up of ten smaller packets also strapped with paper strips.

'Each smaller wrap is worth $10,000, so the bundle is worth $100,000. I had this problem a few operations ago and from memory, that bag, packed the way it is, should hold about $1,100,000.'

Her eyebrows raised. 'Is the other one the same?'

'Yep! Exactly the same. This must have been for local pay-offs. There's no reason to have this much cash otherwise.'

I looked at her, still squatting in front of the million-dollar case. 'I have a suggestion as to what to do with it.'

She looked up, a questioning look on her pretty face. 'Hit me with it, big fella.'

'Let's give it all to the crew. $2.2mil divided amongst eight comes to $275,000 each. As a couple, that means Roger and Jill share $550,000, which should go a long way to setting them up doing what they want. We've just picked up over $4 mil each from the accounts, plus a $250K per week income for a while. That's a good payday in anyone's language, so I'm sure that the others can use a hand.

I mean, look at Alex and Bree. They've got nothing, so this could mean the world to them. Jane, Rick, Terry and Gillian are good people with a long career in the Navy ahead, but having $275K in the bank is a really nice backstop.'

She thought a moment, then jumped up and gave me a long kiss.

'Well done, Harry. You're right. We have plenty of money and it would mean a lot to them. We should get them back in here and tell them!'

I smiled, 'That's an even better idea, but just one thing. Can they handle a lump of cash? Especially our four Navy crew.'

'Yeah. I think they can. It's not as though it's a fortune. Not these days.'

Without bothering to dress, Corrine went and knocked on Jane and Rick's door, then Jill and Roger's, while I did a rough split of the cash into eight piles. It wasn't too difficult, especially as there was a bit more than my first rough assessment, so I was able to make up three bundles, and seven small stacks for a total of $275K for each. There were a few small packs left over that I tossed aside to use for expenses. I only set out four piles and lined them neatly along the end of the bed, leaving the remaining $550K in one bag for Alex and Bree and another $550K for Terry and Gillian.

Jane and Rick came in first, with Jane dressed like Corrine and looking very appealing. She was a bit bigger in the chest than Corrine, but still neat. I can't help it — I notice beautiful ladies' chests! Roger and Jill were wearing mismatched pants and tops which had been hastily dragged on.

It was comical to see their reactions when they spotted the money, as large amounts of physical cash do that to nearly everybody, myself included.

It was Roger who asked the question, 'Ah...what's with the money, Harry?'

Briefly, I explained. 'When we raided Terry and Paula's place, we needed to take any papers which related to EarthCare and their operational planning to make sure they were destroyed. I stuffed a bunch of files into a backpack, but these were sitting there as well with the latches locked so I just grabbed them. We think the cash was for local palm greasing, but it does raise the question of where it came from. Still, it's not our concern since cash only belongs to its current holder.'

Jane and Rick were still staring bug-eyed at the banded bundles and stacks of pretty green notes.

I coughed to clear my throat. 'So, the deal is this, guys and girls. Corrine and I have decided this will be payday for the whole crew. Spoils of war, so to speak. There's four of you here and four piles of cash. It's all yours!'

Jane moved over and touched the pile of green plastic. 'But this must belong to someone? We can't just take it!'

Corrine spoke softly to her. 'Earlier this morning, I spend 30-minutes on-line trying to trace where their funds were coming from without success, but I'm not as good as the Tax Department investigators. Therefore, we don't know who to give it back to, unless you want to just make a donation to the Federal Politician's retirement fund?'

Without looking away from the cash, Jane shook her head. 'No, I certainly don't want to do that! But being practical, as Navy personnel, how can we account for having this?'

'Ah,' I said, 'that's where Uncle Harry's cunning plan comes in. Let me explain. Firstly, you could just take the cash in a bag back to Australia and stow it anywhere you think is safe and take some whenever you need it. That's simple and excellent if you just use it to get small things, but it's difficult to buy big things with cash these days. A used car is fine, but a new car or a house deposit would be very difficult. That's where the second option comes in.

Corrine can set up accounts for you with the National Bank of Vanuatu. We have accounts there and they are numbered accounts which you can access from anywhere. Just keep transfers into your Australian accounts below $10K per time and you won't have the ATO asking embarrassing questions. An accountant should be consulted to keep you legal. Either way, that stack is all yours!'

She finally looked away from the bundles of green. 'How much is here, Harry. It's not a big bundle of notes really. It'd fit in a small gym bag easily.'

I smiled at her. 'Yes, it would and that's a good, unobtrusive way to carry it. There's $275,000 in each stack.'

Her eyes widened and Rick closed his mouth. 'That's a lot of money to me, Harry. Could I really just take it and keep it with me?'

'Sure. No problem with that. Just keep it safe, don't flash it around and keep your lips zipped. Remember what I said; cash is anonymous and belongs to the person who has it in his or her pocket.'

She nodded. 'I'll just go and get some plastic bags. Won't be a minute.' With a final lingering look at what constituted a fortune to her, she left the room, but was back in less than the promised minute. She handed one each to Rick, Roger and Jill and filled hers from the pile she'd been fondling. 'It's heavier than I expected.'

I chuckled, 'There's 2,750 pieces of pretty, coloured plastic there.'

She started to tear up, then gave me a stimulating, full body hug and a big kiss. I got the same from Jill, as did Corrine who got the same treatment and seemed to enjoy it. Rick and Roger confined their appreciation to handshakes and a quick man-hug, although Corrine got the full treatment and looked very pleased with herself.

My parting words to the two Navy crew was, 'Think twice before you start spraying cash all over the place. It'll be gone before you know it and you'll attract the attention of the wrong people. Just be cool with it. OK?'

CHAPTER 6

CRATER HOTEL, LAKE BATUR, BALI, WEDNESDAY

Finally, all four had collected their loot and left for their rooms, still a bit stunned at their change in fortune and deep in discussion about what to do with it. We arranged to meet in the dining room in 90-minutes for breakfast.

Corrine kissed me again. 'That was really good, Harry. I feel good about doing it, but now I'm going to have long shower. I've got some dirt to wash off!'

I nodded, 'Yeah. I feel the same. Away you go.'

She gave me a funny look and shook her head.

'Nope. I want company and my back needs washing really well.'

I try not to argue with pretty, semi-naked ladies so I gladly followed her to the shower and washed her very thoroughly; several times. Everywhere. As a tension reliever, it was a most effective therapy.

The dining room was in chaos when we got there, with people who'd been displaced from their rooms parked in every clear space with their luggage and a mattress or two to perch on, but few were trying to sleep. Nevertheless, the Management was trying very hard to make up for the difficulties and had opened the bar early with all drinks half-price and the breakfast free. That in turn led to an upbeat mood and our crew got stuck in like the rest.

'What's our plan today?' Roger asked.

I grinned around a mouthful of bacon and eggs, washed it down with a slug of cold beer and replied, 'No plan, apart from acting like tourists who've have their plans messed up. Let's just cruise with the flow and see what the Police come up with.'

The mention of Police made the crew nervous, but I hastened to reassure them there was absolutely nothing to connect six tourists with a house blowing up.

There was in fact, a parade of coppers through the hotel and some stopped to talk to selected guests. Finally, we were visited by the Manager with a policeman in tow who was apologetic for disturbing our extended breakfast, but did we see anything last night?

Naturally, we hadn't seen or heard anything until the explosion, so our interview lasted about 30 seconds. I offered to buy the policeman a drink but he gave me the stern look reserved for dopey foreigners who had too much time and money on their hands.

With our cover firmly established, I asked the Receptionist if we could book a cruise on the Lake. Despite the turmoil, she was obliging and mentioned there were some operators that had a highly dubious reputation for safety, but she would make a booking for six with the best one. She had tried it herself, she earnestly assured me, and found the boat clean, well-maintained and the commentary lively, informative and funny.

I paid in cash from my new stash and she said the hotel bus would be ready to go in 30-minutes.

'C'mon crew!' I tried to rev them up. 'The bus leaves in 30-minutes. We're going on a lake cruise.'

There was a chorus of disbelief, but they finally dragged themselves up and got organised. The Manager had somehow been able to get the services of a bunch of glass fitters and they were hard at work in the rooms cleaning up, cutting and fitting new glass. Our room was OK but the corridor was like Central Station on Saturday morning so I was glad we were getting out of the place for a few hours.

We scrambled on the bus with a few others who had heard my request at the front counter and they were fairly happy as well. The trip down the crater wall was exciting, and scenic and upon being delivered to the lakeshore and the boat, we wasted no time in getting well fortified with alcohol. That pastime isn't difficult anywhere in Bali and we found the Lake Batur cruise was OK, but not exactly memorable. The thought occurred to me that if this was the best cruise, then the others would have been quite dismal.

Delivered safely back to shore, we found our happy driver propped up in the local bar, but he assured me he only drank fruit juice on duty.

'No drink and drive Boss,' he said earnestly, 'and no drinking at work. Very good rules. So now we go and then we drink, yes?'

Everyone agreed with a resounding, 'Yes!' And in that frame of mind, we made the steep climb back up the crater. At one point near the top, there was a gap in the trees and it allowed a quick view of the missing house and on looking carefully, one could see debris had even spilled onto the road, although there was no sign of the house itself.

Back at the hotel, the Manager was quick to tell us the Police had told him that two people had died in the explosion and the subsequent fire and there was almost nothing left of them or the house. It was almost certainly a gas explosion and there were no suspicious circumstances to investigate.

'It is an accident that happens too frequently in Bali,' he said sorrowfully, 'not all gas installations are done properly.'

The accommodation corridor was much quieter and the absence of people camped out in the dining room suggested the glaziers had been, glazed and gone. It seemed some of the other guests had gone as well, but there were still a rowdy crowd around the bar that night. We were a tired crew having had no sleep for 36 hours and no one stayed up to party on.

'We check out tomorrow as planned,' I told the crew over another lovely dinner. 'We're booked all the way back to Marina Del Ray and there won't be any Customs checks as we're already cleared in country, and we'll probably head out Friday or Saturday. The cash will be safe if it's just in your normal bags, or you can hang onto it if you like.'

I could see that Jane and Rick were probably sleeping with theirs as a pillow and weren't letting it out of sight for a moment.

THURSDAY

It was another bright, clear day with cool temperatures at the height the hotel was and after paying for everything with my Visa Black, we wearily climbed aboard the mini-bus and rattled off down the back slope of the old volcano, with the satisfaction of knowing it was mission accomplished!

We had some time to waste at the wharf before the fast ferry was ready to depart and were joined by several other passengers, obviously day trippers. It was a comfortable trip and the sight of *Firebird and Seeker* safely moored was welcome. The sight and feel of Sandy was very welcome and there was an enthusiastic hello from Jasper and little Krazy girl.

Sandy was delighted to hear that the operation went so well and even more so to hear about the giant earn we'd made.

'I still haven't gone through the files I grabbed,' I remarked. 'They're in that backpack.'

'I'll do that tomorrow,' Sandy offered, 'and I think we should stay here at least another day or two, to let the six of you get over that gig. Everyone looks so tired.'

I had to admit that she was right, and allowed myself to get talked into at least two more days at Marina Del Rey as R & R.

We all came together for drinks that afternoon aboard *Seeker*, where I ceremoniously handed Alex, Bree, Terry and Gillian a plastic shopping bag with a paper-wrapped bundle in each.

'Presents!' I smiled at them. 'For being good crew persons.'

The rest of us watched in gleeful anticipation as they were all puzzled to get a present in the first place, but the looks on their faces when they unwrapped the bundles of cash was absolutely priceless.

'What's this Commander?' Alex asked, still unable to bring himself to address me any other way.

'I call it 'spoils of war' Alex, and it's your share to do with as you want. I don't know what sort of nest-egg you have put away, but this is for whatever you want to do with it. Corrine can help if you need to put it in a secure Bank account.

The same with the rest of you. You can do what you want with it, but I suggest you spend carefully to avoid the attention of the Australian Tax Department.

'H... how much is here, Harry?' Bree asked, looking tearful.

'Two hundred and seventy-five thousand Aussie dollars, dear girl,' I answered cheerfully. 'Best payday we've all had for quite a while I must say.'

At that, Bree burst into tears and hugged everyone in sight, finally saying, 'Nobody's ever given me something without wanting a lot more in return. I don't know what to say!'

'That'll do; we understand.' Sandy replied, as she hugged Bree.

Gillian followed her example by crying and hugging us hard.

'May I assume, Commander, that this money came from the targets?' Alex asked.

'Yes, it did Alex. We tried to trace it, but the source is extremely well hidden. We'll have to make sure the forensic accountants are still chasing it. I'll call Greg tonight.'

'I do not know this Greg person, but if the money comes from those very bad people, I am happy they are gone and we have some good from them.'

'Well said, Alex. Now, how about we go celebrate at the bar and have a feed?'

Dave offered to hide their cash away in a concealed drawer where they could get at it any time they wanted. Before calling the Admiral, I placed the long-overdue call to Greg.

'*Harry! Just the man I wanted to hear from. How's it all going?*'

'Good thanks Greg. Well, better than good. The job's done with no casualties on our side and apparently no suspicions of foul play from the Authorities.'

'*Oh, that's brilliant, my friend. A lot of people will be happy!*'

'We're hanging around for a while longer having a bit of R & R, seeing as we're here anyway, but there's two things you can do for me if you would.'

'*Sure thing. Go ahead.*'

'Bob mentioned he had a couple of ex-Tax Department investigators who were really good at Forensic Accounting. Can you chase that up and get them or someone like them, looking for the money trail? We had a look using the target's computer, and found the trail is well hidden in a series of offshore accounts and shell companies, but there is an active link still running and paying money into one account. Tell the accounting team they don't need to trace the trail forward, we have that one covered, but they need to trace it backwards. We don't know how long this link will keep working, although we've set diversions in place to keep the payments moving. Tell them to hurry or it'll close down.'

'*Wow! Copy that. Just between thee and me, I presume the on-going payments are going to a good home?*'

I chuckled, 'You may presume such a thing. Call it danger money, but the recipients are well hidden.'

'*Excellent! So there should be no loose ends?*'

'No! That should be tight. Now the second thing I need you to do is ask very delicately, perhaps via our Embassy in Bali, if there were any Australians injured in that explosion beside a hotel overlooking Lake Batur. You could say you've been asked by relatives who haven't heard from people staying in the area. But what I really need to know is if there are any suspicions about foul play. The Police have already said it was just a gas explosion, but we need to keep monitoring the situation in case further evidence comes up. Can you do that?'

'*No problem. It will be a discrete enquiry about possible rello's staying in the area. I presume you'll be another couple of weeks yet?*'

'Yeah. At least that. A little private enterprise job has popped up, but part of our cover was that we were going to be poking around the islands looking for good dive sites, so we're obliged to do so for at least a couple of weeks, perhaps more. Otherwise it could look suspicious to some Indonesian copper with a devious mind, we didn't stick with our declared plan.'

'No problem, mate. I'll get your requests moving while you enjoy yourself.'

'Gee, thanks Greg. Cheers for now.'

While I still had the phone in hand, I placed a call to the Admiral and passed on the good news. He was delighted at the successful outcome and said he'd be passing the message 'upstairs' immediately.

'I have to say, Harry, in the last couple of days, a lot more interest has been shown in your operation from the current occupant of the Lodge. It would seem you and your team have defused a potentially major crisis in Aussie politics.'

'Glad to hear that, Admiral. You can pass on I have initiated discrete enquiries to the Police concerning 'relatives of people who were staying in the area of the explosion and haven't been heard from for a while'.'

'Even better and well done! Now when can I have my gun and sailors back?'

I laughed. 'Not just yet, sir. We have to follow our declared itinerary in order to appear normal, so we have to go cruise the islands and get some diving in first. Then we need crew to get back home to the Gold Coast.'

He laughed, 'No trouble, Commander. I'm just yanking your chain. Paul Davy and his crew are on leave at the moment for ten days, then they'll be on a training rotation for another three weeks. If you can be finished your work by then, that'd be good, but if it does take longer, I think I can handle it.'

'I appreciate that, sir and I'll keep you updated.'

'Thank you Commander, to you and your crew for a truly outstanding job.'

Duty call completed, I joined the rest of the crew, who were well on their way to getting pissed in the lounge bar of the Marina Del Ray. There were some crews off other boats in the lounge and after a while we started chatting with them and the party grew. Some were heading for the good dive sites up off the south coast of Sulawesi or what used to be Celebes, and when they asked where we were headed, I handballed the question to Roger who nodded and said, 'Yeah. The places we wanted to see are off the south-east coast of Sulawesi, but not the main sites that the tourists all get dragged to.'

I thought that he might have dug a hole by saying that, but the pleasantly-rounded woman asking was distracted by somebody else. At that moment, my phone rang and over the party noise, I thought I heard a strange voice but couldn't make out what it was saying.

CHAPTER 7

MARINA DEL RAY, THURSDAY

'Sorry about the noise, I'll just move away from this bunch of pissed boaties... There, that's better. Now sorry, who's this?'

'My apologies for contacting you directly like this Commander, but I just had to talk to you immediately I received the news. I live in a house called The Lodge in Canberra and I am sorry for the mystery; I never trust the security on these things.'

My mind started racing wondering why the PM would call me. 'No problem sir. How may I help you?'

'Oh, you already have, Commander. Very much so and I wanted to say it would appear that you and your crew have done the country a great service by ah...fixing the problem we had and apparently doing so without creating a diplomatic incident. Most impressive! There are few who I can share a confidence with these days, but I would like to explain this business was not so much about this party or that party, but was a plan by a few rogue politians and business men to totally destabilise the Australian Government system!'

I'm buggered if I know how I came to be the confidant to the PM, but said anyway, 'That's roughly about what I gained from some of the correspondence which I've already seen, Sir. I haven't seen a document which quotes names yet, but it might be in the last lot of files I found in the possession of two of the late instigators of this ah...failed enterprise.'

'I'd be further indebted to you Commander, if you would let me know if you do find such a document and ask that if you do, please don't allow anybody else to see it!'

'There's only two other persons who have full access to the documents involved, sir. They are my partner, a Queensland Police

88

Inspector and a colleague from the SAS who was involved in the incident in the desert where I was wounded.'

'Ah, I understand. That would be the 'incident' as you call it, where you earned the right to wear that piece of maroon ribbon?'

'Yessir. That's the one.'

'Very well, Commander. I shan't take up more of your time, except to say I'd greatly appreciate having a private meeting with you and your two ladies just as soon as you return to Australia. I'll have one of my staff get in touch with you shortly, if that's alright?'

'Certainly Sir. Since you're asking, I'd also like to appraise you of all that's gone on with this operation as soon as possible, but I'm still in Indonesia and won't be back in Australian waters for another two weeks. Contact is best made via secure SatPhone. I have the number when you're ready to copy.'

'Go ahead......I have that, thank you Commander. And my thanks again to you and your crew for a marvellous job. I look forward to seeing you soon. Good night.'

I started to say good night when I realised that he'd signed off, so I re-joined the group.

Sandy raised one eyebrow, a trick I'd never been able to master and asked softly, 'Any problems?'

I shook my head, 'Nah! It was just the PM... but I'll tell you later.'

She sat back with a startled look on her face, not sure whether I was yanking her chain or not, so I just held up a hand to forestall any questions.

The rest of the evening went pleasantly and we made several good new friends including Bruce and Heather, the pretty and pleasantly-rounded lady I'd spoken to earlier and her husband. They were a lively couple in their late fifties and sailed a 55 foot mono-hull ketch with two cats and a foul-mouthed African Grey parrot. They weren't into diving so much, but loved meeting and associating with the locals on the more isolated islands, since Bruce was an Anthropologist attached to Queensland University. Unfortunately, they seemed to want to go roughly where we were headed, so we'd have to work out something about that, or else be very careful.

FRIDAY

We all slept well, especially aided by some vitamin nookie and the day was officially rated as slow-starting. I'd told Sandy that Jane and Rick had become a unit and they now shared the forward queen cabin, which left the stern cabin free. She refrained from making any comment about my behaviour while sharing a bed with Corrine, which I took to mean that I had a reputation to live down to; and had succeeded again.

She giggled, 'She said you had an erection she couldn't jump over most of the time! She was most impressed!'

I wisely refrained from responding, particularly as I fancied taking my lovely Sandy back to bed for most of the afternoon. Jane and Rick were sprawled in the sun on the bow trampolines, I was sitting around the cockpit playing with the cats while Sandy dug through the backpack and started going through the files I'd grabbed from Terry's desk just before the big bang.

'You'd better check this out, big dog!' she called as I carefully pried a lacerated finger out of Krazy's mouth — she who always forgets that needle-sharp teeth used in play are still needle-sharp!

'Coming dear. I'll just get a band-aid.'

'Ah. Playing with the Catten again are we?'

'How on earth did you guess? Now, what've you got?'

'This file details the setup of the payment system and these loose sheets at the back name a few names, places and contacts. Is this what our new best friend would be looking for?'

I had a quick skim over the pages and saw they were exactly what was being looked for! They also were pure dynamite and I imagine the individuals named in them would stop at nothing to retrieve them and eliminate everyone who had seen them!

'Holy crap! This stuff could get all of us killed! Keep looking for anything else that's juicy, but I'm sure this is the real deal.'

She returned to her scrutiny of the last couple of file folders while I took the red-hot one and stowed it in a sealed plastic bag down below, where I put it under the old blanket in Jasper's bed which he sometimes retires to when he gets booted off the marital bed. As I came back up to the saloon, Sandy had her head buried in another file and absently said, 'This was in the backpack with the files. I don't think it's ours. I haven't seen it before.'

She flicked a grubby, soft leather roll across the table at me, so I was forced to stoop to catch it. It was about 300mm or so long and about 60mm or so in diameter, and had quite a lot of weight to it, as well as a series of six big lumps along its length.

Naturally curious I started to untie the three leather thong cords which held the long side closed, then the SatPhone rang so I shoved the leather bag in my pocket and answered the phone.

A ridiculously cheerful female voice announced, '*Good morning Commander. I'm Charlie Langley, the private and personal secretary to the person who spoke with you last night.*'

'Good morning to you Charlie, are you always this cheerful?'

'*Oh, most certainly, Commander. Work is too much fun to be grumpy. From what I can gather, you should be the same, living on that lovely boat and having exciting adventures all the time.*'

I coughed, 'Well, Charlie, it is true I do love my life on my beautiful boat, and I do seem to end up in the middle of adventures, but it's not all great fun as the newest bullet hole in my shoulder reminds me from time to time.'

'*Oh dear, I must update your file. I didn't hear about that. Left or right?*'

'Excuse me?'

'*Left or right shoulder, dear man? And it's not as though you haven't been shot before, although I suppose it wouldn't be something you'd get used to.*'

'That'd be left, and no, you don't.'

'Very good, Commander. Now, I've been told to ask if you have located the information which was discussed last night?'

'You are quick! But yes, we have in fact, not ten minutes ago. My partner, Inspector Thomson, is just going through the last few folders to see if there is anything else of value.'

'Excellent! But you are keeping this confidential and the documents secure?'

I chuckled, 'Yeah. There's only Sandy and I who've seen these docs and my cat is sitting on the folder guarding it!'

For the first time there was a hint of nervousness in her voice.

'Ahh...If that's a joke, then ha, ha! But if not, then I urge you most strongly to secure those documents, please! I can also tell you I'm about to land at Bandar Udara Airport on Lombok. The boss sent me in this lovely chartered jet straight from Canberra to collect those files you have. Unfortunately, the crew tell me they have to stay overnight due to flight time blowout or something aeronautical like that, so I'd be pleased if you could arrange accommodation for me. My needs are simple and the crew tell me I have an eighty-minute trip to get to you, so as it is now 11:00 local time, may I request you are available to meet me at 12:30?'

I chuckled again, 'No problem, Charlie, we'll find you somewhere to stay. You can even stay on board if you don't mind roughing it. We have a spare cabin at the moment and you can keep the files safe if you can get them away from my cat. He likes sitting on them.'

'Oh, that's a kind offer, Commander. I accept, gratefully. I must confess I am really intrigued to see your boat that I've read so much about. And is your deckhand Jasper still there too? He seems to feature quite prominently in the various reports I have of your exploits and I'd love to meet him.'

I laughed, 'Oh, yes. Jasper will be here and he'll be happy to meet you too. See you soon Charlie. Bye for now.'

Sandy cracked up when I told her about 'deckhand' Jasper. 'Bad boy, Harry! The poor lady will be thoroughly confused.'

'Not my fault. She was the one who leapt to Jasper confusions and invited herself up here, but I did say she could stay aboard for the night.'

'You did what? Oh shit. I'll have to tidy up the cabin and make up the bed. When does she get here?'

'She was just landing over on Lombok as we were speaking, so she'll be here on the fast ferry about 12:30 or so.'

'Bloody hell! Those files must be considered rather important to go to this much trouble.'

'Yeah. I was thinking that as well. We'd better be careful none of this shitstorm bounces back on us!'

Sandy looked serious for once, 'I've a feeling, dear man of mine, that we're in the middle of this particular shitstorm.'

I called Reception at the Marina office.

'I have a guest, a Miss Langley, who has just flown in from Australia and is coming here for the night. Could I have the ferry drop her off at *Firebird* on the way past when they arrive, please?'

'*That will be a pleasure, Mr Stevens. I'll call our driver who is just leaving the dock at Lombok now.*'

'Thank you very much and we'll all be in for dinner again with one extra.'

'*No problem sir and thank you. I'll let Chef know.*'

Despite being deprived of the pleasure of an afternoon romp with Sandy, I was quite intrigued by this urgent mission of the PM's PPS, just to collect some files. They must be thought to be potentially even more damaging than we'd thought!

While Sandy fixed up the stern cabin, I stirred the sleeping beauties on the trampoline and told them about our visitor.

'Don't volunteer any information, although you probably won't be asked. But if she does, all you have to say is what your part in the operation was. Make no mention of any money. That information stays with us and is nobody else's business.'

They were both cool with that and also most curious about the trip to pick up files.

The fast ferry was only about ten minutes late and the young dude driver who'd taken us to and from Bali, swept up to the stern of *Firebird* with a big flourish and roar of reversed engines, although he did park it neatly beside the boarding platform with a big grin on his face.

Charlie proved to be a small, neat woman, comfortably rounded and possibly aged in her early to mid 40's. The expected beaming smile was on her face and certainly looked genuine as she nimbly hopped onto *Firebird* before turning to be handed her compact overnight bag by the driver who saluted her, then roared off to his parking spot at the head of the main wharf.

At least she was dressed sensibly in long shorts, a loose top and joggers.

She fairly bounded up the steps, hand out-thrust in greeting.

'Commander Stevens, I presume.' she grinned, 'and Inspector Thomson as well. What a pleasure and how exciting to be dropped off right to your marvellous boat!'

Sandy and I exchanged grins as we realised here was a woman who could talk underwater with a mouthful of marbles!

'Welcome Charlie, and we'd prefer to be called Sandy and Harry since you're our guest for the night.'

'Of course, Harry. What a great boat this is and the huge marina just over there with all those other big boats. Wonderful! The boss would love to see this, but he can't move without the tribe of advisors tripping over his heels. I'll have to try to sneak him away sometime. Maybe you'd take him for a bit of a sailing holiday when you get back?'

I looked startled for a moment, trying to imagine the PM on board, but politely replied, 'I'd be very happy to do that, Charlie. Just give me some notice if you can.'

My bluff failed miserably when she said, 'Oh, you would? That's absolutely bloody marvellous. With your background and Sandy as a serving Police Officer aboard, security requirements can be met and we can dispense with the protective tribe! He'd be delighted.

There'll only be the two of us. He never re-married as you probably know.'

'No problem, Charlie. There'll just be Sandy, myself and Jasper as crew.'

'Fantastic! We'll do it sooner rather than later, if you don't mind?'

'No problem. Just call.'

Jane and Rick came aft to say hi and Charlie launched into greeting mode again, insisting on calling Rick, 'Jasper'.

'Actually, Charlie, that's Rick and he and Jane are crew on loan from the Navy. Jasper hasn't come out yet.'

'Oh, silly me. My apologies, Rick. I tend to leap to confusions when I'm excited and this is all so very exciting! So where is the dear lad?'

I couldn't help chuckling as I called, 'Jasper. Come and meet Charlie!'

My big black cat padded silently out of the gloom of the saloon where he'd been sitting watching the circus in the cockpit.

Charlie did a classic double take and an involuntary step back as he stopped just in front of her and for once, she was temporarily speechless.

'This is Jasper?' she asked in a slightly breathless voice. 'He's not exactly what I expected.'

'Several bad guys have discovered so, to their eternal regret,' I said dryly. 'It doesn't pay to underestimate Jasper.'

I bent down and spoke to him. 'This is Charlie and she's staying with us for tonight. She's a friend and a nice lady so please look after her. If you're nice, she might even scratch you.'

Charlie got an odd look on her face when Jasper gave his usual response by turning his head towards me and 'huffing'.

'He just huffed at you,' she said, 'is he annoyed?'

'Nah. He's just telling me not to be silly. That's what he does.'

Before she had time to come up with a response, Jasper stepped forward and held out his huge right paw to be shaken.

Looking apprehensive, Charlie took his paw and gave it a good shake, whereupon he nuzzled her crotch and mewled at her for good measure. She took the nuzzling in good spirit and totally intrigued by his welcome, scratched his head. His version of a purr startled her for a moment, but that really broke the ice as he totally captivated her.

After a minute of that, Sandy laughed, 'C'mon Jasper, let Charlie get out of the sun and I'll show her to her cabin and the bathroom.'

At that, they went below, Jasper following with Krazy cat taking a flying leap off the chart table to land in her favourite position on Jasper's shoulders. To his credit, he hardly flinched as her needle claws dug in to hold herself in place as they padded silently behind Charlie and Sandy.

Sandy re-appeared, leaving Charlie below to wash and settle in. 'That was interesting,' she commented, 'are we really going to have the PM and Charlie aboard for a 'sailing holiday'?

I nodded, 'Yep. Looks like it. We'll take them down the Bay for a few days. I can't imagine that he'd want to go any further afield.'

'They aren't an item, or anything like that are they?' she asked with a lift of her expressive eyebrows.

'Nah! No way. This'll be all above board and they'll play it straight.'

She nodded, 'You're probably right. Still, it may not be too bad; he seems like a nice, down-to-earth bloke and should be better away from work. Charlie is certainly a live wire and seems very pleasant.'

'Yes, she does. But just remember who she works for. If push comes to shove, she'll always protect her boss ahead of any of us!'

Sandy smile indulgently at me, 'Cynical Harry, but probably true!'

CHAPTER 8

MARINA DEL RAY, FRIDAY

'Who's cynical?' demanded Charlie happily, fairly bounding into the cockpit. 'Is it you, Harry? Quite a healthy attitude, being a bit cynical. I don't have enough of it, and gets me into all sorts of trouble.'

I laughed, 'I guess you'd see a lot of it in your job.'

'Yep! Everybody's a cynic and plays political games. Most times it's funny to watch the subtle manoeuvring, but occasionally I get tired of it. This life seems much more appealing and honest. I imagine you'd always know where you stand with Mother Nature.'

'Well, that's right, you do. But that's a very philosophical view, Charlie.'

'I've got degrees in Philosophy, Political Science and Psychology and most times need all three to help cope with the big kids and their bigger egos who I have to work with. Although the boss is pretty good; he tells it straight, which is rare for a pollie.'

I went into the saloon, grabbed the stack of files on the chart table and handed them to Charlie. 'You need to go through these to see if there's anything else you might want to act on. The one file we thought was the most dangerous is the top one. Feel free to set up anywhere to read. You won't be interrupted.'

Her eyes lit up as she grabbed them, hugging them to her chest. 'Thank you, Harry. If this has the information we think it has, it can put some very un-Australian individuals away for a long time; or maybe we can contract your capable team and they'll just disappear!'

I wasn't sure I liked the idea of the Special Marine Strike Force being considered for use as a hit squad, but I supposed we'd done just that anyway, except in this and the previous instance, we'd made the decisions ourselves as to who stayed and who went!

Charlie parked herself in the saloon at the dining table and started reading, while Sandy and I stayed chatting in the cockpit. Jane and Rick had disappeared below and seemed to be doing what I'd planned to do with Sandy before Charlie had lobbed on the scene. While she was occupied, I remembered the roll of eggs or rocks or whatever I'd shoved in my pocket and which was digging uncomfortably into my leg.

Sandy looked at it curiously when I tugged it free of my pocket. 'What is it?'

'I don't know. I didn't have time to open it earlier, because Charlie rang.'

I untied the leather thongs cords binding the full-length flap and peeled it back to reveal six quite large green rocks nested in six pockets the length of the bag, so I dug one out and laid it on the table in the sun.

Immediately shafts of brilliant, deep green fire lanced in all directions from the large cut stone in front of us which presumably was an emerald. It was a medium deep green, looked the same colour from any angle and was cut in a rectangular form with a minimal number of large facets. It was at least the size of my upper thumb and I picked it up reverently, thinking it was probably the most beautiful thing I'd seen, apart from the blue diamonds we'd sold many months ago.

Handing it to Sandy, I hastily dug the other five out of their protective pockets to find two more were the same rectangular cut of the first and appeared to be exactly the same size which made them virtually identical triplets.

The other three, while the same size or slightly smaller, were a faceted oval cut and also were identical. Choosing one, I held it up to the light.

'Bloody hell, Sandy, this is incredible! Remember when we saw Mr Jacobs, the jeweller in Southport and Corrine had some emeralds?'

'Yeah. From memory she kept them.'

'That's right. But I remember him saying that nearly all emeralds have what he called inclusions in them. Little imperfections which reduce the value, although they're accepted as normal. He also said that emeralds are easily broken and can shatter if there are too many inclusions. But look at this one. I can't see any at all and I'm sure he said they were easily visible!'

I passed her that one and selected another at random, holding it up to the light and looking carefully. 'Buggered if I can see any in this one either! But I've just remembered the other thing he said which applied to all precious and even semi-precious stones.'

'What's that, oh wise and clever guru!' Sandy replied, still gazing raptly into the depths of bright green magnificence.

'He said that apart from size, the other three things which determined a really great stone were cut, depth of colour and clarity. Here we have big size, what I think is a good cut, the mid-deep green colour is terrific and the clarity is such that I can easily see through it! They look flawless to me. Just amazing!'

I jumped up, too excited to sit and paced the cockpit. 'Naturally, we'll split with Dave and Corrine, but if these are as good as we think, as two matched sets, they would be worth a lot. I've got to find out!'

'What are you going to do?' she asked, slightly alarmed by my restlessness and not trusting my renowned impulsiveness. 'We're a long way from Mr Jacobs.'

'Yes, but maybe there's a relative of his nearby,' I said, ducking inside to grab the phone; Charlie not even noticing me since she was too engrossed in the files.

'Reception, how may I help you?'

'Hello. This is Harry Stevens on *Firebird*. Is there a gemstone expert in Mataram City?'

'Oh, yes indeed, Mr Stevens. We have the best gemstone experts in Indonesia right there. They will have magnificent stones for you to buy — perhaps for your lovely lady?'

'Yes perhaps. Can you recommend the best one you know please and can I charter your fast ferry or another fast boat to get over there right now? And maybe the driver could show me where the best place is?'

She laughed what she thought was my impulsiveness, 'That won't be a problem, sir. Lennie is here now; he knows where to go and he can pick you up when you're ready.'

'I'm ready now, thanks. Send him on over.'

'Very good sir. Impulsive acts are always the best. I'm sure that she will really appreciate your decision.'

Sandy heard the last part and cracked up.

'You're staying here, Girlfriend,' I said giving her a hug, 'to help Charlie in case she needs anything. It's only about 15 miles each way, so I should only be about an hour and a half.'

She gave me another of those indulgent smiles, 'Yes my dear, darling man. Away with you, but don't take all six stones.'

By way of answer, I put just one of each cut back in the dirty leather roll, tied the cords and had Sandy shove the others in her pockets where they wouldn't clink against each other. I grabbed my wallet, slipped on shoes and a hat and was waiting on the boarding platform as Lennie eased the fast cruiser up beside me.

'We go to Mataram City, boss and I am to take you to the best precious jewel merchant. Is that correct?'

'Yes, Lennie. I need to see somebody who knows much about precious gems.'

'Ah, yes. No problem, boss. Lennie fix it for you.'

The run only took 25 minutes and Lennie had fun with the throttles wide-open; the boat launching itself from wave crest to wave crest and no complaining passengers.

I was surprised at the huge, sprawling size of Mataram City, but Lennie found a place to park the boat where he knew the dudes hanging around the dock and it became apparent they were paid to look after the boat in his absence.

It also seemed his mates owned a taxi, since one was waiting at the head of the dock and carted us through the surprisingly light traffic on roads which were twice the width of Bali's narrow, over-crowded lanes pretending to be main roads. We stopped at what appeared to be a vast, open-air market where it appeared you could buy or sell absolutely anything. It was a seething mass of humanity cheerfully and noisily haggling.

Lennie led the way to a small, unpretentious stall that had some beautiful gold chains, bracelets and other pieces on display at what seemed to be extremely reasonable prices, so I resolved to get some-thing for Sandy before I left. A young man, not much more than a boy, noted my interest, but spoke to Lennie first in Sasak, the main local language.

'You like the gold pieces, sir?' the boy asked politely, in good English.

'Yes, I do. There is some beautiful work there and I may wish to buy some, but first, I would like to talk to a gemstone expert if there is one here.'

He smiled, 'But of course, sir. May I introduce you to my Uncle? He is renowned throughout the Province as the leading expert in all precious stones.'

'And just where is your Uncle?' I asked, suddenly wary.

Another beaming smile, 'My apologies! He is right here, sir, if you will step to the rear of the shop, I will bring him to you and may I also bring a selection of the particular stone you wish to see?'

'No. I wish to have him inspect a stone and make a report. I will pay for his time and expertise and I will look further at the gold work afterwards; but first, your Uncle, please.'

He inclined his head in a courtly gesture before ducking through a bead curtain that clicked and clacked after his passage. Lennie stood near the door, so I said, hoping he'd understand, 'Is this man really good, Lennie? I truly hope I'm not being given the 'dumb, wealthy tourist' deal. That would make me *very* unhappy.'

He knew exactly what I was saying and replied, 'It would be worth my magnificent job if I did not make sure you are looked after properly, boss. This man is excellent and I have brought many foreign visitors here. They have all been very happy with the service, the items and their prices.'

Slightly mollified, I nodded and returned to the back counter which had a powerful light hanging over it. Finally, the boy returned, helping a little old man with long grey hair and a wispy grey beard. He looked to be a hundred, but judging the age of Asian people is difficult for Westerners.

'This is my esteemed Uncle, sir, and he would like to know how he may be of service.'

I paid my respects to the old man, and received a grateful response. 'I have two stones that I would like his opinion on, if he is willing to do that.'

The boy translated and Uncle bobbed his head, muttered a reply and gave a toothless smile, rapping on the finely-polished wood of the counter top with a long, wizened finger. The boy promptly covered the wood with a white velvet cloth and smoothed the wrinkles out.

I pulled the grubby and stained soft leather case from my pocket, untied the cords and shook the two emeralds onto the white cloth. Even without the overhead light, the stones sparkled and glittered with an inner fire, but when the boy flicked the light switch, they seemed to come alive.

The old man came alive too, suddenly reaching for a polishing cloth and carefully wiping all fingerprints off both stones. A loupe appeared as if by magic in his left eye as he grasped the oval stone in a claw-type instrument and held it up to the light.

He took his time examining it, turning it around all ways, all the time peering into its depths. Finally, he muttered quietly, and with slightly shaking hands, reverently placed the stone down and picked up the other one. The performance was repeated and there was the same result as he laid it beside the first, while having a lengthy conversation with the boy.

The boy bowed his head to the old man and then turned to me, 'Uncle asks, what information you want about these stones?'

'I guess I'd like to know if they are any good and if so, what they would be worth. Lastly, an indication of where they came from would be handy, but not essential.'

There was another lengthy conversation in Sasak, before the boy replied, 'Uncle has never been privileged to see such stones and states they are without equal for cut, colour, clarity and the size is excellent. He would like to perform some non-invasive tests if you approve.'

'Go ahead.'

An array of small equipment was produced from under the counter and each stone was photographed, measured, weighed and had a spectrometer fire a beam of pure white light into one facet at just the right angle so that it bounced around inside the stone.

'Uncle says again that both stones are without peer, and are so unusual that few dealers would even contemplate buying them. The rectangular one is 26.87 carats, while the oval is 23.94 carats. The colour is more intense than the best he's seen, yet not too dark. The clarity is superb. There are very few inclusions and they are microscopic in size which is so unusual, most potential buyers will suspect they are fakes. He would estimate the value to be in excess of US$30,000 per carat, but he doesn't know who might be able to buy them! Certainly no one in Mataram.'

'Please tell your uncle I have four more stones — two identical to the rectangular one and two identical to the oval one.'

The old fella must have had some English for he nearly swooned on the spot when he heard that bit of news, but rattled off some more comments.

'Uncle suggests that were you to offer all six stones at auction as two sets of triplets, they will attract the highest price. He would be delighted to make the arrangements to do so from here, or you can wait until you return to your own country.'

'Please, thank your uncle most sincerely for me. I shall consider his remarks and offer carefully. Unfortunately, my friends and I are travelling through the country and we may not be here long.'

The old fella looked me in the eye and spoke English slowly in a strong accent.

'You be most careful with these stones. These stones, have bad history. Much blood has spilled as they passed from hand to hand.'

I got excited again and asked, 'You know where they came from? You know their history? Please tell me what you know!'

He muttered to the boy who went out back briefly, returning with a scrapbook of newspaper cuttings. He selected three and laid them on the counter. Going yellow with age, two were in Sasak and one in English.

Each article had several photos, one of which was of an old ship run up onto rocks, then there was a group of women and children on a beach surrounded by scruffy-looking men draped in guns and bandoleers of ammunition. Another grainy photo in one of the Sasak newspapers showed a number of women and children lying on the ground, their white dresses and shirts covered in large dark patches.

The boy gave me a brief version of the story. 'One hundred and ten years ago, a ship came from Columbia with many persons aboard, immigrating to India because of the harsh and primitive conditions that existed in Columbia. It passed through the Indonesian Archipelago, but pirates lured it onto rocks in a storm. Many of the crew and male passengers died trying to drive off the pirates and save the ship, but when they failed, the women and children were taken ashore where the pirates had a large camp.

The pirates became drunk on the small cargo of brandy carried on the ship and for many days, the female passengers, regardless of age were repeatedly raped until they died. The boys were then subjected to a similar fate. Their bodies were strung up and used for target practice or hacked apart with machetes. There is some evidence of cannibalism, but few of the local tribesmen would talk of that.

A journal was found which belonged to one of the women, where she described six flawless emeralds, three each of two different cuts, being the net worth of a wealthy, extended family. The stones were meant to re-establish the family with new homes, businesses and a new life in India. The description of the stones was very detailed and matches precisely the ones you have in your pocket!'

I was stunned to hear this bloody, detailed history, but the young man carried on.

'Vague reports of their existence came up from time to time, and it would seem they were always at the centre of bloodshed, murder and chaos! Because of their origin, they were even named 'The Columbine Stones', after the name of the ship, and before long, a legend arose that the stones were cursed and everyone who touched them would suffer a fate worse than death. This is the first confirmed sighting of them in a hundred years.'

'But your Uncle doesn't believe in the curse. He touched them!'

He nodded, 'You are correct. He did touch them, but the curse is apparently directed at the owner of the stones. It's not applicable to those who might merely handle the stones in passing.'

I smiled, 'I will be careful, but for now, may I have copies of those articles?'

'Certainly sir. I will be just a few moments.'

Once I had the copies in hand, I felt the need to get moving, so I said, 'I'd still like to look at some of those gold pieces, then I must get back.'

I ended up buying three gold pieces for Sandy; a beautiful chunky coarse-link chain, a bracelet, set with hundreds of tiny rubies, and a necklace with a 5-carat teardrop emerald.

The taxi was summoned and with only a modest dent in my Visa card and a fond farewell ringing in my ears from the old man and his nephew, we headed for the wharf, the sea and home.

CHAPTER 9

MARINA DEL RAY, FRIDAY

Charlie and Sandy were lounging in the cockpit having a chat, when Lennie dropped me off and thankfully, Charlie was too excited about the files to wonder where I'd been.

'The files were just what we wanted, thank you Harry. The one you mentioned has all the critical names and addresses so your parent organisation should be able to round them up in short order.'

I smiled at her. 'In that case, I'm glad your flight wasn't in vain, although it's always a pleasant change to have company.'

'Oh, I wouldn't have missed this for anything. Now the main business is done with, I'm just enjoying myself and having a relax. Of course, the boss will be jealous when I tell him; he loves sailing and would be delighted to be going somewhere on this boat.'

'I suppose it's busy being a PPS?' Sandy asked.

'Twenty-four/seven, I'm afraid. I love being in the centre of happenings, but it never stops! Although I don't have any social life, I'm not complaining too much. I could always leave if it gets too much.

So tell me, where do you go from here if you won't be back in Australian waters for two more weeks?'

'We thought while we were up here, we'd check a few dive sites and do a bit of sight-seeing. There seems to be an incredible diversity in cultures, flora and fauna,' I offered, trying for the intellectual touch.

'Oh, yes. What a marvellous opportunity and what a terrific way to do it on this wonderful boat. But don't you have more crew? Where's the girl you rescued in Afghanistan, for instance?'

By way of answer, I jerked my thumb over toward the Marina.

'See the cruiser closest to us with the white upper works and royal blue hull? That's the other half of the team.'

She looked, then exclaimed, 'Do you mean that huge thing? Wow! That's amazing! Can I have a close look at it please? I'd love to meet your rescuee and the others.'

I checked the time. 'We're due to have dinner ashore in the restaurant in a couple of hour's time, but we usually have drinks in the bar first. If we go over a bit earlier, Dave will give you a tour of the boat and you can meet the whole crew.'

She beamed with pleasure. 'That'd be wonderful, but I didn't bring a cocktail dress since I didn't plan on having to dress up.'

Sandy laughed, 'Not that sort of restaurant, I'm afraid. You'll be fine as you are unless you want to borrow a blouse. You can take a shower to freshen up if you want.'

'I might just do that, thanks Sandy. A shower and a clean blouse will be good.'

While she was doing that, I brought Sandy up to date on the story of the emeralds which fascinated her and she looked at the four she dug out of her pockets with renewed interest and even more careful handling. I could see her mind ticking over as she tucked the four glittering lumps of foul, bloody history back beside the others in the grubby, stained leather roll.

'That means that each of the bigger ones, even sold alone, would be worth around eight hundred thousand US dollars. And potentially a lot more if they sell as two matched sets of triplets with a history! This is like the blue diamonds all over again!'

I nodded, grinning at her disbelief and wonder. 'It is I'm afraid. Sorry about that. But I bought you a few presents while I was over there.'

I handed over the cases the three items were packed in, and she was blown away by the three beautiful golden pieces, immediately slipping the bracelet on.

'Bloody hell, it's heavy! I guess that makes it real gold!'

'That's what they said. It's not 24-carat gold because it's too soft for jewellery when it's pure, but it has only a tiny amount of a metal he wouldn't name as the hardening alloy, so it's very close to pure gold — hence the weight.'

She tried the necklace on and the chunky chain suited her, but it was the emerald necklace that really blew her away and it looked stunning on her with the teardrop 5-carat vivid, green emerald flashing its glorious green fire.

At that point, Charlie came back looking more refreshed and wearing one of Sandy's shirts. Jane and Rick weren't far behind and minutes later we were tying up to *Seeker's* stern. Dave took Charlie on a tour and she was in raptures about the boat and was lavish in her praise of the crew as she met them, passing on the PM's personal message. Even Alex was quite taken with her and chatted quite animatedly for a while, something highly unusual for Alex.

While Charlie was busy, Corrine said while we were away, Dave had the Marina Del Ray shipwrights fit up mounts for the Browning .50 cal machine guns which were leftover ordinance from the last job. He had only given them the bare mounts, saying they were for a pair of high-powered spotlights he wanted to try out, and had them placed at the front of the open upper sundeck.

That excuse for the mounts sounded sufficiently vague enough to mislead anybody, so with Sandy's help, he had brought two fitters back to *Firebird* and under her guidance, had them make a couple of mounting points either side of the Firebird's cockpit to accept the MK47 grenade launcher. I only had one launcher, but it was effective! Jane and Rick were the talented Navy crew who would operate it.

When Charlie was done inspecting *Seeker*, we wandered up the jetty to the bar and dining room where Charlie showed she wasn't afraid to have a wine or three and it turned out to be a happy, fun night.

PART 2: GREEN GOLD

CHAPTER 10

MARINA DEL RAY, SATURDAY

Charlie's ferry left at 07:00 next morning, so there was no chance of sleeping in. After thanking us for our hospitality and the files, she reminded Sandy and me once again of her determination to drag the Boss away from affairs of State and onto *Firebird* for a sailing holiday.

'Contact me before you leave the Archipelago,' she said, 'in case your Navy crew needs to fly out to re-join their boat; we can fly in to replace them. It would be a perfect holiday for him. But even if I can't get the Boss to do it, we'll supply however many crew you need to get back home. Promise you'll think about it? Please?'

I had to say that I would and, in all honesty, it could work out quite well if Jane and Rick did have to get back to work. They'd been with us ten days already, which meant their leave would be over within a week. Any time after that would really be stretching friendships with the Navy.

MONDAY

We stayed at the marina until Monday, spending some of the time re-stocking both boats with everything we might need in a remote area, before departing Marina Del Ray on the hunt for the island of magical, mystical herbs. Dave and I had already had a frank talk with Roger to find out just where we were going, and he told us that the area was NE of Singapore, between Malaysia and Borneo. He wasn't being secretive, because when he and Jill picked up Anna, she'd already been paddling for five days, more or less south of the island. Therefore, he was unsure of the exact location until we had a chance to retrace his sailing track. Unfortunately, Anna hadn't told Roger and Jill exactly where the island with ruins was, so we couldn't start from there.

'I'm sure if we find the right group of islands, we'll be able to find the exact island based on things she said on the trip back to Bali, which is where she left us and flew home. We were seven days getting to Bali and I do remember our average speed for that leg of the trip was five knots as the winds were a bit fluky.'

Much searching of the charts and measuring, ended up pointing to the area known as Ebeling Reef.

'That makes sense to an extent,' I said, 'since there is a lot of pirate activity in that area, because it's right on the sea-lanes from Singapore to the Far-East, China and Japan.'

After much debate, we chose several likely areas to visit to see if any fitted Anna's ramblings.

I found it good to be back at sea, especially after a spell ashore. The sparkling water and fickle breezes combined to carry away all the accumulated bad air, including the tension and stress the clean-up operation had generated. We all settled back into the watch-keeping routine with our Navy crew now familiar with *Firebird* and her systems.

On Tuesday, the first morning out from Lombok, I spoke to Jill and Rick about when their leave ticket would run out.

'There's only three days of our leave left, although normally we go into a training period for a week before standing by for a boat to become available. It might be best if you or I checked in with the Skipper to see what the go is.'

I let Jane, as Petty Officer, call her boss and he confirmed her guess that the crew was about to enter a short training period to prepare for a new deployment. Consequently, he requested that she and Rick return to Darwin by Sunday of the following week at the latest.

'To do the right thing, we should be back by Friday next week, so that's another ten days from now,' she informed me happily. 'Will the second task be complete by then?'

'I really don't know,' I admitted, 'I fear we're going to waste several days hunting for the right group of islands, let alone the right one!'

I explained the problem we'd been discussing, but Jane had a good thought.

'If you have fairly good descriptions of the herb island and the Archaeological island, why not conduct your search on Google Earth? Surely it will be a lot easier and faster to pick the geographical features that you've been told about, like that little rocky headland where the creek runs into the sea.'

I grinned at her, 'Well done! I should have thought of it myself. It will be easier and much faster.'

I called Dave and passed on the new suggestion and like me, he cursed himself for not thinking of it sooner, but said he'd get Jill and Roger on it immediately.

Even with that incredible technology, it wasn't until the following day, Wednesday, that Dave called to say that Jill and Roger had found three islands in one broad area that almost matched the description given by Anna.

WEDNESDAY

The area was shown on the charts as being the southern-most islands in the Riau Archipelago and was called Ebeling Reef.

'Not much of a pirate area I would think,' Sandy commented, looking at where the shipping lanes ran, 'but I suppose there might be less patrolling here by the Indonesian Authorities.'

I agreed and late that afternoon, we sailed into the area, checking out the first island on the list, which was well south of the main group.

'*This won't be it,*' Dave radioed, '*but dawn tomorrow should see us to the first of the most likely ones. I suggest we slow down and take precautions against unwelcome visitors!'*

'Agreed,' I replied, 'But won't ten knots make us inviting targets?'

'True. But at least we're not a fuel tanker. So hopefully, any pirates will ignore us as too small.'

'We can only hope, but be prepared.'

The next couple of hours saw Jane and Rick busy putting their MK47 grenade launcher together from the various bits that were scattered around the boat looking like spare parts.

In the right hands, it was a terribly potent weapon and Jane and Rick had shown they were very good.

The solid mounting positions created by the Marina fitters really held the launcher steady and should allow the MK47 to punch out 40 mm high explosive death and destruction with remarkable accuracy to over 2000 metres. They practiced setting it up and swapping from one side of the cockpit to the other and before long, it only took seconds to move the wicked little auto-cannon over to the other side.

There was definitely an air of heightened tension among the crew that evening as we tracked a large island where the lights of several villages gleamed fitfully in the distance. The tension ratcheted up a notch or three when our digital broadband radar showed several small, but fast boats leave the shore, heading directly for us at 30 knots.

Dave and I had discussed this situation and he smoothly moved in front of us, as his twin machine guns were mounted so as to cover attack from ahead and abeam, whereas our grenade launcher covered the stern sector only. I activated the masthead mounted IR camera and shortly had a clear view of six to eight men in each boat, with what looked like rifles and machetes stacked on the bottom boards out of sight.

I called Dave to tell him they weren't coming out to see if we wanted to buy some fresh fish!

'So, are we weapons free?'

'If they are still approaching at 300-metres, you might lay a burst of tracer across their bows. If they don't stop, then weapons free. Nobody makes friendly night-time visits to passing yachts!'

'*Roger that!*'

I guessed Corrine would have taken over the Browning on the approach side, since as the three fast boats kept coming past the 300-metre mark, a short line of green dots streamed out from the shadowy bulk of *Seeker,* to wink out of existence just ahead of the lead speedboat. It would appear they didn't expect that response, since they abruptly turned away, but then just as quickly turned back, still approaching, but on a zigzag track which suggested they'd been fired at before!

'Weapons free!' I called over the radio and repeated the call to Jane and Rick who dutifully repeated the call at the same time as they fired the first sighting burst. Three rounds fled into the night, before erupting into yellow-orange balls of flame, one of which happened to be right on one speedboat, which transformed itself into a large ball of yellow-orange flame!

The remaining two boats milled around in confusion for a moment, giving Corrine a perfect target back-lit by a small lake of burning fuel. Once more the deadly green fingers reached out almost delicately and swept back and forth across both boats until they too erupted in flame.

'Secure firing!' I called and Jane repeated the call.

'Well done that girl on the .50 cal!' I said over the radio.

Dave chuckled, '*Yeah. She's not bad at all. Do we check for survivors?*'

'Nope! More trouble than it's worth. We'd get no concessions for saving any of their useless necks. They got fair warning.'

'*True, boss. I thought we might maintain this formation for the rest of the night. What say you?*'

'Good thinking. Carry on.'

The rest of the night was peaceful and everyone managed to get some sleep until we had the de-briefing over breakfast.

CHAPTER 11

After the drama of the night, it was a lovely day with a light breeze barely ruffling the surface of the sea and suited our reduced speed since the first of the possible islands were coming up ahead. We had decided to launch *Dragonfly*, our UAV or Unmanned Aerial Vehicle, to let us look at the island better, without getting too close, reasoning that one pirate encounter was enough!

The swell was slight enough that Dave was able to come alongside to let Sandy jump across and for Bree to jump back to replace her in case we needed to quickly go into action. By staying close to *Seeker*, we were able to get the live feed from the UAV, but Roger and Jill didn't get excited, so we pushed on and let *Dragonfly* range on ahead toward the next prospect. It wasn't recognised either, nor were several more we checked out as the day wore on. We did find, however, that using *Dragonfly* sped up the search dramatically as the two boats could maintain a straight course while the UAV darted back and forth, sending high resolution pictures of each island. It probably saved us at least a day, if not two, in travelling time.

By day's end, we had looked at many more and it was hard to imagine just how many islands made up this vast country. With twilight draping its soft, purple mantle over the gently rolling seascape, we closed on a small island which the UAV had confirmed was uninhabited. The plan was to anchor for the night and now we were in the area of the herb island, hopefully everyone could get some decent sleep, although there would still have to be an active watch kept, as we rated these as hostile waters.

With only a light breeze blowing through the night, we kept the anchors on short chains in case a quick getaway was called for, only used red lighting and after a light meal, we set six-hour watches. I had a good 4-hours sleep before Jane shook me awake, reporting all was quiet with no sign of movement. Bree and I were on the morning watch and were in the cockpit where she was telling me her good feelings of having some money for the first time in her life. Her happy tale was interrupted when the radar proximity alarm chimed softly. Muttering a curse and hoping it was just a pod of dolphins or similar, I was disturbed to see what appeared to be two long, narrow shapes leaving shore and heading toward us.

Calling for Bree to quietly wake Jane and Rick and not turn any lights on, I activated the masthead camera and within moments, had a sharp image of two long canoes full of men paddling steadily out toward us. Most had rifles slung over their shoulders and they still had about 500-metres to go when the gunnery team appeared and I quickly briefed them.

'They're getting closer and there's a lot of them. I wouldn't like to let them get too close,' Jane warned.

'Yeah, you're right. It's getting a bit tight for room. Don't these fuckers ever give up? OK, Jane. Light 'em up and to hell with the warning shots. Weapons free!'

'Weapons free, aye!' came the confirmation as the cocking handle was pulled twice and Jane read the laser-generated ranges to Rick so he could set the elevation. Moments later, the familiar banging rattle sounded as a series of red tracer rounds arced toward the canoes, held steady in the MK47's Infra-red sights. Several rounds impacted the first canoe, blowing it in half and wreaking terrible damage on soft flesh, while the second canoe copped the remainder of the burst which effectively obliterated it.

'Cease fire!' I called and Jane responded by clearing the grenade launcher and locking the breech open. Bree had just started to ask about survivors, when *Seeker's* RIB shot out from its stern locker and buzzed over to where a few heads were bobbing amongst a mass of shattered wood fragments. Two individuals were in the RIB as it nosed through the debris field. I hoped none of the bobbing heads still had weapons but Corrine must have been aboard and prepared, for I heard the flat crack of a .22 magnum being fired several times until there were no more bobbing heads!

Bree sucked a sharp breath beside me, but before she had a chance to voice disapproval, Jane spoke with an angry hiss, 'Don't even think about objecting, Bree! Those fuckers would be raping us right now if they got aboard, and all tomorrow and so on until we were dead meat. That's how they think and operate. No mercy! The only way to respond is to hit first and hit harder! Remember, we didn't come here to fight and didn't ask to be attacked.

You've been told the stories about Harry's previous encounters with bad guys, and now you've been involved in several yourself! But have you thought about *why* he and now we always win each encounter? It's certainly not because he's James Bond! But he is well-trained and well prepared to fight, and he's shown us why we need to be the same. *That's* what has kept us alive each time! Also remember almost every time we came peacefully. If the bad guys had left us alone, we would have done the same! But they chose to attack us first, and because we had better planning, better training and better forethought to have better weapons on hand, we came out on top. That's what makes it all seem easy!'

In the dimness beside me I saw Bree nod. 'Sorry guys. I forgot for a moment and I shouldn't have. It won't happen again.'

I gave her a brotherly hug of consolation. 'I'd like to think there'll be no need for you to control your emotions ever again, but I'm afraid life in these parts is held very cheaply. There'll be more of them before this trip's over. We just have to stay ready and trust no one except ourselves.'

Dave came on the horn and suggested we get moving even though it was just 03:30, in case there were more on the island waiting for us to let our guard down.

Ten minutes later, we were idling along at 5 knots, radars and masthead camera working full time as we headed for the next possible island in this group. Sandy wanted to know if she should launch the UAV, but I suggested we wait for dawn, so all was peaceful until the first rays of the new day popped over the horizon and the weird shape of *Dragonfly* floated off *Seeker's* foredeck, then darted off to the northeast, scanning for the next possibility. Unfortunately, it wasn't the target, nor was the two after that, but Roger became excited by the look of the next island which showed under the UAV's HD cameras.

'Roger says the features described by Anna all match, so we're going to do a series of passes to try to confirm things further. Sandy's going to keep it high to avoid detection and it shows as being ten miles away, so they shouldn't see us if we just sit here until we get more data.'

'Righto, good plan. Keep the video feed going.'

We shut down the engines and floated motionless on the quiet ocean, until fifteen minutes later, both Roger and Jill agreed that to the best of their recollection, this was the island. The most telling evidence was the sight of a large, camouflaged tent set under palm trees with a small creek flowing past it and several armed men wandering around in decent uniforms. The island wasn't very big, and only had the one village.

'Roger suggests it would be best if we approached slowly to just off the village and wait for someone to come out to us. He'll do the communicating and intends to use the line that we are friends of Anna and wish to discuss business with the King.'

I thought a few moments, then agreed, 'Yeah. That's probably the best. If we tried to sneak up it would look too suspicious. Open and non-threatening is best, but we'll stay prepared with the big stick!'

'Roger's not too happy about that, but does see the sense.'

'Ok. Retrieve *Dragonfly*, we'll exchange crew again and move in.'

'Sandy suggests leaving Dragonfly orbiting so we can have advance warning if anything shifty is being planned.'

'Good thinking. The ground party will be Roger and Jill, I presume, and they can wear tactical headsets so we can warn them. If the Islanders aren't used to hi-tech UAVs, we might score a decent surprise factor.'

'*Good plan and Roger approves. Do you still want to swap crew? Sandy can operate from there just as easily.*'

We drifted together again and exchanged crew along with the UAV's Ground Control Station housed in a large, waterproof Pelikan case. Sandy was happy to be back and by the time she had set up the GCS on the dining table we were under way for the herb island.

CHAPTER 12

HERBA ISLAND, FRIDAY

We approached the small, shallow bay in front of the village at a leisurely pace, all fixed weapons draped with clothing to break up outlines, but with shooters lounging casually beside them ready to leap into action. Several locals came out onto the beach to look at the two mismatched boats which had come to their small island home, but nobody seemed to be overly concerned as we dropped anchor and rafted side by side.

Finally, a long canoe powered by a new-looking outboard motored out of the narrow creek and headed out to us. Several armed men were aboard, but their rifles were slung over their shoulders in the traditional alert, but non-threatening mode.

As they drew closer, I noticed one man stood out among the locals who were short, nuggetty men. This guy was tall, good-looking and light-skinned with Eurasian features. The boat nosed up close to *Seeker's* stern where as planned, Roger stood alone on the stern board. Interestingly, it was one of the locals who called out in broken English and not the Eurasian man.

'Hello strangers! You have problem with boat? Why are you at this place? We peaceful people. No trouble!'

Roger held his hands out sideways in a universal gesture of peace. 'We are peaceful too. We come to see King Mikhail with a message. We would like to talk to him.'

The local spoke quietly to the Eurasian man who only seemed to grunt back at his words, while making gestures with his hands and I remembered Roger relaying what Anna had said about a mute man who was the right hand of the King.

Stepping up to the stern of *Firebird*, I called out, 'You must be Gilbert. Anna told us about you. I am Harry and this is Roger. Will you take us to King Mikhail, please?'

That got Gilbert's attention and a frown briefly crossed his handsome face. He made more signs to his interpreter, who responded by saying, 'You, Mr 'arry and Mr Roger will come with us. All persons stay on boat. No leave.'

I had a sudden epiphany about Jasper and indigenous superstitions — don't ask me why!

'I want to bring my cat with me.'

That caused another flurry of signing before Gilbert shrugged and gave a sharp nod, so I called Jasper to my side and before we stepped down to the boarding platform, I spoke to him.

'We're going to visit a man in his house. You don't need to like him, but he is friendly. Just stay with me and don't bite anybody unless they cause trouble.'

He delivered his usual 'Huff' to show understanding, but also patted my foot with his paw, which was a new twist in Jasper/Harry communications, although I wasn't sure of the meaning.

When I stood up, I saw the appearance and size of Jasper caused the expected stir amongst the boat crew who looked as though they didn't know whether to bow or recoil in horror. They had also heard me speak to him and saw Jasper's reaction, so that compounded the confusion as to whether the black cat was a God or a Daemon. The result was a general shuffling of bodies to the stern where they crowded against the outboard driver.

Gilbert uttered a bark that sounded like an expression of disgust, before stepping back and allowing Roger, Jasper and me to step gingerly aboard. Despite the natural stability of the boat, we stayed up in the bow to avoid a serious imbalance of weight as the driver growled for some room and got the boat moving the short distance to the shore in the small, flowing creek.

We were shepherded, with the escorts keeping their distance from Jasper, to the side entrance of the huge tent and it was just as

Anna had said. This time we were free to enter at our own pace and Gilbert led us to the big, main room where the fat Mikhail sat at the head of a beautifully made and polished dining room table that could seat twelve in comfort. There was a flurry of signing to Mikhail from Gilbert.

He was snacking on a plate of chopped fruit, but stopped when he saw me tagging along behind Roger, then did a classic double take when he spotted Jasper.

'My, my! A Chausie and more to the point, one where the Jungle Cat F5 gene has gone super dominant! Very unusual and, I would imagine, a loyal and effective companion.' He spoke with a high, clear voice, with excellent diction and just a slight accent.

'He is all of the above,' I replied to the gross creature wearing a purple caftan and looking like the lovechild product of the union between Demis Roussos and a circus tent. I took note that Gilbert stood close behind Mikhail and paid attention to every word said.

Mikhail was in no rush to learn about our visit and finished his fruit platter first. Finally pushing it aside, he said, 'Now, Gilbert said you mentioned names you could only have learned from the young lady Anna, so I presume she has told you everything about the island and us?'

Roger spoke up, 'My girlfriend and I found her near death from exposure and dehydration miles from land. We were sailing a chartered yacht at the time and luckily, I'm a Doctor and Jill is a Registered Nurse, so we were able to treat her effectively. She was in a coma for days, but made a full recovery. When recovered, she did tell us everything about this place and while she was grateful that Gilbert and you had saved her from the pirates, she didn't like being kept prisoner, despite the generally pleasant conditions.'

Mikhail nodded. 'We wondered why she left suddenly, when I thought she had accepted my offer of work.'

Fortunately, Roger seized that opportunity to get down to business with both hands.

'Actually, it's that business offer which has brought us here today,

123

at great expense and trouble I might add, as Anna didn't know exactly where this island was. Luckily. Harry and our other friends have excellent technology which assisted with that search.'

Mikhail looked thoughtful, then waved at the chairs around the table. 'Forgive my bad manners and please take a seat.'

He clapped his pudgy hands and a pretty local girl wearing just a colourful wrap for a skirt around her slim hips and no top, appeared with a tray of drinks and a fruit platter. I automatically had to assess her neat little boobs and mentally chastised myself for always looking at bits of female anatomy, but then thought '*What the hell! Be yourself, Harry. There's nothing wrong with it and to hell what other people think!*'

With that sorted out, I was able to direct most of my attention back to Mikhail, while still keeping an eye on the fascinating way that her neat little boobs bobbed when their owner moved around serving us.

Politely waiting until we drank some juice and sampled the fruit; Mikhail spoke, choosing his words carefully. 'So, am I to understand you wish to enter into a business arrangement with me?'

Roger nodded, 'That is correct. As a Doctor, I can see that both the healing and analgesic properties of the green paste are astounding, and would be extremely beneficial to thousands of chronic pain sufferers. The aphrodisiac properties are most interesting and certainly will be useful for those with low sex drive, although the effects are quite strong and for therapeutic use the paste would need to be diluted considerably. Pure pleasure-seekers would undoubtedly want to use the less diluted version.'

Mikhail nodded, 'I can see that your medical background could be just as useful, if not better in marketing this product as perhaps Anna would have been.'

Roger nodded eagerly. 'It's as a Doctor that I want to enter into a business arrangement with you. This paste can help so many people. The pleasure market is a minor concern, although a less diluted version could be lucrative.'

'What is your proposal, Doctor?'

Clearly, Roger had given this a great deal of thought.

'Simply that we enter into a business deal where I will take as much product as you can generate and market it for both medicinal use and for pleasure. The two markets will be kept separate. You already have some sort of transport arrangements in place, so I suggest you keep them going. The selling price can stay at $500 Aussie dollars per jar, although I reserve the right as a Doctor to dilute the product as required depending on the use intended. Because I will have import fees, approval fees and marketing to pay for, the 200/300 split you proposed to Anna needs to be reversed.'

Mikhail frowned, 'I'm not so sure about changing the division of return. I have expenses too.'

Roger shook his head, 'Nothing like what I'm facing. Anna has already told me of your low production costs and even if you do set up a better production line, it will still be cheap to produce. I suggest the new split per jar of concentrate be 300 for me and 200 for you.'

Mikhail turned red in the face and I idly wondered who would get the job of mouth-to-mouth resuscitation when the heart attack felled him.

'That is ridiculous!' he spluttered. 'I cannot operate on that!'

Calmly, Roger said, 'I'm sure that you can, especially when I start moving a lot more product than you ever have before. You produce the concentrate for me, undiluted and as the medical specialist, I decide what level of concentration suits the market. Also, I will be in the best position to recommend, endorse and dispense the product officially with far more credibility than Anna would have had.

From the limited experimentation Jill and I have carried out, if people kept using the undiluted product all the time, they'd kill themselves. I'm the scientist who can accurately tailor dosages for the greatest effect.'

This time, Mikhail didn't go red-faced, so Roger's words must have been making sense. They certainly did to me.

Cautiously Mikhail said, 'If I did agree to this outrageous proposal, what guarantee can you offer that I will be paid?'

Roger smiled, 'How many jars do you have on hand at the moment?'

Mikhail turned to Gilbert who signed rapidly. 'Gilbert says that we have just over 5200 jars at the moment, although another batch is brewing and within three days will generate approximately another 5000 jars.'

To allow some time to process the numbers, I asked, 'Why does it take so long to make a batch?'

Mikhail beamed, 'Ah! An excellent question and I can give you a short answer. The paste is made from the leaves of a certain variety of bush that only grows on this island. The leaves must be harvested by hand then soaked in the spring water we have, which has many healing properties of its own. After soaking for a week, the batches of soaked leaves are heated gently in a large vat, which is topped up as the mixture reduces. Finally, the concentrate is left and must be filtered to remove any solid matter, then dispensed into the jars. That is why just one batch takes more than two weeks to produce, although it yields about 5000 jars each time.'

'Thank you,' I said, 'that's interesting and I can see the only way to increase production will be to create a second production line.'

He nodded, 'Yes. You are correct and is what Gilbert and I have been doing, but because the village people aren't used to the concept of producing more than they need, it is taking us time to get all phases of the second production line happening at the right time.'

Roger had finished processing numbers. 'Here's my suggestion in answer to your question about payment security. We will take the 5200 jars in storage and will wait until the next batch is finished and loaded ready for shipment. That should total about 10200 jars and represent a value to you, the producer, of $2,040,000.

For these two batches, we are saving you the cost of packaging and transport and will pay a deposit of AU$500,000, either in cash or as a deposit into your bank account. I seem to remember you told Anna you have an account with the Bank of Vanuatu. We do too. As sales are made, a deposit will be made to your account each month based on your share of $200 per jar.

As your new sales and distribution team, we will need the mailing lists of your existing Asian customers whom I believe you've been selling to at AU$750 per jar. We will negotiate a new deal with them and you will get your share. Is this an acceptable deal to you?'

Mikhail and Gilbert conferred in their mixed way, then Mikhail said, 'Gilbert finds that agreeable, but wishes to impose another condition on the deal.'

I looked at Roger and said, 'Ok. What is it?'

'Gilbert must go with you to see how you set up the distribution network. He will not stay too long, perhaps 8 to 10 weeks, then he will return here. Despite being mute, he signs in ASL, understands six primary languages and several dialects. He also has a degree in Economics and an MBA. Despite appearances, he is perfectly capable of fitting in with any social group.'

I chuckled as Gilbert's chin currently sported a wispy beard, his hair was long, although clean and shining and he wore just a pair of ragged shorts. His upper body was impressively muscled and with a dramatic six-pack, he'd challenge our resident weight-lifter Rick for body development, however there was no disguising the intelligent gleam in his eyes.

I addressed Roger, 'I'm good with that, so it's your call. Having Gilbert along to see how things are set up is just the price of doing business.'

He thought a minute, then agreed. 'Very well. That's acceptable. We should type out the terms of the agreement, so there's no misunderstanding.'

Mikhail clapped his hands and the young girl appeared with a note book in hand. 'Mai-ling has already transcribed the terms as discussed. Please read the notes and if you agree, sign down below. Perhaps you have the facilities on your lovely boats to make a copy of the agreement?'

'Yes, we do,' I answered, 'and can do that today, but we need to read the agreement first.'

We read it in Mai-ling's beautiful flowing script and it was as discussed, so we signed it on the spot then watched Mikhail do the same.

I took the document to be copied and accepted Mikhail's offer for Gilbert to show us the production facilities.

'Before we do,' I said to Mikhail, 'I'm also interested in the reports Anna made about the water. She said it seemed to have extraordinary properties to ease aches and pains. Almost as good as the paste.'

He nodded, 'That is true and if you don't mind the climb, Gilbert can take you to the source which is halfway up the tall hill behind the camp. There are mineral deposits which the spring water flows over and they seem to give the water its curative properties. The Islanders have been drinking and bathing in it for hundreds of years and they never get sick. They can and do injure themselves, but no illnesses or diseases!'

'Then I'm definitely interested to learn more, although shipping water out of here would make it terribly expensive.'

Mikhail nodded knowledgeably as he replied, 'There are ways and means, dear boy. I must say it is refreshing to have associates who are free to move in the outside world and have entrepreneurial ideas. We can talk further on this project since you are going to stay for at least three days.'

'I look forward to that, but in the meantime can our crews come ashore?'

'Of course, they may, dear boy. But I must caution all of you about venturing too far from the village, especially over to the other side of the island. Those rebels and pirates who we rescued the delightful Miss Anna from, sometimes land over there and try to make trouble with the locals by stealing some of their females.'

'Oh. I didn't realise they were so close. We did have some trouble on the way here, but that was further south. I hope we haven't stirred up the whole region!'

'Yes, there are many...'nests?' of them in the surrounding islands and they become bolder by the month. The police and the Indonesian Government don't seem to want to do much about them. The authorities believe if they don't chase pirates, then they don't have to admit that they exist. The logic becomes twisted, but the result is a thriving industry, much of it within 50 kilometres of here!'

'Thank you for that information. I hope we don't have to defend ourselves again, but while here, we are willing to assist if you need help.'

'Thank you, Harry. We will talk again and perhaps tonight, you and your crews will join me for a small feast to celebrate our business deal?'

'Thank you, Mikhail, that would be greatly appreciated.'

We exchanged grins, although I wouldn't trust the old rogue for a moment if he thought he could get away with something. I followed Roger and Gilbert outside where the interpreter waited.

CHAPTER 13

HERBA ISLAND, FRIDAY

It wasn't far to an open-sided, thatch-roofed long hut where a long table took up most of the space and a large iron cook pot that looked exactly like the cartoon pot that cannibals are depicted using, and which would have held a person if they were to scrunch up! The hut was set away from the village which made me wonder until I caught a whiff of the vapours rising from the simmering green mass of liquid being stirred languidly by an old man. A quick wave of light-headedness washed over me and it looked like it similarly affected Roger.

'Is that part of the effect?' I asked him.

'From what Anna told us, yes. I hate to think how we'd be affected if we stayed downwind of it for too long!'

I chuckled, aware of the looks I was getting from a number of Islander girls who were tending smaller pots full of a water/leaf mix which I guessed were to be added to the main brew as it reduced down. 'If we do stay, the first thing I'll need is bigger sized shorts!' I commented.

Roger laughed, 'I'm glad you're affected as well. I thought I was some sort of depraved sexual deviant!'

'Yeah. I don't know how these girls stand it being here all day.'

'Maybe they take it in turns,' he suggested.

The interpreter finally spoke up with a grin. 'Smoke make man very hard! Girls always ready for pom-pom!'

That seemed to say it all, so we hastily backed off and told the interpreter that we would like to go back to our boats now.

He referred the request to Gilbert who politely inclined his head and signed a lengthy message.

'Gilbert him say thank you Harry for agreeing to take Gilbert to Australia. Him happy and will do anything to help Harry. Gilbert hard worker and good with boats.'

I stepped up to where Gilbert was waiting well away from the green-goo cook fest.

'Thanks Gilbert. You will be very welcome aboard my boat and I will use your help where I can.'

We shook hands on that and he led the way back to the powered canoe moored in the narrow creek, where crystal-clear water meandered to the sea.

'Hey Gilbert. Can I drink this water?'

He smiled and nodded, so I scooped up a few handfuls and found it to be almost like a fizzy mineral water from a bottle. The taste was wonderful compared to the neutral taste of water produced by the reverse-osmosis process on *Firebird*.

'This is terrific!' I said to him and he signed to the interpreter in reply.

'Gilbert him say water very good for insides. No get sick. Always feel good!'

I turned to Roger, 'There's a testimonial for you! We have to find some way to get this stuff to customers, without it costing a fortune.'

He smiled, 'I wonder if it might be easier and cheaper to bring the wealthy customers to the water?'

I laughed, 'Now there's an idea worth talking over, but they'd have to be kept away from the green goo. There would be a bunch of rejuvenated, middle-aged, healthy sex maniacs running around!'

'But seriously, I'm at least going to work out a way to fill *Firebird's* water tanks with this stuff. I'll have a talk to Dave.'

In the canoe, I asked Gilbert about the Islander's reaction to Jasper and how they regarded him, and after much signing, the interpreter said, 'Big Cat special. His ancestors come from place near this one. Very powerful magic come from this cat. He protect you from danger; always!'

Addressing Gilbert, I said, 'OK. That's good to know, but the Islanders seem to be half afraid of him and half revere him? What's behind that?'

The second-hand answer came back. 'This cat regarded as Demigod. Live for very long time, also fierce when protecting family. You and friends are family.'

That gave me a lot to consider as we nosed up to *Firebird*. 'Gilbert say all crew come to house at 6 hours for feast.'

'Thanks Gilbert. We'll be there, but should we bring drinks? Is alcohol allowed?'

He smiled and shook his head. 'No alcohol on land please. Plenty fruit juice and good water.'

'One more question, Gilbert. What's the name of this island?'

'Pulau Herba.'

I laughed, causing a puzzled look to cross his face, but I just waved, so their boat backed away.

I called a full crew meeting in *Seeker's* spacious saloon and passed on the information we'd received about the green goo and then added. 'We've been invited to a feast tonight around 18:00, but no alcohol. The Islander females usually get around topless, but until we find out what we're allowed to do, we'd all better behave ourselves. The brewing of the green goo really blows inhibitions away, so be careful around the production area. There can often be a set of customs for the Islanders and a different set for visitors.

The water in the creek is amazing. It's like drinking a bottle of Perrier, but has a bunch of minerals that really does marvellous things to the digestive system.'

'What's the story with Gilbert?' Sandy asked. 'Is he really coming back with us?'

'Strange character. But yes, he is coming back with us and he is mute. But he's very intelligent, has a couple of degrees and an MBA and understands a whole heap of languages and dialects. Mikhail seems to defer to him a lot! He's also got the build of a combination of a body-builder and a long-distance swimmer! He's grateful for the chance to travel with us and visit Australia and apparently is very handy with boats.'

'I suppose we can give him the aft cabin.'

'That'll be fine. He seems the sort of guy who will fit in just about anywhere. Oh, one more thing. I asked about pirates and apparently we're right in the middle of one of the biggest groups in the islands, seeing as this is just south of the main Asian shipping route. We were also warned about wandering off across the island. The pirates who grabbed Anna sometimes come here to nick a couple of females, so some more white girls will go down just fine.'

My comment effectively squashed any ideas about exploring, so the meeting broke up for everyone to clean up and dress. I fed Krazy and told her she was on guard duty. To the vast amusement of all six of our new crew, I had another quiet talk to Jasper before we left, about what was happening. I might have made a mistake by saying that the Islanders revered him and his ancestors, because he flicked his tail at me when I'd finished, as well as huffing.

'OK, smart-arse cat! But just watch it, or it'll be PAL only for a week and no human tucker!'

As far as dire threats go, it was one of the worst I could make, so he sulked all the way to shore, only cheering up when a small girl, her parents hovering anxiously in the background, approached Jasper with a woven necklace of hibiscus flowers.

I nodded to her and stopped Jasper who sat and regarded the small girl with what passes for a regal feline look. She stepped closer, he inclined his head so she could gently place the wreath around his muscular neck, then he held out his right paw to her.

With a giggle, she briefly grasped it with both hands, then rushed back to her relieved parents. I bowed my head in thanks to them and was rewarded by one in return, so we proceeded to the tent. We were greeted by a presentable Gilbert who'd not only just showered, but had shaved, tied his long hair back in a neat pony tail and dressed neatly in Western style.

Sandy's enlightened comment was, 'Wow!'

I introduced the whole crew, noticing that Gilbert was just as interested in the ladies as they were in him! With difficulty, I managed to pry Sandy away from him before she embarrassed herself and we went inside to repeat the introductions to Mikhail. Jasper behaved himself, although acting just a bit too regally for my liking, so I squatted down beside him and said quietly, 'Make the most of it, fur-ball, cause back aboard you are just another cat who farts something terrible and drools in his sleep!'

His reply was to turn his head to yawn in my face then swat me with his tail!

Jane cracked up laughing, 'He understood and then told you to get stuffed!'

I grinned ruefully, 'Yeah, he's a cheeky pussy all right. This demigod business is really going to his big black head!'

Mikhail overheard, 'The Islanders are a superstitious people and believe he is. Although clouded leopards are supposed to be extinct, there are still some of the breed in the jungle over on Kalimantan and that's what he is! If you were to see one, you would find he looks identical in shape to them, except he is all black. The Chausie part of the hybrid breed doesn't seem to have taken at all except for the colouring, so you have a virtually pure-bred clouded leopard as a domestic cat. Have you noticed any strange happenings with him?'

I looked at Sandy and laughed, 'If you have the time, I can tell you several things that are straight out of the Twilight Zone!'

Mikhail gave a little titter that passed for a laugh. 'It would appear my dear Harry, for the next few days, starting now, we have all the time we would need. If I can help you understand the origins of your cat a little better, that would be good, would it not?'

We were taken outside to where a long, low-set table had been set up on the sand and a series of beautiful Indonesian dishes laid out. As promised, there was plenty of fruit and juices and jugs of the sparkling water. Sandy soon recognized what I meant about the water.

'We've really got to do something with this stuff,' was her comment. 'It's even better added to the natural fruit juice.'

Although beside her, I was at Mikhail's right hand with Jasper sitting just behind being fed chunks of meat by the serving girls under the direction of Mikhail's efficient and pretty secretary, Mai-ling.

So, with time in hand, I told Mikhail about the mysterious and mystical things we'd seen Jasper do. If he'd had eyebrows, they would have climbed into his non-existent hair-line, especially the giant croc story and healing my shoulder with saliva.

When I'd finished telling of his main mysterious doings, Mikhail commented, 'I find I must raise my estimation of his abilities and powers. Those events are extraordinary, especially when witnessed by many other people. I must undertake some studies on this. The village Chief Medicine Man will be the first place to start. Will it be possible for him to meet Jasper?'

'Sure. Whenever he likes.'

'Mornings are best for him if that would be suitable for you. He doesn't go far from his hut these days due to old age.'

'No problem. Perhaps if you can send a boat out when he's ready. We'll be only doing some maintenance on the boats in the morning.'

The object of this discussion was sitting in a Sphinx pose just behind us, gnawing loudly and messily on a large bone and behaving in a very un-mystical or demi-god like manner.

'On another matter,' I said to Mikhail, 'do you have any form of warning should pirates come raiding?'

He shook his head. 'No, not really. If some Islanders are out fishing or over on the other side of the island harvesting leaves, then we can get some warning, but they don't come to the village any more since I purchased six Kalashnikov rifles and had Gilbert train some men to use them effectively. Although I have done some arms trading in the past, it was all done remotely and was only recently I bought the Kalashinikov's.'

'OK. That's good to know just in case some pirate boss gets it into his head to chase down the boats that took out 84 men and five boats!'

Mikhail blinked before saying, 'I can see you don't mess about Harry. But the survivors will have good descriptions of what you look like and where you headed, so they might trace you here after all.'

I smiled grimly, 'No they won't. All gone!'

'How very...efficient of you. I'm not sure I want to know how that feat was accomplished, but I can't say that I'm sorry. They're all an evil bunch and don't help anyone but themselves.'

'Well. Let's just hope there aren't any chasers on our tail.'

When we returned to our boats, I pulled Dave aside and updated him on the situation with the local pirates and the lack of any form of warning system should they come calling.

'I think we should maintain a full-time radar watch for the duration of our time here, as well as keeping the weapons mounted and ready to shoot.'

He agreed. 'Yeah. We'd be sitting ducks if they came through the night. Do you want two person watches?'

'Minimum. We still don't know Mikhail and the Islanders very well and if one was in the pay of the pirates, then they already know that we're here.'

'That's a lousy, but very likely thought to go to bed on!'

CHAPTER 14

PALU BENWI, PIRATE STRONGHOLD
RIAU ARCHIPELAGO, FRIDAY

It was a small, hilly island, with a second, even smaller one close beside it and separated by a narrow, but deep channel. The two islands were officially listed by the authorities as one island and also as un-inhabited, but were avoided like the plague by the other inhabitants of the area. Over the millennia, the relentless sea had carved a series of caves out of the rocky cliffs on the south side of the main island and in several places some had collapsed to join up to form one giant cave which hollowed out much of the little island's main hill.

Further collapses of the unstable, fractured bedrock created an opening on the east side into the channel between the two islands and all it took to create a usable channel for boats up to 150 feet in length was the judicious application of explosives. Even more careful use of explosives enlarged the internal pool until six boats could fit inside, free from surveillance.

It was tailor-made for pirates and smugglers and for many generations had been used and inhabited by those who embraced that unholy profession. It was also no coincidence that for centuries, the bulk of the world's shipping had passed through the area, although the dawning of the 21st century had brought about sweeping changes to the *modus operandi* of one of the most successful and ruthless groups in the area.

The group's charismatic, but aging leader was struggling with a three-fold problem; his age; his young, highly educated and ambitious lieutenant and his difficulty in understanding the advantages modern technology had to offer. Unfortunately, his young protégé understood and embraced modern technology supremely well, having gained a degree in Electrical Engineering as well as an MBA.

Until recently, the nature of a pirate group hadn't changed for hundreds of years, but now the younger leaders were trying to make their groups more efficient and organising them into profit-sharing societies. This was something the older members had difficulty coming to grips with, but nevertheless, all were appreciating the personal wealth each member was assured was building up rapidly in a Singapore Bank.

It was in this evolving climate that the Benwi group, as one of the top three in this lucrative area was known, was teetering on the destructive edge of revolt and a classic *coup d'état* was brewing. It was classic in the sense the elderly leader was trying to cling to power, while finally realising he had a Sumatran tiger by the tail! On the upside, his young and ambitious lieutenant was his son and they did occasionally speak to each other.

They managed, for once, to communicate so well that over the past few weeks, they had been working out a private deal whereby dear old Dad would be given one last opportunity to show his men he was still a force to be reckoned with. He was then to be allowed to retire gracefully, head still attached, to live out his days in luxury, so long as he stayed away from Indonesia.

The only remaining item to kick start this plan for a bloodless coup, was for Dad to lead the members on his last operation. His son assumed a raid on a merchant ship or better still, an oil tanker would be the go, so he directed their intelligence networks to find out the shipping schedule for the coming weeks.

The task was complicated by the shipping companies who deliberately changed sailing dates, times and routes at the last minute to try to foil pirate plans. Having their captains sail faster or slower also messed with the pirate's calculations of where to strike the target vessel. Therefore, it was almost by accident, a pair of reports crossed the desk of the entrepreneurial Leader-in-Waiting who happened to skim over the handwritten report.

With a curse, he marched into the next room, carved out of the fractured rock at the back of the boat pool, and tossed the grubby piece of paper on his Father's desk.

'What do we know of this, Bapa?'

The grizzled, but still imposing bulk of his Father, leaned forward to look at the brief report, a frown deepening the permanent furrow already there.

'Bah! This is nothing. Two small groups have disappeared and only wreckage found!'

He shrugged expressively and gave an evil grin. 'They are rivals, so this time they cross paths, they fight, they wipe each other out! Sounds like a win to me.'

His son shook his head. 'Look more carefully, Revered Father. The two groups were over three hundred kilometres apart and both disappearances occurred within 24 hours! I find this disturbing.'

The Father snorted dismissively, 'Are you suggesting these two incidents are linked in some way? How could that be? No one has ever interfered with the Brethren!'

'At this stage, I do not know the how, but I see the second group, which comprised 60 heavily armed men, met their fate just 60 kilometres from here! Does it not strike you as strange and unsettling? What if the Indonesian Authorities have finally developed some backbone and decided to send a patrol boat out to destroy some of our number?'

His father frowned again. 'They wouldn't dare! We pay them too much money for this to happen! Please investigate. There must have been an accident.'

His son raised his eyebrows in disbelief. 'Really Father! Two accidents, 300 kilometres apart, within 24 hours? Both of which destroy the crews and shatter the boats into firewood? If you truly believe this fantasy, I fear old age has affected your thinking! With respect, Honoured Father!'

The old man's face grew darker with anger. 'You push too hard, son of mine. You are not Chief yet! Now, go and do as I request and bring the news quickly.'

Knowing when to bide his time, the son briefly bowed his head before withdrawing to the communications room.

Just two hours had elapsed when he again knocked on the door of his father's office.

'I have news, Respected Father. Just before darkness two nights ago, two boats were seen approaching the island which is home to the first of the missing men. There is an unreliable report there were shots exchanged before there was an explosion. It is all we have to go on for now.'

'What were these boats? Were they Navy patrol boats?'

The son consulted his notes. 'There was a large speed boat and a sailing catamaran, and neither appeared to be Navy craft.'

'I will admit that is rather disturbing, but if they are not Military, then I cannot believe they pose a threat to us.'

'Maybe so, dear Father, but we should take precautions.'

There was a hurried knock at the door to interrupt him and a messenger ducked in and handed the son a note, scurrying out before he was awarded punishment.

The son read it quickly, frowning like his father.

'Well, come on. What is it?'

'Two boats which roughly meet the description of the two I just mentioned were sighted approaching Herba Island.'

The Chief laughed, 'What! That strange place with the mad white man who calls himself King?'

'That's the one, Father. In the name of peaceful relations with other Islanders, I have forbidden our men from going there, but occasionally a crew defies the order and stops there to pick some local girls as wives. They are reputed to be unusually passionate and... vigorous and therefore highly sought after.'

The Chief snorted at such rubbish. 'So, you are suggesting the crews of these two boats attacked and decimated two raiding parties and are now at Herba Island? I find it unlikely, but if they are, what would they be doing there?'

The son bowed his head in false humility, 'That is just the suggestion of our analysts, my dear Father. They also recommend a sudden strike by our best crew would be highly successful and eliminate these new raiders who dared to come into our territory to make war on us without provocation!'

The Chief thought a few moments. 'Perhaps, my Son, this could be the raid that we have spoken of. My Grande Finale! Not too involved and with low resistance expected since we will have the big advantage of surprise.'

The son bowed his head to hide his relief at the silly old fool taking the bait. 'That would be a masterstroke, Revered Father.'

'Are they anchored off the village?'

'Apparently, dear Father. What is your plan of attack?'

'Simple! We'll have three boats approach from the north and three from the south, timed to arrive at the same moment. They each make one pass, then establish the circling pattern that has served us so well in the past. Tell the crews we will eliminate all trace of these intruders and take no prisoners.'

'A masterly plan, Revered Father; simple but effective. It cannot fail.'

The double meaning of his words was lost on the elderly Chief who had drifted off into dreams of past glories.

'Excuse me, my Father, but when do you wish to make this attack?'

'Tomorrow! We will strike while the intruders think they are safe. The time will be at dawn so our brave men can see to kill every intruder. How far is it to Palu Herba?'

'Just fifteen kilometres, Revered Father, which will take just 30 minutes to travel. Do you intend to use all six of our RIBs?'

'Yes. We will have ten men in each boat and arm them with our AK-74s. They will provide more than enough firepower to eliminate these arrogant fools.'

'So, you aren't going to use the machine guns?'

'No, they will not be necessary. Sixty AK-74s will be more than enough! And you will be right there beside me, my Son, as I lead my men into battle one last time.'

That wasn't what an ambitious son wanted to hear. Especially when encouraging his father to take on a ridiculous mission like this.

'I wouldn't like to diminish the glory which will be deservedly yours, Father, when you clean the sea of these foreign raiders. I can better serve you by remaining here and co-ordinating the operation on the radio.'

'No, my Son. I want our men to see the old Chief and the new Chief side-by-side, sharing the danger. It will make an effective statement and the word will be spread how we made my last raid together!'

The devious son's heart sank as he realised he couldn't pull out for any reason, or risk losing face in front of the men he wished to lead. He bowed his head in resignation, 'Very well, Most Revered Father, that is how it shall be. The old and the young together. I shall inform the men.'

CHAPTER 15

HERBA ISLAND, SATURDAY

The night had been quiet and as dawn approached, I was making tea for Jane and myself when the radar beeped loudly, indicating the intrusion zone limits I'd set had been breached. Tea-making abandoned, I quickly checked the radar plot to see three fast-moving targets just rounding the island from the north and three more doing the same from the south. 'Bandits!' I yelled. 'Sandy! Rick! Grab your guns, we've got trouble!'

My bellow must have been a good one as two half-naked bodies came belting up the two companionways struggling into clothes.

Even before Rick had finished dressing, Jane had the MK47 cleared for action, a fresh ammo box opened and the first round loaded. Rick made sure that the link feed was straight, before getting another box ready.

Sandy quickly had one shotgun loaded with solid shot and I had another loaded with solid and 'Dragon's Breath' incendiary rounds. Next to us, *Seeker* was boiling with activity and I blessed the plan which had us set two-man watches.

I called out loudly, 'Everyone keep low. They may think they have the advantage of surprise.'

'How close do we let them get?' Dave asked from above me on *Seeker's* sundeck where the two .50cal machine guns were mounted at the forward end.

'No closer than about 500 metres, I reckon. You guys should be able to rake the three from the north very quickly, and I'm hoping the explosive grenade rounds will stop the southern three just as quickly. Don't let a boat get away.'

'Copy that!'

Being rafted together allowed our main weapons to cover both directions without moving, which was convenient. I'd like to say it was carefully planned, but that wouldn't be correct or true; it was just what we liked to do and always did.

'Everybody keep behind cover,' I reminded them. 'These guys won't be armed with just handguns! Those dudes the other night had what looked like AK47s.'

The wait for the RIBs to close to within suitable range seemed like hours, but in reality, was only a couple of minutes. Hopefully, the pirates wouldn't have spotted our action stations movements and would think we were still asleep.

Regardless of what they did think, they just kept on coming straight at us, which made for an easy firing solution.

'They're making it too easy, boss.' Jane said, seated comfortably behind the bulky mass of the MK47 launcher. 'The laser range finder says 800 metres. Do I fire at 500 metres?'

'Yes, thanks Jane; weapons free at 500 metres,' I called out to Dave and Corrine. 'Wait until Jane fires. She's got the laser range finder, then weapons free. Take no chances, wipe 'em all out!'

'Ok.'

Seconds later, the MK47 gave it's now familiar asthmatic barking as Jane, with high confidence in her aim, sent a stream of rounds arcing out in a green stream at the three RIBs. Their drivers either didn't see the winking lights on their targets ahead or were just too slow to react in time, but all three boats, travelling in line abreast were smothered in ugly red-yellow flashes and spurts of seawater. Within seconds, two boats had spewed fire, with one simply exploding in a huge fireball.

The third took hits and swerved drunkenly a few times, then straightened and at a greatly reduced speed, continued on course toward us.

Above and beside us, the loud chugging sound of the two Browning .50 cal guns continued well after the MK47 had stopped, until Dave yelled, 'Stop, stop!'

We were too busy to check how effective they'd been, concentrating on the damaged RIB that was still trying the press home the attack despite an obvious impairment to power and steering functions. Finally, it lurched closer and only two individuals were still standing, both holding on to the steering station. One, an older-looking man, was covered in blood and had one side of his face mostly ripped away. The other survivor wasn't much better, but they were still coming on. I told Jane to hold fire, but if I couldn't take it out, then she was 'weapons free'.

With Sandy standing beside me ready to lay some solid shot on the crippled RIB, I let it close to within 60 metres before I chickened out and laid two rounds of Dragon's breath on them. Even though I'd tried firing a couple of rounds as a test, the results against a real, highly inflammable target were dramatic in the extreme as a huge fireball engulfed the boats and its inhabitants in a shower of burning magnesium at a toasty 2,200° C.

Everything which wasn't already burning or smouldering, flashed into immediate flame, including the two humans who had stood together at the steering console. The physical force of the ball of flame blew them from there into the back of the boat in a tangle of twisted limbs. For good measure, Sandy pumped five rounds of solid shot into the outboard motors, stopping them instantly, so the wreck of the RIB, with bodies piled up in it from stem to stern, slewed drunkenly sideways. With the intense fire rapidly eating away the flotation chambers, the weight of the outboards slowly dragged the stern down.

Bizarrely, one of the men who'd been still standing, appeared to be trying to get up again, but could only manage to shake a clenched fist at us from his position slumped in the stern, before the whole stinking, blazing mess slid out of sight beneath the surface of the uncaring water. Moments later, just the remains of a column of black, greasy smoke marked where ten or twelve men had perished in very nasty circumstances.

Jane and Rick were in a rare sombre mood as they cleared the

MK47, as it wasn't often the results of their expert shooting presented itself for a final close and personal inspection. Further down range, only one boat was still afloat, a column of smoke pouring up to mar the beauty of the early morning sky.

Dave called down from *Seeker's* top deck. 'You'd better get your RIB launched, mate. It looks like you've got one or two swimmers back there. We've got a couple up front, so Corrine's going to check 'em out.'

Sure enough, their RIB emerged from the garage under the cockpit daybed and Corrine and Alex roared up to the north. I kicked my brain into gear and launched ours, Sandy joining me with the ugly little mini-Uzi sub-machine gun slung over her shoulder and handed over my favourite gun, the Grizzly Mk IV .44 magnum pistol.

A few minutes later we were at the debris field. Of the boat which had exploded, there was only an oil slick and some unidentifiable pieces of...things! The other boat sank as we were still 100 metres away, leaving behind more debris, some identifiable and some not, as well as two heads splashing feebly and ineffectively as they tried to stay afloat.

Unfortunately for one of the two, a brown-grey shape flashed under us and struck him so hard he was tossed out of the water, the unmistakable dark-barred and thick body of a large Tiger shark leaping out after it. The shark and its prey nearly fell across the last man, the thrashing tail batting him sideways. While tempting to end his torment with a .44 solution, I nosed the RIB up to him where he scrabbled at the side trying to escape the big shark. It was no threat to him at the moment as it was off playing with its new piece of food. Sandy and I dragged his water-logged body aboard, letting him lie on the bottom boards coughing up seawater. There were no other signs of life around the twin oil slicks, so we headed back to *Firebird*, our captive curled up miserably and still coughing up water.

Back aboard, we hauled him out and sat him on the boarding platform where cable ties secured wrists and ankles and a rope attached his neck to the handrail. He was only wearing the remnants of a shirt with the rest of his clothing apparently having been blown off. Apart from seawater ingestion and terror from the near-hit with the shark, he didn't appear to be hurt, so we left him with his feet in the water to fully awaken him. Gilbert and a few other Islanders had come out to see what was going on and grinned wolfishly when they saw our captive.

'This man pirate!' Gilbert's little interpreter explained un-necessarily. 'What you do with him?'

'We want to find out where their base is,' I told Gilbert, and taking a guess at what they were after, I added, 'then you can have him.'

He nodded and smiled again, leaving little doubt as to the fate of this hapless individual.

We served coffee for Gilbert and his interpreter and sat in the cockpit winding down from the stress of action. I noticed Gilbert was watching the girls closely as they brought out tea and coffee and went about doing normal things to shed stress as quickly as possible. In return, they were all quite taken with his good looks and silent, but good manners.

Finally, our captive began to stir and quickly panicked when he found his feet in the water, so I guessed the encounter with the big Tiger shark had a profound effect on him. As it should!

Between Gilbert and his man, we extracted some story about the old Chief and his son, the succession plan and the expectation of low resistance from us. It also raised the question of 'how did the pirates know that we were at Herba Island?'

'We have informer,' Gilbert's interpreter passed on, 'and that will be our first job. Find person and remove problem.'

'Please ask our captive where their base is. With no Chiefs left, there's no point in him keeping quiet.'

'He can show you on map, but he cannot go back or the others will kill him!'

I went inside and found the area chart and showed our captive. With hands strapped behind his back, he couldn't point too easily, but we worked out the system whereby I pointed and he moved his head to indicate left or right or up or down. It worked and within moments, I was looking at a small, double island with a narrow channel splitting the two.

Our new friend quickly realised he was pleading for his life so details about the precise location of the camp poured out of his mouth. Once his limited memory of personnel numbers and basic security ran out, I clipped his restraints off and passed custody to Gilbert.

'You can tell Mikhail I intend to visit this base and finish the clean up we've started here. It's almost certain there will be a reprisal raid by the rest of the pirates on the village, so they all have to be eliminated!'

Gilbert smiled and made a sound that I was to come to learn meant he wanted to tell me something, but his interpreter said, 'Gilbert want to come too! Me too!' he said proudly.

I shrugged. 'Sure. I don't mind, but we're going to have a good look at this place first. It's only fifteen kilometres away.'

It didn't take long for Sandy to get the *Dragonfly* ready for flight, so twenty minutes later, the odd-looking aircraft lifted smoothly off *Seeker's* foredeck, gained height and flew east over Herba Island in the direction of the small twin islands nominated as the pirate base. Gilbert watched the operation with undisguised interest and appreciated being invited to check out the GCS and to watch the live feed in HD on the big screen in *Seeker's* spacious saloon.

Even at an economical cruise speed, the UAV was over the target site in minutes, so I asked Sandy to place it in a high, wide orbit so we could check the place out.

Both islands were hilly, although the western one had a higher peak and the narrow channel ran north to south between them. A mixture of medium height scrub and low trees covered both islands and there were several narrow, sandy beaches.

'What are these snaking lines?' I asked nobody in particular, stepping closer to the screen.

By way of reply, Sandy zoomed in. 'Walking track!' I exclaimed. 'Not for bloody tourists either! They've got a lookout post up on that peak.'

Sandy left the camera zoomed in and shifted the aim back along the track where it wound around the steep-sided hill.

'Bingo! There it is and there's just the one. Right on top of the highest peak!'

She adjusted the UAV's orbit to give a better view and engaged the AutoTrack function so the lookout post was kept centred in the view all the time. There was a rough shelter with a thatched roof and open sides and what looked like two men inside. Sandy dropped the orbit height so we had a better view beneath the roof and revealed two AK47s or similar and what looked like a field telephone.

'That phone is very inconvenient,' I commented. 'We're going to have to sneak up on them without being spotted and the cave-dwellers alerted.'

'How about at night?' Dave asked. 'Maybe in conjunction with a diversion?'

I thought about that, but shook my head. 'Nah! Any diversion would still cause an alert to be raised.' I looked at Gilbert. 'How many long canoes do you have with good outboards on them and can we borrow some?'

He grinned, apparently thinking what I was thinking, and held up one hand with all fingers spread.

'Five, and it'll be OK to use them?'

He nodded.

'OK. How about this. The long canoes are surprisingly stable, can hold up to thirty people and with a 50 horsepower outboard, are quite fast. What if we mounted a Browning amidships on two of them, take a third for security and towed one of those inflatable kayaks we used on the Pilbara job? We approach the island to within two or three kilometres, then hold position while Corrine takes the kayak and paddles in alone.'

'Shouldn't someone go with her? Dave predictably asked.

'No. One small black-painted kayak would be easily overlooked, but not two.'

Corrine nodded, 'Harry's right, love. We've proved they're easy to paddle and are almost as good as rigid boats. This is what I'm best at; taking out observation posts, so I'm cool with it.'

Dave looked unhappy to see his girl jumping into the frypan alone yet again, so I went on.

'We all wear Tac-net headsets and Mouse should be able to talk to us easily from the lookout post. Once the guards are neutralised, you call us in to where you landed. We can choose the best spot on this UAV flight.'

Sandy, who'd been still watching the return video from the UAV, called out. 'Look here. There looks to be an opening in the hillside half-way down the slope on the northern side and the trail leads right past it. I'll bet it's a back door into the cavern the pirate told us about.'

We all crowded around as Sandy adjusted the orbit yet again and locked the camera onto the opening she mentioned. It was clearly a well-used hole carved out of the hillside with the track running past it down to the base of hill and around to the channel.

After watching some more of the live video, Corrine suggested, 'If I landed a bit further around from where the track reaches the bottom of the hill, then the kayak won't be noticed by anybody on the trail. It'll be the fastest way for me to access the observation post as well.'

'That sounds good,' I said. 'Any other thoughts for the moment?' No one did then, but they would later as a bunch of fertile and active minds mulled over the problems.

A thought occurred to me and I asked Gilbert to follow me forward. His interpreter started to follow, but I waved him down. 'No interpreting necessary thanks sport. We'll be back in a minute. I just need to show Gilbert something.'

The local sank back, clearly torn between duty and orders.

Luckily, orders won as Gilbert followed me out through the port side door to the side deck, then forward to the bow where I mimed showing Gilbert the anchoring system.

What I actually said was, 'I wanted to ask you not to say anything more to either your mouthpiece or to anybody ashore about these plans, including that we're going to borrow the boats, in case word of this raid gets to the informer who we now know is one of the Islanders and reports directly to the pirates!'

Gilbert gazed at me for a few moments with those intelligent eyes, then nodded and made the soft grunting sound I'd heard before which seemed to indicate a 'yes'. Apart from learning ASL, I had found if I phrased a question the right way, it was easy for Gilbert to answer yes, no or maybe which was a big step forward.

I also asked, 'Do you totally trust your interpreter?'

He looked aft, then nodded. He also pointed at the Island, mimed talking and slowly drew his hand across his throat, which I took to indicate what would happen to the informer when Gilbert found him.

'Ok. But if you don't mind, I'd like to keep him on board for the rest of the day while you try to find the informer. We'll make this raid early tomorrow morning and I'd like to be just off the pirate's island by 03:00. Can you plan around that, please? And can you bring six men you trust implicitly and have trained to shoot those AK74s?'

He nodded enthusiastically, pointed to shore and held up six fingers, then pointed to the saloon and held up one, then at himself.

I nodded, 'OK. You can trust and will bring the six trained men, also your man and yourself.'

He nodded rapidly.

'Good, thanks Gilbert. I'd like you and your men out here, very quietly, with the long canoes and extra fuel at 02:00, if you can. I can also supply weapons for you and your man.'

He grunted, nodded and shook my hand.

Shortly after, he managed to convey the instructions to his man to stay on the boats for the day, something he seemed to be happy to do, then Gilbert went ashore to arrange his end of things.

CHAPTER 16

HERBA ISLAND, SUNDAY

In the afternoon of the previous day, Gilbert had come to us in one of the long canoes with two of his trusted and trained men, seemingly on a visit to discuss something, but in reality to have his two men, who were also boat-builders, look at how the tripod mount for the .50 calibre machine guns could be fitted to the canoes. It hadn't taken those two inventive men long to work out a clamp system to hold the weapons secure and only about an hour, using fittings we carried aboard, to mount them in such a manner that they could be removed and re-mounted quickly.

While Gilbert and the men were there, we held a final briefing to make sure we didn't need any more changes, but it had still seemed a workable plan so we'd resisted the urge to fiddle with it, and sent Gilbert on his way.

At 02:00 that cloudy night, three long shadows ghosted up to the stern platforms, with Gilbert and seven grinning Islanders aboard, armed with six AK74s and festooned with bandoleers of extra ammunition and the ubiquitous razor-sharp machetes strapped to each man's waist. I was assured it wasn't going to rain.

While Gilbert's men mounted the .50 cal tripods and the guns on top, I gave Gilbert a pump-action shotgun and two bandoleers of SG buckshot rounds. His interpreter received the same and showed he was perfectly familiar with the weapon.

He'd spent the day with us for security, but after getting his shotgun, Gilbert informed us that they had found a fisherman who's been bribed to inform the pirates of any unusual activity on Herba Island. 'Fishman, him no talk no more!' was the succinct statement from Gilbert's mouthpiece.

It was 02:15 when three long canoes drifted away from our boats with a very mixed and motley crew manning them. Only Sandy, Bree and Krazy cat stayed behind to provide security and to launch *Dragonfly*, which was tasked to provide IR video surveillance of the target site for the whole duration of the mission. I included Jasper in the raiding party, although Sandy was not happy to be left out of the action yet again, and would use either radio or the SatPhone to communicate and provide warning if the bad guys popped out of the wrong hole to surprise us. The UAV had a full eight hours loiter time to watch over us and I figured that should be more than enough.

One long canoe towed one of our inflatable kayaks, still roughly sprayed a dull matt black.

The outboards fired instantly and quietly, and were run at low power until we were well away from the village before they were opened up to full power and the 40-foot long canoes surged forwards, their slender hulls creating very little wash. The hand-held GPS units showed a speed over the ground of 30 knots or 55 km/h, which meant that the run to the initial staging point took just 15 minutes. Two kilometres short of the twin islands, we stopped our little convoy and loosely tied the three canoes together.

I called Sandy on the radio and wasn't really surprised the signal was weak and very scratchy, so I used the SatPhone.

'How's the target area look?'

'*Nothing stirring. Still just two guards up top and both look to be asleep.*'

'Can you do a pass that shows you the sight line from the guard's eye level to the sea on the north side? I want to see if there's a blind spot at our intended landing place.'

'*Standby......Yeah, there is. They can't see closer than about 500 or 600 metres offshore.*'

'Beautiful. Thanks, my lovely lady. You just saved Corrine a long paddle. But please call immediately if either guard wakes and moves. We will move straight into shore while they're asleep.'

'*Will do and glad to be of service, O White Knight of mine!*'

I quickly explained what guards asleep meant to the mission, then had the drivers fire up the outboards.

'One kilometre at moderate speed, then the rest of the way at a no-wake speed. If someone wakes while we're in the visual zone, I don't want any white water to show us up.'

A trio of thumbs-up showed their understanding as we motored straight at the enemy's lair.

After a nerve-wracking period, the SatPhone warbled. 'OK' *said Sandy, 'you should be in the blind spot now and the sleeping beauties are still just that!'*

I had the throttles cut back even more and the well-silenced four-stroke motors settled into a gentle purr which still drove the slender canoes at 6 to 8 knots, with no white broken water to mark our passage.

I looked at Corrine, crouched beside me, clad in dark grey flesh-hugging Lycra, 'Beats paddling, Mouse!'

She flashed a nervous grin, 'Shit yeah! I'm not complaining.'

We closed on the landing place, chosen earlier from the UAV's flyover so it was well away from the path and hopefully from any risk of accidental discovery. Finally, the GPS and the sharp-eyed drivers agreed that the black mass towering over us was the target island and not a Russian aircraft carrier. Gently, the drivers grounded the bows on a rocky foreshore, one man hopping out to hold each bow from drifting off again.

I squeezed Corrine's shoulder as she rose, strapped on her favourite pistol, the PMR 30 with a suppressor which was remarkably quiet, even with magnum rounds, although it was the 30-round magazine which really appealed. A Gerber Mk II combat knife was strapped to one slim thigh and a garrotte circled her waist.

Without a word or any other sound, she slipped over the bow onto dry land and within seconds, was lost from sight. I'd plugged the SatPhone into my Tac-net headset to avoid undue noise and after five minutes, I quietly asked Sandy for a Sitrep.

'Still quiet up top and I have eyes on Corrine moving up the trail.

The tunnel opening into the hill is 50 metres ahead of you. All clear so far. Twenty metres to the tunnel, all clear.... stop, freeze! One bad guy has just appeared, no alarm. He's lighting a cigarette so there goes his night vision. He's just standing there... Oh dear. He's not standing there any longer, his body just slid down the hill about ten metres. His heat signature seems to be fading slowly and Corrine is moving again. All clear to the top.'

I started breathing again and Dave let out the one he'd been holding.

Eight minutes later, Sandy spoke again. *'Corrine, you're almost to the top. About 30 metres and targets still asleep. Just around that slight bend ahead and to the left of the overhanging bush. There, that's them!'*

Corrine's voice came on, slightly breathless from the long climb.

'Ok. Two Tangos down and I'm not touching the landline. Returning down the trail.'

Our plan was to collect Corrine and take the boats around to the channel between the two islands and access the cave via their man-made channel, but when Corrine got back down to the tunnel entrance, she disappeared.

'Corrine is out of sight. She's gone into the tunnel!' Sandy reported.

That stopped our main plan in its tracks, since we didn't know what her plan was and had to just wait.

Finally Corrine called in. *'Just went down the tunnel. There is a guard station just inside the opening, but just the one ex-guard. This would be a good way to gain quiet access for most of our group. Send the boats around to the entry channel ready to open fire when they hear fuss inside, but hurry up, these guys might be expecting relief anytime soon.'*

I looked at Dave, 'I'm inclined to go with her assessment. She's on the spot and it makes sense.'

He nodded. 'Yeah. I agree. Let's do it.'

Within a minute we were all geared up, leaving Jane and Rick on one Browning and Alex and Jill as loader on the other while the drivers manned the motors.

I gave them last minute instructions before following the others in stepping off the long overhanging bow of the canoe onto the rocky beach. In single file, we trotted up the first rise of the trail and five minutes brought us to within 20 metres of the tunnel entrance.

Since I was behind Dave, I had noticed that he had a canvas satchel case slung over his shoulder that looked pretty heavy.

'What's with the man-bag, dude?'

He turned his head and flashed a grin. 'Corrine grabbed a case of these handy, dandy grenades before she resigned from her previous employment, and so I thought being underground, they might come in very useful.'

I chuckled, 'Yeah. Good thinking. As Jane told Bree; if we're better armed, that gives us an edge!'

Sandy came on, *'You're almost to the tunnel entrance and I can't help you from there on. The rest of the island is clear as is the surrounding sea. The UAV will stay overhead, so call when you can.'*

Corrine was waiting for us at the tunnel mouth and re-claimed her H&K MP5 from Dave. Then with a muttered word to keep it quiet, she led the way down the uneven floor of the sloping corridor mostly formed by a fracture in the rock, perhaps caused by an earthquake. We had several red-shaded torches since it was utterly black inside the hill and on the Tac-net radio I heard Corrine say, 'I haven't been further than this, so we need to be careful of what we might stumble into.'

She led the way and after another five minutes a faint yellow glow ahead announced the need for further caution.

The passage abruptly opened out into a huge cavern where the roof was at least 15 metres above our heads and the floor was uneven rock maybe 150 metres across. Water lapped the sides of a narrow channel that connected with the outside through a wide, jagged split in the rock that had been obviously opened up with explosives and led into a roughly circular pool on what would be the south side of the huge space.

Stacks of supplies and material were scattered around in no particular order, mixed in with more random stacks of what could only be looted goods. Toward the back of the cavern where the roof sloped down to meet the floor, a series of rough huts had been constructed from a bewildering array of materials. Other constructions more like lean-tos were apparently sleeping accommodation for the pirates.

The pool and entrance channel were empty, except for a small inflatable dinghy pulled up onto the rocky floor. A tall, bearded Eurasian man was pacing the floor, barking orders to several pirates of mixed nationalities, none of whom looked happy at being told anything by the bearded dude.

'Maybe we have some division in the ranks,' I murmured, 'they shouldn't have been told about the loss of the raiding party, but they also should have been back yesterday morning. It hasn't taken long for the most ambitious character to assert his leadership style.'

Juan the interpreter tugged at my sleeve, 'Scuse boss. This man him say no hear from lookouts on hill and at tunnel. He want one man to go wake sleeping lookouts.'

'Thanks Juan. OK everyone. Fall back up the tunnel a few metres and let Corrine handle him.'

We retreated and a few moments later, as one surly, unwashed individual shuffled into the tunnel to rouse the permanently sleeping beauties, a black shadow rose up behind him and persuaded him to join them. With his body pushed behind a rock, we clustered around the end of the tunnel again, making plans.

'Aren't there supposed to be twenty guys here?' Dave asked.

'That's what the survivor said,' I replied, 'less the four that Mouse has taken out, leaving sixteen. We need to get rid of that bloke giving the orders as soon as we can, so the rest will be easier to deal with. But we'll see what's going on first.'

There was a fair amount of noise in the cavern, hammering and sawing up the back, while shouted orders echoed off the walls as the new leader seemed to be trying to get men to re-arrange the stacks of supplies into a different order. A pattern slowly emerged as several men carried wood boxes of various sizes and weights down to the edge of the pool where they were stacked neatly. As the pile grew, an idea formed in my brain and I said to Dave and Corrine, 'I think they're boxing up loot and stacking it ready for extraction by boat. They must be expecting another boat to swing past now it seems the raid has gone tits up!'

'Makes sense,' Dave said, 'but it means that we need to take these guys out sooner rather than later if someone else is coming to the party.'

Corrine chipped in with the best piece of common sense. 'Forget about the frontal assault plan to come in with machine guns blazing. Let's just whittle them down one by two, as we have been. That way, we don't get shot at! We can start with this self-elected leader bozo. If you can get him over here, I can take him either by hand or with my SD6. It's quiet enough with all this noise going on.'

'Good one, Mouse. Much less wear and tear on our troops! OK everyone, back up the tunnel again about 10 metres and lights out.'

We did that as Corrine faded into the darkness.

'Give me a few coughs, please Harry,' I heard in my headset. So I conjured up a few muffled, hacking coughs and sure enough, Bozo's head snapped around and he called out something in a strange language.

I coughed again, but muffled it more and faced away from the cave as I did.

Impatiently, he stalked over to the tunnel entrance, peering into the blackness before taking a step too far. He didn't react to the black shadow which rose up beside him and with languid grace flicked the garrotte wire over his head and abruptly jerked her hands apart.

I'd practiced the move on dummies and found it takes serious upper body strength to get the desired result, but Corrine had refined the technique so it looked almost easy.

The other thing one learns about this particular stunt is to move out of the way very quickly, something else she'd practiced and refined into a graceful and deadly move.

She'd just moved back against the tunnel wall when Bozo's head lifted off his shoulders slightly, letting a gusher of black-looking liquid spray out in all directions. With the command centre separated from the motion bits, his body fell backwards to thump hard onto the sandy rock floor, his loose head bouncing across the floor, until it came to rest against the foot of one of the men carrying the boxes of loot.

As a conversation stopper, it was a ripper!

Dead silence spread over the cavern like a wave washing back off a sloping beach. The unfortunate worker was frozen in place, his former leader's nose looking like it was nuzzling his left boot. Almost in slow motion, the worker gently placed the box on the floor and delicately moved his foot sideways before turning and joining the slow movement of six or eight others toward the back of the cavern, none taking their eyes off the head or the headless body lying on its back, feet in the darkness of the tunnel.

A click sounded in my ear as the Tac-net opened and Corrine whispered, 'Nobody move or make the slightest sound. These guys are about to freak out and we're gunna play on that.'

I gave her a 'click' in reply and scrunched lower behind a rock outcrop. The rest of the crew were even further up the tunnel and hopefully lying flat since I wouldn't put it past someone braver than the rest, to empty a magazine of 9mm slugs up the tunnel just in case.

Still, it was what we did in the desert quite often. We had found if one shows a ruthless enemy an even greater degree of mindless brutality, it seems to freak them out to discover there is someone or something which is capable of even greater atrocities than themselves. Often, they will attribute the action to the supernatural, a rather bizarre conclusion to draw. In this case, the soundless and apparently invisible removal of a head the moment he'd stepped from the light to the dark was enough to reduce fully half the pirate crew to terrified, near-catatonic wrecks.

The Tac-net clicked again with Corrine's whisper. 'Can someone do a really weird, non-human type scream? Loud as you like and as long as you like, but it has to be really weird.'

'I will try, my Major,' came the deep, throaty whisper of big Alex. 'Wait one.'

There was silence for a few moments before a series of harsh loud grunts blasted down the tunnel into the natural amphitheatre of the cavern, followed by an insane cackling howl that rose in pitch and volume before abruptly cutting off.

It was bad enough being in the tunnel with it, but the sound level out in the cavern must have been incredible.

Silence reigned supreme for several seconds, before a scream erupted from several throats up near the back of the cavern. They might have been triggered by Alex's impersonation of an amorous hyena, or perhaps because I'd crawled up in the darkness, grasped the corpse's ankles and slowly dragged him out of sight, leaving just a huge puddle of blood to mark his violent demise.

Whatever the reason, the screams quickly escalated to the hysterical level with no one making any attempt to settle them down.

I crept up beside Corrine and said, 'How about I ask Jasper for a yowl? Now he's heard Alex, he might get the idea.'

Corrine chuckled, 'That might really be stretching your Jasper-talk, but try if you like. I really want to keep these idiots off-balance.'

So, I put my lips close to Jasper's ears and murmured, 'Can you make a loud sound like Alex just made? Except we want it to sound like it's coming from a big cat. Can you do that?'

He huffed gently, sat back on his haunches, took a visibly deep breath and let loose the most incredibly loud and bone-chilling yowl I'd ever heard! The natural amplifying effects of the tunnel would have made it seem like the cat direct from hell had removed the leader's head and was about to repeat the job on the rest of them.

All previous screams were silenced instantly and a deathly silence held sway.

CHAPTER 17

PIRATE ISLAND, SUNDAY

I keyed the Tac-net radio, 'Boat One, Shadow One, copy?'
'*Boat One copies.*'

'Come and join the party now please. Bring both armed boats right up to the loading platform. All the Tangos are up the back of the cavern and in a state of severe shock. Perhaps just one brief burst up high to keep heads down would be good.'

'*Roger, Shadow. Entering now.*'

Almost silently, the two long canoes slid into the cavern and used their great length to run their bows up on the rock of the loading platform. In that environment, the pair of deadly-looking .50 cal machine guns totally dominated the situation. In the closest boat, Jane triggered a quick three-round burst which was aimed at the roof above the cluster of ramshackle huts and as the thunderous echoes bounced back and forth, large chunks of rock fell and smashed into the huts below, raising a chorus of feminine screams.

'Hold fire!' I barked quickly. 'That sounded like a bunch of females.'

'It was,' Corrine snapped. 'Time to move out, Harry. Let's go troops!'

Her lithe, dark grey-clad figure was up and running for the back of the cavern while the echoes of the .50 cal shots were still fading, our whole crew, also in basic black or dark-grey pouring out of the tunnel after her. On reaching the first of the huts, we spread out, slapping improvised cable-tie hand and ankle cuffs on each pirate we came across.

Most were curled into a small foetal ball and gave no resistance, looking almost as terrified of the wildly painted faces we all sported.

By my count, we'd accounted for all the pirates before we reached a low wall that reached from floor to the low roof, just one metre above the floor.

A small gate with a drop bar securing it was the first clue, as was the terrified whimpering of many females and children by the sound.

Gently, I lifted the bar and pulled the gate open to be struck almost physically by the stench of unwashed bodies living in their own filth.

'Juan. Get up here and tell them that they're safe. Quickly!'

'Yes boss, me come now.'

He knelt by the open gate and called softly in a variety of tongues until finally one girl crawled out, naked and streaked with filth. She was soon followed by many more and it was obvious they were the pirates play toys, to be used and abused as required.

Roger and Jill smoothly took over and organised cleaning, clothing and first aid where necessary. More than a few of the girls spat on the bound, captive pirates and a series of well-aimed kicks landed where they'd do the most good.

Significantly, none of our crew made any move to prevent the former captives from taking out some revenge, as some pirates received a lot more attention from the women than others.

While the medical team was working, Corrine, Dave and I searched the place, starting with the huts. Although rudimentary in nature, they didn't need to be more since they were in a cave where they could ride out a typhoon if necessary. Nevertheless, they were remarkably comfortable inside as each man simply chose the best furniture and furnishings of what was available when they hi-jacked boats and ships.

The hut I really wanted was off to one side of the main group and was a lot bigger. A two-roomed office was at the front and a bedroom hung off the back of it. Along with a desk and a laptop computer, there was a giant, old-fashioned safe in the office portion which was still closed tight. It was about shoulder height on me and more than a metre wide

Corrine headed for the computer while Dave and I checked out the safe. It had combination locks, but they must have been of an early design, because Corrine wandered over, took one look and sent Dave to borrow Roger's stethoscope. She pulled up a comfortable chair and was ready when he arrived back, device in hand. She looked very professional sitting there twiddling the dials, pausing to listen, before adjusting them slightly again. It all seemed to be working all right, since she stopped every few moments to write a number in a little notebook.

Twenty minutes after starting, she spun the second dial and threw the big brass handle over with a loud, 'clack'!

Rolling her chair back, she strained to pull the heavy door open until Dave helped, revealing the contents to be stacked bundles of used US currency in $100 denominations. A shallow shelf at the top held a stack of US$ Bearer Bonds, and shoved to the back of it was a smallish black velvet bag with one big lump and five or six smaller lumps in it, that sent a shiver up my spine, so I automatically shoved it into a pocket which held a handful of shotgun rounds.

'We're going to need some decent bags to clean all this out', I commented, 'and who knows what's in those boxes they were stacking by the dock.'

Corrine was thinking as usual. 'Why not get Juan to ask some of them. We didn't kill them all this time!'

I flashed her a smile and ducked outside, finding Juan and Gilbert watching over the prisoners with Juan talking to those who were able to do so.

'Yes boss?' he asked, seeing the look on my face.

'Please ask some of these men what is in those boxes that are stacked down by the dock. We don't have the time to stuff around opening all of them. We just need to know where the papers and valuables are.'

'Papers, boss?' he looked puzzled. 'Them only good for...' he mimed, wiping his bum.

'Sometimes they can be more valuable than cash or gold!'

I ransacked the bedroom behind the office and found several soft bags and six large duffels. Returning to the office, Corrine had the laptop computer in a padded carry bag and she and Dave were stacking the cash on a table. The bundles were the familiar $10K per wrap and they were stacking them in stacks of ten to make $100K. There were already an impressive number of stacks lining up along the table and the bundles were still being pulled from the safe.

I grabbed the sheaf of bearer bonds and sat at the other desk to flick through them. They were old and issued by the US Government. After a while, Corrine paused in her cash-stacking labour for a moment to say, 'We still should be able to cash those in. They don't issue them anymore, but the old ones are still honoured.'

'That's good,' I said, 'because there's seventy-eight of them here and nearly all are $10,000 each!'

She grinned, 'US$780,000 should help the bank balance a bit more.'

I smiled back and nodded at the stacks on the table. 'That lot might as well!'

There was knock on the outer office door, so I left the bonds, and went out, closing the inner door behind me. We had formed a few strange alliances and I didn't fully trust some of our allies.

Outside were Juan and Gilbert, looking excited.

'What's up, guys?'

'You ask about boxes, boss. We ask pirates and they say much gold and jewellery. Captive from ships. Many ships – many years. This place — him now 'pinish. Other boat, he come take all.'

'OK, Juan. Thank you.'

'OK boss.'

I went back inside. 'Dave. I think you should take one canoe and head back to Herba Island immediately and hustle to get *Seeker* and bring her here. Quick as you can, considering the other boat is expected here soon. Leave Jane and Rick here, if you would and take the other boat. You can tell Sandy to stay put on *Firebird* and keep *Dragonfly* airborne please.'

He nodded, 'Yep! Good idea. I'm gone. See you soon.'

He left and I went on helping Corrine stack the cash, then count it. We used all four of the big duffle bags and a few smaller ones to stow it all safely out of sight and the final, impressive total was US$4.87 million, which converted roughly to a staggering AU$6.878 million. Toss in another US$780,000 or AU$1,101,000 and it was looking like yet another excellent payday!

We lugged the various bags outside and stacked them carelessly with the other crates and boxes.

I checked with Alex who'd been in charge of watching over the clearing out of all the huts and he reported that everything of value had been retrieved and that all prisoners were behaving themselves.

Next I checked with Dr Roger and he reported that many of the women and girls needed a lot more treatment, so I spoke to Gilbert.

'These females all need more treatment. Can we take them to your island for help?'

He relayed we could do just that, but we would need to talk to Mikhail as to what happened to them after they had been treated.

'Thank you Gilbert. That will be enough for now just to get them better treatment. Even though Roger is an excellent Doctor, he doesn't have the supplies to treat them properly. I'm having Dave bring the *Seeker* here as quickly as possible, since there may be a pirate boat on the way to pick up this scum.'

Gilbert nodded, then mimed putting a gun to the head of each pirate.

I shook my head. 'No, sorry mate. Chopping one dude's head off was to make the rest more subdued, but to shoot sixteen men in cold-blood is a bit over the top, even by our standards. Once we have loaded all the valuable cargo, I intend to chase the pirates up the tunnel, then blow up the cavern to ruin the base for anybody else. The left-over pirates can fend for themselves.'

Gilbert thought a moment, then nodded agreement, so I went and brought our crew up-to-date on the latest cunning plan.

With everything quiet for the moment, I walked beside the inlet channel out clear of the cavern overhang to where the SatPhone could see some satellites and called home in the form of my lovely Sandy. She was very happy to hear we were all well, that nobody was missing any vital bits and reported that Dave had just left in *Seeker* and should be with us momentarily.

Shortly after I disconnected, I heard the muted thunder of big diesels approaching. Yelling out to the two long canoes still nuzzling the rocky wharf, I indicated for them to back out of the constricted pool because I wanted Dave to try to fit *Seeker* into the narrow channel and make it to the wharf. Loading all the loot would be much easier if *Seeker's* bow was overhanging the piles of stuff. We also had to transport the freed females, although I was strongly inclined to send them to Herba Island in the long canoes.

It was a welcome sight as *Seeker's* long, royal-blue snout nosed slowly up the channel between the islands until opposite the entrance channel to the cavern, where Dave made a cautious pivoting turn to line it up. There wasn't much in the way of clearance on either side or end as he eased the big boat in, and the whip antennas on the rear wing just scraped gently against the top of the rock arch above the entrance. It was only possible through the use of the clever remote control which let Dave sit right up in the bow and ease the big boat into the tight confines of the inner pool and wharf.

Clever boy that he was, no paint was harmed during the execution of the manoeuvre and shortly, he reported the bow was overhanging the dock area. We'd found numerous ladders, so these were pressed into service to make it easier to load the many boxes and crates up into *Seeker's* cockpit. There were plenty of willing hands to help load the cargo, especially when a report came from Jane, who was waiting outside in the dividing channel, that the UAV had spotted a boat apparently heading toward the island.

It was moving slowly however, and wouldn't arrive for a couple of hours, but we still had a lot to do. I had the crews remove the Browning machine guns from the canoes and re-mount them on *Seeker*, a task that only took ten minutes or so, while I stirred Roger and Jill into getting their patients ready to board the canoes as soon as the guns were removed. The ladies looked a lot better than when we'd released them from their cage and were now clean, external wounds treated and were dressed in a motley assortment of mostly male clothing taken from huts. T-shirts were the most popular garment, worn as a dress on their small frames.

Finally, I was able to get Roger and Jill to start leading them to the dock where we called the canoes in one by one to load them. As that process was happening, Corrine came up, a silly big grin on her face.

'OK. What are you up to Mouse; like, what've you found?' I grinned back, recognising her expression.

'You're going to love this one, boss. I've been looking for the weapons and ammo store, because there's nothing like that around here, and I knew there had to be a decent armoury. Anyway, I've been searching for the last twenty minutes or so and I found it! The pirates put all the bang-bang stuff in a small, separate cave which opens off the old south entrance that looks like its been partly collapsed for years. You'd better come and take a look.'

'You know Sandy took the UAV up to do a high-level sweep of the area and spotted a boat apparently heading this way. It's only moving slowly, but could still be the relief boat for these bozos. We have about 90-minutes before it gets here.'

'Plenty of time for what we have to do,' was her reply as she led the way across the uneven floor, littered with lumps of rock, fallen from the ceiling over the years. The thought occurred to me that the way the rock was fractured, it wouldn't take too much to shatter it. Corrine stopped beside a cave which opened off the old entrance, partly blocked by a rockfall. A battery — powered light did a fair job of illuminating the amazing collection of weapons, ammunition and explosives roughly stored inside.

Much of the older stuff was heavily rusted by constant exposure to salt air and zero maintenance, but there were some newer items in fair condition which caught my eye.

Kalashnikov AK74 carbines were the most popular, with maybe eight or ten looking like they could be used without blowing up in the shooter's face! Ammunition for them was plentiful and since it was in sealed boxes, should still be in good condition. Two things had really excited Corrine; the first being a stack of boxes, each containing an RPG-7 Russian rocket propelled grenade launcher.

We both knew it from the Middle East and had often used it as it was a simple and reliable weapon, and there were heaps of boxes containing High Explosive Anti-Tank rounds for them.

The second thing which had brought an almost orgasmic grin to her face, was a stack of boxes of Semtex high explosive which looked to be in good condition and fairly new. A quick look showed the red-coloured, one-kilogram bricks were packed into light wooden boxes with twenty bricks per box. A quick search located a box of detonators which didn't look too far out of date, a roll of fuse cord and a big roll of Det Cord.

'Now *I* have a cunning plan,' she said with a huge grin. 'We take the usable Kalashnikovs and ammunition as a present for Mikhail and we take two RPG-7s for ourselves, with fifteen HEAT rounds each.

I'm going to add to my depleted stock of plastique by taking a couple of boxes of Semtex, all the Det Cord, detonators and fuse cord. Everything else we leave here and I'll set a long fuse that will give us time to get clear before the whole place blows up!'

'Yeah. Good one Mouse. That's the best thing to do. Mikhail should appreciate the present and I don't mind having my own RPG, except that now I'll have to find someplace to hide it and the rounds.'

'Tough job, Harry, but I'm sure you and Dave will work something out.'

CHAPTER 18

PIRATE ISLAND, SUNDAY

Fifteen minutes later, we had a work party moving the stuff we wanted, to *Seeker*. The good Kalashnikovs were wrapped in oil-cloth and in crates, as was the ammunition for them, so we took all of it. The RPG-7s were in individual crates and it was tempting to take more than two, but they were reusable and would certainly last fifteen rounds each, so we reluctantly left the others. We ignored all the other weapons, being not even slightly tempted by several Russian heavy machine guns which were liberally coated with rust.

Nevertheless, we were happy with our haul and as the last load left, I went with it to make sure it all got loaded aboard, leaving Corrine to do what she loves best – blowing things up! In this case, she had about 70 kilos to play with!

We were running out of time, so I hustled the last few females aboard the long canoes and sent them on their way after telling Sandy what was happening and warning her to keep the UAV well back from the island. Corrine was well known for her excesses with explosives! I had the guards lengthen the pirate's ankle restraints enough so they could just hobble at best, then linked them together with a short rope knotted around each man's neck.

Their hands remained tied firmly behind their backs and they'd been searched for knives or other weapons, so they weren't getting free by themselves.

They were then told to start hobbling up the tunnel we'd come in by and if they took too long, they might find a few hundred thousand tons of island dropping on their worthless heads.

They were reluctant to enter the tunnel, convinced that the Devil himself was lurking in ambush, but after Jasper had torn a chunk out of the first pirates bum, they got the message that life would be much worse if they didn't brave the dark! Unfortunately, I forgot to give them any torches, so I suppose progress would be a bit slow.

It was almost comical when the first man, blood pouring from the huge wound in his backside, tripped over the headless corpse of their former leader lying where I'd dragged him. The first one going down dragged most of the others with him, a mixed chorus of abuse and terror filling the air.

'Do you think they'll get themselves sorted out enough to get clear before this all goes bang?' Corrine asked casually.

I shook my head. 'Doubtful, by the look of it, but we can't wait much longer. How much fuse have you laid out?'

'About 15 minute's worth. But I was just thinking that it'd be nice if we could bag the relief crew as well. Something like 'more bang for your buck'!"

I chuckled, 'Yeah, good one Mouse! It's worth a try, so I might just check with Sandy.'

'*Hello dear. You haven't been shot again, have you?*'

'Very droll, my lovely! Very droll! No, I haven't, but we would like an ETA on the incoming if you can, please?'

'*Anything for you, my dear. Stand by one...we think about 15 minutes tops, so unless you're on Seeker, you'd better think about moving your nice little bum. And Corrine's too, since I'm sure she's with you.*'

'Nicely said, my lovely lady. We are about to do just that. See you soonest.'

'OK, dear girl. If you're going to light that fuse, how about I get Dave to launch the RIB to pick us up? Then he can move out clear of the island on the opposite side to the incoming boat well before bang-time.'

I called Dave on the Tac-net and requested his immediate departure, but asked that he drop off the RIB first. Minutes later, Alex motored clear of *Seeker's* stern and headed down channel toward us, while Dave carefully moved the big boat, an action that looked like a big cork extracting itself from a small bottle neck, back out into the main channel, then moved to the north away from us and the incoming relief crew. I waved Alex over close to where we were standing and said to Corrine, 'Would now be a good time to light the fuse you're hanging onto?'

She grinned, 'Yeah, I suppose so. We can't try to time it any closer, can we? At least they should be even closer in by now and shouldn't suspect anything since there's no one to tell them we've been here.'

'True, O Queen of the Mighty Bang! Light thy fuse and we'll have our good man carry us away in his chariot forthwith!'

She giggled at my attempt at levity. 'You can be such an idiot sometimes Harry, but don't change!'

I patted her neat little bum as she flicked the fuse igniter, checked that it was burning, then we strolled over to where Alex had nosed the RIB up against the rock shelf, the engine still running.

'Is all in order, Major?' he addressed Corrine as was his habit.

'Yes, thank you, Alex. We can re-join *Seeker* if you please.'

'Certainly, Ma'am and Commander. I believe we are about to have company. Is that correct?'

'Yes, that's right. But even though they are still about eight to ten minutes out, we should get out of sight ASAP!'

'Yes Ma'am.' He pointed the bow north up the channel, and opened the throttle. I wasn't worried about the foaming wake we left behind; within thirty seconds it would have dissipated and the waves not long after. Seconds later, we shot out of the confines of the narrow channel and headed north, clear of the two little islands. I called Sandy and she gave us a series of steering directions to rendezvous with *Seeker*.

I thought I could just make out a darker mass against the horizon, when Corrine quietly said, 'Time!' And told Alex to chop the throttle.

We rocked to a halt, the idling motor barely a murmur in the background.

'Bloody damp fuse!' Corrine muttered. 'Nobody looks after their gear properly these days.'

I was about to comment when night turned to day as a stark white light lit the ocean in all directions like the flash gun of a giant camera. The image which burned into my retina was that of the entire top of the island lifting off like an inverted cone sitting on a colossal ball of fire. The other part of the image was that of a long, brightly painted native boat with the characteristic high raked bow, keeling right over sideways as the blast caught it just entering the channel.

The blazing light lasted long enough for me to see the boat roll completely over, before righting itself, except that it was missing everything above the waterline. Needless to say, it didn't remain on the surface long and had disappeared before the light faded.

And that was about when the thunderclap hit us with a physical force that actually flattened the low wind waves and left me with ears that produced some odd ringing sounds.

By the way they were massaging their ears and noses, I guessed that Corrine and Alex had the same problem. Although half deaf and with flashing lights rendering my eyes almost useless, I turned to Corrine in awe. 'Fuck me, Mouse. How much of that bloody stuff did you use? I thought there was only about 70 kilos left!'

She squeezed her nose and blew gently to equalise the inner ear pressure, then answered, 'Well, there was 70 kilos left in the boxes we opened, but there were a few more boxes behind those ones.'

'Oh, shit! Just how many more boxes were behind those?'

'Oh, a couple of hundred, I guess. I didn't really count them all, so there could have been more.'

I couldn't help but laugh. 'You really did it this time, Mouse. I've seen you blow up a lot of stuff, but turning a peaceful island into a volcano is a first, even for you! You just destroyed an island with five or six tonnes of Semtex. But don't worry; the plan was to collapse the cavern, but this'll do the job nicely. I mean, why bother to drop the roof on the place when you can vaporise 80% of the entire island instead!'

She beamed at me, 'You say the nicest things sometimes Big Dog! I'm so glad you see it like that.'

I glanced at Alex who looked as bemused as I was, 'Back to the boat now, please Alex.'

'Certainly, Commander.' He engaged gear and we motored quietly toward *Seeker*.

Once aboard, I asked Dave to get going toward Herba Island, little splashes marking where small, and some not so small pieces of the pirate's lair were happily returning to the sea.

HERBA ISLAND-SUNDAY

The long canoes had returned ahead of us, with Roger and Jill to look after their patients and I'd asked Gilbert and Juan to accompany them to explain the situation to Mikhail.

I had hoped to be able to pass the responsibility for the rescued females over to Mikhail and the Islanders, since I had no idea where they all came from and didn't want to have to sail all over the Indonesian Archipelago taking them all home.

The sky was becoming light in the east by the time Dave dropped the anchor and eased the big boat in to raft up against my lovely *Firebird*. As always following action, I was especially pleased to see my equally lovely Sandy, and Dave, Corrine and I agreed that we needed some R & R before we looked at the mass of stuff we'd taken from the pirates, or talked to Mikhail.

Still, there was one job that took precedence over even R & R and that was to stow the green box holding the two RPG-7 launcher tubes and the smaller boxes of thirty rounds for them out of sight. They went into my forward dressing room on the single bunk which is usually Jasper's bed when we have visitors he doesn't want or need to meet!

I'm sure we weren't the only ones taking a couple of hours break to re-connect with civilisation and reality. Re-connecting with

Sandy was especially good, to the extent that we were still in bed around 10:00 when a discrete knocking on the door admitted Jane's pretty face to inform us that Gilbert had been out to say that Mikhail would greatly appreciate a visit by Corrine, Dave, Sandy and me at midday for lunch.

Since 12:00 was still two hours away, we both agreed that another hour could be more enjoyably filled in by my doing the same to Sandy. That worked so well that it was after 11:00 when we shuffled aft to the shower.

Finally cleaned up, we found Dave and Corrine having tea and coffee in the cockpit, a bunch of long and short boxes piled up on the daybed.

'About bloody time!' Corrine said with a grin. 'Don't you two know when enough is enough?'

'Never!' was my reply as Sandy handed over a mug of tea. 'So we're all summonsed to his Royal Highness's presence for lunch huh?'

'Yep. If he wants to talk about the rescuees, we thought we'd give him his presents.'

'Good idea,' I said, 'but what do we do with the rest of the loot? I mean there's a shitload of cash, bearer bonds and there's supposed to be gold in the boxes which were packed by the pirates. I reckon they'd have all the good stuff packed away first.'

Dave, usually a voice of reason and a calming influence to Corrine's volatile nature, responded with a positive, 'We keep it all and share some with our crew! Roger and Jill wanted the green-goo business and have offered us a cut for bringing them up here, so for their share in things, how about we let them keep all the income and say our expenses are covered by our combat pay?'

Sandy and I nodded, then she said, 'It might seem greedy but as you say, I'd like to hang onto it and look after Jane and Rick, Terry and Gillian, and Bree and Alex.

The four Navy dudes have a job and a career, but some extra cash doesn't hurt, but Bree and Alex have no home and no job. We have to think carefully about what we're going to do with them. I know we've already handed over some cash from Terry and Paula's place, but we can afford to set them up with a Vanuatu numbered account so they can do whatever they want.'

Nods were all the agreement necessary, so Sandy finished with, 'How much we give them will depend on what we find in all those other crates and we should do that privately – somehow! I know that I'm rich, thanks to you guys, but I really like the idea of being seriously wealthy!'

We all joined in laughing as we loaded Mikhail's presents, then piled into the RIB ourselves and headed for shore.

CHAPTER 19

Mikhail's idea of lunch wasn't as lavish as the feast he laid on for our first night on Herba Island, but it was a working lunch after all and fruit is supposed to be healthy so it wasn't all bad.

Today, Mikhail was in all his regal splendour wearing a shimmering gold caftan trimmed in deep scarlet. Little designs were worked into the fabric and even to my non-fashion-conscious eye, the cloth was magnificent, even if the body it concealed didn't quite qualify for the front cover of Esquire magazine.

'You and your people have been busy, Commander. Gilbert speaks highly of what you have achieved and is most impressed. That nest of pirates has been in existence for several hundred years or more, but I gather you have rendered the island virtually useless?'

I nodded, 'Indeed Mikhail. We were fortunate with our planning and all the crew worked well together. However, we brought you some presents from their armoury before we blew it up.'

He raised his eyebrows, or would have if he had any that is, and watched with interest as Dave and Gilbert unwrapped the bundles of Kalashnikovs which had been left lying on the carpet flooring. His piggy little eyes fairly gleamed with pleasure as eight AK-74s in good condition were revealed.

'There's a stack of ammunition for them as well, but we'll drop that off tomorrow,' I said. 'So, with a bit of luck, you can train up some more guards in case another group of pirates decide to come calling.'

'Indeed, they will be put to good use Commander, and I must thank you very much for them. But now we must discuss these females you have brought to our Island.'

I shrugged, 'I didn't have a lot of choice. They were captives, kept in appalling conditions and apparently from various islands all over the area. They needed medical treatment, which they received from your new distributor, Dr Roger and Jill, but they need more care and I believe Dr Roger has already treated the worst cases with the green-goo. He says that they are reacting well to it.'

'But what is to become of them?' Mikhail asked. 'Surely you don't expect me to allow them to stay here do you?'

'That's up to you,' I replied, 'although it would be our preference, given they are the only witnesses to what happened on that island. I would imagine they would be good workers and should assimilate into the local community quite easily. If there are some who don't wish to stay, then let them leave on the next supply boat that calls. I have neither the room nor the time to run a shuttle service all over the Indonesian Archipelago dropping off kidnapped females. And bear in mind that most will have had husbands and family killed by the pirates.'

He looked unhappy with my argument, so I added, 'Why don't you ask the village chief and the elders what they'd like to do with them? I think you'll find a strong vote in favour of keeping them here as workers as well as keeping their mouths shut.'

He finally nodded. 'You speak good sense. I would have to consult the chief and elders anyway, so I'll do that very soon.'

'May I ask how the latest batch of green-goo is proceeding?'

He smiled, 'Splendidly! In fact, my Head Brew Master tells me brewing is complete and the mix is cooling today and overnight, so that tomorrow the crew will commence filling the small glass jars. He expects to create in the vicinity of 5250 jars of the 'green-goo' as you call it and the filling and packing into cartons should be finished by the day after tomorrow which should be Tuesday.'

I beamed, 'Excellent! As lovely as this island is, we do need to get moving in case more pirates decide to enact some payback for our efforts of earlier today.'

He looked suitably grim. 'Yes. That is a serious consideration.

Already word has spread that there has been a catastrophic eruption of a long dormant volcano which has destroyed the best set-up pirate base in these waters. So far, involvement by an outside party has not been suspected. Sudden volcanic activity isn't entirely unknown in this area and as there were no survivors to tell the true story apart from the women, as you mentioned, it is hoped none of them will talk.'

'Good. Are there any other issues we need to work out?'

'I'll finalise the details of the distributorship with Dr Roger tomorrow and there is just Gilbert's transportation back to Australia which I hope is still going to happen.'

'Yep. That's no problem. I'm going to lose four crew in a few day's time, so his services will be welcome.'

Mikhail beamed, 'Thank you! I'm very grateful. He's been like a son to me, but he needs to get a taste of civilisation every so often.'

I wondered about that and asked, 'But what about Singapore or Kuala Lumpur? They are much closer than Australia.'

He smiled, 'Ah yes. But Gilbert likes to mingle with persons of European stock rather than Asians. Just for the stimulation of being with different people, I mean.'

I got a strong feeling there was a lot more to this than Mikhail was letting on but kept my mouth shut, since Gilbert would be a great asset on the trip back to the Gold Coast.

'In that case, we will take our leave now, thank you Mikhail, and will call in tomorrow. We might just visit Dr Roger and his patients briefly before we return to our boats.'

He inclined his head and replied, 'You're welcome, dear boy. Gilbert will show you the treatment area and anything else you might need. Oh, and thank you again for my new carbines. They are lovely.'

I'd not heard an AK-74 being described as 'lovely' before, but few things on this island could be described as normal! With Gilbert's guidance, we found the hospital was one of the ubiquitous long huts, open at the sides, but with heavy mosquito netting draped over all the openings. There were two rows of makeshift beds and we saw Roger's patients were doing quite well. In fact, under the influence of the green-goo, several ladies and girls were looking happy and relaxed.

'This is a really good test run for the stuff, with multiple patients mostly suffering light injuries. It really is marvellous!' Roger enthused, as Jill bustled about behind him checking their flock.

'I must grab a carton for *Firebird*,' I said. 'I'd like to try it out myself as well as have some on hand for genuine medicinal use.'

While Jill fetched a carton of thirty jars from their make-shift storeroom, Roger grinned, 'I was told a few minutes ago this new batch is more potent, rather than less, so I'll have to experiment with the percentage of an inert oil, maybe jojoba, to dilute the effect a little. Unless you actually want to see people fornicating in the streets?'

I grinned back, 'Might be fun to see the Gold Coast Council's reaction, but otherwise, no thanks. Chaos is never a good thing, even that!'

CHAPTER 20

HERBA ISLAND, SUNDAY PM

Sandy hung onto the carton of green-goo as we boarded the RIB and returned to our boats.

'That all went well,' Corrine said, 'especially the plans for the women. I'm glad they won't just be sent away without a home to go to.'

'Yeah. I was a bit concerned too, but that's a good outcome.'

Sandy chuckled, 'I think it was the gift of the AK-74s that swung the deal. He nearly had a wet dream when he saw them!'

'True,' I said, 'but we'd better ferry all the AK rounds ashore before we forget!'

'Good thinking,' Dave added, 'we'll drop the girls off and load up immediately.'

By the time we'd done that job and Mikhail was better off by ten thousand rounds, dusk had set in and the bar was opened for a mild celebration. Roger and Jill arrived back in time to join in and reported all their patients were doing extremely well, having been treated with both the green-goo and the amazing healing, rejuvenating water that flowed so carelessly into the sea.

'How did you go with Mikhail about the business arrangements?' I asked Roger.

'Really good, no trouble at all! We transferred AU$500K from the account you kindly set up for us, into Mikhail's bank to act as a semi-permanent security deposit. We get it back if we dissolve the business deal, but when things are going well, we deposit $200 per jar sold. If we dilute the stuff, we sell more.

I've got the list of the existing Asian customers and there are a few hundred of them, so that'll keep us busy just with them. There's more detail about the shipping from here, but there's no problem with that.'

'How are you going to set up for Australian sales on both the medical and the recreation side?' I asked, curious.

He smiled and shrugged, 'We're not sure yet. In fact, we don't even have a place to call home, so we thought we might travel back with you to the Gold Coast if you don't mind and set up there.'

'Aren't you going to need an office, simple examination/treatment rooms, secure packing and dispatch space and some basic lab facilities?' Corrine asked.

He looked at Jill and nodded ruefully, 'Yeah, that's right. But we have some cash left over from your generosity, so we should be able to rent a bit of space in a medical complex. I've learned the Gold Coast has become a bit of a medical mecca! If we can get set up fairly quickly, we hope to be able to start paying you guys your share.'

Corrine glanced over at Sandy and me and Sandy gave a slight nod, so she said, 'What if we consider that debt wiped out by the way you've helped us with our job. And then, how about we remain as business associates and invest in you two and your plans for the green-goo?'

They glanced at each other again, before Roger asked cautiously, 'That sounds interesting. But invest how and under what deal?

Corrine stayed with the plan. 'We would just be your backers, silent partners if you like, and would expect a share of profits at some point. We have done rather well out of the last few operations, so this could be a good investment for us. It would be up to you to decide what facilities you want and how to set them up. You can rent if you really want to, but we can afford to fund the set-up of your own specialist Medical Centre by way of either a purchase of property or a new build if that's the best way to go. We'll have a chat with Harry's accountant, Mike Adams about that side of it, but suffice to say, funding won't be a problem for whatever you want to do.

You can stay on board while you work out what you want and

decide where you want to live. I know Sandy and Harry will agree that the Gold Coast, with all its flaws, would be an excellent place for a clever Doctor and Nurse to set up a specialised practice with an amazing product.'

'Here, here!' Sandy added. 'We support all that! Maybe you could set up as the 'Chronic Pain Relief Clinic', or something like that. And for tenants in your own medical centre, only have practitioners who have natural healing to offer. Establish the Asian connection by having an Acupuncture Clinic and a Chinese Remedial Massage Clinic.'

Roger and Jill looked stunned and the rest of the crew clapped approval. By mutual agreement, we decided not to say anything more for now.

'That sounds terribly exciting,' Jane said, 'and if I didn't have a career in the Navy, I'd like to be involved in something like that!'

The rest of the Navy crew joined in agreeing and that in turn, called for another round of drinks.

I asked Roger, 'When is the last of the new batch expected to be bottled?'

He looked relieved to be back on a safe subject. 'By tomorrow midday, so from our point of view, we can leave as soon as you're ready. The female rescuees are recovering just fine now and the village medicine man will keep an eye on them. The ones in better condition are looking after the ones who are still bed-ridden. Anyway, the upshot is, we don't have to be here any longer.'

'OK, thanks. I also don't see any need to stay longer; does anybody else?'

The chorus of negatives decided the issue and we planned to leave as soon as we had loaded the final portion of the batch of green-goo tomorrow.

I decided to keep Gilbert on *Firebird*, since the port aft cabin was free, now that Jane and Rick were bunking together in the forward queen.

The impromptu meeting broke up with the others dispersing to their cabins, but four of us, as the executive, adjourned to *Seeker's* upper sundeck where we had a small amount of privacy.

'We wanted to talk to you two,' Dave said seriously, 'since we've had a chance to have a quick check of the contents of those crates and boxes.'

I looked around, 'I didn't see them when I came aboard. Where are they?'

'We moved them into our cabin, since there is plenty of room and the weight is just aft of the balance point.'

I smiled, 'Good thinking, but what did you find?'

Corrine unfolded a piece of paper. 'Two boxes held records and accounts of their raids over the years. Historically, someone could find them fascinating, but there's bugger-all in it for us. I recommend pitching them overboard.'

'Most of the other crates had jewellery, golden candle sticks and plates; stuff which could have come from churches, but nothing terribly high in value although it would probably add up to a decent amount.

However, it was the last three crates which were small, but very heavy and contained gold ingots! Lots of them! Here are samples of the two types.'

Dave passed around a 112 x 52 x 9mm flat gold bar that weighed exactly one kilogram and was the standard bar for small trades within the industry. The second bar he passed around was considerably heavier, weighing in at 12.4 kg and measuring 255 x 85 x 35 mm. It was what is known as the standard-size bar and was normally traded between countries and held as gold reserves.

'The small one kilo bar is valued at $58,100 Aussie, while the big fella is priced at $720,440 Aussie, all at current rates. There is one box of 6 standard ingots weighing a hefty 77kg, but is worth $4.322 mil Aussie.

Then there are two boxes of the little one kilo jobbies with 70 bars in each. They work out at $4.067 mil each box for a total of $8.134 mil. The overall total in gold bars is $12.456 mil Aussie!

If we add in the cash and the Bearer Bonds, we took a total of $20-odd million, or something close to it in this last raid'.

'Holy crap!' said Sandy.

'Fuck!' was Corrine's more earthy comment, as I had a sudden flash of memory.

'Ah, fuckit!' I cursed. 'Sorry guys. I clean forgot in all the excitement.'

'What the hell are you mumbling about, Harry?' Corrine asked, looking at me oddly.

'This!' I exclaimed, digging through the voluminous pockets of my cargo pants, finally pulling out the black velvet bag that clicked as I shook it.

'It was pushed up the back of the top shelf in the big safe, behind the Bearer Bonds. I shoved it in my pocket and promptly forgot about it!'

Sandy reached over and gently took it from me. 'You're waffling, my darling man. Please be quiet for a moment.'

I did and watched as she untied the drawstring and shook the contents out onto the soft, padded top of the table. Several cut stones fell out, gleaming a dull sort of red in the weak light, followed by a much larger stone that looked nearly black in the low light, then came two more of the reddish stones. The smaller ones were round cut, but the bigger one was a beautiful teardrop shape, a good 75mm long and 35 mm wide.

The roundish smaller ones looked to be about 30mm or so across

'Crap, Harry! You've done it again,' Sandy breathed, 'we've got to see these in good light.'

'Ok, but let's wait until tomorrow in the daylight to inspect them properly.'

The other three reluctantly agreed, but then Sandy spoke up, 'Since we've come into Indonesian waters, we've picked up a great deal of money and there's more to come in the shape of those six emeralds and now the seven new stones which may be good or may be worthless, but either way, we four, who weren't broke to start with, have just gained a minimum of $20 mil. That's another $5 mil each and if the old man in the markets is to be believed, those emeralds with their bloody story are going to fetch another one or two!'

We were all waiting to hear where she was going with all this, but I thought that I knew.

'I suggest those crates of gold and silver ornaments be given to the crew to share equally! How they can be valued and sold, I don't know, but it's probably best if it was done back in Australia, if you think we can get them out of Indonesia without trouble. Even divided eight ways, there still should be enough to boost their earnings, and if we think it isn't enough, then we could tip in a bit more each without feeling too much pain.'

She sat back, but there wasn't any discussion as we all agreed to the proposal without reservation.

'Where are the crates and how many?' I asked.

Dave chuckled, 'We've put them in our master cabin with the gold bars since we have the most room. Alex and Bree have decided to share a bed, so we moved them out of the two bow cabins into one of the VIP twin cabins and Terry and Gillian volunteered to move into the two bow cabins, since they'll be leaving in two or three days anyway. There are four medium-sized crates, but they'll need to be properly checked and inventoried.'

Sandy spoke again. 'I just had a thought in reference to my earlier comment about getting this stuff out through Customs. Perhaps much of it could simply be sat around on both boats in plain sight? Particularly on *Seeker!* I mean, everything inside is very up-market, so I imagine to a Customs officer, a couple of sets of golden candelabra and a set of gold plates on the dining room table would be expected, as would other silver and gold fittings and ornaments. I can't imagine they'll bother too much about personal jewellery if all the females have some in their lockers or even were wearing some smaller pieces. There are also the concealed lockers where the guns are hidden so a lot of the smaller stuff can go in there. That way, we could spread the loot over the two boats in a way the makes it seem as though we just like lavish living. After all, that is our image!'

I nodded. 'Not bad, dear lady. That would work, so let's tell the troops tonight and they can play at hide-a-treasure during the trip back to Lombok and Marina Del Ray. It'll be much easier to clear Customs there as they know us pretty well by now. We can fly the Navy out to Darwin from there, and we might be collecting a couple of passengers at the same time, but I'll let you know tomorrow if that's on or not.'

Dave chuckled and rubbed his hands together, 'Oh my goodness. Mysterious passengers now, Harry? Love it!'

I gave him a rueful grin, 'You may live to regret the thought, but I have to make a phone call or two.'

We broke up the meeting and I went to make the calls before we all got together for dinner and the fun of telling the crew about their new windfall.

'Harry! Wonderful to hear from you. Is everything alright?'

'Hi Hilary and good to talk to you too. Yes, everything is alright now, but we've had a few adventures along the way. This was supposed to be a peaceful trip, but several pirate groups had other ideas! Anyway, I'll be pleased to bring you and the Admiral up to speed on that at a later time. It should be worth a good dinner and a few reds!'

'We'll hold you to that, Harry and gladly supply the dinner and the reds. So, what can I do for you?'

'We're about to leave the eastern part of the Archipelago for Lombok and the Marina Del Ray and should be there Wednesday, if 'Mr Murphy' stays asleep! So by Thursday, your four sailors will be released from temporary detached duty. Can you arrange to fly them out of Bandar Udara International Airport on Lombok on Thursday, whenever it's convenient? Bear in mind they'll be carrying some odd pieces of hardware in their checked luggage. I don't know if their Diplomatic passports will get them through Security without problems, but I figured you'd know how to handle that one. Naturally, I'll keep the unused ammunition with me for now.'

She gave a hearty chuckle. 'Rest assured I do know how to handle
that. It won't be a problem. Just call me on Wednesday evening when
you're at the Marina and I'll pass on their travel arrangements.'

'That's great, Hilary and thanks very much. I'll call you then.
Bye for now.'

With one box ticked, I took a deep breath and called the other
number I'd been given.

'Harry! Wonderful to hear from you! How is everything?'

With a strong feeling of Deja Vu, I plunged headfirst into the
deep end.

'Pretty good thanks Charlie, although we've had an eventful
week or so. It would seem the pirates in this area don't like visitors
very much. Still, we're all here and they aren't, so from our point of
view, that's what matters

'My goodness. You do live an exciting life! Is everyone alright?'

'Yeah, all good thanks Charlie. But the reason for my call was
to...

'You're going to invite the Boss to come sailing with you! You lovely
man. If Sandy wasn't there, I'd kiss you. I might do that anyway – I'm
sure she won't mind. You must have known that Parliament is in recess
for several weeks, so what's the plan? When can we come? I've got a heap
of stuff to arrange so you've got to give me at least a few days!'

Finally, she did run out of breath and I was able to get a word
in. 'Jesus, Charlie. Belt up a moment will you and I'll answer your
questions!'

'Sorry, Harry. I get a bit excited about really fun things sometimes,
and this qualifies, but I'll be good. Please go ahead.'

'Thanks. Now the deal is, we're heading back to Marina Del Ray
at Lombok where you met us last time and we'll be there Wednesday sometime. Our four Navy crew will be flying out sometime on
Thursday. Admiral Stallman's secretary is trying to get them out
under Diplomatic passports as they'll be carrying some Navy equipment which the Airport Security wouldn't really approve of, so...'

'Yeah, I know Hilary. She's good value. Give me her number and *we'll work out a deal to fix that little problem. I presume they need to go back to Darwin?'*

'Bloody hell, Charlie. You're doing it again! But here's Hilary's direct number... now, as I was saying, anytime from Thursday on will be fine for you and the Boss to come aboard. Our plan would be to clear out of Lombok and head east along the island chain almost to Papua-New Guinea, head down to Australian waters at Cape York, then down the coast. Our home is the Gold Coast, but you and the Boss can bail out at any point that suits.'

'Got all that, Harry. I think I can make that fit in really well. Basic casual clothes I presume?'

'Yep. No cocktail frocks and dinner jackets or ties are required this trip. Are there any particular dietary requirements we need to be aware of?'

She laughed, 'Oh no. He's a man of simple tastes and high office hasn't spoiled him, thank goodness. He eats just about anything, but he does like seafood, and doesn't mind a beer or two and the occasional rum.'

'Geeze, Charlie. He's going to fit right in with this bunch then; that's our main diet!'

'Glad to hear that. Leave the rest to me, but remember he really likes sailing and is looking forward to your catamaran and your cat too. I haven't told him about Jasper, I want to see his face when they meet!'

'Charlie, you can be a little bit evil sometimes. Take pity on the poor man! Anyway, I've got to keep moving, we've got some treasure to divide up.'

'Treasure? What sort of treasure?'

I chuckled, enjoying the tease. 'Why, pirate treasure of course. Is there any other sort? Anyway, I'll tell you all about it when I see you on Thursday. Oh, I meant to ask. Are you bringing any security dudes, because if you are, there's just one cabin left on *Seeker*, but none on *Firebird?'*

'No extra security. You, Sandy, Alex and Corrine are the professionals and that's enough to satisfy requirements. I'll deal with the ACP.

Anyway, that'll do for now. I'll call if something else comes up and vice-versa. Bye Harry.'

I made the disconnect and sat back with a sigh, wondering if we'd just stepped out of the frying pan onto the very hot plate.

CHAPTER 21

HERBA ISLAND, SUNDAY PM

At least dinner was a huge success since Bree and Gillian had worked their neat little bums off in the galley to make a beautiful roast lamb dinner with all the trimmings like roast 'taties, pumpkin, carrot, tinned green peas and real lumpy gravy. What a feast! Then for dessert, I made the announcement to the crew.

'On behalf of my fellow conspirators, Sandy, Corrine and Dave, I'd like to thank you all for being such great crew and doing such a terrific job of knocking off all those bad guys. We couldn't have done it without you!

Therefore, to show our appreciation in a more tangible form, we have decided that the four crates of assorted gold and silver items and jewellery, currently clogging up Dave and Corrine's stateroom, shall be divided equally among you. You've all had a bit of a financial kick-start courtesy of the late and very much un-lamented Terry and Paula, but wait, there's more!

This will, we hope, better compensate you all for the risks you've taken to make sure we all came through unscathed from a series of attacks. Dave and Corrine have been sorting through the crates and the collection is surprising, to say the least, so we're hoping you, too, will be pleasantly surprised by what's there. Mouse?'

Corrine stood and consulted a sheet of paper.

'So far we have a complete dining setting for ten with dinner plates, bread & butter plates and a full set of cutlery, knives, forks and spoons all in what feels like 24K gold. That means they're all bloody heavy at about 35 kilos! We're guessing the gold alone is worth about $1.45 mil, but at auction it might realise quite a lot more as a proper antique dinner set.'

'Then there is a remarkable collection of jewellery pieces, most with mounted gemstones, but there are a lot of solid gold chain necklaces which are worth a lot just as gold, but generally worth more as worked jewellery.

We have no idea what the jewellery might be worth and some of the stones might be non-precious, but since nearly all the pieces look to be old, it's likely that the coloured gemstones are precious stones too. I'd have to say though, based on what we've seen in the past, this collection could be worth several million if presented at the right auction.

Therefore, we'd like to think the eight of you could be dividing up 3 to 4 million dollars if the collection is handled properly.'

There was a generally stunned silence following that revelation, until Alex spoke up. 'It would appear, Major, that an accurate assessment of the items is impossible at this time. I am guessing you have a person you would trust to make a realistic valuation of all these items?'

Corrine nodded, 'Yes, we do. He has handled some items for us in the past, and has been utterly reliable.'

'In that case, I vote we defer the division of this magnificent gift you have given us, until such time as your assessor has had a chance to examine all the items. I presume that he is back in Australia?'

She inclined her head. 'Yes indeed, Alex. He's on the Gold Coast in fact, so it will be several weeks before we can get the stuff to him. Does everyone else agree with Alex's proposal?'

Heads swivelled back and forth, then eight hands were raised.

'OK. You all agree we will take the items to our dealer and get his best valuation possible or the best options to get the most for it all, perhaps at auction. Is that a fair summary of what you'd like? I might add he charges a 1% fee for handling the deal.'

'That seems low,' Gillian said, 'almost too low. What's the catch?'

Dave spoke with a very dry tone, '1% of 6 to 8 million still comes to $80K and that's a tidy fee for a few phone calls.'

'Oh,' she said, then thought a few moments before asking, 'would it be all right if we could look at the stuff? I mean, just to see what we have?'

Corrine laughed. 'Of course you can. In fact, if you give us a couple of minutes, we'll spread the stuff out on the bed so you can see it properly.'

Gillian gave a beautiful smile. 'Thanks Corrine. That'd be great.'

Fifteen minutes later, Dave popped up from the companionway leading down to the cabin area and called, 'Come on down, lucky people, and see what you've scored!'

They all traipsed down below, Sandy and me following. The master suite was easily able to hold the whole crew, but for some reason, there was a log-jam at the doorway.

'Move along,' called Sandy, 'plenty of room down the front.'

When I got inside, I saw why there was a hold-up. Dave and Corrine must have been laying stuff out before dinner, because the bedside tables were groaning under the weight of the gleaming golden dinner service, neatly stacked in order, while the bed was covered in a bewildering and glittering array of jewellery, ranging from dozens of simple gold rings through ornate bracelets of intricately woven gold filigree or solid gold and silver, then came the necklaces.

They were of every size and design possible and ranged from simply magnificent through to utterly stunning!

Like the delicate gold chain with a 15-carat tear-drop emerald set in a spray of small rubies and diamonds that created a red, white and green pattern with the big emerald as the focus. There was even a delicate gold tiara set with diamonds and rubies that Gillian asked if she could model, so I took pleasure in carefully placing it on her head and letting her see it in the dressing room mirror. She almost broke down into tears to see how it looked.

'It seems such a shame it all has to be sold. I didn't realise just how beautiful some of these pieces would be. They're stunning!'

'Well, if you all agree, there's no reason why you all can't take any piece you fancy right now to keep.'

Her eyes lit up. 'Could we?'

'Dear girl, it belongs to all of you now. You can do what you like so long as you all agree. But bear in mind that some pieces may be a lot more valuable than others.'

'Oh. I hadn't thought of that.'

'So, do you want to ask everyone if they want to take one piece each?'

They did and the motion was soundly defeated on the grounds there could be a big imbalance in value between different items and could cause dissention later on. Gillian reluctantly agreed, but had a lovely time touching pieces which had once been worn by Queens and Princesses.

Finally, Corrine was able to chase the last of them out so they could pack everything up and get to the bed. There was a very upbeat mood amongst the crew that evening, as I'm sure they all remembered Dave's casual comment of '6 to 8 mil' value. It isn't rocket science to work out the result of dividing eight million by eight persons!

CHAPTER 22

Next day, before we did anything else, Sandy and I joined Dave and Corrine on *Seeker's* upper sun deck to look at the new find of precious jewels. With little ceremony, Sandy tipped the stones out onto an old towel.

Six large, round-cut, red stones, about 30mm across bounced onto the cloth, cheerfully clinking and rattling together. They were a stunning, deep, rich-red in colour that positively glowed in the bright sunlight which also showed their perfect clarity. It was, however, the single large, cut stone that caught and held everyone's attention.

In the dim light last night, it had looked a dull, lifeless dark colour, almost black, but in the daylight it was an amazing shade of deep, royal blue and we all knew where we had seen that exact shade before. It was a round cut, measured about 30mm by 20mm, and it was Corrine who whispered a little breathlessly, 'Even though I wouldn't know a carat if it bit me on the bum, I'd bet it weighs exactly 42 carats!'

'No bet,' Sandy replied softly. 'This is the parent stone to the '*Firebird Blues*' Mr Jacobs told us about. Remember, he joked when he asked Harry if he happened to have in in his back pocket? Well, here it is and we've got it!'

Idly, Corrine poked a finger into the tumbled pile of vivid deep red stones. 'These aren't more of those red diamonds, are they Harry?'

I shook my head, still staring at the amazing collection of beautiful, precious stones. 'No, Mouse. I don't think so. We are close to several major ruby producing areas, so I'm inclined to think they are rubies, and particularly fine ones at that. With that colour and clarity, they should be valuable. When we get them to him, Mr Jacobs is going to be ecstatic!'

Sandy woke from her reverie to add, 'I can't wait to show him the *Columbine* emeralds with their dreadful story, and now we have six stunning rubies and this huge blue diamond that's Mother to the *Firebird Blues*. I feel like getting on the first plane we can and taking them all to him!'

I chuckled, 'Yeah. I feel the same. These are stunning, and to turn up the Mother Blue is amazing, but when you think about it, maybe not such a coincidence. After all, the pirate's lair had been there a very long time, and with its location in the centre of the main shipping lanes, it's a wonder there weren't more rare stones.'

Corrine looked up from poking at the big blue. 'Maybe there were, but remember that the supply boat drops in every few months, so it would take away excess stock.'

I mentally kicked myself, 'I'm a dick and you're right again. Of course they'd take good stuff away to convert to funds for the operation.'

With reluctance, we stowed the amazing stones back in their leather wrapper and hid them in one of *Firebird's* concealed lockers, before Sandy and I went ashore with Roger and Jill. They wanted to check on the patients first, pick up the rest of the latest batch of green-goo, and then say farewell to Mikhail. The refugees were recovering well, aided no doubt by the wonderful water and the green miracle that was applied judiciously by the medicine man. They were a happy and grateful bunch and we felt really good about having saved them.

Mikhail was cordial and happy to be finally doing the deal for distribution of the green-goo, as well as having his man Gilbert, go along to check all was above board. The cartons of green-goo were packed into larger cardboard boxes which we sent out to *Seeker* separately. Finally, we rounded up Gilbert, who had packed modestly and headed back out to the boats.

I was keen to get underway as quickly as we could and let Sandy get Gilbert settled in the stern cabin and explain the workings of the boat to him. He carried a small notebook with him to write messages which proved very useful, although I still intended to learn to sign in ASL.

It was just before midday when we left, with several of the long canoes escorting us south for several miles until they turned back with cheerful waves and calls. Dave and I had looked over the planned course earlier and decided to bend the legs to remain as clear of land as possible to avoid any further encounters with pirates.

The crews settled in quickly and barring incidents, we expected to arrive at Marina Del Ray on Wednesday afternoon. Gilbert was a surprise asset and as he had indicated, was handy around boats. We walked around the decks of *Firebird* a couple of times where I went through the arrangement for sail handling and he picked it all up very quickly. I stood two watches with him and after that, he didn't need to be told anything twice.

Since the breezes were generally light, we spent most of our time motor-sailing, so with Jane and Rick still aboard, watches were easier and we all had more downtime.

Sandy and I even had time to fool around sampling the 'green goo', checking out its various effects. Sandy had never been shy when it came to sex, but under the influence of the green goo, she was amazing! When I applied a small amount to where Corrine had suggested were appropriate places, I must confess I felt a lot more...potent than I ever had before, to the extent that Sandy finally cried 'Enough'!

Thereafter, when we tried it again, we used a lot less of it for a much more controlled result, but for now, we both noticed the lingering effects of the first concentrated application.

SANDY ON WATCH

On Tuesday morning, not long after our trial run with green-goo, Jane, who got on really well with Sandy, found her on watch in the cockpit and came up to her giggling her head off.

'What's going on?' Sandy asked with a smile, but had to wait for Jane to settle down to get an answer.

'I was just down checking stocks in the lower pantry when I bumped into Gilbert as he was coming out of the shower,' she said, 'and you *know* he's got an amazing body. I mean, I thought Rick was well-built, but Gilbert is something else again! Anyway, he just had a towel on and because the passageway is a bit cramped there, he had to squeeze past me to get through. I happened to be facing him and I felt the most incredible erection against me! I mean the thing was enormous and I swear I could feel it still growing as he wriggled past! He wasn't trying to be a smart-arse and actually blushed.

He made a soft sound that might have been a 'sorry' but I was too amazed to really notice.

When he was past, I managed to get a look at its outline through the towel before he turned away and honestly Sandy, that thing is seriously monstrous; it's very long and thick! Taking it in would be a real challenge but very interesting!'

Sandy was both stimulated and fascinated by the younger girl's story and asked frankly and with great interest, 'So are you saying you're thinking of trying him on?'

It was Jane's turn to blush, and she gave a half-hearted giggle. 'Oh, I don't know. I mean Rick and I have been having a bit of a fool around, but it's just that and nothing serious and it'll all stop when we re-join the boat. But last night, we tried some of that green-goo Corrine gave us and I can't believe how I still feel the effects!'

It was Sandy's turn to blush as she admitted to doing the same thing with similar effects.

Jane laughed, 'We really are a good pair, but to answer your question, the way I feel at the moment, I probably could go and knock on his door. Rick's asleep, but I'm too wired to settle!'

Sandy shrugged. 'If that's the way you feel, go for it! It sounds like Rick isn't going to be too concerned and if you don't do it, you'll always wonder what it would have been like! That's my take on it, anyway.'

Jane eyed her shrewdly. 'Do I assume that you'd maybe like to try him yourself?'

Sandy blushed again and gave an embarrassed half laugh. 'Well, if he's anything like what you say, it could be an interesting experience, but maybe only at the right time!'

Jane giggled. 'You might have fun talking Harry around to let you do that.'

Sandy just flashed her version of the 'Mona Lisa' smile, as Jane turned away to head below, indecision obviously competing with raw lust for control of her emotions.

Sandy checked the sea and sky, but both were empty and the radar, cranked out to max range, showed nothing. She knew Harry was asleep and apparently Rick was too, so there was only the gentle purr of the starboard engine at 50% power to intrude on the soft sound of water sliding past the sleek hulls.

The aft cabin was located just outboard of the cockpit, and had a couple of hatches open for ventilation, so Sandy grinned to herself when she heard a knock on Gilbert's door and a few portions of a one-way conversation. She was prepared to dump a bucket of seawater down the top hatch if it sounded like things weren't going well, but after a remarkably short interval of silence, the expected sounds of activity in the stern cabin seemed relatively normal, under the circumstances.

Normally she wouldn't deliberately listen to another person's pleasure, although on any small boat with everyone living in such close proximity, it's next to impossible to be totally discrete.

Still, with the aftermath of green-goo still running rampant through her blood stream, Sandy found that Jane's occasional descriptions were perhaps a little bit graphic for comfort as they generated too many vivid mental images!

Fortunately, it wasn't a prolonged session, but even so, Sandy found it more comfortable to sit up in one of the bows for a while until the activity had peaked. She waited until all had been quiet for a while before venturing aft again, thankful there wasn't a repeat.

It was quite a while before Jane re-appeared, obviously washed and cleaned up, an expression that was a mix of pleasure and something else on her face.

Sandy pulled her over to the other side of the cockpit and asked, 'Are you alright?'

Jane smiled. 'Oh, my goodness, yes! I'm fine. Maybe a bit sore, but no problem!'

'Oh. Well that's good then. I ah... take it things went well?'

'Quite stunning, but I won't go into details except to say I didn't know men like Gilbert existed. He told me, by writing in his pad, how he came to be at that island. He's from an island east of New-Guinea where there are a number of babies born each year who grow to be as... well, overly well-endowed as he is, so normally, when they grow up enough, the tribal elders kick them out. No other tribe wants them, so most perish or turn rogue, but Gilbert, although of mixed parentage, got lucky and was adopted by Mikhail. He's had to behave himself around the Herba Island women who are traditionally ah.... small, or else the elders would kick him out from there as well. Despite that, he has had lots of female admirers on the Island, although they're afraid to upset the elders by having it off with him, so frustration levels are high most of the time. That's why he has to visit Western civilisation every so often.'

'Wow! That's quite a story all right. Amazing, but what must that whole rejection thing and the current situation do to his psychological makeup?'

Jane shrugged. 'He seems reasonably well balanced to me. I mean, he didn't start frothing at the mouth when I took my clothes off! In fact, he was very gentle and considerate.'

'Are you going to tell Rick or pretend it didn't happen?' Sandy asked out of curiosity. 'It doesn't matter to me either way and of course, I won't say anything to him.'

Jane looked thoughtful, 'I'm not sure. We fly out tomorrow

afternoon, so part of me wants to spend that time with Gilbert. But then I have to work with Rick, although there's always the rank separator present.'

'Probably best to tell him.' Sandy suggested gently.

'Yeah. You're right.'

I woke naturally, checked course and wind on the repeater instruments on the bulkhead above the bed then padded aft to freshen up. Washed and dressed in my favourite old boat shorts, I went up top to find Sandy and Jane in deep conversation which they broke off as I appeared. I thought I heard Jane say that Sandy was right.

'Geeze Jane, you shouldn't tell Sandy she's right. It goes straight to her ego!'

That nearly earned me a backhander, but I'd become good at dodging when I got cheeky.

'Everything going well, First Mate?'

She snapped a two-fingered salute that wasn't in official use by any known Service. 'Aye aye Skipper! Everything in the green and no bad guys in sight.'

'Good oh then. Carry on.' Her foot, irreverently planted on my bum, hastened my exit from the cockpit to do a round of checking things on deck for wear and chafe, something that's a constant battle on a sailing boat, with so many ropes running in all directions looking for something to rub against. It seemed our two Navy crew were in a slightly subdued mood that evening, but I put it down to the fact that tomorrow their luxury holiday afloat with the rich and infamous, which had been mostly spent battling pirates and getting shot at, would be over.

I logged a mental note to check with Sandy, the crew counsellor, to see if there was anything I should know about, but then also reminded myself it was more urgent to call Charlie after dinner and give her a positive ETA for our arrival at the Marina Del Ray.

'*Good evening Harry. All is well, I trust?*'

'Hi Charlie and yes, all is well. I just wanted to give you an updated ETA now we're close enough. We should be at the Marina Del Ray at 12:00 tomorrow. Have you had any luck in making arrangements to export our four Navy crew and their cargo?'

'*C'mon Harry. This isn't Dodgy Bob's Travel Agency you're dealing with here. This is me, the professional! If I didn't fancy you so much, you lovely man, I'd get offended! Of course, I've got it organised, dear.*

They simply fly out in the aircraft we fly in on! Everything's done with all top-level VIP diplomatic clearances so there's no inspections and they'll be flown straight to Darwin to hook up with their boat.'

'Bloody marvellous, Charlie. I will certainly have to kiss you now. So what time will you and the Boss be landing?'

'*We've had to push the schedule back four days, I afraid Harry. The Boss has some urgent business to take care of first with the British PM. However, I can confirm that fifteen hundred hours on Sunday is the scheduled ETA and it's my job to make sure that they all stick to that!*'

'OK Charlie. Shame about the delay, but that can't be helped. From a security point of view, since I seem to be the new de-facto Chief of Security to the PM for this run, Sandy and I will meet you in the general Aviation Terminal and we will be armed.

Please tell the Boss to wear a baseball cap and sunglasses like every other mug tourist and he's not to do any gladhanding or recognising anybody! We'll be with you from there, keeping everything low-key.'

'*Yeah, Harry. We have done it a couple of times, but not like this.*'

'It's simple! Tell him to keep his head down, and not to look any official in the eye. Is his passport in his name?'

'*Pretty close; it's a normal passport in the name of Andy Friar, not his usual diplomatic one.*'

'OK. If you're on a civilian jet, you'll clear Customs in the VIP lounge of the General Aviation Terminal so that'll be painless. We'll be there, but keep reminding him to only speak when he's spoken to. If some ratbag tourist reckons he recognises the Boss, tell him to say that he's a distant cousin.'

'*OK Harry. We'll do as you say and fingers crossed.*'

'Good oh, Charlie. See you Sunday at 15:00 at the GA Terminal. Stay safe.'

   'Thanks Harry. Bye now.'

PART 3: THE PM

CHAPTER 23

MARINA DEL RAY, LOMBOK, WEDNESDAY

After breakfast, Sandy raised the excellent point that we were to have three guests, but only two cabins.

I gave her a cheeky grin, 'Are you sure that Charlie isn't going to bunk in with the PM?'

'Behave, dearest. That's not happening. I'm putting the PM in the forward queen cabin, of course and Charlie will have the aft double, but Gilbert will have to go across to *Seeker.*'

I shrugged. 'Maybe Charlie will take a strong and immediate fancy to Gilbert and want to share with him?'

For some reason, Sandy erupted into a fit of the giggles which took some time to subside. I was tempted to push for an explanation, but got the feeling that she'd tell me in due course – when it suited her!

'Well,' she demanded, 'do I tell Gilbert he has to go to *Seeker?*'

I shook my head, 'No. I want to keep Gilbert close. Apart from being a useful boat hand, there's something about him we haven't been told yet and I need to find out what it is.

For now, let's put him in our dressing room. It has a door and a deck hatch and the single bunk is more than big enough. We'll have to have quiet nookie for a while, though.'

For some reason, that set Sandy off again with the giggles bit, so I left her to compose herself and sort out the housekeeping with Gilbert. Meanwhile, I did the important Skippering stuff which consisted of making sure the water was still sliding past in the right direction and checking the chart plotter for the progress of the little red dot up the yellow course line toward our destination. Its predictions were correct as usual as we were approaching the marina harbour by 11:30 that morning. As before, Jasper's presence aboard meant that *Firebird* had to lie to a mooring buoy, while *Seeker* was able to tuck into a cosy marina berth and they could walk to the bar.

Gilbert and I had only just finished securing *Firebird* and checking for any repairs that might be needed, when Sandy met me as I swung down into the cockpit. The big cheesy grin on her lovely face was fair warning she was planning something I probably wouldn't approve of!

'Sweetie,' she said, and I knew I was in deep doggy do-do! Gilbert did too and flashed me a quick grin, before disappearing into the galley.

'Yes, dear,' I replied casually, 'what can I do for you?'

'I was just thinking,' she said, and my spirits plummeted in anticipation of a really bad idea about to be aired. 'Now that our visitors are delayed for four days, let's take all those lovely stones and go visit Mr Jacobs at Southport!'

It wasn't as bad as I'd thought and in fact was a pretty good idea. I'd been busting to have the emeralds checked out and now was the chance to do it with our favourite expert! I kissed her and said, 'OK. You go toss a few things in a bag, not forgetting the rocks, while I call for a booking out of Lombok, the boat ride to get to Lombok and to make sure Mr Jacobs will be there for us.'

Fizzing with excitement, she happily trotted below while I grabbed the mobile and let my fingers do the walking. In short order and thanks to the efficient staff at Marina Del Ray, we had two return seats booked on the 16:00 flight out of Lombok Bandara International Airport that afternoon, and the fast ferry would pick us up in fifteen minutes. My next phone call was to Mr Jacobs in Southport who was surprised and pleased to hear from me. I made an appointment for 10:00 tomorrow, which would be Thursday and even though he refrained from asking questions, I could hear the excitement in his voice as we said goodbye.

I had a quick talk with Dave and Corrine and suggested everyone could just goof off for the next few days, so long as there were no instances of loose or boozy talking off the boats. When Sandy appeared after fifteen minutes, packed and ready to go, she shooed me down below to get changed.

'Fresh clothing is on the bed, you scruffy old fart. Make sure you put it all on!'

'Yes, dear.'

A few minutes later, I was back on deck and took the opportunity to dig the stones out from the stash in one of the small backpacks where she had them, before spreading them amongst all our pockets. Then the fast ferry arrived in a welter of white spray, roaring engines and grinning crew, so we hopped aboard and waved goodbye as our flamboyant driver shoved the throttles open and roared out of the bay. The usual 90-minute trip was cut dramatically by the youthful driver who ignored such niceties such as passenger comfort, so we were showing our ID to the gate girl at the airport in just over the hour.

HARRY & SANDY, GOLD COAST

'Well, here we go again,' Sandy commented dolefully. 'I hope the bad guys pick some other aircraft to blow-up today. What if someone decides today would be a good day to have a home-grown terror incident that would make good headlines and attract a few more martyrs to the cause?'

Sandy hates flying.

'Well! Aren't we Miss Happy Pants today,' I replied, trying to be disgustingly cheerful just to wind her up, 'although you might care to notice that even though we're flying Air Asia, the crew seem to be mostly Aussie.'

She looked belatedly around the cabin, 'Oh, yeah. So they are. That means we'll only get shot down by a Stinger missile from some activist on the ground! And while I'm at it, stop being a smart-arse for a while. You know I hate flying!'

At that point, with the little old lady sitting beside me looking a bit green around the gills with all the talk of activists, blowing-up aircraft and Stingers, I whispered in Sandy's shell-like ear, 'Knock it off Princess, before this LOL beside me calls for the Air Marshall to come and arrest you for disturbing the passengers!'

She peered past me. 'Oh. OK. Sorry.' and subsided back into her seat, content to just mutter softly to herself under her breath.

The take-off was a bit rough on my arm as Sandy had it in a death-grip and this girl is no weakling! The LOL beside me mistook my wincing and pained expressions for an acute attack of a fear of flying syndrome also and patted me gently on the un-affected arm.

'Try not to be concerned, young man. There are two pilots up the front of this thing and they both look like they know what buttons to push!'

I thought it best to avoid the inevitable complicated explanation and whispered a polite 'Thank you' to her, before turning back to Sandy and commenting helpfully, 'Did you know that these things have only got two engines?'

'Yes!' came the terse reply.

'I've heard that they can fly on just one, but they have to dump most of the fuel and baggage to be light enough to do it.'

She glared at me. 'So what's the point of being able to fly on one engine, if you don't have enough fuel to be able to get anywhere with it?'

I gave her my best ingenuous smile. 'Dunno! Bloody good question to ask a pilot, though.'

'How about you shut up and let me suffer in silence. And that better be your silence!'

Which sort of set the mood for the rest of the flight, so I took the opportunity to catch up on some sleep, a move which avoided the conversational clutches of the LOL who was disappointed her big manly neighbour wasn't going to play ball by chatting all the way back to Australia.

It was a lot of flying just for a quick visit, since we had to go via Perth, so we weren't disembarking at Gold Coast airport until 06:00 the following morning. As usual after a long night on an aircraft, we felt grubby, with gritty eyes and a bad taste in the mouth. However, striding down the steps into the soft and salty morning Gold Coast air was a welcome relief from the air-conditioning.

It was a welcome relief for my arm as well. Sandy recovered quickly with her feet on the firm, non-mobile ground and as we walked to the terminal asked, 'Are we going to catch up with anybody while we're here?'

I shook my head, 'No! I'd like to stay under everyone's radar if we can. To help with that, we'll get a motel room here in Coolangatta and hire a car to go see Mr Jacobs at 10:00, then after that, we have the day free. If you brought your bikini, I might let you take me to the beach. It'll make a nice change to just perve on you and not to have to think about anything to do with boats, pirates or dodging bullets!'

I might have said once or thrice that Sandy in a bikini is a treat for male eyes, and quite a few female ones as I'd found out over the last couple of years!

We processed through Customs without any problem, although the discreet flash of an ACP warrant card made sure no one wanted to know what all the lumps in our pockets were. Five minutes later, with carry-on baggage only, we were signing up for a rental car and only had to walk about one kilometre to find the fool thing! Finally, we were clear of the airport and heading into Coolangatta to a 4-star hotel on Griffith Street, with Greenmount beach just over the road, and the shopping centre two blocks behind it.

The first order of business was long, hot shower, but because the hotel owners had insisted on installing a giant shower cubicle with dual overhead showerheads that would have fitted the entire Wallaby Rugby team, we showered together. That in turn led to the inevitable and a fair amount of the hotel's hot water ran to waste, but we did feel a lot better afterwards. Then there was just time for a quick snack, before the drive north up the M1 motorway, taking the Southport turnoff and heading east again for the CBD.

Mr Jacobs was still in the same shop where we had first met him but it had obviously had a bit of a face-lift and looked clean and tidy. Mr Jacobs himself looked the same and greeted us like old friends, as well he should since we had helped him make around $350,000 and a great deal of prestige from the marketing and sales of some very precious gems we had brought to him for assessment and valuation. A pleasant young lady, introduced as Miriam, his 25-year-old granddaughter who was learning the trade, accompanied him this time. Being attractive, well spoken, highly intelligent and knowing what she was talking about were great assets to have.

We were treated to tea and coffee, served by Miriam, before Mr Jacobs said, 'I presume you have something of interest for me to sell?'

I took the lead on this one and replied, 'We've been in the Indonesian Archipelago for a while and have come across a collection of antique gold and silverware which I think might be of interest to a good auction house; perhaps like the one who sold our gems last time around.'

He smiled, 'Ah, yes. They still talk about the public reaction to those magnificent gems!'

I handed him the list of items that the girls had compiled, along with Sandy's iPhone which she had thoughtfully used to take a series of hi-res photos of the items when they were spread out in Dave and Corrine's stateroom. By the time he had carefully read through the list, Miriam had downloaded the photos and handed the phone back to Sandy.

She then brought the photos up on the shop computer screen and when they both had studied them carefully, he said, 'That is a stunning collection, Mr Stevens, particularly the 24-carat gold dinner set. I don't think that I've ever seen anything like that before. When will the items be available?'

'They're currently still in Indonesian waters, but we expect the boat carrying the whole collection will be back here within a month. We've flown on ahead to take care of this business.'

He raised his eyebrows, 'That is a long trip just to see if I was interested in a collection of gold tableware. Is there perhaps something else that I would be interested in?'

Sandy looked at me with an expression that said, '*Stop fooling around with him and get to the point!*'

I relented and said, 'Well, yes there is the small matter of some pretty stones that came our way. so we'd like your opinion on them.'

His smile broadened and his eyes glittered, 'Excellent. I told Miriam this visit would produce something special!'

He flashed a quick grin at Miriam who stood beside him, quietly taking everything in.

I made a show of patting pockets, feeling lumps all over my clothing, since I'd taken some of the one's that Sandy had as well. Finally, after another glare from Sandy, I produced the first of the green '*Columbine stones*'. As Miriam spread Mr Jacobs' favourite white velvet sheet across the counter top, I passed the stone across to his shaking hand.

He shook his head in wonder. 'I don't know how you manage to do this, young man, but every time you and your lovely lady visit my shop, you have some amazing stones to show me! I won't ask how this comes about; instead, I'll just be so glad you have chosen me to show your magnificent finds to the world. Now down to business and even without looking further, I can see this is a stone of very rare quality.'

He held it up against the sunlight streaming in through the overhead skylight and drew a sharp breath, before passing it to Miriam, while he dug his loupe out of his top pocket.

'Do you see, my dear, the lack of obvious inclusions. Now under magnification, I can see that there are the slightest traces of them, but they are so faint and therefore quite invisible to the naked eye. That is so rare, it would make some people suspicious, but the fact they are there at all is proof this is an example of the finest quality emerald and not a fake.'

By now, Miriam had expertly screwed her own loupe into one eye and was examining the stone.

'Yes, Zaydee, I see the inclusions, but as you say, they are faint and invisible to the naked eye. It really is a stunning stone.' She passed the stone back to Mr Jacobs who laid it reverently on the white cloth.

'As I am somewhat used to your ways by now Mr Stevens, I don't suppose that you have a twin to this in your back pocket, would you sir?'

Unable to help myself, I shook my head ruefully, earning another kick from Sandy.

'No. I'm afraid I don't have a twin to it.' While I was speaking, I dug in my pockets, but it was Sandy who had the other matching pair in her breast pocket, which made interesting jiggles as she dug them out.

Sandy handed them over and he eagerly inspected them, before passing them onto Miriam. While she looked carefully into their depths with young, sharp eyes, he became thoughtful.

'They are without a doubt, the finest emeralds I've ever seen or even heard of, although there is a legend about six stones of supposedly flawless quality which came from Columbia in the 1900's. There were all the ingredients of legend; a shipwreck, pirates, wholesale murder, rape, sodomy and even cannibalism.

It was supposed to have happened in Indonesia somewhere, and is a really dreadful story, but it is claimed the stones were unprecedented in quality, although they haven't been sighted for over a hundred years.'

I didn't say anything as both Sandy and I had developed a flair for the dramatic, so as she carefully dug a folded sheet of paper out of her jeans pocket, I found the pocket with the other three emeralds in it. I let Sandy lay the copies of the newspaper stories in front of our jeweller and gave them a few moments to read them.

I then dug out the other three stones and carefully lined them up in front of him.

Having read the reported story with rapt attention, they both stared mesmerised at the second set of triplets which were a little larger than the first three and were cut slightly differently.

Miriam said in a hushed voice, 'Zaydee, it is true. The legend has been proven. The stones are described quite well enough for the provenance to be un-disputed. But they are supposed to be cursed.'

I shrugged. 'We've survived this far. If there was a curse, I think it's been used up on the very bad guys we took them from!'

Both Mr Jacobs and Miriam looked up sharply. 'You do seem to lead an interesting and exciting life, Mr Stevens. And you too Miss Thomson. I would like to hear this story one day in the near future. It's not often a legend of this level is exposed as being true. The ramifications for the sale of these are enormous! I presume you wish to sell these?'

We nodded together, 'Yes, please Mr Jacobs. But I must warn you we have more, so perhaps you should complete your preliminary inspection before we move on.'

The dear old man was blinking with the news of additional gems to check out and it took Miriam all her time to get him moving on the measuring, weighing and spectrometer checks while she went to make more tea for all. I noticed she double-checked that the front door was electrically dead-bolted before she moved.

By the time she was back with the welcome mugs of strong, sweet tea, the old man had finished his checks and took the hot mug gratefully, sipping carefully on account of his shaking hands.

'Mr Stevens. Miss Thomson. I seem to remember in reference to the blue diamonds, saying something like, '*Never have I seen such perfection in gemstones!*' Well I have to say it again! These stones, by any standard are flawless! The fact there two sets of identical triplets is incredible, but when one adds in the legend which has been built up around the Columbine Stones over the years, then I have to say you have the situation where you could almost name your own price.

Collectors and investors will flock to have a chance to see and bid for these amazing stones. Physically, I can confirm they are virtually in another new classification for colour and clarity. They measure 24.8 carats for the smaller ones and 26.4 carats for the larger. The cut on both is quite superb. But you say you have more treasures?'

He motioned to Miriam, who carefully placed the stones in two rows in a shallow, silk-lined tray and set it aside.

'Now,' he said with a cheeky grin, 'titillate my senses further, if you please.'

CHAPTER 24

With more pocket searching, I prolonged the moment slightly until I produced, one by one, the six rubies I'd found in the pirate's cave. I placed them carefully in a line on the white velvet until all six were flashing their gloriously deep red signal all over the room in a hundred tiny shafts of pure light. The effect was stunning and even Mr Jacobs and Miriam who must see similar sights all the time, were momentarily silent.

The old man dragged his eyes back to the source of the light show and picked them up one at a time to examine them more closely. Miriam followed suit and all was quiet for a while, until Mr Jacobs removed his loupe and sat back with a sigh as he eased his aching back.

'I find myself running out of superlatives, Mr Stevens and guilty of repetition when I say that these, too, are flawless! Please bear with me and I'll just weigh and measure them.'

'Between 33 and 35 carats each,' he announced proudly. 'Well-cut and nearly as hard as diamond so they wear very well. Once again, the colour and clarity is virtually in a new category, so the value is difficult to judge, but I would hazard a rough guess at around 1.5 million each!'

Sandy did the vice-grip routine again, but on my leg this time. 'I didn't think rubies were even close to the value of diamonds,' I said, when I had gathered my own whirling thoughts.

He smiled at our reactions, happy to be scoring some points off the chief point scorer in the room for a change. 'Normally, that is the case, but when you get the incredibly rare combination of superb colour and virtually perfect clarity, that's different!. The price heads for the stratosphere, to coin a phrase. The auctioneers will have a field day with these offerings.'

I coughed gently. 'I'm afraid that I'm guilty of saving the best 'till last. We do have just one more item to show you.'

He didn't have to try hard not to look surprised, but chuckled as he motioned again for Miriam to place the six rubies in the same tray as the emeralds, 'I should have known. Very well, 'knock my socks off' as my lovely granddaughter likes saying!'

I felt in another pocket and withdrew the 42-carat blue diamond, that was the Mother stone to the *Firebird Blues*' which had gone to auction. Giving it a rough polish on the front of my shirt, I placed it on the white cloth in front of his disbelieving eyes.

'You found it!' He breathed. 'You actually found it! The Mother Blue! This has to be the one! Oh, my dear man and lovely lady! You have no idea what turmoil you are about to cause in the industry! I said collectors would be coming in droves, first for the emeralds, then for the rubies, but to get the Mother of the Blues is a coup beyond description! Let me check it over first, then we must plan on how best to present these to the gemmological world!'

He busied himself with various pieces of equipment for a few moments, while the beautiful and enigmatic Miriam peered intently into the depths of the large, deep blue diamond, a small tic of her right upper cheek muscle the only indication of the tension we were all feeling.

The old man gently took the stone back and ran through his basic tests for weight, size and used a small desk-top spectroscope. 'As I expected, 42 carats as reported; cut down from its original 93 carats to create this beautiful stone and the six smaller stones you have already sold. I will be happy to say this is the Mother of those six, but naturally these will all have to be tested more fully before certification can be issued.'

Sandy and I nodded, familiar with the process by now. 'We understand and are happy to leave the stones with you for that purpose, if you will supply a receipt and a photograph of each set of stones.'

He beamed, thoroughly approving of our belated sense of security. 'Of course, Miriam will attend to it immediately.'

While she made busy with the task, Sandy found her voice and asked, 'But how should the sale be managed, not forgetting all the other stuff that's coming on the boat?'

He glanced at his granddaughter briefly. 'I have been thinking about it and must admit the additional stones you conjured up, have made me change my thoughts a little. I believe we should approach the same House as last time and suggest they build a special event around your offerings. Although there are a great number of beautiful items in the collection, if they were to call for more items in the same vein, there would quickly be sufficient to make a full, but very special auction event. We would have to wait for your boat to arrive with the other treasure items, in any case, and then the checking, cataloguing, photography and advertising will take extra time, so the auction would not be for at least two months, maybe three. Is that acceptable?'

I looked at Sandy, our thoughts coinciding. 'No problem, Mr Jacobs. That will suit our timetable nicely.'

He and Miriam smiled, 'I'm glad we are in agreeance. Once word starts leaking out about the stones, which we will insist be the stars of the auction, intense interest will build quickly. The stones will be kept in a safe deposit box in a high security vault, although only Miriam and I will know where, since I keep several in current use at any one time.'

'One final point I must mention, Neither Sandy nor I will be the ones bringing the assorted treasure items to you when the boat arrives back on the Gold Coast. The two people who will be arranging the drop-off will be our partners, Corrine Johns and David Robson. They are the owners of the boat carrying the treasure and were the original owners of the red and the blue diamonds. However, to maintain security, I will give them a letter of introduction from myself and if you have a piece of paper, I will give you a sample of my signature to compare to the one on the letter they will produce.'

'That will be most satisfactory, Mr Stevens. I will ensure there are no problems with the delivery and the arrangements for the auction. I will send an email message when I have more information.'

I added *Firebird's* email address under my signature, and that seemed to conclude our business, so after the usual pleasantries and assurances that our stones would receive the finest and safest care, we were ushered out of the shop by a grateful pair of jewellers. Although we were close to the Southport Police Station where Sandy normally worked, we made it back to the rental car without seeing anybody we knew. Driving away, Sandy was silent for a while, concentrating on avoiding the worst of the traffic, but then asked, 'Even though he's not sure of prices and we've seen how auctions push prices up, we could be looking at upwards of $20 million for the stones!'

Inevitably, I'd been thinking along the same lines, so was able to reply, 'Yep! At least that if not more. Every stone in the lot was large, flawless, had perfect clarity and intense deep colour, so all the important boxes were ticked. The old bloke was right; the gem collectors will go nuts over this one, especially over the discovery of the Mother of the Blues, which is a magnificent gem in its own right. I wouldn't be surprised if the end result is closer to double that amount!'

That statement caused Sandy to swerve violently as she nearly ran off the road, then she had to pull over and lean across to give me a big hug and kiss.

'So, our share could be up around $10 million?' she asked in wonder.

'Yeah! Quite likely!'

'Fuckin' hell!' was her response, and although she doesn't often use strong language, it did seem appropriate for the occasion. Somehow we made it back to the motel where Sandy insisted on celebrating our continued good fortune in traditional style, which drew no complaints from me. After that, we finally made it to the beach, with Sandy in her bikini and she drew all the attention expected. It was a relaxing afternoon which rolled slightly drunkenly into an even more relaxed evening.

We spent a fair chunk of Friday travelling and wearily landed back on Lombok on Saturday morning, to be met by Dave and Corrine who wanted a full debriefing on the gem situation. They were delighted with the report and the plans, so it was a happy crew who boarded the fast ferry back to Marina Del Ray, our pussies and our home.

Being just tired, but not really jet-lagged, we recovered after a good night's sleep, although both Jasper and Krazy had insisted on sticking close to us in case we disappeared again.

CHAPTER 25

MARINA DEL RAY, LOMBOK, SUNDAY

I called Reception to arrange a fast ferry pickup for six persons at 12:30 since I'd decided to take Sandy as extra cover. They were delighted we were back and were swapping guests immediately.

... 'Yes, that's right. Four of our crew are flying out to go to work, and my lady and I will meet the two who are flying in by chartered jet. We need to be at the airport shortly before 15:00. Can the driver organise that?'

... 'Oh yes, of course. Lennie. Great. He'll wait for us too, will he? There will be four of us coming back.'

...'Very good. Now are there any other passengers scheduled to travel either way on the ferry?'

...'No? Excellent! We'll be ready to depart by 12:30 and we'll meet Lennie at the ferry jetty.'

...'Thank you.'

There wasn't much time to kill so amid the usual last-minute round of checking to make sure they had everything, we herded the four Navy crew into the RIB and ashore to the ferry where Lennie was waiting, the twin outboards idling as they warmed up. The farewell with the rest of the crew was slightly emotional, as it is between people who have worked closely in the ultra-high stress situation of combat, but at least, these four had some real war stories to tell their mess-mates! I'd told them the actions against the pirates wasn't classified as we were going to report to the officials at Marina Del Ray that we'd been approached by armed men on two occasions, but we'd avoided being boarded. I wasn't going to mention the attack off Herba Island or our reprisal raid.

Despite the presence of two attractive females, Lennie restrained himself and only launched the fast ferry off every third or fourth wave top, getting us to the ferry terminal in good time to meet the mini-bus for the airport run. Naturally, the driver was a mate of his and they had to have a chat before we settled in for the 35-kilometre run to the airport. Following the directions given to me by Charlie, he parked at the GA Terminal and there were more slightly emotional scenes where they all thanked Sandy and me for potentially making them all rather wealthy!

I wondered how many would stay in the Service when each had more than a million dollars in the bank.

Promptly at 15:00, a familiar shape in the form of an RAAF Challenger 604 business jet landed and taxied in off the main runway to the Executive jet parking area in front of the small terminal.

'Oh, shit!' I cursed. 'Why did they have to come in a RAAF aircraft? That's like holding up a bloody big neon sign!'

Sandy patted my shoulder. 'Settle petal! We'll cope!'

I was conscious of the weight of the Grizzly pistol pulling at the waistband of my shorts in back under the tails of the colourful and clean shirt Sandy made me wear. I carefully checked around the terminal, but there were only a few people in sight and just one armed security dude near the Customs station, although he did have a H&K MP5 sub-machine gun slung across his chest in a quick-action sling.

The door of the Challenger opened and the stairs deployed. The female Flight Sergeant came out followed by a distinguished-looking man in a dark grey business suit, carrying a briefcase and followed by two RAAF persons, a male and a female carrying two bags each. The Sergeant escorted them as far as the terminal gate, then returned to the aircraft.

Puzzled, we visually tracked the man as he entered the terminal followed by his aides who all flashed their passports at Immigration & Customs, then walked past us to the bathroom facilities. There was no further activity at the aircraft, but then from within the terminal, a RAAF Officer with the four narrow bands of a Group Captain appeared, and walked briskly to the Customs desk where he flashed a passport and was passed through immediately.

The Flight Sergeant popped out of the aircraft doorway and met the Group Captain halfway across the tarmac, saluted, then escorted him to the aircraft. He climbed the stairs, but she returned to the terminal, stopped by the Customs desk and called for our passengers. She said something to them and they walked straight through Customs and were escorted by her out onto the tarmac and into the aircraft. The door closed, the engines started and the sleek aircraft taxied to the runway.

Sandy and I didn't wait to watch the take-off, but left the nearly deserted terminal and re-boarded the mini-bus. The two RAAF aides from the jet had shed their uniforms and were now wearing casual shirts over knee-length shorts, cut in the current style.

Charlie jumped up and greeted me effusively with a big hug and a kiss for good measure, then gave Sandy the same treatment.

The man stood and was about my height, lean and fit with a good head of sandy-blonde hair which needed cutting and his pleasant, open face had a huge smile. His grip was firm and I was treated to a quick man-hug from the PM.

'Hi Harry, I'm Andy Friar and very pleased to be here to meet you finally. And you must be Sandy. It's a pleasure to meet you too. Even though Charlie has told me so much about both of you, I've got a lot of questions, but we'll have time for that.'

'It's a pleasure to meet you too, Andy,' I responded, determined to maintain the informal atmosphere. 'I loved the piece of deception in the terminal. Slick!'

'Oh, Charlie gets all the credit for that,' he said cheerfully, giving her an appreciative glance. 'One of my assistants and I did just what we were told to do. But it was quite well done, I thought.'

I grinned back, his infectious smile easy to take. 'Bloody marvellous, I reckon. We didn't know what the hell was going on until I recognised Charlie.'

I motioned to the driver and he coaxed the tired old vehicle into motion, joining the stream of taxis and private vehicles leaving the airport as passengers from the two commercial jets which had just landed, raced for their resorts or businesses.

Conversation wasn't easy inside the mini-bus, being more akin to sitting inside a metal garbage bin rolling down a concrete walkway, so we held off the conversational bit until we could hear ourselves think.

There wasn't much chance to chat at the ferry wharf either, but Sandy and I took the chance to have a look around for anybody taking an undue amount of interest in us, while Charlie shepherded Andy on-board and got their bags stowed. He was obviously used to being mothered and went along with good grace, a happy little grin permanently on his face. It was that grin which made me think maybe this was the first time in years he'd been let off the leash.

I saw Charlie answer her Sat-Phone a few times, but they were brief conversations and she took very few notes in her diary, which never left her side. It was a scenic run, threading through a number of islands and always staying close to the coast. It was also the shortest part of the journey being only about 12 nautical miles, which at 30 knots took just 24 minutes before we wheeled up to the stern boarding platform of *Firebird* in Lennie's usual flashy style.

From the time the marina came into view, Andy's head was in constant motion checking everything out and even more so when it became clear the big, white catamaran was to be his home for the next few weeks. Gilbert was in the cockpit, neatly dressed and ready to help with guests and bags. I'd already clued Andy and Charlie in to the fact that Gilbert was a mute, making sure to point out there was nothing wrong with his hearing or level of intelligence.

I'd forgotten to check with Sandy about Gilbert's accommodation, so I quietly asked her while our guests were getting out of the ferry and taking bags up to the cockpit.

'Did you sort out Gilbert's bed?'

She gave a brief giggle, but replied normally. 'Yes. I did what you suggested and made up the dressing room bunk. He has plenty of room, doesn't mind sharing with Jasper and said he was perfectly happy to be there. He said he'll try to disturb us as little as possible.'

I chuckled. 'Like I said earlier, I was afraid it would be the other way around!' I received a friendly smack on the bum for that.

Up in the cockpit, Andy was staring around, quite intrigued and interested. 'Where's this fellow Jasper I've heard so much about?' he asked as we joined them. 'He sounds like a capable fella!'

'Oh, he is,' I grinned, 'although looks can be deceiving. I'll just fetch him out.'

Andy looked around, 'Out? Out of where?'

I called softly and my big cat made his usual dramatic appearance, scaring the hell out of Andy who was still looking around as Jasper stepped out of the saloon where he'd been lurking, keeping an eye on the newcomers.

'Crap!' was Andy's comment. 'What the hell's that?'

'That's Jasper. I'll need to introduce you properly as he's part of your protection detail.'

Andy managed to look incredulous. 'Your overgrown cat is going to protect me?'

'Better than I can in some circumstances,' I said seriously. 'Anyway; Jasper, this is Andy and he's a friend who is going to be staying with us for a while. We are also protecting him, from some bad men who might be trying to harm him.'

Jasper huffed as usual and went into his sniffing routine, which Andy put up with, but looked even more dubious as he stepped over to Charlie, sat and held out his right paw to be shaken.

'That's a good trick to teach a cat, I must say,' he commented, clearly certain that the whole Jasper myth thing was bullshit.

I sighed, only slightly theatrically and said, 'I didn't teach him anything, not that, nor anything else. He shakes hands with people he knows and likes, purely by choice. How about you talk to him directly?'

To his credit, Andy immediately squatted down and looked Jasper in the eye at the same level. If he felt silly addressing a big cat, he didn't show it. 'Hello Jasper, can we be friends? I'd like to be your friend.'

Jasper looked at him, cocked his head, and then gave a 'merow' before gently nuzzling Andy's face.

Andy looked up and laughed as he expertly scratched Jasper behind the ears, 'Well I'll be buggered! I didn't believe he could actually understand what people say, but that was rather convincing. If he can do half of what I've heard, he's amazing!'

'Now that you're friends, he'll defend you as strongly as he would Sandy or me.' I decided not to mention Jasper's kill rate in defence of his family, in case he felt intimidated about sharing space with a killer cat!

I asked Sandy to show Andy and Charlie to their cabins and to give Andy the boat briefing. After they'd gone below, I saw Gilbert scratching Jasper's belly.

'Sorry to have to move you out of the stern cabin. I'm not sure how long they'll stay, but hopefully you'll still be comfortable.'

A smile lit up his handsome face, then he shook his head, before pulling his notebook out and writing, 'No problem. Just happy to be here and to help.'

I patted him on his muscular shoulder, then checked the time. It was still too early to go ashore, so I settled down to wait for Andy and Charlie to appear, which wasn't long, Andy bubbling over with enthusiasm about *Firebird*.

'What a great boat, Harry! You must show me the sail arrangement tomorrow and I love the way you've set the systems up. Fascinating.'

I smiled. 'Glad you like it, and she sails well, but how's your cabin? Enough room?'

'Yeah! Heaps of room for me. I didn't expect a three-room suite on a sailing cat.'

'Our friends on the other boat, *Seeker*, who you'll meet shortly, have a three-room master cabin, but their boat's a bit bigger than us,' I chuckled.

'Is that the boat which has been travelling with you? With the SAS soldier you rescued in the desert?'

'Yes. That's the one. Corrine and one of the crew, Alex, are trained soldiers. Dave's very handy as well. Bree is a great cook and Roger and Jill are the medical team.'

He laughed, taking a long drink of the beer Sandy had brought out for us. 'Sounds like you've got all aspects covered. You mentioned you and Sandy were armed when you met us at the airport, but do you really consider that there's a risk of somebody wanting to take me out?'

'Yes I do, Andy. You read those papers with names and addresses that Charlie retrieved from us?'

He nodded.

'Well. I'm not privy to your plans for dealing with those people who tried to destroy the democratic system of Government, but if I were them, I'd be trying to take you out first. I don't think it's entirely coincidental that Charlie tried so hard to get me to agree to take you on a sailing cruise with no set itinerary!'

It was too much to expect Charlie to be embarrassed. She just looked pleased with herself I'd finally realised what was going on. 'Sorry for the deception, Harry,' she said, looking anything but. 'I thought getting the Boss away at very short notice without the security that's like a neon sign, would be the best way to disappear for a while.

And this is the perfect place to hide out. All the comms we need and as you say, no itinerary!'

I grinned as well. 'OK. I don't really mind, so it's just as well we're fairly well stocked with weapons, although we had to send the MK 47 grenade launcher back to the Navy.'

Andy looked faintly shocked to hear that. 'You must have mighty powers of persuasion to prise one of those off the Navy. Whose soul did you have to surrender to get that?'

'Nothing dramatic like that. I just had to take Admiral Stallman and his PPS Hilary on an overnight sail up the West Australian coast from Onslow to Port Hedland. He loved it!'

Andy chuckled. 'Yes, he would. Alan loves his sailing. He's done the Sydney-Hobart race six times so far.'

'No wonder he wanted to come on this trip! We nearly had him and Paul Davy, the Skipper of the patrol boat *Glenelg*, along as well.'

'That would have gone over well with our Indonesian friends if something had gone wrong with the pirate attacks,' Charlie said in a dry tone. 'I can see the headlines now. "Australian Navy 2IC Admiral and Patrol Boat Skipper take part in raid on a pirate base in Indonesia"!'

When the laughter died down, I replied, 'That's probably why I didn't take them. But I've been meaning to ask, has the money trail investigation uncovered anything? I know my friend Inspector Greg James of the Southport Police got that ball rolling early.'

Charlie knew the answer to that, and replied, 'We took over the investigation and they've had some success. We're starting to see evidence of massive tampering with the Union Superannuation Funds to provide much of the funding of EarthCare and more particularly, EarthSquad and the Pilbara base you took out.'

I was disturbed to hear that, even though it was half-expected. 'Oh, bugger! That could be another hornet's nest about to be stirred. I can't imagine a worse bunch to upset. They'll be gunning for all of us, while trying to cover their own arses. Just as well we've still got the .50 cal's!'

Andy raised a cautious eyebrow and asked the question he probably didn't want answered.

'Salvaged from the EarthSquad arsenal before it all went tits-up!' Sandy said cheerfully. 'They've come in handy already and I won't be surprised if we have to re-mount them again before this trip's over!'

Andy mimed plugging his ears, while we laughed.

Soon after, we cleaned up, changed where necessary and took the

RIB over to *Seeker*, leaving Jasper in charge of boat security, assisted by his rapidly growing assistant, Krazy cat.

CHAPTER 26

MARINA DEL RAY, LOMBOK, SUNDAY EVENING

Andy was delighted to meet Corrine and their crew, impressed by the size and intelligence of Alex Chetty, while Corrine's small size and demure appearance masked her deadly nature. While they chatted and played 'get to know you' over beers and wines, I took Dave aside and brought him up to date on the latest news from Charlie.

'Therefore, we could have two groups trying to knock off the PM and Charlie's talked us into this fun cruise so he's got a chance to dodge them? Is that the case?'

I nodded, 'Yeah. I'm afraid so. I just found out as well and I'm not happy, but the whistle's blown, the ball's been bounced and the PM is in play, so to speak!'

'Bloody hell, mate! Surely there would have been somewhere else to stow him for a while? I mean, how long do we have to keep him away from prying eyes, and should we even be taking him up to the restaurant?'

I nodded. 'Yep. Wondered about all that myself, but Charlie seems comfortable with the idea.'

'Humph!' he grumped, 'it's all very well for Charlie to be 'comfortable', but we're the security detail and have to defend him if either of those two groups get a sniff of where he is! Can't we disguise him a bit? You know, with some make-up?'

I nodded thoughtfully. 'Not a bad idea, old mate. Let's get Charlie and Sandy in on this.'

Dave was still a bit wound up and said, 'I think we need to throw this onto the table for everyone to think about. Everyone's at equal risk, and any one of the girls might have an idea about what to do.'

'True, but let's have a quick word to Charlie first.'

'I'd like to keep this new information on a need to know basis, and only four of you qualify for that status!' said Charlie.

'With respect, that's crap!' Dave replied. 'As I've just said to Harry, we're all exposed to the same risk and we are all going to have to fight if it comes to that, so a small crew like this, needs all the Intel it can get. It keeps the trust in each other strong.'

'Dave's right, Charlie. It's the only way we can work. Even something as simple as asking if someone can do a make-up job on the Boss so that his features are changed enough so that he's not instantly recognised, will make the crew ask why? And we're not going to lie to anybody in the crew. We've been through too much together to start the lies!'

Charlie nodded. 'Yes, you are both right, and I'm sorry – I've been too long around idiots who can't be trusted to shake the drops off their dicks before zipping up! We'll do it your way Dave, and have a round table.'

'Excellent choice, dear lady. It'll be for the best, especially as we are supposed to hide the Boss until the leaders within those two groups are taken out or otherwise immobilised. Does that, in fact, summarise our job?'

She finally had the grace to blush a little. 'I'm sorry Harry, sorry Dave. I thought I was being a bit clever with my little piece of subterfuge, but I see now it's all wrong. I must learn to be upfront with people I trust and not play politics with them.'

I held up my hand to forestall any more breast-beating. 'Apology accepted, so let's get back to the group while they're still in a listening mood.'

We re-joined the rest of the crew who were politely chatting with Andy, but wondering what was going on with our breakaway group.

'Sorry to be rude and leave you all, but we've been made aware of a couple of situations that change the complex of the voyage we were about to start. The cause of this current situation is the previous operation down in the Pilbara you all were involved in; except Charlie and Andy, of course and they received all reports.'

I raised my eyebrows at Charlie, 'You did pass all reports in full onto Andy, didn't you Charlie?'

She was caught out again, and looked down while chewing at her top lip. 'Not in full, no. There are times when the PM needs to be able to look a reporter in the eye and say truthfully, *I know nothing about that*.'

I nodded at her bowed head. 'Understood! However, I would have thought when those names were placed in your hands, your ACP security advisors would have connected the dots and raised the alert level to critical. Additionally, you had the money trail investigators identify the source of much of the funding. Did they really think the people who happily transferred millions of 'Other People's Money' into that whacko project, were just going to sit back, shrug their shoulders and wait for an ACP officer to knock at the door?'

It was one of those rhetorical questions and fortunately Charlie didn't try to answer it. Andy looked a bit disturbed and asked the right question. 'May I presume from your statement, Harry, since I haven't previously been advised of all this, that you and Dave believe the threat level to me personally, to be high?'

'Andy, we believe the threat level to you is extreme. There is almost certainly one bunch gunning for you and they are the names on the sheet of paper we found. Naturally not them in person, but they'll have either put out a contract, or hired the right crew to do the job. Added to that is the strong likelihood the Super Funds bandits will be pro-active on this one. To their way of thinking, they'll reason if they can knock-off the PM, nobody will want to continue the investigation and it will all fall apart.'

Charlie still looked upset, as well she should, but Andy patted her gently on the knee in a magnanimous gesture of forgiveness, and showing the decisiveness which had carried him easily to the top political position in Australia, he said, 'I'm glad you stopped the recriminations; they don't help, but obviously you recommend we should proceed on the basis there is at least one group looking for me and maybe two?'

I smiled grimly. 'Yep. Exactly that. We can't afford to pretend otherwise. In many ways, Charlie has done the right thing by bringing you here, and there was a fair attempt to keep your identity secret, but just the fact of the RAAF CL604 aircraft visiting Lombok will have raised a few red flags somewhere.

Therefore, we need to fuel to utmost capacity, provision the same, then disappear for as long as we can or until we know the bad guys are shut down.'

I thought a few moments, while everyone in the know, recognising the signs, kept quiet.

'OK. I've mentioned the fuel and food requirements. Bree and Sandy are in charge of catering. Make sure we have stuff that everybody likes and don't forget Jasper and Krazy, although there should be plenty of the dry stuff. Don't forget booze since it might be hard to get in some areas.'

I looked at Charlie, 'How secure will it be for you to communicate through your office? I presume the official word is the PM is on holiday at an undisclosed location?'

She nodded, almost back to her usual effervescent and competent self. 'Yes, that's exactly what we released to the media. As for security in the office, and being totally objective, I guess that there could be leaks since no one is aware of the threats and would probably talk quite naturally outside the office. What's the alternative? We need to be kept up-to-date as to how the search is going.'

I nodded, 'Yep. Understood. Do you have one person who is across most of this stuff and you trust not to speak to anyone?'

'Yes. I have an assistant, Alice Lawson. She knows pretty much everything that crosses my desk and she knows how to keep quiet.'

'That's good, but think about this carefully. If an unknown person rang Alice on her personal mobile, what could that person say to her which would convince her that any information she was asked to give to this person would be relayed straight to you?'

She thought only a few seconds, then grinned at Andy. 'Last November, the Boss was waiting for the Chinese Ambassador and their Foreign Trade Minister to come and sign a new agreement, when he grabbed a biscuit with dip from the tray of snacks. Unfortunately, a blob of dip slid off and landed on his pants, right on the crotch. We had just sent his spare suit to the cleaners to be refreshed, so we had to get him to take his pants off and stand around in his green budgie-smugglers while Alice and I sponged the pants clean and dried them with a hair dryer.

We got them done seconds before the Chinese delegation were announced! It was a frantic day and we forgot about the incident, so even though it wasn't a secret, nobody else knew about it. If your contact mentioned the 24ᵗʰ November, Chinese delegation, dip on crotch of pants and green budgie-smugglers, that should do the trick.'

'Excellent. I'll pass that on to my contact. Is there anything else we need to discuss?'

Alex half-raised his hand and asked in his deep voice with the appealing South African accent. 'Commander. Is it your intention to remain in Eastern Indonesian waters for the duration?'

I nodded. 'Yes it is, Alex. I thought it might slow any bad guys down a little if they had to work in a foreign country.'

'I agree, Commander. It would have that effect, but please remember the southern arms of Sulawesi are home to the Bugis people who have for centuries made piracy a way of life! So we may have more than just Australian bad guys to contend with.'

I looked at Alex, but then directed my question at Charlie. 'Good point, Alex. Should we need more resources, that is ammunition and or weapons, I trust we can call on the Navy again?'

'Hell yes!' was her emphatic reply. 'Although we must avoid having a patrol boat actually enter Indonesian territorial waters unless it was a dire emergency.'

'Of course. We want to keep as low a profile as possible.'

Andy had been following the whole conversation carefully. 'What's the risk level of encountering pirates?'

'In all honesty, fairly high Andy, but not as bad as in the Straits of Malacca or where we we've just come from.'

'OK. So, are we prepared?'

'Yes. Apart from plenty of small arms, including four sub-machine guns, we have two Browning .50 cal's and two RPG-7 grenade launchers.'

Andy raised his eyebrows at that listing. 'That seems a very heavy weapons load for two pleasure boats,' he observed dryly. 'I presume they were gained as 'spoils of war'?'

'Yes. Exactly right, Andy.'

He paused a few moments before saying, 'I might have missed something, but in light of this increased threat, why don't you just sail clear of Indonesian waters and transfer me to a patrol boat? They are far better equipped to defend me and it saves you taking the risks they are paid to face.'

'Good point Andy, I considered it when I found out what was going on, but the problem with the patrol boat is security. All the crew have phones and tablets and even innocently, one could give away the fact that, 'the PM's aboard' and the word would spread. Additionally, it would take at least two days to get a boat close to here, if one was able to leave immediately. The delay would more likely be four or five days whereas we will be gone tomorrow.

However, security would be my greatest concern, even with the Skipper imposing a comms ban. I know what enlisted troops are like.'

He and Charlie looked thoughtful. 'Hmmm! That's a fairly light-weight argument, but I'll go with it. I presume you think like I do, when I see our cover of two pleasure boats in a foreign country is still the best way to keep from being noticed.'

'Yep. That's the basis for the whole setup. The weapons are last resort. But let me give you another point against you hiding behind the Navy's grey wall. What would be the reaction by the press when an Australian Navy patrol boat is attacked by a swarm of high-speed RIBs armed with RPG-7s and small anti-ship missiles, and is holed and sunk?'

Andy nodded thoughtfully, 'I get your point, but do you think that sort of firepower is likely to be used by the groups you say are looking for me?'

I smiled grimly, disturbed by his lack of appreciation of what a few determined men with too much money can achieve. 'The short answer to that one is 'Yes', and the longer one is that they will use whatever it takes to get the job done!

Tomorrow, after refuelling and re-provisioning, we check out and wander east looking at dive and fishing spots. I believe that you have an open-water certificate?'

'Yes, I do and I'm looking forward to making good use of it.' he replied with his grin in place again.

'Good.' I looked at the girls before saying. 'Now there's one final thing we have to do and that's to disguise Andy sufficiently so he won't be recognised in the bar and restaurant. Ladies? Any takers to re-decorate the PM?'

That drew a laugh, until Bree stuck her hand up. 'I was a receptionist at a Special FX company in Sydney for a while and one of the artists showed me a few tricks. I can give it a go using what we have here.'

I looked at Andy, 'OK for Bree to make you less obvious?'

'Sure. Just so long as I look better afterwards,' he joked.

We had a few more drinks while Bree exercised her talents on the PM, using what make-up Sandy and Jill had been able to put together, which wasn't much as neither were really into using it. Nevertheless, Bree showed she did have a real talent by using diluted mascara as a darkening agent and the blush brush with a trace of lipstick to redden some areas and to shadow others so the final effect, if not exactly flattering, didn't look like the PM in the slightest! In fact, he looked quite gaunt and the discrete shadowing under his eyes gave him an overtired, unhealthy look.

'Try not to smile too much,' she advised, deftly putting on some finishing touches, 'it'll spoil the effect.'

He gave her a grin as he surveyed the damage in a small makeup mirror, 'I'm afraid I can't offer you a job as my makeup girl, based on that. But you do have a serious talent!'

Bree beamed with pleasure at the praise, as she tidied things up and we decided to test public opinion by heading for the restaurant.

In any event, no one even gave him a second glance. Our friends, Bruce and Heather from *Misty* were still there, being grounded with engine problems and having to endure the traditionally long wait for spare parts to filter through the Indonesian postal system.

They were fooled completely to the extent that Bruce, who was a retired Professor of Political Science at Monash University, even got into a discussion with Andy over some controversial political issue and both had a lovely time debating the pros and cons back and forth, despite many attempts by Heather to shut them both up!

Sandy and I were hard pressed to keep from laughing out loud to see them carrying on, but everyone had a good time and we parted company with the Tandy's again, wishing them well with engine repairs.

Back on board, everybody was sagging, so it was off to various beds. It was slightly odd to have Gilbert in our dressing room, but he was such a good guest, we were hardly aware of him, so since Sandy was happy, I was too. He only passed through our cabin a couple of times, considerately knocking softly each time, but we were too tired to fool around so it didn't matter. Something was niggling at my memory to do with Sandy and Gilbert, but it eluded my feeble mental search so I went to sleep.

THURSDAY

Next morning was busy as Sandy and Bree made out provisioning lists then went ashore in the RIB to get what they could or acceptable substitutes. As soon as they'd gone, I moved *Firebird* to the re-fuelling dock after I'd unrolled and re-connected all the Flex-Tanks. If the re-fueller was surprised at the quantity of diesel that a sailing boat took, he didn't show it, being happy to be paid. Dave had brought *Seeker* over to the dock as well, as the marina hadn't yet set up a mobile fuelling barge. If the fuel bloke thought I took a lot, his eyes nearly popped when Dave finally said 'stop!' Both boats had been getting low on the standard tanks.

By the time we had the boats back in position, the girls returned with several RIB loads of provisions. Andy and Charlie pitched in on *Firebird* unloading and stacking stuff where Sandy could sort what went where, but within 30 minutes, we had everything stowed. We took the necessary walk up the marina to the Customs and Immigration post. The two officials were very helpful in issuing clearance for the boats and their crews to explore East Indonesian waters for the next few weeks en-route to their home port of South-port, Queensland, Australia. The hundred dollars each that Dave passed across might have helped somewhat, but who's to say?

He also paid the marina fee with a healthy tip added for the Reception crew and was assured of a warm welcome the next time we visited.

CHAPTER 27

MARINA DEL RAY, LOMBOK, MONDAY

At 11:00 we motored away from the marina complex and headed north up the west coast of Lombok. Once clear of the confines of the little harbour, I hoisted all sail and with a light, but steady breeze from the SE, we slid quietly and smoothly away from civilisation for a while.

I'd had a chat with Sandy, Dave and Corrine before we left and we decided that since we weren't in any rush, *Firebird* would set the pace under sail alone as the winds were typically light and out of the SE through October, although it was officially the start of the monsoon season. We'd been dutifully warned about tropical storms which could brew up with little warning with the early onset of the monsoon and both the forecasters and the locals said that this year it was coming early.

Accordingly, the skies were grey with heavy, rolling cloud, as if Mother Nature felt obliged to occasionally live up to man's pathetic guesstimate forecasts. As usual, the mood of the crew changed once we were at sea and into a new routine. Charlie appointed herself Sandy's helper and her eternal cheerfulness kept spirits up. Andy admitted he'd had the best night's sleep he'd had in years and felt good.

I'd already come to rely on Gilbert's help with boat handling since he'd proved to be extremely competent whether motoring or sailing. Andy was keen to get his hands on the wheel and he too proved to be useful and knew how sailing boats worked. With *Seeker* idling along 50 metres off one rear corner or the other, we followed the rough plan we'd formed which was to head up toward a group of small islands which lay like a scattered patch of freckles across the face of the Flores Sea, north east of Lombok. Those small islands stretched up almost to the western arm of Sulawesi, an area I thought it best to avoid, after Alex's warning. I was considering taking a bit of a chance by visiting the southern portion of an extensive area of shallow reefs and lagoons well down south-east of South Sulawesi which promised excellent shallow and open-water diving.

We weren't trying to make distance, so the mood was relaxed and laid back and I reflected on how this time out, we were a very mixed crew on *Firebird*; a current PM, his PPS, a Eurasian mute with a mysterious past, a serving Queensland Police Inspector and me, a shot-up, busted-arse, ex-SAS Major.

Those moments of idle thought reminded me I needed to make contact with Greg James, who was still our contact for the passing of information. Therefore, with the boat being steered by Andy, and with Gilbert lounging in a cockpit chair being chatted to by Charlie, I took the Sat-Phone out of its charging cradle and punched up a familiar number.

'*Hi Harry. How are things going? I haven't heard from you for a while.*'

'Gidday Greg. Things are going alright now, but we've had a bit of excitement, although that all over now; we hope!'

'*Bloody hell! When you say you've had a bit of excitement, it means you've had to fight off some serious bad guys. Is everybody and everything OK?*'

'Yeah. It is for the moment, but there's a situation brewing which we need you to help with. It's to do with the financial investigation you had going.'

'*Oh, dear yes! Our two ex-Tax Department Investigators were really getting somewhere when someone in the Prime Minister's office, of all places, snapped them up. I had the strangest phone calls about it, and was told the ACP would be looking after things from that point on. Some person called Charlie. All very mysterious! Anyway, how can I help?*'

I chuckled, looking out at the mysterious 'Charlie' playing with

Krazy cat as she lounged back with her feet up. 'I need to set up a communications link via a cutout, which is you. I have two new persons aboard, one of whom needs to remain invisible for a while due to the fallout from the last operation and that financial investigation. We may have some serious heavies looking for this person and I don't want to take chances with comms.'

'Ahh...Is this person fairly high up in the general scheme of things?'

'You could say that. In fact, about the highest. But I wouldn't say that; even in your sleep.'

'Shit, Harry! You really have stepped straight into the poo-bucket this time. Don't tell me how you managed to get into this shitstorm, but Bob and I want to hear when you get back! Tell me what I've got to do.'

'Thanks, mate. What you need to do is call a lady named Alice on the number I'm about to give you and prove to her satisfaction that you truly represent the correct person. The proof is in the form of a short story, or at least the basic facts of it and this is what you must say. On the 24th of November last year, a Chinese Trade Delegation was about to arrive; there was dip spilled on the crotch of the Boss's pants and Alice and Charlie cleaned it off while the subject stood around in green budgie-smugglers.'

There was silence for a moment or two, then he replied, 'Green budgie-smugglers, eh? Really? And Alice and Charlie cleaned it off! Seems like there are a lot of Charlies involved in this situation you're up to your neck in! I don't suppose they're one and the same?'

'Maybe,' I replied airily, 'and maybe it wouldn't pay to speculate too much at the moment! Once you've established yourself with Alice, we need her to keep you updated with all news about the financial investigation and anything else which is truly vital, particularly if there's any word about bad guys picking up our trail. Tell Alice she is to pass any routine office stuff onto Deputies, not to us. Also tell her this link through you, is to be the only channel of communication. The usual phones will be shut down.

Give her your personal mobile number and perhaps go get a few cheap pre-paid mobiles as burners, but if you change, tell both of us first. And watch out for the wrong people asking questions, as in, keep your head down, sunshine.'

'*OK Harry. I've got all that. But it's sounding a bit serious if you've got the big dog there and are playing hide and seek with the bad boys!*'

'Yeah, it is serious, but if we can stay under everyone's radar long enough for the investigation to roll over the right rock, we'll be fine.'

'*I just turned up the political page of the paper and it says the PM is taking a well-deserved holiday in an undisclosed location. I guess that's the truth, isn't it?*'

'Yes, but don't say stuff like that again where others might hear you.'

'*Sorry mate. Good point. But why not use the Navy to do the guard-ing? All those guns and grey-steel must be better protection than two smallish boats.*'

'Funnily enough, the subject raised the same point less than 24 hours ago and the same answer applies. We're the least likely place the top dog would hang out and we can blend in with the boating background easily when we have to. The Navy would be a tough nut to crack, but if it came to a fight, the publicity would be very damaging.

At least for now, he is happy to stick with the 'hide in plain sight method'. It remains his call.'

'*Fair enough! I'm glad you've at least considered it. I'll get on and call this Alice sheila and see what she has to say. I'll call as soon as I have anything to report. Stay low, Harry. Bye now.*'

'Cheers, Greg and thanks mate.'

GREG JAMES, SOUTHPORT, MONDAY

'*...This is Alice. Who is this please, and how did you get this number?*'

'Hi Alice. My name is Greg James and I'm an Inspector with the Queensland Police in Southport. I've been given your private number and asked to act as a contact person by a person you know very well, and to verify that I have really been in contact with this person, I've been told to repeat some excerpts from a happening at your workplace some time back. May I proceed?'

'*Very well, Inspector. Convince me if you can, but you have just 30 seconds before I hang up!*'

He chuckled, 'If I can't convince you in 30 seconds with this story, I'll hang up and save you the trouble.'

'*25-seconds, Inspector.*'

'Bloody hell Alice! OK, here it is. On the 24th of November last year, a Chinese Trade Delegation was due within minutes; dip spilled on the crotch of the Boss's pants and you and Charlie cleaned it off while the subject stood around in green budgie-smugglers. Now, how did I do?'

'*OK. That's something only three people know, so I have to accept it came from Charlie. But I need to know how you got involved!*'

'That's fair. I know where your Boss is now, because of the two people who now constitute his protection detail. One happens to be a fellow Police Inspector and the other, a very good friend who is an Australian Commonwealth Police under-cover operative. Charlie has asked me to act as a communications link for you to covertly pass on any information you may have or come across which concerns any attempts to find the Boss or talk of doing him harm. Specifically, one group may have been associated with the recent events in WA that concerned attempts to overturn the Australian system of Government. A second group may be the source of the finances which funded the abortive coup, since there are active efforts underway to trace and confirm the source of that funding.'

'*You are privy to top-secret information, Inspector, some of which even I didn't know. As I'm prepared to do what you ask, the only news I can add to what you know, is there are stories coming from street informers, that a small group of powerful business people with close ties to the Opposition Party, have issued a contract for the timely demise of our subject. We have also heard a newly-established security company who calls itself the peculiar name, 'Stainless Associates', may have accepted* the contract for a fee which is rumoured to be around twenty million dollars!'

Greg was silent for a few moments before asking, 'I don't suppose you've heard who is the boss of this 'Stainless Associates'?'

'Not his full name; just that he calls himself, 'Mr Xavier'.'

Greg felt a sudden chill and was silent for a bit longer, then said decisively, 'Before we make contact again, I need you to buy two or three, pre-paid basic mobile phones, no frills, and use one to text me the number. Don't discuss any of this business with anybody using this phone, which will only be used for personal communication. It can be intercepted and may be in the very near future. Only use the pre-paid mobile for stuff to do with the Boss. Oh, and I've been asked by Charlie to say that you are to pass most of the Boss's stuff to the Deputies. Only the most important things should be passed on to her via myself. That's all we should say for now until you get those anonymous mobiles. Bye.'

He hung up without waiting for an answer, fingers crossed that she would get at least one 'burner' phone and contact him on that.

He immediately got online to the database that listed the status of all convicted and incarcerated prisoners and was appalled to see that Terry 'Xavier' Johnson had won his appeal against his sentence due to 'irregularities in obtaining evidence' and had been released four months ago.

Another search under the heading of 'Investigation Services' showed that 'Stainless Associates' was a new listing with its head office in Melbourne, and offered 'First Class' discrete investigations at all levels; Missing Persons a speciality; Bodyguard Services by trained ex-Military and ex-Police Force members.

With a sigh, he reached for the phone again.

CHAPTER 28

We had just finished a lovely feed of BBQ lamb chops with fresh vegies, smothered with real lumpy gravy and finished off with a perfect apple crumble and fresh cream that Charlie whipped up, when the SatPhone sounded off again.

With Sandy's direction, I wiped the last spot of cream off my chin and grabbed for it.

'Hi again Greg. You're working late.'

'I made contact with Alice as requested and all's OK with her, but she passed on some bad news.'

'Go ahead. I'm sitting down.'

'It seems the political group you punched in the nose have put out a contract on your guest. But wait, there's more! The contract is for $20 million and has been taken up by an old friend by the name of Terry Johnson, aka Mr Xavier!'

'Bullshit! That prime turdburger is locked up tight.'

'Not any more. He got out four months ago on appeal over 'irregularities in obtaining evidence'. It sounds like he's picked up those of his old crew who aren't locked up and set up the same business under the name of 'Stainless Associates'.'

'Rude prick! Still, he always was a cunning bugger and knew how to trace people. If he's only had the contract a short time, we may still be a few jumps ahead. But that's bad news all right and not what I wanted to hear. OK Greg, thanks for that and keep the contact with Alice alive. We need info as soon as it happens.'

'Will do, Harry. Take care.'

I re-joined the crew and brought them up-to-date. Sandy well remembered Mr Xavier and the ruthless band of killers he employed who gave us such a hard time while chasing us all around Bass Strait and Southern Victoria three operations ago.

'I really don't like that man,' she said, 'he's cunning like a fox and doesn't give up. If he does manage to get onto our tail, we're going to have to do some quick shuffling to get away!'

Both Andy and Charlie looked somewhat alarmed.

'That's a sizeable contract price,' Andy said with a lop-sided grin. 'I've always wanted to know what I'm worth.'

'Bugger all if they really do nail us!' I replied. 'He might use ex-coppers and defence force dropouts, but they're scum who were kicked out for nasty behaviour. There's not a single redeeming feature amongst the lot of them. This Xavier character also likes to throw money at situations, so if we are found, expect to be hit with everything. Still, we shan't worry about that until it happens. So, if we stick to the plan, we're going to be very hard to find as well as having a good time.'

That bold statement drew a round of heartfelt applause, following which, we introduced Charlie and Andy to the delights of an NQ tea or two for a night cap and sent the off-watch to bed. I shared the watch with Charlie, while Sandy had Andy and Gilbert. We tried to let Andy have a good night's sleep, but he insisted on doing his bit and really enjoyed the different routine. As I expected to be at our first stopover island by morning, one night of broken sleep wasn't a big hardship.

TUESDAY

Sandy woke me at midnight and told me the kettle was hot as she pulled her clothes off and climbed into bed. She didn't seem to notice or care that Gilbert was passing through as she tossed everything in a heap on the small seat against the side of the hull, and I saw the gleam of approval in Gilbert's eyes as she climbed up into the elevated bed.

I had wondered several times about Gilbert's sexual persuasion, as he'd seemed indifferent around the ladies up till now, but seeing him appreciate Sandy's naked body was perhaps a sign that he was heterosexual. I made another mental note to ask her opinion about Gilbert's persuasion next morning.

Charlie and I spent a quiet watch with only the sails up and no engine running. We were due at the island just after dawn, so there was no rush and the light but steady night breeze kept us moving at around 10 knots. I learned more about Andy and also a little bit more about herself. Getting right to the point, I asked, 'It seems to me in the job you have, there wouldn't be much time for personal relationships?'

She laughed, 'No, there's not. So, I grab what I can. One-night stands are the rule, unfortunately. I've had a few live-in boyfriends, but they don't last because they can't take me getting a call in the middle of the night, or anything else for that matter, and having to rush off to do something for the Boss.'

She chuckled again. 'My trusty vibrator usually gets a good workout!'

Absently, I said without really thinking, 'I suppose it wouldn't do you any harm to try some of this interesting herbal paste we've collected in our travels?'

'What paste is that?'

'It's made by the islanders from the leaves of a bush that grows exclusively on their island and apparently it has quite remarkable properties. They sell small quantities at high prices to an exclusive market in SE Asia. Corrine has tried it and says it is a strong pain-reliever, a rapid healing agent, especially for bruises, and damaged muscles from sprains. The other effect seems to be that it is a powerful aphrodisiac! Sandy and I gave it a go and it was, well... dramatically effective for a long time!'

Charlie laughed, 'That really does sound interesting. Have you got some?'

'Yep! Why, do you really want to try it?'

She looked around, 'It's a quiet night, so why not. It can't be harmful if they've been selling it.'

I shrugged, thinking it might liven up a slow watch watching Charlie check out the stuff that Sandy and I had already tried, to our great satisfaction. 'OK. I'll go get the jar.'

I found it in a drawer in our cabin. Sandy sleepily asked, 'Whatcha doing?'

'Charlie wants to try some green-goo. Might be interesting!'

She gave a small laugh, 'I'd say it'd be more than just interesting and if I wasn't quite so sleepy and warm, I'd come and have a look, but I'll settle for a full report in the morning.'

'OK. Back to sleep my sweet.'

'Yes boss.'

I took the jar and returned to the cockpit, patting Jasper on the way. With Gilbert in his normal bed, he'd taken to sleeping on the dining table seats although he could have slept in with him at any time. Krazy cat had long ago adopted the chart table as her perch and bed.

I unscrewed the cap of the jar and let Charlie have a sniff, the familiar pungent aroma apparent as soon as the cap loosened and I experienced the slight light-headedness I'd felt before.

'Wow! That's a strong smell, but it's strangely pleasant,' she commented, 'so what do I do? I don't have to rub it on my very personal spots, do I?'

I laughed, 'No, you don't have to. Although Corrine says you can if you want the effect to be even stronger, but just behind each ear is a good starting spot and only with quite a small amount.'

She gingerly dipped a fingertip into the jar and smeared some behind each ear where the skin is able to absorb it into the bloodstream more readily. I capped the jar and sat back to watch and note the effects so I could tell Sandy.

After a couple of minutes, Charlie reported, 'Those spots have become quite warm and there's a pleasant, tingling feeling slowly spreading out from each side.'

A minute later, with a giggle, she said, 'That tingling is spreading down my chest and it's starting to feel really pleasant!'

I could see how her chest was feeling pleasant, but when she saw me checking out the bumps in her shirt, she just giggled. 'I did say! It really does feel...really... very... oh, my... good!'

I was intrigued to see that she was starting to fidget and looked like she didn't know where to put her hands. She rubbed her palms on her thighs several times and scratched her belly.

'My goodness me, Harry! This is quite an amazing experience for me. I'm always quite shy and retiring in a social setting, and never get drunk and do crazy things, but my skin is jumping so much, I need to do something. Would you mind if I took my shirt off?'

She didn't wait for my reply and quickly stripped her shirt off, followed by her bra! I smiled at her. 'Of course not, dear lady. You can do whatever you want to when you're here with us. No recriminations, no storytelling. What happens on the boat... etcetera!'

'Thank heavens for that!' she said, sitting back, her hands now cupping and rubbing her nicely rounded boobies which suited her slightly chubby body, but nevertheless stripped down very well.

'Where is the tingling feeling now?' I asked, trying to distract her.

'Oh, that! It's down in my crotch, naturally enough, so before I make a fool of myself, I'm going to have to go to my cabin for a few minutes. Just talk amongst yourself for a few minutes, if you don't mind.'

Out of curiosity, I asked, 'Just out of curiosity, if you weren't worried about making a fool of yourself, what would you do?'

She looked at me and said bluntly, 'I'd take my pants off and try to convince the nearest handsome, virile man to do the same, then join me on that lovely big daybed for some internal massage therapy!'

I laughed at her honesty. 'I'd love to oblige, but just for the moment, perhaps you should stay with Plan A and go below for a break.'

She jumped to her feet and gave me a long passionate kiss which almost had me heading for the daybed, but I resisted and let her go with a fond pat or two on her backside in parting.

Minutes later, the lack of engine noise allowed the buzz from the stern cabin to float up through the open hatch along with Charlie's summary of the effects of the green-goo on the inhibitions of middle-aged females.

It was more like twenty minutes before she was back, flushed in the face, but obviously more settled.

'Shit Harry! That stuff's dynamite! I mean one reads the wild claims which are made for aphrodisiacs and it seems like none really work, but that stuff is pure gold. How much is a jar worth?'

'The Asian market has been paying $750 for it, but under the new distribution system, new stock will be $500 per jar.'

Her eyebrows lifted. 'So just now I had a ten to fifteen dollar hit.'

I grinned. 'Yep. Something like that! But the cost doesn't matter so long as it works. It seemed to work well for you, from what I could hear.'

She grinned delightedly. 'Oh, did it work? And it still is, I have to say, but the sensation has eased off slightly! I truly didn't think it would do anything, but it blew me away, along with my inhibitions. I've never taken my top off like that before.'

I gently reminded her that not only was she still topless, but she'd left her shorts down below, although the pair of pink panties which clung precariously low on her hips, sort of preserved a tiny smidgen of modesty.

She glanced down, giggled and made no attempt to cover herself any further. 'Doesn't worry me. Does it worry you? No? Then fuck it! They can come off too. Let's see how long it'll take before I feel the need to get dressed!'

As she dragged the panties off and flicked them aside, I smiled at this alternate Charlie, no longer the PPS to the PM, but a pretty lady who'd temporarily parked her inhibitions in her bedside table and was having a wonderful time!

If it could shake Charlie out of her normal strictly-controlled attitudes to the extent that she was happy to take her clothes off and proposition someone she didn't know all that well, this was an excellent testimony for that part of the product's attributes!

'How about I put the kettle on?' she said brightly. 'That might help settle me down.'

'How do you feel right now?' I asked, 'I mean, does it make you feel uncomfortable?'

She laughed as she got up to go inside, happy for me to be eyeing her body off. 'Uncomfortable? Hell no! I feel great! Probably the best I've felt in years. It's just a good, happy feeling. Oh, and I still feel very horny too!'

She was out shortly with two mugs of tea and thoughtfully laid a towel out before she sat and asked about the origin of the green goo. I saw no problem with telling her that Jill and Roger were the new distributors and that hopefully supplies would be more regular.

She nodded thoughtfully. 'In my circles, that stuff would sell like hot dogs at a footy match, so if they want to, we can talk about discrete advertising.'

'That'll be a big help and I'm sure they'll take up your offer, but remember, it's a legal herbal ointment which also has remarkable healing properties.'

'Yeah. Good point. There's no need to be too stealthy about it.'

We chatted about this and that for another 30 minutes, before she gave a little shudder and started to put her clothes back on, to my great pleasure as I've always enjoyed watching ladies dressing. Although the undressing bit is more exciting what with the anticipation thing and all that.

'Starting to wear off?' I asked as she tucked herself into her bra and pulled her shirt over the top.

She grinned and shook her head. 'No way! Still there, but I was getting a bit cool in the breeze, that's all. There's still a wet patch on the towel and it wasn't getting any smaller!'

I laughed with her, enjoying her ribald sense of humour in her affected state, then checked the time and saw that as it was 05:00, it had been nearly two hours since she'd first rubbed it on. That was also just an hour until the change of watch. As we were almost on the Equator, there was almost no difference in the length of day and night, so dawn tended to occur around 06:00.

After a careful check around visually and on radar, we brewed two more mugs of tea and while Charlie took one to Andy, I took one to Sandy. Unfortunately, it became quite cold while I relieved my arousal and frustrations to Sandy's great delight, as she considered a couple of big 'O's' to be the best way to start the day. I had to agree and was grateful Gilbert didn't do a walk through. Or maybe he did and I just didn't notice.

CHAPTER 29

THE ISLAND, FLORES SEA, TUESDAY

We tried not to take too long away from the cockpit, but when got cleaned up and presentable, Gilbert was on watch, grinning happily when he saw us, indicating that he was happy for us. Andy wandered out shortly after and I presumed Charlie had taken herself to bed. I stayed up to make sure we made the expected landfall although there were rain showers about and visibility was poor, however the radar plot showed our island just 5 miles ahead. The chart showed it to be small and uninhabited; just a palm-tree covered dot in the ocean with white sandy beaches and a gap in the fringing reef on the south-east corner.

The island was shaped like a sharply-curved boomerang with the hollow part on the north side so the two arms gave good protection from the west, east and south, while the fringing reef cut the swell to near zero.

At 08:10, *Firebird* made the run in through the gap in the reef, with all sails furled and both engines running hard to stem the ebbing tide rushing out through the deep and narrow entrance. *Seeker* had a much easier time on our tail as we carefully motored around the lagoon in water so clear it looked as though it was only a metre deep, although the depth sounder promised that the real depth was more than 4 metres.

We were able to nose up close to a beautiful, white sandy beach, dropping the lightweight stern anchor on the way in, then the main bow anchor. Backing down to set it, we ended up held securely between the two, just metres off the beach and bow in.

Our guests were utterly delighted to see such a beautiful place, even on an overcast and gloomy day. 'Stunning, Harry!' Andy exclaimed, stretching his arms out. 'Is it safe to go swimming? The humidity must be near 100%!'

'Sure Andy, it should be but I'll just have a look around. I won't be long.'

Nothing untoward showed on the camera scan, including armed locals in long canoes, so I gave Andy the thumbs up and he leapt in. Charlie wasn't too far behind him, hoping I guess, the water would dampen the lust that was still surging through her bloodstream. She'd changed into a bikini which seemed to work pretty well for an older lady a little on the chubby side, but who was definitely worth a second or third look!

Gilbert and Sandy came up from below together, Sandy giggling at something Gilbert must have signed or done, and followed the other two over the side. I thought I'd keep watch for any lurking 'men in grey suits', so I dug my Grizzly pistol out from its concealed little locker under the helm station.

With the radar set to perform a 30-second sweep every ten minutes and the proximity alarm set, I felt comfortable we had some early-warning system in place. I strolled around the deck, scanning for any movement other than the four bodies off our sterns. Dave had parked *Seeker* alongside as usual and had rafted up. Corrine, Jill, Roger, Bree and Alex were in the water as well, splashing around, laughing and generally making enough fuss to attract any sharks if they were around, so I stayed extra vigilant and climbed up onto the saloon roof to get a better view.

Up there I was looking down on the swimmers and noticed Gilbert and Sandy were staying close together, and Charlie was chatting with the big man Alex, although Bree seemed to have him well under control, so that wasn't going anywhere. Finally, and without any unwelcome visitors, the swimming party slowly broke up as they left the water one by two, until just Sandy and Gilbert were left, hanging onto the stern platform together. Andy and Charlie were in the cockpit, chatting and drying off while *Seeker's* crew were doing the same next door.

Sandy was giggling and Gilbert smiling as they continued to hang onto the stern swim ladder and I suddenly realised it was a curiously intimate scene. So as not to intrude, I stayed back from the edge of the cockpit roof, just keeping them in sight. I could see that Sandy's face had a devilish grin on it which I knew from experience meant she was doing something of a deviate nature. Then I noticed that while she was holding on with one hand, the other was down between them. She seemed to be doing a lot of giggling and talking, but then tossed her head back and gave a delighted laugh. I couldn't see Gilbert's face, but his body language was fairly unmistakable. Very soon after that, Sandy backed off, waved her hand back and forth in the water between them a few times, then climbed out, leaving Gilbert by himself to paddle around, no doubt waiting for his body condition to return to normal.

I went down to meet Sandy and hand her a towel after she'd rinsed off with the freshwater shower. It was obvious she was aroused as I handed over the towel with a big grin.

Speaking softly, I said, 'You're a cheeky lady! If I didn't know better, I'd say that you just gave Gilbert a hand-job!'

She giggled again and kissed me. 'Of course, I did, and he's an amazing man! I'll tell you about it later, but for now, how about some breakfast?'

I kissed her back, then scraped a something off her shoulder and flicked it overboard. 'Great idea. Then you can tell me all about your devious plans!'

She smiled, but shook her head, 'Nope! No devious plans, I'm afraid.'

'Really?'

'Yes, really!' She gave me an enigmatic smile as she hung up the towel and headed for the galley, Charlie in tow.

After breakfast, we adjourned to our cabin for a little talk. 'OK,' I opened with, 'tell me Gilbert's story.'

So she did, starting with his home island near New Guinea; how it was a tribal custom to cast off all the exceptionally well-endowed men once they had fully developed; the string of rejection by other tribes and Islanders, then finally ending up with another outcast in Mikhail, who was the first person to help him by sending him to be educated and giving him a purpose in life as well as steady employment.

I shook my head in wonder. 'All this drama in his life started because his cock was too big?'

'Crudely put, as usual, Harry. But yes, that about sums it up.'

'And could I also crudely say that in his current situation he's suffering from acute sexual frustration because none of the indigenous girls can or will comfortably take him?'

She nodded, 'No, most can't comfortably, but the main reason for them being made outcast is the Headman in each village is wary of a pregnancy producing another super-stud male baby.'

'Bloody hell. What a fuckup! Ok, tell me this. You gave him a hand job so you're freshly qualified to tell me; is he really so big that it's a problem?'

She grinned excitedly, 'Oh, yes! Like you wouldn't believe! That trite phrase, 'hung like a horse' springs to mind. I mean, proportionally, he's no freak. It's not grotesque or anything like that; just very big!'

I thought a moment. 'Is he hoping that Caucasian females can handle him?'

She giggled, 'He already knows most can. Why do you think Jane was acting a bit odd the last couple of days she was with us? She bumped into him, literally, coming out of the shower and his towel slipped. That's when she told me she couldn't help herself. She said if she didn't, she would always be wondering what it would have been like!'

I grinned at her excitement which had started showing again and said, 'Do I see a big neon sign in giant capital letters that says, 'Sandy wants to go to bed with Gilbert to see what it would be like'? How's that for insight?'

She smacked me across the arm. 'Smart arse!'

'Well? Am I right?'

She drew a deep breath as if to object, then let it out before nodding. 'Yeah, you're right, but I'm not going to. I would never risk any damage to our very special relationship over this, even though I know you'd say you were happy with the idea, and obviously there were those times when we both had a bit of a fool around with several girl visitors over the last few years.'

I nodded understanding, 'That's a fair call and I won't try to say what I would have thought about it until it happened, so we'll let that slide. But now you're got Gilbert stirred up, is it going to be a problem?'

She nodded, 'Good question, even though I didn't suggest to him I wanted to go further, I do have a bit of a cunning plan. I thought I'd steer Charlie in his direction and vice versa!'

I chuckled at her deviousness, 'I'm sure that Gilbert would be delighted to take her on, but how will Charlie react to the suggestion?'

'Oh, I'm sure she will. From what you've told me about her reaction to the green goo, she'll be more than happy to. I'll have a girl-talk to her, so that will sort that out.'

'OK. But on account of your highly skilled right hand, maybe you'd better have that talk with her sooner rather than later! He is sleeping in our dressing room at the moment don't forget!'

She giggled, 'Good point. A stirred-up Gilbert would be a challenge. I'll go see Charlie now.'

I left her to her 'girl-talk' and went up top to check the weather since it sounded like the wind was blowing up a bit.

Up top, it was blowing up a lot, so I dialled the digital radar to weather mode and was rewarded with the picture of a red, amorphous blob, surrounded by a rainbow of colours.

'What's that telling you?' Andy asked, peering over my shoulder at the display. 'I've not seen a display like that before.'

I pointed to the screen, 'This is the new digital, pulse-compression, broadband radar. These circles are range markings in nautical miles and the coloured mass with the red centre is a strong thunderstorm with very heavy rain in the centre. The colours around it indicate diminishing rainfall intensity. It's 3-miles away, heading this way and will be here in about twelve minutes.'

He marvelled at the image for a moment, then asked the right question, 'Are we secure here?'

I nodded, 'Yep! We have a second anchor, but the one I've laid out is big, well-dug in and will hold us securely. I dropped it almost on the beach so the angle on the chain or scope, is nearly horizontal which will give the best holding power. We won't move, but it will be very noisy for a while. Excuse me while I secure everything outside.'

He came out with me to help and as we checked the lashings on items of deck gear and anti-chafe wraps on the anchor-chain bridle, I saw Dave doing the same on *Seeker*. I also lowered the sheet of copper attached to a length of thick copper cable into the water directly under the mast, so any lightning strike to the masthead would be passed hopefully harmlessly straight into the water.

I tossed the towels that were hanging in the cockpit into the saloon and called out to Sandy and Charlie to close their hatch. Charlie stuck her head up through the hatch to ask why as she was quite un-aware there was a storm coming. The grey murk surrounding us hid the monster quite effectively and it was only the rising wind ahead of it which sounded the alarm.

With everything secure on deck, I went back into the saloon where I set about stowing all portable electronic devices into the microwave oven, and a purpose-built shielded locker.

'What's that for, Harry,' Andy asked, setting himself comfortably at the dining table, Krazy cat preparing to curl up in his lap.

'Our mast is a giant lightning rod and there's a chance we'll get zapped. The oven and this locker will protect all the portable electronics from being fried by electromagnetic radiation. If you've got anything you want shielded, bring them up and I'll put them with the other stuff.'

He slid out from under Krazy's furry little bum and went to his cabin, returning a minute later to hand over two phones and an e-book reader.

Just then, a sharp increase in wind strength announced the imminent arrival of the monsoon-generated storm, the mast making its usual mournful droning that sounds almost supernatural in origin. Our anchorage was well-sheltered from this storm, although being covered in palm trees and not hills, we copped the full force of the wind that topped out at 55 knots in the stronger gusts. That was strong enough to make *Firebird's* rigging emit a high-pitched shriek which made Andy look concerned, even though he must have experienced his share of bad weather on the Sydney-Hobart races. Of greater concern were the stabbing tongues of lightning that repeatedly hit the island with tree-shattering force and grabbed everyone's attention!

And that was in addition to the utterly torrential rain that seemed, at times, as if we were parked under a waterfall. This was my first experience of boating in monsoon weather and it was an eye-opener. The storm took nearly 20-minutes to pass and we were lucky not to receive a direct lightning hit, although quite a few strokes impacted the water close by, the instantaneous clap of thunder frightening the girls and making our ears hurt!

I was interested to see the water boil at the point of the strike and I wondered why the mast was spared, while remaining thankful it was.

Then, as quickly as it had engulfed us, the black-hearted monster grumbled its way off across the water, now beaten as flat as a pancake by the rain, while still stabbing baleful strokes of vivid blue lightning at the uncaring sea. The sun broke out briefly through the still-roiling clouds, creating a haze of humidity you could almost cut with a knife. I heard *Seeker's* generator fire up and guessed that Dave had turned on the air-con, so I did the same.

But before I settled into the comfort of the dry, cool air, I decided to take the pussies ashore for a run and a play in the sand. This would be their first opportunity to have a run since we left Herba

Island and Jasper was letting me know. Charlie came with us, so while the cats peed, pooped and played in the wet sand, we explored some of the little island. The only sign of human activity was a rough palm frond hut tucked into a small grove of trees near the centre of the island.

'Probably just an overnight shelter for fishermen or coconut gatherers,' I surmised. 'There's nothing here for long term habitation like fresh water, so we shouldn't have any issues with visitors.'

Charlie didn't have much to say as we wandered about, finally returning to where the RIB was pulled up, the pussies still romping around close by, although as we sat on the inflated sides watching the feline play, she said, 'I want to thank you for being a gentleman last night when I was rather affected by the green-goo. I've never behaved like that in my life, but I have to admit I loved every minute of it. Absolutely amazing stuff! I might buy some off Roger and Jill.'

She took a deep breath and said, 'I can still feel the effects of it, but not very strong now, so Sandy's talk earlier was rather opportune.'

I had a brief visual flashback to my darling girl in the water with Gilbert, giving him a hand-job, but didn't vocalise that thought! Being the confidant on highly personal matters to a female who was a relative stranger wasn't my strong point, although I did chuckle and say lamely, 'Well, I'm glad she was helpful and I really hope it works out well for you.'

She smiled, somewhat hungrily I thought, and said 'I'll make sure it does!'

'Come on. We need to get back and for you to go and cool off!'

Charlie laughed while I rounded up the kitties, dusted the bulk of the sand off them and loaded them in the RIB. Back aboard, she washed the sand off her feet and went inside while I persuaded Krazy to hold still while I brushed half the beach out of her coat. Jasper was easier, having very short fur like a dog. I avoided hosing either of them off since the consequences of two cats shaking themselves dry over everyone in sight were not good.

I checked with Dave to see if there'd been any damage from the storm, but apart from a few large palm fronds landing on the foredeck, all was well, so I returned to *Firebird* took a shower on the stern then went into the air-con with just a towel around me.

CHAPTER 30

AN ISLAND IN THE FLORES SEA, WEDNESDAY

Since we'd had a very late breakfast, it had done duty as lunch, but I was still surprised to see the saloon was empty and dual sets of snoring sounds were coming from the port hull. I went below and found Sandy propped up in bed chatting with Gilbert who was sitting cross-legged at the foot of the bed. He started to get up when I came in, but I smiled and waved him back down, earning one of his charming smiles for my gesture. Sandy was still wearing her bikini and Gilbert had on swim trunks.

'Hi Hon,' she said. 'Are the pussies happy?'

I pulled my towel off and tossed it on the small seat against the hull before climbing up on to the bed where I lay like Sandy, propped up on the pillows, but under the sheet. 'Hi yourselves and yes, they are now. Much happier now. But Andy and Charlie have retired to quarters, and I gather from Charlie that everything is OK.'

She glanced at Gilbert briefly, smiled and said. 'Yep! Everything's sorted.'

'Excellent. In that case, you two carry on your discussion. I'm going to read this book I've been trying to get into for ages. It's supposed to be good and the author is Australian.'

I read while Sandy and Gilbert carried on their slightly awkward conversation, with lengthy pauses as Gilbert neatly wrote his side of things in his ever-present little notebook. Finally, and I missed Sandy's parting comments, Gilbert got up, tapped me on one foot in acknowledgement of my support, I presumed, and headed aft.

I looked at Sandy who was stripping her bikini off before slipping between the sheets. 'Is Gilbert making a house call?'

She giggled, 'Yep! It's a wonder that you didn't notice the huge bulge in his shorts! I don't know where he puts it all!'

'Well,' I said, putting my book down and turning to her, 'you may not know where he puts his but I know where I'm going to put mine!'

She giggled and delightfully accepted my offering, which took care of the rest of the afternoon.

As the light faded and Sandy seemed to have drifted off to sleep, I eased away from her, pulled the sheet up around her and left.

I poked around the cockpit for a few minutes, but the wind was still blowing and rain squalls were chasing through at regular intervals, so I put the kettle on. The noise brought Andy out of his cabin to have one with me. We sat around chatting and scratching the cats for quite a while, before Charlie and Gilbert joined us. Much to Andy's amusement we watched them come up from the same cabin.

Gilbert was his usual silent, affable self, while giving no indication of their earlier activities, but Charlie, while not saying much, had a satisfied smile on her face that just wouldn't go away.

The squalls eased off a little as the evening folded in around our snug little anchorage, although the area forecast suggested tomorrow morning would be clear and sunny, but storms would again be a feature in the afternoon. With that prediction in mind, I hopped across to see Dave on *Seeker*.

'Gidday mate,' he greeted me, 'I was just coming over to see if you wanted to join us for dinner? Bree has whipped up roasted, marinated chicken legs and wings with bickies and dip and stuff. Finger food, really but she does a terrific marinade!'

I grinned, 'Excellent! That girl's a bloody marvel in the galley. I'm so glad we kidnapped her.

Anyway, they've all been asleep over my way, but I think everyone's awake now. I'll tell them in a moment, but I was looking at the forecast and thought we should stay here as long as we can, since it seems to give good protection from these storms.'

He agreed, 'Yeah. Might as well and it saves fuel.'

'OK. With that in mind, how about we whip everyone into action in the morning and have a bottom scrub session? Apart from the usual helping with speed and fuel efficiency, we don't want to be carting Indonesian barnacles back to Aussie. Remember that outbreak at Eden?'

'Yeah, I do, mainly because it's where you got involved with Janice, Angie and Zoe. And that led to us staying out of jail and getting our grubby mitts on the first *Seeker*!'

'Not to mention a fortune in cash and jewels from Xavier's stash. It's just as well you've changed boats. Now he's free and on the warpath again, he just might be looking for the boat and his stash!'

Dave nodded soberly, 'Yeah. We were talking about that earlier. He's not just going to ignore the loss of so many millions. Maybe hanging around an un-named, uninhabited little island in Indonesia would be a good place to hide for a while.'

'Amen, brother! I'll go call the crew to table.'

I sent them across to *Seeker* while I went to rouse Sandy. I found her just awake and trying to drag herself out of bed, so I told her dinner was on.

'Yum. I'm starving, but I need a shower first. I'm a bit sticky and smell of nookie!'

Now she mentioned it, there was a strong, musky reek to the air, so while she went aft to clean up, I opened the ports and hatches, letting the moist, humid evening air flush out the cabin. The air-con would have done the job eventually, but the fresh air was better. I made the bed while I was at it and laid out some clothes for her from the pile she'd left earlier.

Even though it was a simple feed, Bree had made it taste very special and a few drinks helped the evening pass pleasantly, with several rounds of NQ teas to smooth it off. I mentioned my plan for a bottom scrub on both boats and everyone was keen to get involved, especially as it would help with speed if we had to run. Everyone was tired at the end of dinner, with little enthusiasm for staying up, so Dave and I decided to cancel the watch system and rely upon our radar alarms, my masthead camera which I set into auto-sweep, Infra-red and motion-detect modes. We also set our perimeter defence system, and I had a new and augmented controller for both boats which we hooked in and powered up.

On that note, we all went to sleep happy, sated and secure.

THURSDAY

I was up early as usual and was greeted on deck by Jasper, Krazy and a beautiful, clear sky which had the washed-out, pale blue colour which seems to occur after a tropical storm. The air was cooler than yesterday afternoon, the wind was calm, so the glassy smooth, crystal-clear water was very inviting. I took a good look around and still didn't see any predators, so dropped my shorts and dived in.

The water was like silk against my skin, almost too warm, but refreshing anyway. My splash must have alerted Charlie, because she appeared a few minutes later in her bikini and jumped in. She didn't take long to discover that I was naked and gamely decided to try it herself, although she carefully left her bikini on the boarding platform.

'Wow! That feels really great!' she enthused. 'I must admit, I've never swum naked before. It feels really good!'

Naturally, I got an erection, but if she noticed it, she was too polite to say anything. Or perhaps compared to Gilbert, mine was nothing to even comment on! I made another mental note to subtly try to see what all the fuss was about.

We paddled around in the cleansing water, before getting out and drying off, Charlie dressed in her bikini again and settled in a cockpit seat while I went into the galley where Sandy was making a big pile of scrambled eggs.

She kissed me, and then said with a grin. 'Did Charlie enjoy skinny-dipping? I don't think she's done anything like that before.'

I grinned back, 'Yeah. She did, and you're right, it was the first time. But then she hasn't had Gilbert in her bed before either!'

'True. Someone distracted me, so I didn't get to find out how it went, but maybe she'll tell me today.'

I smiled. 'Fair enough. Those eggs look good.'

By the time everyone had messed around doing this and that, it was almost lunchtime before we managed to chase everyone into the water for the big bottom clean. Dave and I had dug out the scrapers and scouring pads, as well as the Hookah captive breathing gear. Both boats had an electric motor-driven compressor with a small reservoir, and two 50-metre hoses with full-face mask and regulator sets. Once we got them moving, everybody wanted to get wet, but we needed a shark watch, so Alex volunteered to do first stint, armed with the H&K MP5. Andy and I donned the Hookah gear and did the bottom bit on *Firebird*, while Sandy, Charlie and Gilbert kept their heads above water and scraped the upper sections. Jasper couldn't resist having so many bodies in the water at once and jumped in, swimming from boat to boat and head-butting every bum he could get to.

That little trick was enough to get everyone laughing and really enjoying themselves, so the work went quickly and easily.

I did see Charlie and Sandy with their heads together several times, and there were several pointed looks cast at Gilbert, who just smiled back wherever he caught one of them.

After a while, Dave got out and relieved Alex on shark watch so he could have a swim and Sandy and Bree got out long enough to make up a huge pile of sandwiches they laid out on *Seeker's* stern board, along with a bucket of Pina Coladas which went down dry throats way too easily. The float I normally used for holding painting and cleaning stuff, was pressed into service to hold the leftover food and the bucket of cocktail.

It was moved, along with the party, into the shade under *Firebird*, which was a lovely place to escape the glaring sun and toward the bows, was just shallow enough to stand. Over to the southeast, however, the afternoon monsoon clouds were starting to pile up into huge billowing masses which looked solid enough to walk on. They were building so quickly, that even at a long distance, one could see the roiling masses pushing upwards into the cooler upper air where they gained additional buoyancy and surged aloft even faster! That level of atmospheric activity was the sign we were in for another round of storms during the afternoon, so it was just as well we had done the work and had the R & R party underway early.

I swam inshore along the anchor chain to check how well the anchor was buried and was pleased it had performed superbly yet again by burying itself deeply out of sight and not moving since our arrival. I checked *Seeker's* on the way back and it was just as secure. The party under *Firebird* was still gathering steam as the level in the bucket of Pina Coladas lowered, and all the ladies started shedding their bikini tops, Jill and Charlie included. I was pleased to see Charlie parking herself beside Gilbert and chatting happily. She even knew some ASL signs, which helped communication considerably, and they seemed to be getting on well.

I moved up beside Sandy and said softly, 'I notice Charlie is staying latched onto Gilbert, so I presume all went well?'

Sandy laughed. 'Yes. Apparently very well. I'd told her Gilbert was hung like a horse, and warned her that he looked rather awesome at first sight, but unless she was particularly small, I was sure she'd have no problems and lots of fun!

She didn't tell too many tales, but said that my initial assessment was pretty accurate, and he was very gentle and considerate.'

She giggled. 'She did say though, he has amazing stamina and added something about needing rubber sheets!'

'Suffice to say then, both are happy with the arrangement.' I chuckled. 'We might even get our dressing room back.'

She nodded. 'That'd be good and Jasper can have his bed back.'

'Well done my dear lady! They make a lovely pair. Anyway, this afternoon looks like being a repeat of yesterday by the look of the storms building up so we might have to take to our bed! Do you think you could cope with that?'

She grinned, 'Gee. That would be terrible! Whatever would we do? Have you got any good books to read?'

'Ha, ha! Very funny! Here, have a top-up of Pina Colada. Obviously you're not pissed enough yet; you've still got your pants on!'

CHAPTER 31

Promptly at 14:00, heavy, threatening clouds totally blocked the sunlight. Dave and I moved out from underneath *Firebird* to eyeball the approaching storm and it looked like it was going to be almost a repeat of yesterday's effort. The main cloud mass was just a few miles away and seemed to be tracking straight for us again; vicious forks of lightning stabbing spitefully at the water as if practicing what they were going to do to the island and our two puny boats.

We broke the party up and sent everyone back to their respective boats to check that every loose item was secured and all hatches closed. There was a queue for the stern shower, but since it was only to wash the salt off, each one didn't take long. I saw Andy, with a bit of a glow on, admiring Sandy's naked body as she climbed aboard, not having bothered to put her bikini back on. He also checked out Charlie fairly closely, although she did have hers on and had Gilbert closely in tow. With little else to distract him these days, I wondered how long he'd want to stay celibate in the erotic and exotic atmosphere which boats and the tropics generate so easily. The lack of any un-attached females might slow him down a bit!

The permanent undercurrent of sensuality was something most land-bound persons, with the pressures and distractions of the teeming activity surrounding them all the time, don't really understand, since you had to be on a boat and away from land to appreciate it.

I went forward and lowered the heavy copper earth plate into the water below the mast, then went aft to help Sandy stow the party left-overs and the cleaning gear. We'd not quite finished the task when the storm hit. It was a teeth-rattler all over again and

270

I suddenly remembered Charlie hadn't given me her phones and tablet to secure in the EMP-proof locker, so I hastily went below into the port hull and knocked on her door.

I thought I heard her call out and opened it in time to see a naked Charlie just about to become extremely well acquainted with Gilbert all over again. That seemed a good point to back out, although with all the noise from the storm, I don't think they would have noticed if the full ASO paraded through the cabin playing the 'Colonel Bogey March'.

The storm was a virtual copy of yesterday's effort, even down to the fact we escaped being struck by lightning yet again. The wind was just as strong and gusty, but the anchor and gear held us steady. Twenty minutes later, the wind suddenly dropped, the rain diminished slowly to a soft drizzle and the crews retired to their cabins. Except for Charlie and Gilbert who were way ahead of us.

Sandy giggled, 'Charlie seems to be trying to make up for years of nothing much, all in a few days!'

'Good luck to her if she can do it all with Gilbert. That might let you and me get re-acquainted.'

And we did just that while the dull, rainy and humid afternoon slid uneventfully into a wet evening. The exercise and the cocktails had knocked everyone down, so there was only a bit of grazing for tea by those who felt hungry enough, followed by an early night.

SATURDAY

I'm normally up at dawn, but my faithful furry alarm system woke me ten minutes early by gently chewing on my foot, then batting my face with a huge paw. I came awake, aware of the huge black mass of Jasper sitting beside my head, paw poised in case I closed my eyes again. I listened and thought that I could hear a faint squeaking noise over Sandy's soft snores, so I pushed him away and rolled reluctantly out of bed.

Our re-acquaintance had been lengthy and extremely pleasant, so sleep had been in short supply. I fumbled through the pile of assorted clothes on the cabin sole for my shorts.

Jasper led the way up top, where I disarmed the electrified safety rail system, before venturing into the cockpit. There was the first hint of pearlescent light in the east, heralding the daily arrival of the sun, as Jasper trotted down the starboard stern steps where he lay down and gave a loud 'Merowl'! Nothing seemed to happen, so he repeated it several times until a large black and white snout rose silently from the water right beside the boarding platform, nearly touching Jasper's foot in the process.

Never having seen one up close before this, I didn't immediately recognise the baby orca for what it was, but then images clicked into place, of the black upper half of the massive jaw, white lower half and an oval white patch just behind each huge, expressive eye that was regarding me with obvious interest.

Jasper mewled with delight to see his new playmate up close and patted the glistening white under snout with one paw. The baby orca, a fully paid-up member of the dolphin family and not a whale at all, seemed equally pleased to see Jasper and opened his or her mouth to utter a rapid series of clicks, squeaks and squeals. Like a dolphin, it also seemed to be grinning at its new human friend. The cockpit fridge had some baitfish stored, so I broke open a 2 kg pack and returned to the stern to stand beside Jasper.

From remembered images of Orcas, I realised this was either a growing baby or a very young juvenile and wondered where Mum and Dad were. The Orca seemed quite comfortable to have me stand beside his or her head and when I opened the pack of fish a bit more, it opened its mouth wider, exposing an impressive set of gleaming, white teeth and fired off a set of squeaks and clicks that sounded like it was excited.

I tipped the bag into the gaping maw and with one gulp and a blast of fishy breath, the two kilos disappeared. The baby orca slid back into the water and cruised back and forth a few times, the distinctive, tall, slender black fin standing up proudly. I had read that male orcas had a tall, straight tapered fin, while the female's fin was curved back more like a shark. The article had gone on to say in juveniles, the difference was not so obvious, so I thought that we'd have to wait to see if our visitor cared to roll over and let us see if we could pick the difference that way.

Meantime, baby orca was still swimming back and forth, lifting its head clear of the water and calling in a manner that strongly suggested I should go get more food! Jasper joined in with a mewl or three it seemed to reply to, so I took the hint and fetched out three packs of fish, thankful they weren't frozen. Tearing the packs open, I scattered the fish in a steady stream into the calm, clear water, marvelling at the speed and grace with which the orca darted in to grab most of the fish before they hit bottom, just 4-metres below.

After that feed, baby orca had a bit of a play around, then came back to the boarding platform and poked his head right up on the platform so about one third of his body was out of the water. He, and I had decided it was a he, nuzzled with Jasper, both of them vocalising in their own language, but knowing Jasper's history with wild creatures, they were probably communicating on a mental level as well.

I quickly walked for'rard and called down to Sandy through the deck hatch to come up and bring the video camera. Not waiting to see if she was moving, I hastened back to the stern where the two totally different creatures were still communing happily, but in silence this time. Krazy cat had joined Jasper and she was quite happy to sit beside her big brother and be inspected by their new friend.

Behind me I heard Sandy say, 'Why does Jasper always bring the strays home? Although I suppose at least we didn't have to feed that 26-foot crocodile up at Cape York, parked across Dave's stern board. I wonder where this little fella has come from?'

I looked at her, standing on the top step, wearing just a tiny pair of panties, obviously grabbed off the pile in haste, video camera recording the amazing scene in 4K resolution. She videoed some more, then Charlie appeared with Gilbert in tow, awakened by our voices.

'What's going on, guys? We heard the fuss.'

'Walk slowly and talk softly, please Charlie,' I said. 'We have a visitor and he and Jasper seem to be communicating.'

She and Gilbert moved quietly up to where they could see, Charlie giving a squeak of fright, while Gilbert made a sound like satisfaction, before signing slowly to Charlie who translated. She must have really been learning ASL from Gilbert and not just fooling around all the time!

'I think Gilbert is saying the orca is a young juvenile and has been separated from his mother. Maybe the storm last night did the job, but he needs her protection. We can feed him for a few days, but he needs to catch fresh fish himself and he's wary about going out past the reef into deep water. There are large sharks that would tackle a juvenile orca and maybe a rare saltwater croc would too, so we need to find his Mum.'

'How the hell do we do that?' I asked Gilbert, who went into a flurry of signing, prompting Charlie to tell him in no uncertain language to slow down while she worked out what he was saying. At that point, Andy wandered up on deck to see what was going on and Charlie had to explain to him, before she could tell us what Gilbert had said.

'Gilbert says the baby orca will eventually call his mother with his cries. They carry a long way in water. We just have to keep him safe until she turns up.'

'Great,' I muttered, 'how do we keep a ten-foot-long, 500kg juvenile orca safe until big Mumma shows up?'

Gilbert's hands flashed again, drawing another curse from Charlie.

'He says if we just keep feeding him, he'll stick around and it would be even better if we get in the water with him. They are sociable creatures and with your very special cat looking over him, the young orca will stay here until his mother comes.'

'Well. I guess that we'd better get fishing in that case. There are four more bags of fish there, but we'll need some for bait, so he can have three bags now and that should hold him for a little while.'

That started the great fishing expedition and we got the *Seeker* crew up and involved. Within the hour, both RIBs were manned with three persons each and out on the reef edge, lines over. Because baby orca wanted to hang around *Firebird* where Jasper was, we had to be careful where we dropped a line in case he snapped at a fish being reeled in. Sandy and I volunteered to jump in with Jasper, and Gilbert was right, he was delighted to have company. He swam around in tight circles, and then slowly nosed up to each of us in turn, poking us playfully but gently in the chest, or in the bum from behind with his big, blunt nose.

He then settled under Jasper and very gently rose to the surface, my big cat perched on his broad, gleaming back. Jasper looked absurdly pleased to be perched there and even more so when the orca with his head up so Jasper wouldn't wash off, slowly swam around Sandy and me, then around the two boats, before depositing him back at the boarding platform

He was extraordinarily gentle around us and let Sandy scratch him under the chin, something he clearly enjoyed. We left the water to be replaced by Charlie, Gilbert and Andy who commented, 'This can't be any worse than facing a hostile Senate!'

In fact, he seemed to enjoy himself enormously and splashed and wrestled with the baby orca as much as the others did.

We managed to keep two crew either in the water, or on the boarding platform at all times and the young orca seemed to like it.

Finally, the fishing parties returned with a generous catch of Snapper, Coral Trout, Grouper, Parrotfish and Wrasse.

'Can't miss with a baited line out there,' Dave boasted, 'our fingers were getting sore pulling so many in. I hope our new friend is hungry?'

I laughed, 'I think you'll find he is. Anyway, here he is now. Toss a few and find out.'

Sandy had named him Willie of course, so as he nosed up beside where Dave had pulled in, he was tossed a selection of beautiful fish of all varieties and they all went down into a seemingly bottomless pit. Twenty or thirty went that way before he gave a polite, but fishy burp and slid the upper half of his body back in the water, making *Firebird* lurch. After that feed, he seemed content to just swim around the two boats, stopping at times to slide up onto either *Firebird* or *Seeker's* stern to have a rest or just commune silently with Jasper, who was a constant companion, or to check out his new two-legged friends who gave him fish on demand. Dave, Alex and Roger set to filleting the remaining thirty or so big fish, carefully saving the carcasses and a few more whole ones for Willie.

Sandy had been on-line checking on, 'How to Care for your Pet Orca', or a similar bit of web nonsense but couldn't find anything to add to what Gilbert had already told us.

The morning drifted along in much the same way; some more fishing to feed Willy and to replenish our own stocks; some swimming to play with Willie; a trip to the island to let Jasper and Krazy have a run on the beach. Krazy spotted a lizard which scurried out of the sun and into the shade and leaf litter, and set off in quick pursuit. She quickly discovered, however, that a lizard in its own environment is hard to catch, but by the time she'd made that discovery, she was well into the centre of the small island.

Fortunately, big brother Jasper had seen her run off and trotted along behind. He re-appeared with a black bundle of paws and legs dangling unceremoniously from his jaws which were clamped lightly onto the scruff of her neck.

The midday build-up of massive clouds was less than yesterday and looked as though we might be spared a storm.

When Sandy and I got back from the kitty run around lunchtime, Andy took me aside.

'It looks like we're going to be drifting around these islands for a while, doesn't it? I mean there's not been any new information from Alice for a few days.'

I nodded, wondering where this was going. 'Yes, you're right. We just don't know how quickly the investigation teams from Treasury and the ACP are moving on the dual problems. I don't want to risk chasing them up, so waiting is the only thing to do, as frustrating as that is!'

'I understand that, but my request is rather more self-motivated. I'd like my lady friend Lara, to join us. Apart from keeping me happy, she'll be an asset to the crew since she enjoys cooking and will be happy to help with housekeeping as well as being an excellent sailing hand. She's been on a couple of Sydney to Hobart races with me. I'd really appreciate it if you could set this up sooner rather than later?'

I thought a moment or two, seeing some problems being caused, but in the long run, keeping our main man calm, happy and comfortable counted for a lot.

'I don't have any problem with having her join us, Andy. The only issue is getting her here without attracting the wrong attention.'

He smiled, seeing the job all but done. 'That's easy. I'll have the RAAF VIP aircraft fly her into the nearest airport and we'll go pick her up.'

I think the horrified look on my face revealed my thoughts. 'What? What's wrong with that?'

I smiled gently to settle him down. 'That's the last thing we need to do, I'm afraid. There's a good chance she's already under some sort of surveillance, whether you're in town or not, so if the RAAF fly her out to anywhere, it's very high profile. Even the press monitors the movements of those aircraft, along with the Opposition, trying to prove how much of the taxpayer's money you're wasting by swanning around on junkets!'

His face fell. 'Oh. But how can we do this? I'd really like to have her here with me.'

'Don't worry. I'll work it out. Does she have a personal mobile reserved just for you?'

'Yeah. I had to set that up so we had secure comms. We mostly use the iPhone iMessage service I was told was pretty secure.'

'OK. That works for me. I'll work a few things out, then when I tell you, I'll get you to message her. You have a private code to identify yourself, I presume?'

He nodded, 'Yep. Sure do.'

'OK. I'll get onto it, but may I also presume she's free to travel at very short notice?'

'Yes. No trouble there.'

I left him and retired to my Operations Centre, the chart table I usually share with Krazy cat, where I got on-line and consulted several diverse websites, taking lots of notes. Finally, I called Greg James and told him to expect a call from a lady named Lara and to pass on to her the following information. I read it out carefully and had him repeat it all back. Once that was verified, I asked about the hunt for the money trail and the second group, headed by my former nemesis, Terry Xavier Johnson, chasing the PM.

'Nothing new, I'm afraid, Harry. Except that Xavier is driving his troops hard to find a sniff of your guest's whereabouts. For your ears only, I can say one of his men got so pissed off by the bullshit that Xavier churns out, that he's turned informer for the brownie points and some cash for now. I'll feed any Intel along as it comes through.

In the meantime, I'll wait to hear from this Lara lady and at the moment, I do not want to know who, what or why! Just tell me later.'

I dragged Andy away from a lively political chat session with Charlie, Sandy and Gilbert in the cockpit.

'OK. I'd like you to send a text to Lara, identifying yourself and asking her to immediately text Inspector Greg James of the Southport Police on this number. You can say she should be prepared to travel at very short notice exactly as per the instructions from Greg, and to pack minimal clothing. She can trust him implicitly.'

'When do I text her?'

I handed him the SatPhone and the code sheet for sending text messages, 'Right now! Tempus Fugit!'

He pasted a happy smile on his dial, didn't argue and got to work, fingers tapping, finally looking up with a grin. 'All done! When will we hear if that's worked?'

'Hopefully, in about fifteen minutes, but now I need to warn Dave he's got a run to make.'

There was no secret to be kept, so I told Dave and the others that, God and the Indonesian Domestic Airlines system willing, a new crew member would be joining us on Monday afternoon.

'You need to do a run, please mate, to the island of West Nusa Tenggara and the city of Sumbawa Besar. There's a river with a wharf just inside the mouth which looks accessible for *Seeker* and by taxi. It's at the end of a narrow street called Jalan Kampung Padak. Her aircraft gets in at 16:30, so if all goes well, Lara will be there around 17:00.'

'I'll go and meet her,' Andy spoke up.

'Uh, uh!' was my reply. 'There's no way you can afford to be seen in public, even in a foreign city. There are way too many tourists. You can't leave here, I'm afraid.'

Dave said soothingly. 'That's all right Andy. I'll go myself and meet her at the airport if you can get me a photo or image of her and write out a note recognisably from you. Say she should trust me and do what I say.'

He nodded acceptance, 'OK. Thanks Dave. I'll download her photo and do a note.'

With that in hand, I told Dave, 'The distance to the wharf from here is about 68-nautical miles, so depending on sea-state, two hours each way should pull it up for you. I don't know about refuelling facilities. Nothing is obvious and un-official stuff could be contaminated.'

'I won't bother refuelling,' he replied. 'We haven't used very much and keeping the speed down on this run will help even more.'

'OK, thanks Dave.'

Over a lovely roast lamb dinner that Charlie and Bree had whipped up, I updated everyone with the latest news on the search, although I left out the news that Greg now had an informer in Xavier's camp, planning to tell Sandy, Corrine and Dave privately.

A couple of my now infamous NQ teas each, created a mellow mood and with Willie announcing his presence by making his usual clicks and squeals around the boats on a regular basis, we talked through the usual diverse range of subjects which a group of adults from such a wide variety of backgrounds normally will.

It was getting late when I announced I was tired and headed for bed. I fed the kitties, set the radar proximity alarm and the perimeter defence system and went to bed with fingers crossed that the events I'd set in motion wouldn't bring the bad guys down upon us and spoil the mood in our idyllic little world.

CHAPTER 32

LARA, CANBERRA, SATURDAY AFTERNOON

In the Australian capital city of Canberra, in the upmarket suburb of Yarralumla, a neat and unpretentious house was tucked away from casual scrutiny by a thick band of tall and lush privacy bushes. The curving street was lined with classic Australian eucalypt trees which were highly decorative until they shed bark everywhere and dropped the occasional massive branch on a parked car, seeming to remind visiting humans they were intruding on Nature and 'She' was not always happy.

Inside, a tall, slim attractive blonde woman in her early 40s and with a shapely and generous body shape, was rapidly packing some clothes and other odds and ends into a designer backpack and a soft Gucci overnight bag. She wore tight, pale-blue jeans and one of her favourite comfortable tops, a rough and baggy linen shirt in a burnt orange shade which was two sizes two big, with its tails hanging down to mid-thigh. The weather forecast was for fine conditions and 26°C for the next few days, despite the fact that autumn had arrived only a week earlier with a blast of icy wind from the south in typical blustery fashion as if to say, 'Here I am!'

Lara had been cleaning up after a simple sandwich for early lunch, when she was galvanised into action by the text message from her dear Andy, the hidden code phrase convincing her it was legitimate. As per Andy's instructions, the subsequent texting session with the unknown person called Inspector Greg James was a bit unnerving, but she dutifully followed the complex set of instructions he sent back. Finally, after double-checking she had her passport, plus the sizeable stash of spare cash she kept tucked away and her credit cards, she locked the little house and waited outside for the taxi. The trip to the airport wasn't long and as he easily negotiated the light Saturday afternoon traffic, she casually mentioned to the driver that she was going to the Gold Coast for a week's holiday.

With the taxi's radio blasting out the blow-by-blow description of the clash between the Canberra Raiders and the Penrith Panthers in Melbourne, she doubted if the driver heard a word she said, but he did manage to drop her at the Departures terminal just in time to catch her flight.

As instructed, she made no attempt to hide her movements and with no checked baggage, she quickly exited the terminal after the 90-minute flight to the Gold Coast Airport and took the first taxi to the Novatel Surfers Paradise Hotel, a high-rise, 4-star hotel pretty much right in the middle of Surfers Paradise, being just a half-block from Cavill Avenue. Of greater interest to Lara was that just 50 metres away down Beach Road to the west toward the Nerang River, lay the Interstate Bus Exchange.

Her room on the 11th floor was, nevertheless, very comfortable and showed signs it had been recently upgraded. Her balcony faced north with stunning views of the start of the Broadwater marine playground which stretched all the way to Moreton Bay and Brisbane. By leaning out slightly, she could also look down Beach Road to the Bus Exchange and the river beyond.

At 15:00, soon after she checked in, a tall, strikingly-attractive blonde, with long hair that hung down past her shoulder blades, and who moved with an almost feline grace, strode confidently through the foyer to the lift bank, a small, wheeled bag in tow. Although many eyes were on her firm, well-developed body, none thought to question her for being there. Such is the power of disguise of a confident and attractive female.

Lara had just come in off the balcony and had a pee, when there was a soft knock at the door. Without opening it, she called, 'Yes?'

'Room Service, Lara. Your chariot awaits! Greg sent me.'

Code correct, Lara opened the door to see a tall blonde with a slightly jaded expression on her pretty face.

'May I come in?' The stranger asked, as Lara kept staring at her.
'Oh...Sorry. Of course, please do. I'm Lara.'

Her visitor smiled in a way that lit up her entire face. 'That's
OK. I'm Amanda, otherwise known as Senior Constable Amanda
Burke of the Southport Police.'

They shook hands, and then Amanda looked around the room.
'I don't know what they told you, but I'm to stay here, taking your
place for two or three days, then disappear. You're paid up for five
days, so the Hotel won't get concerned.'

She pulled the long, blonde wig off and handed it to Lara, revealing her normally short blonde hair which was a fairly close match
to Lara's. Likewise, their body size and shape, especially their boob
size, were very similar.

'Change your shirt now, and keep the wig on 'til you get on the
aircraft in Sydney. You'll pass an ID check with long hair, but don't
run around the airport without it. There are way too many eyes
around there. When you leave here, put your sunnies on and try to
walk out with a few others as cover. The Bus Terminal is 50-metres
down Beach Road and here's your ticket. It leaves at 15:45. And
please remember; talk to the least number of people you can.'

While Amanda was talking Lara stripped off her lovely burnt
orange shirt and put on a dark grey one that fitted her more snugly.
Under Amanda's appreciative eye, she changed her tight jeans for a
baggy, but comfortable pair of khaki cargo pants. Despite being 8
or 9 years older than Amanda, the two looked sufficiently alike to
pass as sisters. Within ten minutes of Amanda entering the room,
Lara was reasonably transformed into a different person and bore
a passing resemblance to the long-haired blonde who had entered
the hotel shortly before.

On her way out, the success of the mild transformation was confirmed when one of the porters who'd helped her check-in, quietly
said to her, 'I haven't seen you work here before. Are you new to town?'

Smiling inwardly, Lara replied, 'Yeah! Just in from Melbourne.
Thought the change of scenery would be good!'

His parting comment as he nodded and waved her goodbye was, 'Looking like you do, you should get a lot of business!' Still grinning to herself, Lara left via the side entrance onto the old Gold Coast highway, then dodged through the traffic as she trotted across the road to the entrance to Beach Road. It took only a couple of minutes for her to walk down to the Bus Interchange, where she flashed her ticket to a bored girl at the check-in counter and was pointed in the direction of her departure bay where a immaculate two-level Coach was waiting, its engine rumbling softly.

The kindly, middle-aged driver checked her ticket again, and said, 'Sit anywhere, Miss. Upper deck, up front is a softer ride and we won't be full tonight, so you can claim the whole seat. If anyone troubles you, there's a button to press that alerts me and I'll sort it out. We leave in ten minutes if you want to grab some sandwiches from the shop. The first stop won't be until 7.30 pm.'

Although she'd been dreading the Coach journey, Lara actually enjoyed the different experience, at least for the first few hours, although trying to sleep, even across two seats, was uncomfortable. The ride was comfortable, although the inevitable pick-up attempts started within 30-minutes of setting out. One was a surfie type who was full of himself and seemed puzzled when Lara rejected his smelly, unwashed body.

The other attempted pickup was an older guy who looked like he should have known better, but turned out to be just a serial talker who only wanted an open ear. Lara allowed him to sit across the aisle from her for a while, but finally had to send him back downstairs so she could get some sleep.

SUNDAY

They pulled up at the Sydney Airport International terminal almost on time at 08:00 Sunday morning, and Lara wearily thanked the driver for his care and kindness before stumbling into the terminal to find the Virgin check-in desk. Her flight was due to depart at 11:45, so she had plenty of time to clean up and to her delight, she found that she could have a shower there.

As a refresher, it was almost as good as a full night's sleep, and Lara felt a great deal better afterwards. With a clean body and a change of under and outer wear, and her long blonde wig comfortably in place, she felt and looked like the suave, confident lady she usually was.

As Amanda had suggested, the check-in staff and the customs officials didn't worry about such trivial matters like hair length, and were happy to stamp her passport and confirmed that she could get a 60-day visa on landing in Bali without any difficulty.

She found the right gate and was waiting for the boarding call when she had a sudden 'Oh-shit!' moment as a thought popped into her mind. She had agreed to be part of a charity fund-raiser function on Tuesday evening and as co-organiser, knew her participation was depended on. In a bit of a panic and trying to think of appropriate excuses, she quickly fumbled her phone out and dialled her co-organiser's number.

'Hi Maureen. I only have a few minutes as I'm about to catch an aircraft out of the country.'

'...No. This has only just come up. Literally just last night and I've been racing around ever since.'

'...Yes, I'm very sorry, but this was totally out of my control.'

'...No, I can't. It's sort of secret and that's all I can say.'

'...Yes, yes. I know it does, but there must be someone else who can step in! My role wasn't that important.'

'...No Maureen, I really can't stay and that's it!'

'...Well, I'm sorry you feel that way. It really isn't my fault.'

Just then the boarding announcement was made for her Bali flight and she waited until it was over before trying to speak again.

'...Yes, that's my flight and yes, you have excellent hearing, but please keep that piece of information to yourself. Walls have ears and all that stuff.'

'...No, I don't know when. That's a bit up in the air for now.'

'...Anyway, I really have to go, and I'm really sorry about the fund-raiser. I hope it goes well. Bye now.'

Boarding was uneventful; she had a row all to herself and they departed on time.

Nearly six hours after boarding, the aircraft landed uneventfully in Bali at Bandar Udara International Airport at 16:30. She was pleasantly surprised to find the Customs and Immigration officials weren't overly officious and she could get a 60-day visa without a problem. Once clear of that necessary piece of official business, the notes from Greg James showed she had a room booked at the Bintang Bali Resort, just 1.5 kilometres away for the night and most of the next day. Her flight out to Sumbawa Besar wasn't until 15:30 the next day, Monday, although it was only a one-hour trip.

Mindful of the security aspects drummed into her by Greg James's message, she elected to hang around the lovely resort the rest of the afternoon and to eat in the restaurant that evening. More excited than she expected by the thought of the reunion with Andy on the morrow and the romantic-sounding boat cruise, she really enjoyed her meal, but over-indulged herself with the lovely, smooth-tasting cocktails the happy little barman was only too pleased to keep making for the 'lovely Missy!'

'Fuck! I am so pissed!' She muttered for the fifth time as she stumbled on her way back to her room. She literally bumped into two couples in a similar condition who laughed with her as they tried to find their rooms and somehow, she ended up joining them for a bit of a nightcap in one of their rooms. Someone produced a bottle of Baileys and a bottle of Butterscotch Schnapps, and because she adored Cowboys, her trip to 'Hangover Central' was assured!

Around 03:00 am, she finally managed to extricate herself from their excessively hospitable embrace and even more surprising, found her own room just two doors along where she collapsed on the bed fully dressed.

MELBOURNE, TERRY XAVIER JOHNSON, SUNDAY PM

In a stark, plain office, in an anonymous tower building in Melbourne's CBD, a quiet, unassuming man of medium height, slightly portly in build, but dressed in a beautiful grey silk Armani suit that would have paid the mortgage for several months on an average Aussie home, sat behind a plain desk. Three chairs were lined up on the opposite side and they held his three most trusted lieutenants who had survived the last massive police raid and the temporary incarceration of their boss.

They knew these days, when in the Boss's presence, you held your tongue until spoken to. The Boss's legendary temper, which had usually been kept under such tight control, had been freed to wreak havoc on those he judged had failed him. Since his release following appeal, there were many who had been judged to have failed him and Melbourne's current wave of building activity provided convenient and permanent resting places for them. Especially when a concrete pour was scheduled for the following day.

'Mr Peter,' he said, looking at the slight man on the left of the row. 'What's the latest on surveillance of the Subject, if you please.'

Peter cleared his throat before speaking. 'We have been keeping track of the movements of all the usual associates of the gentleman, mainly those who are on more personal terms with him. Additionally, we have been monitoring their phones, both mobile and landline. It was only this morning that we intercepted an interesting call made by Miss Lara Bishop to a close friend. Do you wish to hear the recording?'

Xavier flapped his hand. 'No, no! Get on with it. Just give me the gist of it, please.'

'Very well. Miss Bishop was explaining why she couldn't be at a charity fund-raising dinner and her reason was she had to leave the country suddenly. So suddenly, in fact, she was calling from the airport and almost forgot to notify her friend who is the other co-organiser of this function.

That in itself didn't raise any red flags with us, except because Miss Bishop is the subject's secret girlfriend, we watch her movements closely and at this moment, we have a watcher who has her in a bar overlooking Surfers Paradise beach, drinking a large glass of chardonnay and listening to a rather mediocre live band!'

'So, what's the problem if she's on the Gold Coast right now drinking piss in a bar?'

'That is what is interesting, sir. We followed her to the Gold Coast and know where she's staying, and we have a positive sighting of her by one of our operatives who has seen her before, so he's certain it is she. His only comment is she's let her hair grow. Therefore, if she didn't want to go to this fund-raising dinner, she chose a ridiculously elaborate and devious way to duck out of the obligation!

Consequently, the obvious implication is she's on the Gold Coast to meet up with the Subject. I'm reliably informed that a meeting with another boyfriend is extremely unlikely.

With the high number of tourists always moving in and out of the place, it isn't a bad choice to hide out. Anywhere smaller and the gentleman would stand out too easily.'

Xavier thought those words over. 'It does make sense. Therefore, you're convinced she's on the Gold Coast?'

'Yessir. The eyes-on surveillance confirms her presence. We believe the phone call from the airport was an elaborate ruse to convince her girlfriend she was flying to Bali.'

'Bali? How the hell did bloody Bali come into the equation?'

'During the phone call, a boarding call could be heard in the background. We believe she went to that trouble to reinforce her story about leaving the country, and this lends weight to the theory that she's meeting someone of importance who wants to remain anonymous. As she's the gentleman's girlfriend, he is the logical choice!'

Xavier thought again. 'It still makes sense, so I tend to agree with you, Mr Peter. It points towards a well-planned setup to meet with the Subject. Very well! We shall move ten operatives into the Gold Coast area immediately, but none are to get too close to Miss

Bishop. I do not want her to get suspicious that she's being watched. In fact, have the man who is on her at the moment make sure to avoid close contact. Watch from a distance, but I want all public transport points to and from that den of iniquity watched 24/7, and particularly watch her hotel closely! If she goes anywhere else, I want to know about it immediately. Is that understood?

Oh, and hang on a minute; send someone reliable who can use his or her brain to Bali to have a sniff around. Just in case some sort of double bluff is in play!'

Three men made it very clear that they understood, before they were dismissed.

AMANDA BURKE, SUNDAY PM

Amanda was having a lovely time pretending to be Lara Bishop. She had a bundle of cash, a short-term credit card and no other duties except to stay away from anyone she knew and to behave like Lara would if she was waiting around for her lover to arrive. Sitting in various pubs and sucking up what Lara would drink wasn't too hard a task either.

As far as surveillance went, she'd spotted one guy in particular who always seemed to hang around, but never getting too close, which suited Amanda since she didn't want to test out the close resemblance thing too much.

For that reason, she decided Lara would lead a fairly quiet life while waiting and therefore after finishing her Chardy, she wandered back to the hotel and asked the concierge to book her a table in the restaurant for dinner at 7pm. In the small mirror behind the concierge's desk, she saw her watcher stroll into the foyer and upon spotting her, veered sharply off into the bar. She was tempted to have some fun with him, but restrained herself for now, at least.

CHAPTER 33

BALI, JULIET, MONDAY PM

At the same time, the stylish, tall woman with the long blonde hair passed through airport customs without incident, although she did attract a lot of attention. Although her well-used passport proclaimed her to be Juliet Davis; that was not the name they burdened her with at birth. At times, she had trouble remembering what her real name was; such are the disadvantages of using false identities all the time.

Ground-side at the airport was a seething mass of humanity as hordes of tourists arrived to take the rooms vacated by the opposing hordes heading back home, sunburnt, half-pissed and broke. A large section of a wall was taken up with hundreds of glossy brochures extolling the virtues of the many hotels, resorts and houses for rent. To be fair, most upmarket Bali accommodation was, by Australian standards, good quality and reasonable in price.

Juliet stopped to scan the display and was immediately besieged by touts trying to get her attention, but she brushed them away, concentrating on putting herself in the shoes of the elusive Lara Bishop who, she thought, wouldn't want to get buried in the centre of Denpassar. With that reasoning, she might book into a nice hotel or resort fairly close to the airport for easy access both coming and going. Finally, through the mass of brochures, one stood out, being for the Bintang Bali resort, and just 1.5 kilometres from the airport. It even had a Courtesy Bus that could be alerted by picking up the phone handset on the small counter below the wall of advertisements.

A polite voice in excellent English was happy to book a room and advised she would be picked up directly, so that minutes later, she was being escorted to a clean minibus along with several other new arrivals and whisked through the insane traffic to a quiet oasis of a resort which suited her perfectly. Once at Reception, she used the line that her twin sister had gone missing and had last been reported as heading for Bali and this was her favourite Resort.

That request, along with a photo dug up from media files, showed no positive response.

Frustrated for no good reason, Juliet went to her room and after a relaxing shower, thought things through. There was no real reason to suppose that even if Lara Bishop had made it to Bali instead of lazing around the Gold Coast, why should she necessarily stay at this Resort. Answering her own question, she just had one of those feelings which all good investigators get, that she was on a trail that wasn't too cold...yet!

Determined to make the best of the situation, she dressed and headed for the restaurant where she had a delightful meal, made even more so by the personal attention of the barman who insisted on bringing her a selection of special cocktails to get her approval. She wasn't normally a heavy drinker, but the happy atmosphere with lots of new visitors keen to party and the super smooth and powerful cocktails arriving in a steady stream had her head reeling. The alcohol caught up with her about dessert time and after that, with the wobbly boot firmly on, she decided on just one nightcap at the bar before going to bed. Through the fog of alcohol, she almost missed something the barman quietly said to her as she slowly sipped his latest creation.

'Sorry,' she slurred, 'I missed what you just said.'

He smiled indulgently, 'I remarked that you like my cocktail creations as much as the other Missy who looked like you and was here only two nights ago.'

She tried to focus on his open, honest face, but that proved extremely difficult, so she closed her eyes, which helped, and asked, 'What was she like, this other Missy? I'm looking for my sister who's gone missing and was supposed to come here. Reception didn't recognise her photo.'

He looked around, before leaning forward and huffing in disgust.

'Pah! They know nothing out there! I hear everything and because my sister is the Housekeeper, she tells me about the other Missy who looks a lot like you. Unfortunately, she drank many times too much and the next morning had to be assisted to wake up, get cleaned up then take a taxi to the airport.

Juliet seized on that statement.

'Did they know where she was going?'

Her co-conspirator lowered his voice even further. 'My sister, she say Missy had seat on Wings airline to Sumbawa Besar, one-way. She was ill and my sister had to help her into the shower and help her dress and checkout or she would've miss the flight. Would have been big problem for your Missy if she missed that aeroplane.'

The inference was practiced and subtle, but Juliet was well stocked with handout cash, so she slid a $50 note across the bar-top. 'This is for the trouble your sister took to help my sister.'

His face lit up. 'Thank you Missy. She will be very grateful for this reward!'

Juliet waved his profuse gratitude away, then asked, 'Where would my sister go from this Sumbawa Besar place? Is it an International airport or a cruise ship terminal or something?'

He chuckled, 'Oh no Missy. It is quite a large city, but it does not...how do you say...connect with anything else. There is some good diving in the area. Did your sister like the diving? Maybe that is why she went there, but you would have to ask the diving companies if they have seen her.'

Juliet almost shook her head about the diving suggestion, but stopped and thought that if the place was a bit of a dead-end, maybe Lara had taken a boat somewhere or, her mind racing along a slippery, alcoholic path, maybe she had been picked up by a boat as part of the elaborate escape plan! With fuzzy, random plans wandering about her slightly scrambled brain, she finished her drink, thanked the barman and finally found her room.

Next morning, she was up and about early, heading back to

the airport with a plan in mind and the 'lost sister' story ready to invoke the sympathy vote. Unfortunately, the Airline, even slack as it appeared to be, wouldn't budge on releasing passenger's names, regardless of how much cash she showed or cleavage she displayed. With all avenues of investigation exhausted in that direction, she sat in the airport coffee shop for a while mulling things over, before marching back to the Wings counter and booking herself on the next flight to Sumbawa Besar.

It wasn't departing until 15:00 the next day, Wednesday, so she had plenty of time to kill, some of which she used by reporting to Xavier, who was delighted she had made what was possibly a positive contact, but he still had a set of eyes physically on a person they believed was Lara on the Gold Coast, and until he resolved that puzzle, he told her to stay on the trail and report back soonest.

She had a quiet night at the resort, enjoying another excellent meal, but went light on the cocktails. There were some new guests in the restaurant and when she moved to the bar after dinner for a nightcap or two, a group of three couples invited her to join them rather than drink alone. She wasn't really in the mood for socialising, but joined them with good grace and found, to her surprise, she was soon enjoying the easy banter and chatter between the group of friends who obviously knew each other well and were polite enough to include Juliet in the conversation.

Although her resolve not to drink much tonight had pretty much been washed away by the invite to join the group, she wasn't too pissed to realise that she was receiving a healthy dose of interest from two of the men, both of them construction contractors from Melbourne, and that their wives were well aware of their husbands interest and apparently didn't mind.

Juliet had recently indulged in a bit of fooling around with a couple, and while initially she found it quite exciting, the hit and miss aspect to such an encounter had made the outcome rather less satisfying. Still, she didn't have to get up early, and they were an attractive and happy group, so she was prepared to go with the flow and see what developed.

What developed was she received the inevitable invitation to come with the party back to their room where they could be more comfortable and with the barman happy to sell them a few bottles of cocktail ingredients, they cheerfully and noisily traipsed off to a room similar to hers, except it had internal doors to the rooms on either side.

A few more heavy-handed drinks later, music was turned on, lights were dimmed and clothes started coming off. In her present mellow mood, Juliet wasn't opposed to joining in and as the atmosphere was still happy and relaxed, she soon found herself naked on one of the beds, propped up against some pillows, a super-strong drink in one hand, having an in-depth political discussion with a man and someone's wife. The fact they were naked as well, didn't seem to detract from the lively discussion, although at some stage, when the inevitable coupling happened between her companions, it seemed to be regarded as a minor, but enjoyable interruption to their discussion, after which it was resumed where it had been paused. In due course, Juliet was politely invited to take part and was pleased to find it was all easy-going, low-stress, and with lots of laughs and giggles to show it was all in good fun.

WEDNESDAY

The Wings Airline plane trip to Sumbawa Besar was exciting to say the least, leading off with a 40-minute delay before boarding, apparently due to some re-fuelling issue. Then once aboard, there were three attempts to close the cabin door, either because someone had been left outside, or the fool thing wouldn't align properly. Finally, some ground crew wrestled it into place so the pilots could get on with starting the engines.

Naturally, in accordance with Mr Murphy's dictum, only one

wanted to stay running. The other one belched clouds of smoke and the occasional spiteful gout of flame, before finally succumbing to the efforts of the flight deck crew and/or the prayers of the passengers and consenting to stay alight. The cabin crew were totally unperturbed by the whole circus, standing around chatting until the pilots were convinced the recalcitrant engine would remain functioning so that taxiing to the runway could happen.

A monsoon-generated storm over Lombok tossed the 5th hand Boeing 737 around like a leaf in a gale, causing half the passengers to be violently ill, something Juliet avoided by a whisker. Their arrival at Sumbawa Besar was not called a landing by any stretch of the imagination, although it was a testament to Boeing's build quality, that they could taxi to the terminal under their own power. Shaken and stirred, the motley collection of passengers disembarked thankfully.

Sticking with the only plan she had, Juliet found the information board in the terminal and looked up dive companies. There were six or eight to choose from and all seemed to be in the same area on the waterfront, so she snagged a taxi and asked to be taken to where the boats docked.

The driver's English wasn't the best, but he seemed to get the idea of what she wanted when she kept repeating 'boat wharf'.

'OK Missy! I find boat place for you.'

Barely five minutes later, they turned off a wide boulevard with only light traffic and were driving down a narrow street lined with houses jammed closely together, dodging small kids, dogs, cats and chickens, with no sign of water, when he suddenly stopped on a concrete wharf on the bank of a river.

There were a few boats tied up there, two being smallish sailing boats, one flying the Australian flag, as well as a long, low powerful-looking boat with fully two-thirds of its length open cockpit with a gaily decorated awning covering it. A straggle of divers with armloads of equipment were walking away from it to a waiting mini-bus, with Sumbawa Besar Dive Charters painted on its sides.

Telling the taxi driver to stay put, she headed for what looked like the boat's Skipper, a tall red-haired man hosing the boat down with a disgusted look on his face.

'Excuse me,' she said politely, 'I wonder if you could help me. I'm looking for my sister who might have come here on a diving trip. If I showed you her photo, would you mind seeing if you recognise her?'

He looked briefly at her before saying, 'Yeah, but give me a minute. I need to hose this chunder off before it sets. Bloody amateurs! No matter how many times I tell the useless pricks to spew over the side, what do they do? Stay seated and spray the boat, themselves and friends with their recycled bloody lunch! And it wasn't even rough today! Fuckin' wallies!'

He finally turned the hose off and gave her a more careful inspection, head to toes and when apparently satisfied with her physical appearance, nodded. 'OK. Show me, but I've gotta say I'm not the only dive charter operator around here. In fact, this isn't even my normal berth; I'm usually further up the creek, but I'll see if I know her.'

Juliet handed down the image of Lara lifted from a charity function publicity photo. The man looked at it carefully, comparing it to Juliet several times.

'Yeah, she looks like you, I'll say that.'

Juliet grimaced. 'That's good, because we're sisters, but do you recognise her?'

He shook his head. 'Nah! Haven't seen her before, but I wish I had. How about you though? Are you interested in doing some diving? I know the best spots and I'll do a really good rate for you.'

Disappointed, she shook her head, 'No, thank you. I just need to find her. She went missing from Bali and although I've managed to trace her this far, she could've gone anywhere from here.'

'Unlikely,' the big man offered. 'Tourists really only come here for the diving which is world-class, but there's not much else, just a few bars and restaurants. They fly in, dive for a few days, then bugger-off back to the fleshpots of Bali. If your sister got this far, she's either back in Bali or she hooked up with a group on a boat. That's the only other way out of the place.'

'Bugger! How could I find out if she jumped on a boat?'

'You could try asking some of the other dive crews. They might have seen her. Otherwise, I don't know. There's no harbour control here. Boats can come and go as they please.'

'Fuck it! OK, thanks for your time anyway.'

'No problem. If you change your mind about going diving, come and see me first. I'm Mike McGee, but people just call me Big Mike.'

She gave a faint smile. 'Thanks Mike. I'd better keep moving.'

'OK, if you must. The other dive boats are further up the creek toward town. Your taxi driver should know where they are. I can tell him anyway, unless you speak the dialect?'

'No. Afraid not, so that'd be a big help, thanks.'

He swung easily up onto the wharf, a good-looking, confident man who towered over even her tall frame, and ambled over to the taxi, gently pushing through several locals who had come out of their neat little houses to see what the fuss was about and had been chatting with the driver. Mike rattled off a set of instructions to the driver, but was interrupted by a local who spoke rapidly, pointed to the little house closest to the river, then back at himself. He spoke some more, with Mike listening carefully. Finally the little fella fell silent and Mike turned to Juliet. 'You can be lucky sometimes. This man, who lives in the house just behind us, says two days ago, a big power boat came in here one afternoon and tied up for a couple of hours. There were a bunch of foreigners on board, but one of them got off and was picked up by taxi. He came back after an hour or so with a woman who looked a lot like you.'

Juliet felt like kissing him, but restrained herself. 'That's fantastic! I don't suppose he heard anything about where they were going?'

Mike talked briefly to the local again. 'Nope. No luck there, but he took some photos of the boat with his smart phone. He's just gone to get it.'

One minute later, the little man was back, a big, gap-toothed grin on his face, and a new iPhone in a tattered case in hand and with the photo icon already selected. He carefully handed it to Mike who expertly swiped his way through the series of photos.

Turning to Juliet, he handed her the phone. 'This boat is a serious bit of gear! It's almost in the super-yacht class and is a rare boat to be visiting here. In fact, I'm not sure how he made it over the bar to get in here in the first place.

They aren't good photos, but I can tell you that it's an AB100 Super Cruiser, designed and built in Italy. They are fast and luxurious. If your sister has gone off on it, she's doing all right for herself.'

Juliet was busy flicking through the photos, but there wasn't one of her 'sister'. 'Please ask him if I can send these photos to my phone?'

Big Mike did so and with the little man's nod, Juliet rapidly typed in her address and hit the buttons to transfer the series of photos to her own phone. With that done, she handed the man his phone along with a $50 note that made him bow and stammer his thanks, before she turned to Mike.

'Is there somewhere we can have a drink and a talk? I need to ask you some questions and get some advice. I'll be happy to pay you for your time.'

'No need for that and I'll be happy to have a drink and a chat with you, but you'll have to give me a few minutes to finish hosing my boat down. Then we can have a cold beer aboard or at a bar uptown if you wish. You can pay off your taxi, too. I've got a car here and I'll run you to wherever you need to go later.'

Juliet wasn't sure about the 'later' bit, although he was an attractive man and maybe taking another one for the Company wouldn't be too much of a chore in this case, even though she was still feeling the effects of all the extra attention she'd received the previous night. Therefore, it was in a pleasantly anticipatory mood she dutifully paid off the taxi and watched it roar off in a cloud of dust and indignant chickens, before returning to sit on a steel bollard, watching Mike finish hosing the vomit and salt off his boat.

Mike proved to be a mine of information, as well as a genuinely nice guy, so Juliet extracted all the information she could about boating in the Archipelago and where a boat like the AB100 might go to hide out. That was before she let him think she couldn't resist his manly charms and finally dropped her pants to join his on the floor of his cabin.

In fact, he proved to be an entirely satisfying lover, to the extent that over a late dinner uptown, she revised her opinion and elaborated on the 'missing sister' story a bit to suggest there was a sizeable inheritance involved and an enterprising Skipper with a fast, long-range boat could do quite well by continuing to be helpful.

She also convinced herself that having a local expat on side would help the search considerably.

Between cleaning up and heading uptown for dinner, she stepped onto the wharf for privacy and made a report to Xavier.

'...So that's the state of affairs, sir,' she reported, having delivered all the pertinent facts in the weird manner the egomaniac demanded, 'and I'm confident he'll remain silent and helpful, especially if some money is passed his way.'

'*Very well Miss Juliet. You've done an outstanding job and I'm pleased. With your local knowledge and new resources, I'm making you the Operative-in-Charge of the six operatives whom I'm sending, and you are to charter three long-range aircraft for them to conduct an aerial search based on the information you have gained. The authorities don't need to be involved if it can be avoided, but if any questions are asked, we are contracted to scout for movie locations and will need lots of local extras when the time comes.*'

'Understood, sir. Accommodation is limited in this town, so I'm booking into the Samawa Transit Hotel near the airport, which should suit the other operatives in particular. I'll book six more rooms to make sure we have a secure base in one place. As this is Wednesday late afternoon, when should I expect the other six?'

'*Miss Julie is making the bookings now. They will fly out on Jetstar at 09:15 tomorrow and arrive Bali at 13:15, then fly in on one of the domestic flights, getting to Sumbawa Besar at 16:30. Are you able to meet them? There will be four men and two women, and three of them are pilots, but that knowledge should be kept private.'*

'Understood sir. I'll have a sign with Adams written on it for identification. Is there anything else that I should be doing?'

'Not that I can think of at the moment, thank you. Please report when you have more information.'

CHAPTER 34

SEEKER CREW AFTER PICKING UP LARA, MONDAY PM

With the last mooring line dropped off, Dave carefully pivoted the big boat around, the stern just clearing the wharf and allowed the current to carry them toward the shallow entrance. With a touch more power, they picked up speed and headed for the messy array of small waves breaking across the entrance bar. The big, sea-kindly boat barely noticed the waves and with the water-jet drives, the shallow water was not an issue.

Corrine stood beside him at the wheel, as out on deck Bree and Alex took in the protective fenders and stowed them in the bow locker.

'She really must have rubbed you up the wrong way!' she observed, looking at the way Dave had his jaw clenched.

He nodded, 'Yep! She did that all right. Snotty bitch! Her greeting was, 'Who are you supposed to be?' and that was after she'd eyeballed me top to toe, sneering at how I was dressed! She can go get fucked as far as I'm concerned! I thought we were doing something nice for the guy. Not importing some Nazi bitch to give us a hard time!'

'No. That doesn't sound too good', she commented, 'and not what I'd expected as the girlfriend to such a nice guy like Andy. We might just leave her out there in the cockpit and turn the wick up a bit on the way back. She actually looks like she's got the 'Mother' of all hangovers, so maybe she just needs to sleep.'

Dave erupted, 'I don't give a flying fuck how she feels. She's a rude, selfish, stuck-up bitch, so she can contemplate her rudeness over the next two hours, and I might just happen to open the taps a whole heap more to help rock her off to sleep!'

Corrine couldn't remember when she'd last seen Dave in such a state, so she just sat with him as *Seeker* set a fairly straight course, cutting just past the western tip of Pulau Medang, then direct to their little hideaway island. They'd cruised down relatively quietly at 30 knots, but in a move which lifted Dave's mood considerably, he opened the throttles until the big boat was skipping nicely across the small swell at around 55 knots, the twin V16 diesels bellowing their spine-tingling song. At that speed, the boat really came alive and the crew gathered in the saloon with the side doors open to enjoy the ride.

Strangely, no one seemed to give their new passenger a second thought, as she appeared to be trying to sleep in the chair where Corrine had first pointed her. They all knew from experience. that the noise levels out there would be high, so it was unlikely she was getting much rest.

Corrine finally took pity on her and went out to invite her into the saloon and was disturbed to see the tear tracks down her cheeks. She tried to talk to Corrine, but the noise level was a bit too high for comfortable chat, so Corrine dragged her reluctantly inside and closed the doors. She parked her on the white leather lounge at the rear of the saloon where she was out of the way. Jill came over to see her in a professional capacity and after finding out she was suffering from both a severe hangover and near-terminal remorse, spoke to Roger who went to his medical kit and passed over a couple of tablets for Lara to take.

'What are they?' she asked suspiciously.

Roger sighed at her tone, but replied with exaggerated patience, 'I'm a Doctor and they'll settle your stomach and make you feel better in general. You also appear to be severely dehydrated, so plenty of water, starting now, is required, otherwise you will become worse.'

'You're a real Doctor? As in medical and all that stuff?'

I Ie sighed again. 'Yes, dear, I actually am, and Jill, my fiancée, is my theatre nurse.'

'Oh! I'm sorry for doubting you. I don't know what's got into me the last few days. Maybe it's all the ducking and hiding and subterfuge. I'm not used to this level of stress. Is Andy OK?'

He regarded her with a neutral expression. 'Yes. He's fine and has been enjoying himself playing at being a boatie like the rest of us!'

She finally smiled, transforming her forlorn look into a radiant one. 'Oh, I'm so glad. He does love boating of any sort and badly needed to get away from all this horrible business. I don't suppose he's told you anything about it? The mess in West Australia, I mean.'

Roger smiled dourly. 'Actually, the people you see here were some of the ones who told him. They and the others you'll meet soon, were the ones at the sharp end of things in the Pilbara and also in Bali for the clean-up!'

Lara's eyes opened comically wide in surprise. 'Oh, shit! I didn't know that! No wonder Dave is so pissed off with me when I acted like such a goose!'

Jill had been listening in and tugged Roger aside for a moment, although Lara didn't even notice.

'I reckon she's a prime candidate for a dose of green goo behind the ears. It really should settle her down. She's a bloody mess at the moment and we'll be there in about 40-minutes!'

Roger thought a moment, and then nodded. 'Yeah. You're right again; it must be that female thing you keep telling me about. I'll go get some.' He dodged her elbow with practiced ease and went below to their luxurious cabin, finding a partly-used jar in a drawer.

Lara looked up as he approached, the small green jar in hand. 'What's up Doc?' she said with a tired grin. 'I've always wanted to say that for real.'

'This is a herbal treatment I'm trialling and so far have seen remarkable results. It will settle those feelings of paranoia and anxiety you seem to have. I can assure you it will have no bad effects; in fact, you'll probably feel rather good.'

'Oh! What the hell, go ahead. Where does it get applied?' she asked, sniffing at the small jar. 'It smells strongly of something, but it's quite pleasant.'

'It goes on just behind your ears, if I can just rub a small amount in. It's a transdermal medication for rapid take up!'

He rubbed a reasonable amount behind each ear, before capping the jar and slipping it into his pocket, watching her carefully.

'How much longer till we get there; wherever 'there' is?' she asked.

'About another 30 minutes,' Roger replied, 'especially if Dave backs off the power a bit.'

'I heard that, you wuss. Where's your sense of adventure?'

'I think I left it back in Bali,' Roger replied semi-seriously.

'Oscar Mike Golf!' came an exclamation from Lara. 'What the fuck is this stuff? It feels great, but it's like an almost instant high! Wow! What a buzz!'

Roger and Jill chuckled. 'It's just a herbal remedy which has a lot of healing power. It's made by islanders on the far side of the Archipelago and they've been using and trading with it for years. There are definitely no harmful side effects. Jill and I have tried it without any problems.'

Jill giggled. 'That is, if you don't count not being able to keep our hands off each other for a couple of days!'

Lara giggled, definitely relaxing, 'I can understand what you said. Is that an official side-effect?'

Jill grinned, 'Yep. Although we prefer to think of it as a side-bonus!'

'I can't wait to see Andy,' Lara said wistfully, 'I feel a workout coming on! And speaking of that, can I apologise to Dave and Corrine for being such a bitch earlier?'

'Hang on a second,' Roger said, stepping up to the helm station at the forward end of the long saloon area and getting Dave's attention.

'How about you throttle back and let Alex take over. Our guest has something to say now we've settled her down.'

Dave thought a few moments, and then shrugged. 'Sure. I'm into forgive and forget, especially living in close quarters. How did you settle her down?'

Roger grinned. 'Our new cure-all; the green-goop, of course.'

Dave had a good laugh. 'Yeah. That'll do the job. I pity Andy when we get in, he won't know what hit him! Anyway, let's hear what she has to say.'

He throttled back to a relatively sedate 30 knots and handed over to the competent Alex, before moving aft to where Lara sat looking nervous. He and Corrine stood in front of her, looking impassive, and waited while she cleared her throat.

'I wanted to apologise to you for my ridiculous behaviour earlier. It was uncalled for since you're just trying to help Andy. I won't make excuses, but I'm not really the cast-iron bitch I pretended to be earlier. That must have been my evil twin and I've sent her home, never to show her face again. Ever!'

She tried to avoid putting a pleading look on her face, trusting that Dave would be reasonable, and he was.

'Yeah, OK. Apology accepted and let's say no more about it. I gather that you're feeling a little bit better?'

Lara nodded at Roger. 'Yes, thanks to Dr Roger. That green paste is magical! I felt like death warmed up earlier and now I reckon I could run a marathon!'

Dave chuckled, and said cryptically. 'It's good alright, and the effects usually last quite a while, so make the most of it!'

CHAPTER 35

THE ISLAND, MONDAY PM

It was with a real sense of relief I saw *Seeker's* sleek bow poke around the corner of the island, slowing as we watched. Willie was out of the way, having parked himself mostly out of the water on *Firebird's* boarding platform, his broad head halfway up the steps, where Jasper and Krazy crouched, silently communing with each other. Jasper seemed to be teaching her more of his habits every day. Even *Seeker's* arrival didn't faze the big mammal, although the tall, blonde woman, who I took to be Lara, nearly freaked at the sight of the massive black and white body which looked like it was climbing up the steps, trying to catch the two cats.

Once Dave had anchored and rafted-up, Lara stepped across and hugged Andy so hard I saw him wince. Andy introduced her to Sandy, Gilbert and me, although Jasper had to forego his usual ritual with a new passenger, as the mental discussion with Willie took his full attention. Andy then took Lara below to stow her clothes, and as both seemed to have an itch which needed urgent scratching, I didn't expect to see them for some time, especially with Lara feeling, as I'd been told, the full effects of the green-goo.

The girls had planned a simple evening meal of mostly finger foods, so we broke out the cocktail dispenser and settled in for a pleasant evening. Every so often, Willie would swim past clicking and whistling happily, which made Gilbert say, via signs, that the more he sounded off, the better chance his Mother would hear him and come to collect her wayward offspring.

Andy and Lara belatedly joined us and finished off the food, although Lara delicately shuddered when Sandy offered her a

306

cocktail. 'I'll just have a mug of coffee, thanks. Can I get it myself? You don't have to wait on me.'

Sandy smiled patiently, 'Actually, I was just going to show you where things are, so you can help yourself anytime.'

Lara smiled, 'Oh yes, of course. Christ, you all must think I'm such an idiot!'

'Don't beat yourself up too much. It might have been self-inflicted, but alcohol excess is still poisoning and knocks the body around pretty badly. The green-goo helps, but it'll take another day or two before you're back to normal, so take it easy.'

'Thanks Sandy I appreciate that. That stuff was a blessing, although t must say the side effects were a pleasant bonus!'

Sandy grinned. 'Yes, they are.'

'Well. I can give it a 10 out of 10 for effectiveness and for settling me down when I so badly needed to,' Lara said earnestly, 'anyway, thanks for the pep talk and I'll be right to make the coffee now. I'll be back out in a minute.'

I had heard about Lara's less than grateful greeting with Dave and was keen to see how she would fit in with the rest of the crew, but there seemed to be no problems so far. Shortly after, I heard the Sat-Phone ring, and went to answer it.

'Hi Greg, how are things with you?'

'Not bad, Harry, but they might start warming up for you, although the situation is hard to read at the moment. Our informer says there's been a leak of info to the Stainless crew about Lara's movements. Amanda is still being followed and some of them think she's Lara, but there's some conflicting info which puts her on a plane to Bali. Therefore, we can expect a lot of crosschecking. Apparently, at least one operative has been sent to Bali to poke around and ask questions and we're not sure if it's a male or female.'

'Ah, bugger! How can that have happened?'

'Don't know yet, but we're pushing our man to get more.'

'Good oh, but don't push him too hard. We really need him to stay in place and keep the Intel flowing. And you'd better give

Amanda the heads up. She'll need to be extra cautious not to get too close to any of these characters.'

'Yeah. I've already done that but you know what she's like!'

'Yes, I do. And that's why she has to play this gig straight. That bloody Xavier is a devious and ruthless piece of shit!'

'She's been told. Do you still want her to do her disappearing act on Wednesday?'

'Yes, please mate. But make sure she disappears from somewhere very much in public. Maybe from someplace like SeaWorld, but definitely not from the hotel. That would focus attention much too closely on the one place where they might find out about the I.D. switch. Tell her to leave her bag in the room with those Lara Bishop I.D. letters and notes. If it gets lost in the shuffle, she can replace everything with the Commonwealth credit card she's been flashing around, but not until after Wednesday.

And tell her to stay out of social circulation when she's off-duty. There'll be a bunch of guys looking for tall, well-built blondes all over the Coast for a while.'

'I'll do that, mate. But how about I send her away for a week or two? She could go relieving in a country station until all this mess dies down.'

'Yeah. Great idea. It'd be a really bad thing if Xavier got his grubby little paws on her at this stage.'

'OK Harry, it's all I've got for now. I'll let you get on with it.'

'Thanks Greg. Cheers, mate.'

I passed the news onto the crew, but motioned Lara to follow me into the saloon.

'Can you think of anything that you did which deviated from the plan we gave you? Just think through all your movements from when you got the text from Andy, to when Dave met you at the airport.'

She thought a while, and then shook her head. 'No, I can't think of anything that was off-plan. I didn't see anyone I knew and I didn't talk to any strangers about why I was here, even when I was pissed!'

I pressed her further. 'Did you call anyone? Like maybe to cancel an appointment?'

'No, I.... oh, fuck! I called my co-organiser of a charity fund-raiser to tell her I couldn't make it because I had to leave the country in a hurry.'

I nodded grimly. 'Yep. And what reason did you give for having to leave the country?'

'I said it was a secret and I couldn't say!'

'OK. And where were you when you made that call?'

She thought a moment. 'I was in the departure lounge at Sydney Airport. I remembered to call Jan just before they called for the flight to board. In fact, I had to hang up quickly because they called for boarding while I was on the phone.'

'Ahh... shit!. That's what caused the leak! They heard the PA call in the background. We couldn't figure out how they caught onto the Bali connection.'

She looked stricken. 'But.... but that means they were listening to my call. I was on my mobile. They can't do that!'

'They can and still are. All mobile calls transfer to a land-line, at the nearest tower, so they can make the intercept anywhere after that.'

I chided her gently, conscious of her still-fragile nature. 'That's why we have to be so careful not to make any calls to anybody.'

Her face crumbled, 'Oh...shit! I've done it again! But I didn't mean to do the wrong thing!'

'Nobody is suggesting that,' I said grimly, 'but mistakes can hap-pen so easily, we have to be on guard all the time and not take any chances. So, no more phone calls! Please! Not to anybody for any reason, regardless of how important it might be to you. I hope you turned your phone off when you left Sydney?'

She nodded. 'You have to on the plane anyway, and I didn't get around to turning it back on again.'

'Good! Leave it that way. In fact, take the battery out as well, please, right now.'

She did as I asked, then when she returned, she asked in a more practical mood, 'How much damage has this caused, do you think?'

'We don't know. It could be bad. Amanda, your stand-in on the Gold Coast, is doing a terrific job of distracting them, since the watcher is convinced that she really is you, so the Bali thing is being considered a clever piece of misdirection, although he has sent one of his operatives to Bali to sniff around to see if there is any trace of you.'

'Oh. What happens when Amanda just disappears on Wednesday?'

'We're hoping this Xavier character will think you've gone to ground with Andy, and will keep looking around the Gold Coast. We're planning to let slip some information via the press that will help reinforce that belief. A grainy photo and a brief report about a 'sighting of the PM on a remote Gold Coast beach with an un-named woman' might do the trick!'

She gave me an admiring look. 'That's simple but inspired, Harry! You have a real talent for misdirection planning.'

I smiled modestly. 'Sometimes those ideas work. I've had a lot of practice in foreign deserts. We can only hope this one does as well, or we've really in a pile of trouble.'

She then asked an excellent question, 'If we know who these people are, why can't they be arrested and we can stop all this worrying and enjoy a lovely cruise on your beautiful boat?'

'Because they haven't done anything wrong, and it's not an offence to go looking for someone. Private Investigators and the media are doing it all the time. We need to wait for them to do something illegal, or have our financial wizards find the shadow men behind the search. Until then, we just keep dodging and hope our investigators move quickly.'

'That makes sense. We'll just keep our heads down.'

'Yep. Low profile and make the best of our situation. We are on a pleasure cruise, after all.'

That drew a laugh; one of the first I'd heard from her as we re-joined the others in time to hear them saying goodnight and heading for bed.

TUESDAY AM

I normally wake early and get up just before dawn, but this time it was Jasper who tugged on my foot until I sat up quietly, then he left. I hastily pulled on shorts and a shirt and headed up top, leaving lights off to preserve my night vision. Jasper was waiting in the cockpit and led me up to the bow. Nothing appeared to be amiss on either boat and there were no other boats in sight.

Touching his sleek head with one hand, I felt him quivering with what I recognised as excitement! He was staring out toward the reef, just a few hundred metres away although I still couldn't see anything, when suddenly I heard a faint whistle and a distant splash.

Jasper gave a soft mewl which wasn't an alarm sound and I remembered Willie. Another splash sounded closer and a series of squeaks could be heard. Jasper tugged at my closest hand, before trotting quickly back to the cockpit. When I arrived, he was down on the boarding platform, so on impulse, I turned on the blue LED underwater lights and was amazed to see a massive black and white shape flash through the pool of soft blue light, followed by the smaller form of Willie.

Apparently, Mum had found him and he'd brought her around to say hello!

I hurried below to rouse Sandy and had her grab the video camera again and start recording. Joining Jasper on the stern platform, I waited to see what would happen next, which was the sight of Willie drifting up through the shallow water under us, to shove his big head up on the platform, forcing me to back up a step, although Jasper stood his ground and nuzzled the wet snout of his new big friend. I must admit that even though Willie was a juvenile, it was still un-nerving to be that close when he opened his big jaws, breathed a cloud of fishy breath over us and gave us a happy, toothy grin.

That was nothing compared to Mummy doing the same trick a few moments later, even though she'd not been around us before.

She surfaced just behind Willie, carefully inspected the situation before gently nosing in beside her offspring. The effect of 7-odd metres and around 4 tonnes of aquatic mammal nosing up onto the stern made *Firebird* lurch and dip violently and even Jasper retreated to the top step so Big Momma could get enough of her huge head right up the steps to be comfortable. I was naturally way ahead of him in beating a strategic retreat to the relative safety of the cockpit!

To say it was a bizarre sight was the understatement of the year, to see mother and son orcas grinning at us from less than a metre away! The jerking of the boat roused first Charlie and Gilbert who came sleepily out to see what the fuss was about, and it was comic relief to see their faces, although Gilbert became quite reverential about the two mammals.

Charlie dashed off to rouse Andy and Lara, while Sandy kept recording the encounter, particularly when Jasper sat in front of mother orca and patted her lower jaw with his right front paw. She made a series of soft whistles and some clicks, before sliding slowly off the platform, to float head-up just clear of Willie's tail, one big expressive eye focused on all of us. Willie seemed to be saying goodbye to Jasper and also to we humans who had fed him so well.

Finally, Mumma fired off a series of much louder squeaks and Willie took the hint, nuzzling Jasper one last time before he too slid back in the water beside her.

The two orcas swam several laps around both boats where Dave and his crew were up and watching, then Willie launched himself into a leap that took him two metres or more clear of the water, before landing with a mighty splash, just clear of *Seeker's* stern.

We thought that was that, but Mumma must have felt the need to show Junior how it was really done.

Despite the shallow water, she headed away, then turned and accelerated at an incredible rate, before launching her 4-tonne bulk, many metres clear of the water and covering fifteen metres or more horizontally, before landing with a massive splash that sent a foaming, breaking wave smashing into *Seeker's* stern.

The pair headed out over the reef into the deep water surrounding the little island and were gone, leaving us feeling exhilarated, yet strangely flat, such had been the brief, but emotional connection we had all made with these wonderful creatures who had graced us with their presence and touched us all with their magic.

Jasper cast a wistful look after the pair, then climbed up onto the daybed, gave a big sigh and put his head on his paws. Little Krazy cat sensed his mood and quietly joined him, stretching out along his back, her little paws kneading his muscular neck.

CHAPTER 36

THE ISLAND, TUESDAY

Now that we had Lara settled in, Andy asked about doing some diving on the surrounding reef and drop-off, so we started planning the dive. After that, I dug out all the gear, and then started filling some tanks, while Andy and Dave cleaned and checked the regulators.

With no other land close by, the tide run was minimal, more like a slow drift that was convenient and restful as it carried us along the face of the drop-off where we speared some beautiful snapper, coral trout and parrot fish that were the best eating of all.

The fact that they were difficult to de-scale and fillet, being particularly slippery with scales off, just made them more worthwhile.

Although I had an open-water certificate, I didn't have a passion for diving like Dave and Andy did, especially being super-keen to repeat the dive after a rest. They weren't going deep, so a quick consult of the dive tables gave the minimum rest period. Which pretty well set the pace for the day. Fill tanks, Dave and Andy would rest, and then dive. Repeat as necessary. I cleaned their catch and we had beautiful fresh fish for lunch.

Bree minced a whole heap and made a large batch of Thai fish cakes, only mildly spiced, for the evening meal.

The only real change to our routine occurred when two long sailing canoes with four men in each, swung past the island and cautiously came in over the reef, before nosing up on the shore close-by. Charlie said Gilbert would go ashore to talk to the men, so I ran them in, but it turned out they were just fishermen who came to inspect the potential for a coconut harvest occasionally.

Their own island, which was part of a group of four, was about

15 miles away to the northeast, and had about 250 locals living there, most of them fishermen. We bought some fish off them for the sake of relations, but I was wary of them and the other islanders, especially when the fishermen departed in an obvious hurry, motoring out using the big outboard bolted to the stern of each canoe, instead of sailing.

Back on board, I called a crew meeting and explained my concerns.

'It's not necessarily these blokes who might cause us trouble, even though they left with indecent haste, but maybe the others they'll speak to as soon as they get back. They might get the idea to make a profitable, nocturnal visit to the two flash boats!'

Charlie spoke for Gilbert. 'He says those men are alright, but their islands are probable pirate hangouts, so you are right to be careful.'

Noting the concerned looks on the faces of the girls, I said, 'I don't think we should rush off, just because some locals have spotted us, it was bound to happen anyway; but we will take precautions, day and night from here on.'

I addressed Sandy and Corrine. 'Let's get all the weapons out and check them over. We'll re-stow them so they're more accessible, but maybe mount both .50 cal Brownings on *Seeker* with a couple of towels tied over them. Ammo boxes under the seat beside them. If we're going to get trouble, it'll most likely be tonight, so we can be ready.'

Dave made the dry comment. 'It really makes it easier if they come at night. There's no doubt about their intentions that way.'

No one felt like indulging in any fun activities after that, although the fish lunch went down well. It didn't take long to set the machine guns up and with yet another storm pending, the covers for the Brownings were changed to a large piece of plastic sheeting each, tied down securely.

Small weapons were dug out of their hidden lockers, disassembled, cleaned, lubricated then put back together. Magazines were filled and all crew except Charlie said they were willing to be armed. Andy asked if he and Lara could have some practice and liked the look of the neat little PMR-30s in .22 magnum with the 30-round magazine. I set them up with one each, showed them what was where and tossed a couple of empty wine bottles overboard.

They banged off a few rounds each before getting the feel for the well-balanced gun and Andy shattered his bottle with the fourth round. Lara took two rounds more, but both showed a flair for the potent little gun as Lara fired a couple more rounds at the splash mark, then ejected the magazine, cleared the chamber and handed it to me with a grin on her face.

'That's a nice little gun. Those magnums have a healthy kick for a small calibre and having 30 rounds is a big advantage.' Andy commented.

'Yes, for a small bullet, it has a lot of stopping power if you can quickly put several hollow-point bullets into a target. I'll show you both how to field strip it, then you can keep them with you for now, since you know the most important thing about each one; they work. I'll get you an extra magazine each as well. We have plenty.'

He grinned. 'Good point, thanks. And I won't ask where all these guns came from.' He waved his hand at the array of weapons strewn across the cockpit table on an old towel.

'Spoils of war, actually Andy. All taken off the bad guys at various times and put to good use against more bad guys.'

He laughed, 'I like that!'

It seemed like we were preparing for war, but after the previous encounters with pirates where we saw how ruthless they could be, we were wary of anybody who came calling with weapons. Andy, Charlie, Lara and Gilbert had yet to be tested under fire. And so the afternoon wore on into storm time and we copped a small one which still dumped a lot of rain along with the usual colourful presentation of arcs and sparks.

Naturally no one could settle or start any jobs or games, so it was almost with a degree of relief when shortly after the rain and wind stopped, the radar sounded an alarm.

I brought up the camera and zoomed in to maximum, panned around onto the NE direction and was rewarded with a distant image of three long canoes heading for the island, carefully keeping it between us and them. Unfortunately for them, our mast was more than high enough to see over the tops of the tallest palm trees on the island. Half the crew crowded around to watch the approach.

'What do you think, Harry?' Dave asked. 'Will they land and wait for nightfall, or keep coming now?'

I watched their approach for a few more minutes, then replied, 'I think they'll keep coming. The fact that they're almost here in daylight shows a high degree of confidence in the outcome. I reckon they'll come around the island and play up the 'poor fishermen' routine. Maybe even say that they're going to stay the night and collect a load of coconuts.'

'Hmm. Fair call. What's our plan?'

I spoke to everyone gathered in *Firebird's* saloon.

'We play this cool. No weapons in sight and with the covers on the .50 cal, but only loosely draped over. Otherwise, they should be loaded and ready to make instant bang-bangs. Keep all other weapons loaded and close to where you are sitting or standing. If they board us, we let them, in which case, I'd prefer that they come over the stern as usual, so the hot rails can have first crack at them.'

Dave nodded agreement, 'I presume they'll try to talk their way aboard in a nice way first?'

I shrugged. 'Hard to say, but we need to be ready for any tactic. Fronting us in daylight means they'll have to come close and talk nice for a few minutes at least, which should give us enough time to suss out their intentions. I mean, they might just want to sell us a heap more fish!'

'Geeze you're a funny bloke Harry,' Corrine replied dryly. 'As if!'

That raised a general laugh which died quickly as the masthead camera showed the three canoes, each packed with men, hugging the shoreline and about to round a small point of the island just a few hundred metres away.

'OK everyone. Action stations, just like we discussed!'

There was a concerted rush for the various positions we had allocated and within seconds, there was a small group of drinkers in *Firebird's* cockpit and more were up on the sundeck on *Seeker* where Corrine and Alex would be close to the Browning's.

The canoes rushed down on us in seconds and wheeled around to nose up to the stern on both boats, where the head-count in one boat wasn't right, but as my brain tried to make some sense of that, an unusually tall islander stood up in the bow of one canoe and called out in passable English, 'You want buy more fish? We good fishermen! Got lots of different fish.'

By way of inducement, he waved a limp, smelly old snapper which looked and ponged like it'd been dead a week. I was tempted to buy it, if only to keep until I could jam it up his smelly arse, but he needed to be defused before he got the rest of the crew worked up.

I pasted a drunken smile on my face and pretended to consider his offer, but then shook my head, 'No, I don't think so, my good man. We already have plenty because we bought some off a boatload of your mates a few hours ago.'

Naturally, he wanted to argue the toss, so I didn't say anything when he stepped off his canoe onto *Firebird's* boarding platform and up a few steps close to where I was standing, just behind the closed safety rail gate. Just holding my hands and arms close to the electrified safety rail system made the hairs stand up and prickle my skin and it made me wonder if I'd over boosted the system.

The tall islander slowly stepped up to me, holding the limp carcass of the snapper out to me as if close proximity to the stinking artefact would change my mind about it. As he came closer, his attention abruptly switched to Sandy, Lara and Charlie sitting at the table with Andy and Gilbert, glasses of wine and cans of beer in front of them.

His smile came over as a leer as he said, 'Maybe pretty ladies would like to see excellent fish,' and in his haste to get closer to Sandy, he pushed at the gate with his free hand.

There was a fearsome 'crack' like a small explosion as the current shorted out the few brain cells he had left, a dancing blue spark jumping repeatedly from the metal gate to the nearest, highly sensitive portion of his anatomy, despite his hand being reflexively clamped to the top metal tube of the gate. His feet and legs were doing a weird sort of a dancing shuffle, until one of the other men darted up from the canoe and grabbed him by his free arm, meaning to pull him back to safety.

That heroic action just resulted in the second chap copping a heavy dose of the same medicine that stood his hair on end before wisps of smoke rose from both and they collapsed backwards down the steps, their shirts flying up to reveal a handgun in the leader's waistband and a huge, odd-looking submachine gun somehow stuffed under the shirt of the second guy. Their violent demise produced shouts of alarm from the rest of the crew, some of whom tried to push the canoe away from the unseen killer, while the others started to extract handguns and more of the odd-looking sub-machine guns from under seats and scraps of canvas.

That was the signal Corrine and Alex had been waiting for and the deep, the hammering beat of the pair of .50 calibre Browning machine guns sounding the death knell as they raked the three boats with brief three-round bursts, chewing through soft flesh like a hot knife through butter. I was impressed that Alex was almost as good as Corrine with the big gun and economical with the rounds as well.

As for the attack force, they had ceased to exist in just a few seconds, although their canoes floated just astern of us.

Suddenly, Charlie let out a scream and I spun around to see three naked and dripping Islanders creeping down the side deck on the opposite side to *Seeker* where they couldn't be shot at; long, razor-sharp machetes clenched in their hand. I started to raise my Grizzly .44 pistol, when there was a blur of black and with a loud, unearthly yowl that raised my own hackles, Jasper launched from the cockpit like a black, furry missile, taking the lead islander by the throat and driving him back against the second man.

He gave a jerk and a quick twist of his head and a spray of blood misted the air above the two fallen men and their black nemesis. The third man was still in the process of working out what was happening, when Jasper spat something overboard before equally efficiently interfering with the breathing arrangements of the second man. Another cloud of dense pink mist shot up and while Jasper took the time to spit another chunk of flesh over the side, the third man turned to run, keening a high note in sheer terror!

He'd barely made three paces before he was hit from behind as Jasper grabbed a succulent mouthful of gluteus maximus and rather painfully separated it completely from its owner. I didn't think the human throat could make such sounds, or so loudly, but the stricken pirate set some sort of record that evening. When Jasper paused to spit that large chunk over the side, the man leapt over the bow into the shallow water, blood streaming from his ruined bum. As he gained his feet in the knee-deep water, Jasper stood on the bow, sized up the situation then leapt almost delicately onto the back of the hapless man, where one bite of his jaws on the victim's neck ended his noise and suffering for good.

'Good boy, Jasper!' I called, while Charlie, Lara and Andy looked on, horrified. 'Swim back here. That should wash most of the blood off.' So, my lovely, lethal cat paddled strongly back to the stern where I let his artificial turf boarding mat hang over the end of the platform. I had the fresh-water shower and some shampoo ready. He liked to be shampooed and stood quite still, grinning happily while I worked the nice-smelling stuff into his fur, particularly around his face and muzzle. I gave his other end a wash while I was there and he at least tolerated that!

I wasn't quick enough though, to grab him before he bolted up the steps into the cockpit, where he shook himself half-dry over everyone. The yells and screams of abuse at least provided a minor distraction which I took advantage of, by going for'rard to tip the two carcasses overboard. I had to use the high-pressure hose to shift the blood-stains, though it didn't take long to clean the mess off, letting the tide and a few reef sharks apply their highly efficient version of traceless body disposal.

Back in the cockpit, Andy, Lara and Charlie were still coming to grips with what had happened, looking rather bemused since it had all been so fast, bloody and noisy.

Dave had managed to grab one canoe and used it to round up the other two. We quickly checked for any signs of life, but they were all long gone, along with many assorted body parts. The search also showed they certainly had not dropped in for a chat about fishing, as each man had two or three guns or knives! We collected all the weapons and piled them on the stern board, before tackling the grisly task of heaving the bodies overboard. There was nothing we could do about the few bullet holes which decorated the woodwork, so we tied the steering handles on the outboards in the fore and aft position, started the big motors, pointed them in different directions out to sea, then put them into forward gear. At low power, they set off on their final voyage, the amount of fuel left guaranteeing a strong element of mystery which would confuse any investigation if somebody ever came across them.

Back on board, Dave and I carted our pile of weaponry up to the cockpit of *Firebird* and dumped them carefully on the table in front of a still shell-shocked Andy, Lara and Charlie.

Finally finding her voice, Charlie asked rather breathlessly, 'Harry! What the fuck was all that about?'

I smiled gently and quietly replied. 'I'd guess it was what passes in this area for the local pirate crew. The earlier visit by the islanders was happenstance, but they apparently thought they'd be rewarded for telling the pirates about the rich, white trash on their flash boats with their even flashier females!'

I waved my hand at the pile of handguns, which included seven or eight of the odd-looking sub-machine guns, razor-sharp machetes, and sundry knives and pre-cut lengths of cord. Nudging the cord lengths and the machetes, I said to Charlie, 'They came well prepared to look after you girls up while they made sure all us guys had been shot and dumped over the side!'

'What do you mean?' Charlie asked, genuine curiosity over-riding the particularly nasty mental picture my words had generated.

'Because it's the way they function. We saw a similar level of preparedness in the pirates we encountered over near Singapore. They generally aren't very bright, but they are ruthless.'

'Oh.' was her subdued reply. 'But won't they be missed by their families?'

I nodded grimly, 'Yes, bugger their little black hearts. They'll be missed all right, and their families knew where they were going. We've got to get going immediately and clear the area. It's going to be a long night!'

I turned to Dave who was examining one of the sub-machine guns and said, 'I had planned to head for an uninhabited little island around 328 nautical miles ENE from here, although I was hoping we could do it at a leisurely pace. Still, with a head start, we should get beyond their reach, and if we can stay low profile for a while longer, we should be safe from reprisals, so let's get going now.'

He agreed, and immediately left to start and let the big diesels warm up. I did the same and while that was happening, Corrine came over to inspect our weapons haul.

'Oh, these are nice,' she said appreciatively, picking up one of the sub-machine guns.

'What the hell is it?' I asked. 'It's got the look of a Kalashnikov, but I'm not sure.'

'You're almost there. It is a Kalashnikov, but it's a copy of a Russian Vityaz-SN sub-machine gun and built in the good old USA, by Kalashnikov, USA. It's called the KR-9M, with a 30-round mag and 750 rounds per minute of standard 9mm parabellum ammo. It's light, reliable and highly regarded, but I wonder how they got here? I mean the normal AK-47s and AK-74s are everywhere, but not these little darlings! And look here,' she got excited, picking up what looked like a smaller version of the KR-9M.

'OK. I'll bite. What are they except a small version of that other thing?'

She grinned. 'Pretty close again, Harry. It's a KP-9, the pistol-sized version of the KR-9 in 9mm also, and although it's huge for a pistol, it features a 30-round staggered magazine, plus the long 9.25" barrel makes it very accurate for a handgun. This one looks as though it's been modified to have a selectable semi or full-automatic feature. That's useful! Anyway, I might just grab a couple each of the KR-9s and KP-9s, seeing as you seem to have a shitload of them!'

'But seriously,' she called, hopping over the rail to *Seeker* with her armload of lethal weaponry, 'you should get Greg or your own mob onto tracking down who's selling these things over here. They aren't healthy in the hands of pirates. See ya!'

CHAPTER 37

AT SEA — EASTBOUND, TUESDAY/WEDNESDAY

Within fifteen minutes, with dusk closing in swiftly as is usual in the tropics, we were on our way. Initially, we tracked to the southeast, before heading for the uninhabited Pulau Kakabia. Although we weren't in the routine for night cruising, it didn't take long to get back into the rhythm. I took first watch with Andy and Lara, while Sandy had Charlie and Gilbert for the midnight to dawn watch. Everything went smoothly. The evening breeze was light from the south providing some extra drive, meaning that only one engine had to be run at a time for us to maintain a steady 14 knots, the dark bulk of *Seeker* maintaining station, 50-metres off our rear quarter. Fuel stocks were good and food was as well, especially with *Seeker's* big freezers topped up with fish.

Dawn on Wednesday found us in the middle of the emptiness of the Flores Sea with no other boats of any description in sight, a really good thing which helped everyone relax a little, even though we should have been well out of range of the pirate's lair. I was pleased Lara didn't seem prone to motion-sickness and she was able to put the horrors of the attack behind her. She even looked to be enjoying a bit of blue water cruising out of sight of land. I had laid out the desired course on the Chart plotter and it informed me that at our present speed, we would arrive at our desired destination at 18:30 that evening. Being after dark, it wasn't the best time to be arriving at an unknown island, so I examined our track to see if we could shave some distance off of it, but that would bring us in amongst inhabited islands, so the only other option was to increase speed.

I called up Dave and explained the situation. He was happy

with an increase to 17 knots since he was only running on one engine out of the three available and more comfortable with our new arrival time of around 16:00 that afternoon in the vicinity of Kakabia Island.

The rest of the day went peacefully. We ate, slept a little, ate some more, played with the kitties and after lunch, the girls took to the trampolines for some sunbaking. It wasn't long before first Sandy, then Charlie started stripping down, although since they only started with two items of clothing, it wasn't much effort to become naked.

Lara looked amused at first, then interested as she inspected the bare pair, then shrugged and peeled off her own bikini. She had a lean, well-toned body that was generally neat and tidy and fortunately, she wasn't prone to any false modesty.

Naturally, we three males carefully inspected the ladies from the safety of the cockpit, but after 30-minutes or so, Andy offered to mix them some drinks and act as waiter.

I chuckled, 'Watch out for your tail on backwards! It could get you into some fearsome trouble with that lot!'

Gilbert grinned with us and helped Andy make some cocktails, something Lara had finally started drinking again in small doses. He helped Andy carry the drinks forward where the ladies gratefully received them. Andy and Gilbert also had one each, which was rare for Gilbert. They retired to the bow to give the ladies space, but were called back and told to park themselves and socialise.

It wasn't long after the second drink had been served, when the first suggestions were aired that Andy and Gilbert should do as the ladies had and get some sun. Andy thought about it, then after a few more suggestive comments, he did just that and stripped off. I was amused to see that he must have been working hard on body control.

Obviously, Charlie hadn't seen the Boss fully naked before, and certainly not in such a relaxed setting. As the main one encouraging him to strip, Lara obviously didn't mind him being on display.

Sandy being Sandy, was always interested in naked men, and ladies too for that matter.

Then Lara started on Gilbert who at first, politely shook his head and smiled. But then Charlie encouraged him as well.

'It'll be alright, dear man. Truly it will. You're among friends. Sometimes you've just got to go along with things.'

I didn't think he would do it, but then he shrugged and took his shirt off, displaying that magnificent torso covered in rippling muscle. His natural bronze skin colouring didn't need the sun, but even to my decidedly female-oriented eye he looked impressive. All three girls were egging him on, Lara not knowing what Sandy and Charlie did about Gilbert's special endowment, while Andy couldn't understand what the fuss was about, apart from the girls getting a bit pissy.

Charlie had to encourage him again before he finally took his pants off and the expressions on the faces of Lara and Andy was priceless, with Sandy trying hard not to giggle. Gilbert had his back to me so I couldn't judge his appearance for myself, only having Sandy's description to go on. He stayed sitting down and Charlie kissed him, which must have stirred things up a bit, as I could see Lara's eyes grow wide again.

For the sake of decorum, Gilbert remained sitting, and naturally, I was called upon to deliver the next round of drinks, so with the faithful autopilot engaged, I dutifully mixed, delivered, and then poured. Gilbert declined a top-up as I noted that he was indeed impressive and we exchanged smiles. The rest were happy to accept more of the potent brew and they were all getting a bit of a glow on.

I found Lara to be more to my liking and up close she was still a tidy and attractive lady and I caught Sandy giving me a knowing look and an indulgent smile. Pleading Skipper-type duties, I beat a hasty retreat back to the cockpit, before I was asked to strip as well.

What with the sun, the relaxing motion of the boat and three stiff cocktails each, there was a certain amount of low-key fooling around going on up front, accompanied by lots of giggling from the girls, but it didn't seem to get too out of hand, so to speak. Sandy finally found her bikini bits and came back to sit with me.

'Getting a bit too hot up there darlin'?' I asked, tongue firmly in cheek!

She laughed, 'Yeah. It is a bit and has nothing to do with the sun. It's the usual equation; boat, plus sun, plus cocktails equals fooling-around time, so I thought I'd leave them to it!'

I looked forward and saw that the two couples were indeed fooling around with considerable enthusiasm and seemed to be enjoying themselves enormously!

At around 15:45, the radar beeped for attention, showing a growing target which was the island Kakabia. Thankfully, we'd not sighted any other boats and had remained out of sight of land, so our arrival should remain unnoticed for a few days at least. It was a small island, just 1200 x 500 metres and heavily timbered right down to the water's edge. It was surrounded by a shallow coral platform reef, and had two potential anchorages on the western or more protected side.

One was a small inlet which looked shallow, but had two small, pure white beaches, while the other spot was a larger white beach with a deep blue hole some 250 metres long just off the beach. For a measure of concealment, the small inlet looked a better choice and the blue hole was just a few minutes away in the RIBs. There was a deep-water anchorage on the eastern side, encircled by two arms of long, skinny shallow reef with an entrance down in the south-east, the whole thing looked like a wine-glass. Enclosing a bay that was a kilometre square, made it a large body of wave-protected water, but little wind protection.

Having less draft, I took *Firebird* in first, Dave hovering just off the reef. With the forward-looking sonar showing a clear 3D-image of the bottom ahead, we nosed gently in, and as usual, I sucked in a deep breath as we crossed the reef. But although the gin-clear water looked shallow enough to wade ashore, the depth sounders showed a minimum of 3 metres all the way into the little bay.

I called Dave in and it did look alarming to see such a big boat nosing into the tiny bay with apparently not enough water to float it. We'd checked the tides and with barely a one metre tide range, the wonderfully-sheltered anchorage was going to be ideal.

Before I'd even laid the anchor properly, the ladies were in raptures about the glaringly-white sand and the lush vegetation ashore. A stern anchor was essential to keep us in the one spot, so Dave waited until I found enough room and water depth for him to raft up.

With two hours to sunset, everyone wanted to go ashore. Since there was no indications of anyone living there, we all went and wandered around, finding the ground rough with broken and eroded limestone making walking less than pleasant. As if to make up for the rough interior, the two tiny beaches were lovely, with fine, white sand the kitties loved rolling in.

Back aboard, with darkness fallen and happy hour progressing well, I thought I'd better check in with Greg and let him know about the pirates, even though they had nothing to do with our mission.

'Good evening, Harry. Good to hear from you. All is well I hope?'

'Hi Greg. They are now, but we had a spot of bother with the locals at an island not far up from Bali.'

'Oh shit! How many casualties?'

'Oh, about twenty-seven I think,' I replied casually. 'Some were a bit chopped up so it's hard to be certain. Just for the record, they had serious intentions, and came well-armed. Corrine suggested you should make some enquiries about who might be supplying sub-machine guns and machine pistols made by Kalashnikov USA, to pirates in this area. The Indonesians might be interested, so it'll give you something to talk about.'

'Bloody hell, Harry. You really are a trouble magnet! I'll have to have a yarn to Bob about how we approach that one, but it will need to be kicked upstairs quick smart!

'Yeah, you're right. It might be better if I toss it at my people; they're better suited to handle the international side of shit like this.'

'*That would be better, thanks mate. But just minutes ago, Alice called with info from her tame informer, to say your best mate, Terry Xavier Johnson is finally on your trail! Even though he was certain Lara was on the Gold Coast, based on the call that Lara made from the airport, he sent a female operative to Bali to sniff around, and she booked in at the resort Lara stayed for the night on her way through. Someone must have talked, although how they found out her flight details we don't know, but to cut a long story short, she traced Lara to a place called Sumbawa Besar and even has photos of Seeker at a wharf, taken by locals. They reported seeing a tall blonde woman who looked like Lara getting aboard, then it left.*'

'Bloody hell! How good are these people, or more to the point, how slack has our security been?'

'*I hear you, mate, but it's hard not to leave a trail when other people are involved who don't know they shouldn't talk.*'

'Yeah, I know. Sorry mate, I'm just blowing off steam! Do we know what Mr bloody Xavier is planning on doing next?'

'*He's sending several crews to that Sumbawa place, with orders to conduct a search of likely islands by air. They've worked out you'd be avoiding inhabited ones, and you'll most likely be heading east, so that narrows the search area.*'

'I suppose that's logical, but there's still a lot of water to fly over. We've just cleared the scene of the latest raid and found a new, deserted island, so I figure we'll be okay for a few days at least.'

'*You're probably right. It'll take them a couple of days to get the troops in place on the ground, and even longer to organise aircraft and so on.*'

'I forgot about the travel delays, but you are right. We might have a few days grace.'

'*That's the idea. Don't go charging off all over the Archipelago again. We'll keep you informed, because our inside man seems to know what's being planned within minutes of it happening. So that's a measure of security for you, at least!*'

Although worried by the security leaks, I was still hopeful we did have several days peace before we had to run or fight all over again.

I passed on the essence of Greg's information and Lara went on a guilt trip all over again.

'I'm sorry, Harry. I got so pissed on those bloody cocktails, the housekeeper had to wake me up and help me get ready. Reception already knew about my flight out because I had to give them my checkout time.'

'That's OK, Lara. Apart from getting pissed, you couldn't have helped the rest of it. I'm just concerned because I know how tenacious Xavier can be. He's cunning like a fox, so it doesn't take much to get him on a trail. We must accept they'll find us at some time, and be prepared for them.'

Andy spoke up, 'I know we've covered this before, but now we know they're getting closer, couldn't we make a fast run south to international waters and call up a patrol boat?'

I nodded understanding, 'We certainly can do that, but we understand Xavier's mentality quite well from previous encounters Also, Dave and Corrine used to work for him, so we know he won't stop just because the boat you're on is grey instead of blue. And a privately-organised attack directly on a Navy boat would be impossible to keep quiet, therefore the publicity would open up the whole West Australian debacle. Your Government would be not just ousted, but torn to shreds and scattered to the four winds. That was the original plan of these idiots who wanted a Dictatorship!'

Andy reluctantly agreed. 'Yeah. It certainly could go that way. So, we might as well stay here and dig in, instead of trying to find some other hiding place?'

'That's right. And remember, they haven't found us yet.'

CHAPTER 38

PULAU KAKABIA, THURSDAY

The reminder that our old adversary was closing in had created a sombre mood the night before and it persisted into next day. It showed in many small ways. Laughter was cut short and not too many jokes were told or played. Small jobs were started but rarely finished and nervous mannerisms were on display.

Despite the uncomfortable walking environment, we did go for walks, but with joggers on for foot protection. Looked at in full daylight, the island was a lot higher than I'd thought, with a north-south spine poking up all of, maybe, one hundred feet above sea level, but it would help to break up the worst of the winds if we should get more storms; which was an absolute certainty with the monsoon season in full swing.

The exercise helped everyone's mood, especially since we had taken the pussies with us and walked over to the other side of the island. The hike over wasn't too much fun, but we planned to wander back via the beach even though the dense scrub came right down to the water's edge in many places. It took Krazy cat about fifteen minutes to get tired of climbing over and around lumps of limestone, so she either bludged a ride with the nearest human or jumped on Jasper's back and dug her claws in as anchors.

There were two, much longer stretches of pure white sand beach on the east side, although the water looked shallower, but it might have been the same optical illusion we encountered coming in yesterday. The only piece of strategic information I gained out of the walk, was that the rough terrain would slow down any land party who tried to come at us from the dry side. The thought prompted me to have a quiet talk to Corrine when we got back.

Finally, we were back at the boats, safely tucked into their snug little harbour, where a swim was necessary to wash the sweat off, followed by a big feed of toasted sandwiches for lunch. That afternoon, Sandy and I took the RIB and Jasper around to the peculiar deep hole that wasn't far from our little bay. It was an intense, deep blue colour and to our delight, it was full of turtles of all shapes and sizes. Perhaps it was a nursery since no major predators could get in there, although the hole was also teeming with fish of all sizes and descriptions.

I had some snorkelling gear with us and was soon over the side checking out the parade of underwater life. The turtles were totally unafraid, although I was sure some islanders must have found this seafood supermarket. Still, I had a great time paddling around being nudged by turtles and had to give Sandy a go with the gear so she could see for herself.

She finally came back, totally entranced with the spectacle and excited about all the bumps and rubs she'd received.

We hung around for a while, then returned to the boats to tell the others over an early round of 'five o'clocker's' about our discovery. Plans were made for everyone to head there tomorrow morning and get some video of the spectacle, and it provided another useful lift in everyone's spirits.

JULIET DAVIS, SUMBAWA BESAR, THURSDAY

Juliet finally chased a highly amorous Mike out of her bed soon after breakfast had been delivered to the room, after extracting a promise he would help her find charter aircraft. Following her talk with Xavier the previous night, she kept to the background story that Lara, Juliet's 'sister', needed to be found since she was a co-heiress to a large fortune. The story to be given to anybody else, was that she was going to be the female lead in a big-budget movie and had chucked a hissy fit and bailed out of contract talks.

The crew arriving later that day needed the aircraft for the search, and she thought she might put Mike on retainer to help as the local contact. They might even need to charter his boat, depending on how the search developed.

'You are going to help me today, aren't you?' Juliet asked. 'You did promise.'

He gave her a cheeky grin as he padded naked to the bathroom. 'Yeah, Babe. I'll help you. I know most of the charter pilots here anyway since they all seem to like diving. And fortunately for you, I don't have a charter today.'

'Great! Hurry up in there so we can get going. There's lots to do and time's wasting.'

His word was good and he did indeed know most of the aviation community and on Juliet's behalf handled the discussions with one company in particular who had, he claimed, the right sort of aircraft for a long-range search.

'This won't be cheap,' he warned her, stopping in the tiny carpark, outside the slightly rundown-looking offices of the company of his choice.

'How much not cheap?' she asked, impressed by his all-business manner.

'You want three long-range aircraft, so you'd better be prepared to shell out between $1500 and $2000US per hour. Each! That does, however, include pilots and fuel and they'll probably throw in lunch!' The last was delivered with a grin.

Juliet was slightly shaken to think each hour of the aerial search could cost up to US$6,000!

'I'm glad you told me that out here. Let me check in with the Boss briefly and make sure he's wants to go ahead.'

She got onto Xavier straight away.

...'Yes sir. That's a rough estimate my advisor has given me before we talk business with the charter company. I just wanted to make sure it's what you wanted.'

...'Yes sir. That's no problem. I have the card so long as the funds are there.'

...'Thank you for that, sir. I'm sure we can make it happen. I have a lot of confidence in our new associate.'

...'Thank you. I'll tell him.'

She re-joined Mike, waiting several cars away, smiling in reply to his raised eyebrows.

'All good?' he asked.

'All good!' she replied. 'My credit card is full to bursting with dollars, apparently. But,' she added hastily, 'there's no need for anybody else to know that!'

He smiled, 'Of course not. On that basis, shall I negotiate?'

'Sure. But perhaps you can refer back to me occasionally.'

'Absolutely! Tag team is always a good approach.'

They went inside and Mike was immediately and happily recognised by the petite receptionist, before she went to fetch the manager. He was a medium man; medium height, weight and looks, but was happy to see Mike and to be introduced to Juliet as Josh Tellman, another expat Aussie.

'Come into my office and be comfortable.' He ushered them into a spacious but spartan office with windows on two walls; one showing a view of the airport and the tarmac in front of the office and hangers which comprised the company headquarters. The other window showed the interior of the huge hanger which the offices were built inside of.

Although not familiar with the general-aviation scene, Juliet did notice the floor was freshly painted, the mechanics and engineers wore neat and clean uniforms and the aircraft parked inside or being worked on were clean and tidy. Except, of course, where inspection panels had been removed, in one case turning a sleek aircraft into a gutted skeleton which looked as though it'd never fly again.

After giving Juliet a few moments to take it all in, Josh looked from one to the other expectantly, so Mike led off.

'Juliet has asked me to help her organise some aircraft charter, so naturally, I thought we'd come here first.'

Josh's attention sharpened at that and he drew a blank writing pad closer. 'I appreciate that, Mike. I hope we can help, but what's the job and what do you need Miss Davis?'

'I'm looking for my sister. She walked out on a business deal worth a great deal of money and it's stalled until we can get her to come back. I have traced her to Bali and then to here as of last Monday, when she was seen boarding a large and expensive power boat which headed for parts unknown. I'm prepared to pay handsomely to find out where.'

Mike chipped in, 'It's an AB100, Josh. Pretty rare bird anywhere outside the Med, let alone here.'

Josh's eyebrows raised, 'That is a rare bird. Bloody fast too, from what I've heard.'

Juliet resumed the background story. 'We don't know who owns the boat or who else is on it, but it would seem they will be keeping their heads down and staying away from inhabited areas.'

'Ok. That's the why, but what do you want us to do about this? We charter aircraft, not boats. Mike's your man for that.'

She smiled, 'I have six people flying in from Bali this afternoon who will form three two-person teams. I would like to charter three of your longest range and endurance aircraft, plus the planning skills of you and your staff to go and search for this mysterious boat she left on.'

Josh let out a deep breath, 'Three long-range aircraft to search islands. Do you know how many islands there are in Indonesia, Miss Davis?'

Juliet smiled, despite his slightly patronising tone. 'At last count, something over seventeen thousand islands, most of which are inhabited. I want to look at the ones that aren't inhabited, and lie within a reasonable boat range of this place. I have reason to believe my sister and her friends will be working their way back east and then on down to Australia.

Therefore, based on that bit of generalisation, you and your pilots should have an excellent idea where suitable islands are, so the search isn't needle in the haystack stuff, but with good and careful planning, just a case of visiting likely prospects. A boat like that can't be hidden easily, I wouldn't think.'

Josh thought a few moments, studying Juliet carefully. Reaching a decision, he jotted a few notes on the pad beside him and said, 'OK. You're right. That information does reduce the search considerably, although there are still hundreds of uninhabited islands, for one reason or another, so the task isn't quite as simple as you suggest, but maybe we can do a reasonable job of checking out the likely ones.'

Juliet smiled, 'Thank you. So, we can do business?'

'I think so,' he replied. 'Do you have a budget limit we have to stay within?'

'No!' was her short answer and her expression didn't encourage questions.

Josh's smile was immediately wiped off his face and he got straight down to business.

'Without a budget limit, it becomes easier and considerably more effective.'

He flashed a remote over his shoulder at a large TV on the wall and within seconds, it came alive displaying a blue screen.

'I can't give you what I'd like to, because they are committed to other work for regular customers, but I do have two aircraft in particular which will be excellent for this job. Here's the first.'

He tapped at the computer's keyboard and a high definition photo of a twin engine aircraft flashed on the screen.

'That looks nice,' Juliet lamely commented. Josh smiled indulgently, used to uninformed public comments.

'Yes. It is very nice. It's a Beech King Air B-350. It's fast, with long range and endurance and it's comfortable and that's a good thing if you're going to be staring at the ocean for hours on end.'

Juliet nodded, 'OK. That sounds good. Do you have three of them?'

He laughed. 'At times I wish I did. Unfortunately, there's barely enough work to keep this one paying its way. But it's available right now for three days before it has a pre-booked charter.'

He eyed her carefully again. 'The hourly rate is US$1800, including a pilot, fuel, food and I'll throw in a flight attendant. Every hour over the first ten, I'll reduce the rate to US$1500 per hour and that's a bloody good deal!'

If he thought she was going to faint or throw a wobbly, he was disappointed. She made a note in a small notebook, smiled and said, 'Next?'

He stabbed at the keyboard again and a similar-looking aircraft replaced the first one.

'Older brother to the first one,' he said briskly. 'Beech B-200GT. Almost as fast and has similar range. It's just older and slightly more worn, but still comfortable and will be most effective in this job. The rate is US$1400 per hour which I'll reduce to $1100 per hour after the first 10 hours.'

Juliet made another brief note, then looked up.

'Good. That's two, now for the third.'

Josh flashed another aircraft on the screen and even Juliet could see the difference...it only had one engine!

'This is a Kodiak 100 Series II. It's like a small version of the Cessna Caravan, except it's cheaper, just as fast and has the same range. Being single engine, and even though it's rated single-pilot IFR, I'd recommend it be sent along the coast to the east. That way, it will be over or close to land in the remote chance there is trouble. Being slower, it doesn't have the range of the big twins, although it does have nearly 10 hours endurance. By staying coastal, it can refuel as required. The rate for it will be US$1200 per hour and I'll lower that to an even $1,000 after ten hours.'

Juliet made more notes, before looking up. 'Great! My teams will be here this afternoon, so I'd like to launch the search first thing tomorrow morning if that's suitable.'

Josh nodded, 'No problem there. Shall we say a 07:00 departure?'

'Yes, that's OK. But now I'd like to have a briefing with your pilots and for them to come up with a list of potential islands. We may be throwing a lot of money your way over this business, but I'm not going to waste it, particularly since we only have three days for this first effort.

Oh! I forgot to mention, the information about my sister is strictly confidential, so for the pilots, ground crew and anybody else who asks, the cover story is, we are from a movie production company scouting for deserted island locations. I'll indicate on a map the limits of the search, then everyone can chip in with what they know. Is that all right?'

With a grin, he said frankly, 'No problem with that at all Miss Davis. $4,400 per hour buys a lot of attention around here. I'll just go and round up all our spare pilots, although our Chief Pilot is the most experienced and he's off-duty today, but I'll call him in anyway. Give me a few minutes to organise things, then we'll move to a briefing room. I'll send Indah in with tea or coffee.'

'Tea for me, thanks Josh, NATO-style,' Mike said.

'Coffee for me please. White and one.' Juliet asked.

'Coming up'. He whizzed off, appearing in the hanger moments later, rounding up pilots and anyone else who could contribute anything to the briefing; starting the process with the engineers of making sure the chosen aircraft would be ready for the morning.

CHAPTER 39

JULIET DAVIS, SUMBAWA BESAR, THURSDAY

Their drinks arrived with a selection of sweet biscuits. When they were alone, Juliet said, 'Josh seems genuine.'

'He is. He's one of the last independent operators and keeps his aircraft and pilots in top condition, and because of that, he has the lowest turnover of staff of any of the expat operators I know of. He'll get the job done. With him, it's not just the money — he wants to see customers go away happy. That's where the repeat business is; happy customers!

He does lose some pilots to the airlines, but that's the way young, low-time pilots are. Always looking for the chance to move up to bigger aircraft. It's the ultimate 'boys and their toys' game. They all want to be a Boeing 747 or Airbus 380 Captain.'

She laughed at his description, grateful for his easy-going expertise in most matters. 'You seem to know your way around aeroplanes well for a charter boat operator.'

He smiled, 'I should. I'm a pilot with both helicopter and fixed-wing licences and keep my medical and IFR ratings current so I can do the occasional job for Josh if he has a temporary pilot shortage. I used to work for him and was the first pilot he hired soon after he started. When I told him I wanted to try something different, he helped me get the boat and start the dive business, so I owe him a lot.'

Her mind churned over possibilities. 'So, you can fly all these aircraft?'

'Sure. In fact, Josh has me down to do a charter in ten day's time in the B-350 since pilots are always running out of hours.'

'That's good to know. I'll have a think about how that could be useful.'

Mike looked at her, trying to determine if she was really serious and what was behind the thought, but she kept a good poker-face which gave nothing away.

Josh slipped back into the office, announcing, 'I've got the three pilots who'll be doing the job, along with two engineers and my Chief Pilot is almost here. Let's go to the briefing room.'

A large map of the entire Archipelago with some surrounding areas, dominated one wall of the utilitarian room. She met the three pilots and the other staff.

Josh led off. 'OK, Miss Davis. Perhaps you'd care to show us the area of interest, then the boys will chip in from there.'

While mentally changing to the movie location scout story, she was handed a whiteboard marker and told to draw in the area to be covered on the plastic-covered map.

'We would like to base out of here, Sumbawa Besar and require a small island that's a typical tropical island, complete with white, sandy beaches. Forget any island that's inhabited or big. Certainly forget any mainland islands. Maybe include this string of islands just north of us, and then follow the path of islands just south of the west peninsula of South Sulawesi. If that makes sense?'

She looked around expectantly and received nods of encouragement, so she resumed.

'Then past that last area down from South Sulawesi, there are a couple of small, isolated islands. They might be good prospects too. Then look at the islands south of SE Sulawesi, and after that, if we haven't found what we're looking for, we'll try the islands east and north-east of Timor, but not the main islands. So basically, we want to stay local if we can, but if there's nothing of interest here, we want to work to the east rather than go west.'

She sat down again as the eight staff, plus Mike, started firing suggestions back and forth across the teak table. Josh was equipped with his writing pad and kept taking brief notes, sometime getting up to measure distances on the map.

After 30-minutes of lively discussion, the chatter dried up and

Josh turned to Juliet.

'Well, we seem to have a list for you, but it's quite comprehensive and may need more culling, but we can do some of that on Google Earth.'

'Good idea,' Juliet said, 'but Google Earth won't show what's actually there now, will it?'

'No, it won't. Good point.'

'OK. I don't think I can help with the cull since I don't know the area at all. But perhaps you need to be more exacting in the culling. An inhabited island is obviously out, as is one that is too close to an inhabited island. Without giving too much away, we will...ah... be making a lot of loud bangs and don't want to have to fend off irate or overly curious islanders.'

'Oh, OK. That'll help cut a lot,' Josh commented, 'OK guys. In light of that, let's run through them again.'

Juliet was pleased they were being so helpful and appeared to be enjoying the challenge to find what she was after. The lively discussion went on and Indah turned up with platters of tangy and tasty finger food for lunch, during which Juliet had to fend off many questions about the 'movie' they were scouting for.

'Sorry guys, I've said all I can for now. You can imagine how paranoid about secrecy the production companies get, but I had to tell you a little to make the search for the right location easier.'

They took the rejection good naturedly and carried on through lunch with the casting of the various pilots, engineers and female flight crew into increasingly outlandish roles. All the banter caused great hilarity and reluctantly they returned to culling islands.

Finally, they were left with just thirty-five good prospects and the next job of allocating them in a logical order to visit began. The Kodiak single-engine aircraft was nevertheless allocated a run along the coast to the east, although the best chances lay in a line along the chain of islands right over past SE Sulawesi that Juliet had already indicated on the wall-map.

These island targets were split between the two twin-engine

King-Airs and the crews made up their flight plans.

With still more than two hours before her crews were due to arrive, providing the Wings aircraft was on time, a rare event, she was advised, Juliet was pleased at how the planning had gone so well.

The arrival of two new faces, a male and a female pilot, the female with four stripes and the guy with three, brought the news that a line of thunderstorms was rapidly forming to the east and due to hit Sumbawa in a couple of hours. The two were an unlikely pairing, but were cheerful and constantly threw off at each other, although their post flight briefing to Josh was delivered in a totally professional manner.

They also brought an interesting piece of news from their last landing point at Padang on the Island of Selayar in South Sulawesi Province. The refuelling crew was talking about two long canoes which had stopped in for fuel and supplies, having made the long journey from a group of islands not far north of Sumbawa. The canoes were manned by several family groups, where the females were distraught with grief and the men were in a towering rage about what seemed to be an unprovoked attack on three canoe loads of fishermen, by the crews of a big, power boat and a sailing catamaran. The missing men were family members and were apparently on a fishing trip. The ridiculously large number of fishermen in each canoe wasn't explained, especially since the normal fishing crew was just three or four, not twenty-five per boat.

The fishermen had apparently been slaughtered without reason and there were no survivors. They glossed over the details of how the families knew so much without actually being there, but suffice to say, the families wanted to catch up with the murderous foreigners to exact payback. They weren't sure where they had gone, but there was a report from a young boy and his brother who were out fishing on Wednesday afternoon, of a large powerboat and a large catamaran rounding Pulau Madu and heading northeast.

Initially, Juliet didn't register fully what she was hearing, and it was only when they were about to leave for the Arrivals Terminal, she thought of a few questions for Mike's ears only.

'That story of the attack by two foreign boats on the islanders. What's the go with that? Is it a put-up job or what? I can't imagine a couple of boatloads of tourists going berserk and killing what was it...seventy-five islanders on a fishing trip?'

Mike laughed, 'Of course it was a put-up job, but regardless, something odd has happened out there, to drive two family groups to make such a long journey. That area has a bit of a reputation since there have been several other incidents where boats have disappeared, never to be seen again. Piracy is always suspected, but because they never seem to do anything particularly obvious, and there are no witnesses or survivors, the authorities can't do anything. It's nothing obvious like what happens over in the west towards Singapore.

What I took from Reg and Yvonne's story was that maybe there were a couple of cruising boats staying at a small, uninhabited island, and some villagers got a bit greedy and thought they might have a pick of the goodies. Maybe the visitors were armed and prepared to use their weapons; most yachties these days have at least a shotgun aboard for self-defence. But wholesale slaughter is a bit far-fetched.'

'Ok. Are those islands on the list?'

'Yep, they sure are. We'll hit them early tomorrow.'

OK. Just checking.'

They reached the arrivals area to be told the aircraft was almost on time, and was hoping to land before the arrival of several very nasty squall lines associated with an active thunderstorm. It just made it onto the ground, touching down as the first howling gust of rain-laden wind slammed into several aircraft parked on the tarmac, then barrelled like a solid wave of air and rain across the airfield before striking the Wings Boeing 737 midway through its landing roll-out.

The aircraft became airborne briefly, then slammed back onto the ground before it slewed off the runway onto the wet grass, where it performed a graceful pirouette while still sliding toward the apron in front of the terminal. Apart from the huge showers of mud slung up by the wheels when they were going sideways, the manoeuvre almost looked as though the aircraft was taking a shortcut to the terminal, except it stopped well short, still on the grass.

As if such antics with a B737 were normal, the crew shut the engines down, then presumably due to the driving rain, kept the doors closed as they waited calmly for the portable air stairs to arrive. It wasn't until an hour later when the first busload of wet and bedraggled Wings passengers was delivered to the terminal. Juliet's crew were not dropped off until the third busload and were quickly passed through to the groundside portion of the terminal.

She only knew two of the new crew, a competent woman called Clarissa and a man called Tommy, who introduced the other four as Rick, Jim, Abel and Sara. Of the six, Sara and Abel seemed to be the least experienced and a few brief questions revealed they were recent imports from the UK and qualified for Xavier's employment by having been kicked out of the London Metropolitan Police for repeated reports of arrest brutality.

She introduced Mike, then suggested they hold questions until she gave them a briefing at the hotel. Once they had checked into their rooms and washed away the memory of the flight, she called them into her room where she told them of the culling work and gave each a copy of the short list produced, then laid out the plans for the next two or three days.

'Everyone takes a small overnight kit with them, please. Just in case your aircraft can't get home that day.' They all nodded, not asking any questions, so she went on to tell the story of the supposed attack on the innocent Islanders, letting Mike explain the reasoning behind the conclusion that the innocent Islanders were opportunistic pirates.

'Therefore, the crew who visit the island where the presumed pirates came from, will check-out the couple of un-inhabited islands not too far away. They are all not far north of here.'

Clarissa looked at the copy of a map Juliet had the hotel produce for each of them. 'What about the report of foreign pleasure boats slipping around that island well west of here? Any small, deserted island out that way would be high on the list of likely targets, and an excellent chance of finding Miss Bishop.'

Juliet nodded, 'Yes, you're right, but we're going to tackle things systematically. Can I presume no one has any major objections to us working that way?'

Several heads shook. 'Excellent! The crews have already worked the flight plans out and wheels-up is at 07:30. The initial search will be flown at high altitude to reduce the risk of being spotted, but any possible sightings of the AB100 in particular, will require closer checking somehow. We obviously don't want to spook them into making another run for it, so I suggest you stay as high as possible and use the stabilised binoculars we provide.'

She looked at Clarissa, 'Did Xavier give you any of the Canon stabilised DSLR cameras with long range lenses?'

Clarissa nodded, 'Yep! Each team has one.'

'Good. Also, you will each have a Sat-Phone to call back here where Mike and I will co-ordinate the search and the results, if any.'

Clarissa spoke up again. 'What action do we take at this stage if we make a positive ID of the boat?'

'To be honest, I don't know, but I'll be talking to Xavier later to get his plan for that. At the moment, he thinks that Miss Bishop is still on the Gold Coast. In his opinion, this is just a good, but long shot, which is why I believe he hasn't planned too far ahead yet.'

Clarissa was happy with that, and with no further questions, they broke up for the evening, most heading for the bar & restaurant, but Mike and Juliet ordered their meal to the room as she grabbed her own SatPhone and called home.

CHAPTER 40

JULIET DAVIS, SUMBAWA BESAR, THURSDAY/FRIDAY

'Xavier.'

'Good evening, Mr Xavier, this is Miss Juliet with a progress report.'

'Proceed.'

'Certainly Sir. I am still in Sumbawa Besar and the surveillance crews have arrived. The charter aircraft are booked and the company has been most helpful in planning the operation, although they have been told the movie location story and have accepted that.

My new assistant is proving to be extremely useful and is a great asset to the operation.

We have reduced a long list of potential hiding sites to manageable numbers, thanks to his efforts and those of the charter company staff.

We have received fresh reports from two charter company pilots who picked up talk from locals of a strange incident which occurred at a small island not far north of here, where it has been claimed that two boat-loads of foreigners had slaughtered seventy-five fishermen in three long canoes on a fishing trip.'

'Continue.'

'As a result of that incident, two family groups made the long and hazardous journey to the east hoping to catch the foreigners who were sighted by another fisherman rounding the tip of Pulau Madu and heading to the NE. There are only one or two tiny islands along that track, before the coast of SE Sulawesi is encountered, so the small islands are high on the priority list and will get at least a high level overflight tomorrow.

The search aircraft are launching tomorrow, Friday, at 07:30

local time so all the high potential sites will have had a high-altitude check by the end of the day, at which time I will make a further report.'

'*Excellent work, Miss Juliet. My faith in you has been well justified. However, if I may I solicit your opinion; based on what you have already learned first-hand, how likely is it that Miss Bishop is somewhere in the Indonesian Archipelago, rather than on the Gold Coast?*'

Without hesitation she replied, 'At least 95%, sir.'

'*Really? That high?*'

'Yes Sir, I'm afraid so. I feel the other operatives are following an elaborate red herring and someone on the other side is very clever at deception. Which leads me to ask, what are your instructions if we do gain a positive ID on them?'

'*I have the very worst memories of one person who qualified as being clever at deception. It would be too much of a coincidence if he were involved with this operation as well, but we shall see. As for your question, we want them alive, but we must keep them totally isolated, therefore, the base requirement is a snatch and run operation, keeping the 'target' unharmed. I consider the others in his party expendable.*

Thank you, Miss Juliet, for an excellent report and it sounds as though you have things under control for now. I will take your thoughts on board and will consider them carefully. If you are able to prove you are right, I'm ready to move another twenty operatives into the area immediately.

Xavier clear.'

SUMBAWA BESAR, FRIDAY, JULIET

Following another pleasant night with Mike, both in and out of bed, Juliet was awake, refreshed and waiting in the carpark by 07:00, ready to see the teams airborne, even though lift-off wasn't for another 30 minutes. There were two stragglers, the newcomers, who were scheduled to make the coastal run in the single-engine

Kodiak. After suitably chastising them and handing out a 'last chance before you're out' warning, she shooed them into the hands of the aircrew for the day, playing Mother Hen and making sure each team had a SatPhone, stabilised binoculars and maps. The charter company supplied food and drink.

Juliet and Mike returned to the hotel and set up the room with maps, radios, phones and writing materials.

'Bloody hell, I hate waiting,' Juliet grumped to Mike.

He grinned back annoyingly, 'I can see it's going to be a long day.'

'Yes, it will be,' she shot back, 'and even longer if you're going to be a smart-arse all the time!'

He patted the air between them in a gesture meant to settle her down, and fortunately, it worked.

'I'm sorry,' she apologised. 'There's a great deal hanging on this, so I'd really like to be the operative to track the man down.'

'Fair enough. You've worked hard and deserve a break.'

She smiled unexpectedly, 'Sure. But in a male-heavy organisation like Stainless Associates, any female has to be twice as good just to be allowed to stay on the team. They're mostly just a bunch of swinging-dicks!'

His reply was interrupted by the trilling call of the SatPhone with Clarissa of team #1 calling.

'Go ahead, Clarissa.'

We've just flown over the island where the attack was supposed to have happened, but there's nothing to see. We're just coming up on the inhabited island where the fishermen who were involved are supposed to live and I can see several villages with lots of long canoes on the beach or in the water. There is one big native power boat nosed up on the beach in front of the biggest village and it's one of those 80 to 100-foot jobs with the high bow and a cabin down aft.

There's no other activity there or close by. Clarissa clear.

'Thanks Clarissa, Base clear.'

Juliet looked at Mike. 'That was a necessary waste of time, since there's no way those two boats would have stayed at that first island after the attack or fight or whatever the hell it was, but we still had to check!'

'You're right. They would have been moving before the smoke had even cleared, but was it them over at Pulau Madu?'

She gave a predatory grin, 'I really think it must have been. Look at the map. It's 275 nautical miles from the island where they were, to the sighting point. They were sighted at about 14:30 Wednesday which is 20 hours after the attack is supposed to have happened and that gives them a cruising speed of about 15 knots which would be right for a big sailing cat. I'll bet that AB100 goes a lot faster!'

Mike checked distances and times. 'Yep! It all fits, but where did they go from the sighting at Pulau Madu?'

'Now that's an interesting question! But a better question would be, where would they want to go?'

Mike thought a moment. 'They have to avoid any populated island, so that rules out going too far north or north-east, unless they push for the chain of islands south-east of SE Sulawesi, and that's a long way off track if they were edging toward Australian waters.'

She beamed at him. 'Exactly! I always thought they'd want to stay close to Australia if possible, so therefore, they either stop at Pulau Kauna or Kakabia, which are both uninhabited and not far from where they were sighted, or they make a 90° course change to the south-east and head for the islands east of Timor. But that's an extra 450 miles or so from where they were spotted, so why would they waste time and fuel?'

'OK. I'll bite 'cause I'm sure you've got the answer. Why would they go where you think they have?'

'Because,' she exclaimed, 'there are two uninhabited islands in that direction and they aren't far. There's Pulau Kauna and Pulau Kakabia, but Kauna doesn't really have a safe anchorage, whereas Kakabia has several good places if their boats have shallow draft and that catamaran certainly would.'

Mike broke in on her excited deductions, 'I know the specs on the AB boats and they're all water jet drive so even the 100-footer will be very shallow draft.'

'Alrighty! I reckon that they picked Kakabia for all those reasons and should be there now.'

Mike grinned at her. 'Makes sense to me. So that'd be why you asked for the second King-Air to head directly for Pulau Madu first, then high-level search from there. Cunning plan, lovely lady! And looking at this chart, it's about a 60-minute flight time to Madu, then just 6 minutes or so to Kauna and another 8 minutes to Kakabia.'

She nodded, 'Yep! They should be reporting at Madu shortly.'

Mike just had time to relieve some bladder pressure before the Sat-Phone rang with Tommy reporting that they were just passing Pulau Madu at 15,000 feet altitude, which the pilots considered being the best compromise between hard to see from the ground, but able to pick up excellent ground detail with the powerful Canon 18 x 50 stabilised binoculars.

'I might stay on the phone for the moment, as Pulau Kauna is just ahead and the other one, Pulau Kakabia is a bit further on up to the north-east.'

'That's fine Tommy. We have high hopes for Kakabia as Kauna doesn't seem to have much in the way of a safe anchorage.'

'Yeah, I'd go along with that. We're just coming up on it now, although the island looks pleasant, the surrounding reef plateau looks shallow. Gee, these Canon binoculars are sweet as! I can clearly see individual palm fronds and even the leaves. Oops! It just slid back under the wing, but there wasn't anything there — not even a cultivated area of coconut palms to attract other islanders.'

'Understood. We didn't expect anything there really, but we had to check.'

'No problem. It's a great time of day for flying before the cumulo-nimbus build-ups happen this arvo. We need to be on the ground by then, preferably back there. Even Sara seems to be enjoying herself. OK. I've waffled on enough, back to work.

We're just coming up on Kakabia and it's got that really strange-looking reef shaped like a wine-glass poking down to the south-east. Doesn't look like there's anything there, though.... Hang about...Got 'em! There's a little bay up on the north-east corner and the two boats looked like some of the rocks that poke up in the bay, but now I've spotted them, they stand out enough. I've got Sara taking photos.

There's a catamaran and a powerboat which is much bigger than the cat. I dunno how her skipper fitted that monster into the little bay, but he did. Do you want us to get a closer view?'

'No way! You're forbidden to go any lower. Just get what hi-res photos you can and we'll get what we can from them.'

OK Boss. No problem, but how about we bend our course a bit until we're out of sight, then we can curve around and do another fly-over, but we'll stay offset by several miles to be less obvious and we'll get a different view with the camera.'

Juliet thought a moment before replying, 'OK. That's approved, but no lower and no more passes after those two! Understand?'

'No problem. Even if they do spot us, the pilots tell me air traffic is fairly regular in this area, so we shouldn't stand out'.

'OK, Tommy. Change of plan. If you're fairly sure the power boat is the one I showed you photos of, I'd like you to return to base immediately. We need to see those photos blown up as much as possible.'

'On it. I'll tell the pilots now and we should be landing in just over an hour.'

'Thanks Tommy. I'll have Mike pick you up. Bye.'

As promised, 90-minutes later, she let Tommy and Mike into the room. Holding tight to the carry handle, Tommy hefted a camera with a massive white lens up onto the small dining table and unlatched the cover on the side of the Canon EOS 5DS, where the precious SD card lurked, waiting to surrender its secrets.

Mike took the card and while he was opening its files, Juliet looked the equipment over.

'That's some lens!' Juliet observed. 'Is it 600mm?'

'No. It's a Canon 800mm F/5.6. And definitely needs a tripod, even with the excellent image stabilisation. At 15,000 feet, at this hour of the day, the King Air was smooth, so with luck, we should have some useful shots.'

By the time Juliet had finished examining the lens and camera, Mike had the SD card loaded onto the MacBook Pro laptop, and had hooked the images to the huge UHD TV dominating the wall above the writing desk.

He started scrolling and immediately the quality of the photos was apparent. The huge lens and the 50MP stabilised camera made a potent combination and the photos could be zoomed in without pixilation. The best ones showed the two boats, a large sailing catamaran and an even larger power boat nestling side-by-side in an impossibly small inlet on Kakabia's north-west shore. Zooming in on the nearly overhead view, showed several people on deck, but apart from being able to pick male from female, they couldn't say for certain if their target was aboard.

'Terrific photos, Tommy,' Juliet enthused. 'I'm convinced that it's the same boat that picked up Lara Bishop from the river wharf. What do you guys think?'

Both Tommy and Mike agreed that even from the different perspective, it looked the same.

'Going on circumstantial evidence, how many AB100s are running around Indonesia at the moment, hanging around deserted islands? That'd be way too much of a coincidence!'

She looked from one to the other, 'So you're happy that's the boat?'

They both nodded.

'OK. And a woman who looked exactly like Lara was seen to be delivered by taxi and got on board an AB100 at the river.'

They nodded again, with Mike adding, 'There's only so many co-incidences which can be strung together. I think you could safely call your boss and tell him the target's found!' Juliet thought a few moments, before slowly nodding with increasing confidence, 'I'll do it first before I cancel the rest of the flight search. The boss has funny ideas sometimes, and it doesn't pay to stick your neck out too far.'

...'Good morning Sir, this is Miss Juliet.'

...'It's gone well, thank you. In fact, we believe we've found the target.'

...'No, not close-up. But we do have HD photos taken from the aircraft by Mr Tommy who is with me now.'

...'Yes, I realise that, Sir. But the photos are of exceptional quality and we have compared them to the photos of the boat which collected Lara from Sumbawa Besar wharf and are in agreement they are the same.'

...'No, Mr Tommy was under strict instructions not to get too close and he acted accordingly. Our observers don't believe they were spotted, but even if they were, the pilots advise the area is on a regular air route. They say there is a fair amount of air traffic, so we believe the targets shouldn't be spooked into running again.'

...'No, they didn't get close enough to identify faces, so naturally I cannot guarantee Miss Bishop is aboard.'

...'Well, of course we have to be sure. That goes without saying, but the only way would be to have feet on the ground.'

...'Oh, I see. Yes, we can do that.'

...'Very well Sir. I'll organise it immediately, but looking at the area charts, there won't be time to get in and out today, although we could get two operatives on the ground this evening.'

...'No Sir. Even that's stretching things way too far, but I should call you with results by this time tomorrow.'

...'No Sir, impossible. The distance to the island from the closest airstrip is 158 kilometres and the observers will have to hire a powered canoe, so even at best speed each way, it will take 3.7 hours.'

...'I will do that Sir, and report as soon as I have a result. Miss Juliet clear.'

CHAPTER 41

JULIET DAVIS, SUMBAWA BESAR, FRIDAY

Juliet had taken the unusual step of allowing Mike to sit in on her conversation with Xavier, because she needed his local knowledge and because she didn't really have a lieutenant to talk stuff over with, he was nominated. However, she was still being careful not to reveal the ultimate target to him as she wasn't sure of where his loyalties lay, or what his reaction might be to the knowledge that he was assisting in the manhunt for the Aussie PM. Chasing a reluctant heiress was one thing, but a manhunt for the PM was on a totally different scale!

'I gather that he wants feet on the ground to get photo proof of Lara being aboard the cruiser,' Mike said interrupting her musings.

'Yep. He really doesn't want to accept she's up here and not on the Gold Coast. It's all an ego thing. If she's up here, it means he's been deceived by the clever bugger who's behind all this sleight-of-hand stuff and that gets right up his nose.'

She sighed. 'Anyway, we have to get a small team out there ASAP, so what's the best way?'

Mike observed shrewdly, 'This boss of yours is being uncommonly persistent and seems to take this all personally. It should be just a job, really.'

Juliet reminded herself to be careful with her reply. 'Well, all I can say is that with the amount of money involved in this inheritance thing, he's being paid a great deal to find her and bring her back to Australia.'

He nodded non-committedly as he got up and looked carefully at the large map they'd taped to one wall.

'I had a drop-off once out here at Taman Nasional Takebonerate. It's a dirt strip and only 650 metres long, so it'll have to be the

Kodiak100 'cause the King Air won't fit. Your operatives should be able to hire a long outrigger canoe with extra fuel for the run out to the island. That looks like about 85 to 90 nautical miles and if the outrigger is powered properly, it should be able to maintain 25 knots which will take around 3.5 hours each way.

If the crew get going shortly and with flight time about 80 minutes, by the time they land and organise a boat they should be able to be on the island, unseen, a good hour before dark. That's enough time to take photos and get away under cover of darkness.'

Juliet nodded, 'That'll work for me.'

'OK. So who's your best crew to do this job? Two will be enough, but they need to be good on the ground. I get the feeling that these people shouldn't be underestimated.'

Juliet thought a moment. 'I might send Tommy. He's been around and used to be British Police SWAT equivalent.'

Mike chuckled. 'That makes him over-qualified for this little job in that case, so he should do it easily.'

'Alright. I'll call him in and get it happening, if you wouldn't mind advising Tellman Aviation they can recall the other two aircraft for now, but to be ready to send the Kodiak thing out to whatever the place was you said.'

'No problem, although it's just as well Josh has got three Kodiaks. They're perfect for short, rough strips. I'll make some other phone calls as well and try to organise a boat for this afternoon. I know a bloke on the island who might be able to help.'

He got busy with the room phone as Juliet flashed him a quick smile of thanks and used her mobile to call Tommy back to the room.

Two minutes later, there was a rap on the door and Tommy strolled in. 'Hi Boss. What's the go?'

'Our boss wants photo confirmation Lara is on that AB100, so I'm sending you and one other to get it.'

He gaped. 'Aww, c'mon Juliet. What do want me to do, walk on water? Or maybe parachute in?'

She knew him well from past operations and smiled indulgently while he had a little rant.

'None of the above, you drama queen! Mike has it worked out. You tell him, please Mike.'

Mike went back to the chart taped to the wall. 'Two of you, with camera, will fly back to the same area immediately, except that you will land on a large island which has several villages and a couple of small towns. It's called Taman Nasional Takebonerate and is the closest airstrip to Kakabia Island.

A local woman called Lintang will meet you with transport and take you straight to the wharf on the east side where, I've been promised, Lintang's husband will have an outrigger canoe ready and waiting, fuelled and provisioned.

Lintang proudly told me that it's one of the fastest rigs around and can easily outrun a Patrol Boat, which might give you an idea of her husband's part-time occupation!'

Despite his misgivings, Tommy gave a bit of a grin. 'So, we're to hook up with a bunch of pirates?'

'No, no! Just one. There will just be you, your partner and Arief. His only part in the operation will be to get you there, wait and bring you back. The timing will work if you leave in the next half-hour, giving you plenty of time to fly to Taman Nasional Takebonerate, get to the canoe, then get to the island. You should make it with just enough light left to get across the island, take some happy snaps and get back to the canoe.'

He finished pointing the way on the chart, sat down and turned the rest of the briefing over to Juliet.

'Your job is to get to the island, preferably with some daylight left, and without being spotted. Take what photos you can, showing the AB100 and Lara as well. Then get out without being spotted again and get the photos back here urgently. You must try really hard not to be seen. Take food, water, a Sat-Phone and this envelope to pay Lintang and Arief. Who do you want to take with you?'

'I might as well stick with Sara. She seemed on the ball this morning and did a good job with the camera. The experience should be useful seeing as she's new to the Company.'

Juliet nodded, 'Okay. That's fine. Now get going. Your aircraft will be ready by the time you get there.'

He sketched a salute, flashed a cheeky grin and left.

'Will he be all right?' Mike asked.

'Yeah! He's pretty experienced and is steady under pressure. I don't know how Sara will be, but like he said, she needs the experience.'

TOMMY, FRIDAY

He knocked on Sara's door and gave a big grin when she opened it wearing just brief panties and a T-shirt.

'Nice, partner. I especially like the little satin bow and where it's placed!'

Sara poked her tongue out, saying in her British accent, 'Haven't you got anything better to do than inspect my crotch?'

'Unfortunately, yes! We have a job, so get dressed. We're going out again to get photos on the ground at the island where we saw the boats.'

She looked surprised, then excited as she waved him in. 'Keep talking while I dress.'

Tommy didn't mind watching as he talked. Sara was reasonably attractive with a nice body he'd like to get to know a lot better, but he knew if he tried to fool around on the job and Xavier heard about it, he'd be toast.

'C'mon! Start talking about the job and stop thinking about getting into my pants,' she said with a grin, taking her time about pulling on a baggy pair of shorts and a loose shirt over the T-shirt.

'Oh, yes. Well, the deal is we jump back in another aeroplane and get dropped off at some island that's as close as we can land to Kakabia Island; there's a fast outrigger long-canoe organised to take us to Kakabia. We land there in daylight, having snuck in without being spotted, make our way over to where those two boats were anchored, and you get some photos of the boat, but also of as many people as you can. They are particularly interested in the Lara woman. She's the tall blonde with the fairly big boobs.'

Sara playfully stuck out her 34 B chest, 'Like mine, did you mean?'

He grinned, and said diplomatically, 'That's right, just like yours, yes!'

'Good answer, dude. Maybe there's hope for you yet.'

'Thank you. Very kind of you, but for now, we'd better go. Don't forget the camera but have you got a more normal lens for it, instead of the elephant's dick thing you used this morning?'

She laughed, 'Did you mean that lovely Canon 800mm F/5.6 prime lens?'

'Yeah, that's the one. Still looked like an albino elephant's dick but I must admit it did a superb job. The boss is really pleased!'

'Good. But I'll put on a smaller 100-400mm Tamron zoom. Long reach, but much more compact and lighter than the big fella.'

She tossed the gear and a jacket in her backpack and said, 'I'm done. Let's go.'

Tommy stopped briefly at his room to grab a jacket and slip a compact Glock 19 in his pocket along with a couple of loaded magazines, and five minutes later, they reported at Tellman Aviation reception where their pilot from the morning run was waiting.

Five minutes after that, the single-engine turboprop droned into the humid air, leaving the circuit to climb to an economical cruise height of 10,000 ft on a heading of 065° direct for Taman Nasional Takebonerate.

While the pilot expertly dodged the afternoon thunderstorm build-up's, they chatted about the job and wondered, as all employees do, about the reasons behind it and the possible outcome of the present job. Neither felt the present mission was going to be much of a problem, but being careful, they went over the area chart and planned their approach to Kakabia Island as well as the best landing place. With homework done, they settled in to have lunch and relax as best they could, commenting that the Kodiak wasn't anywhere near as comfortable as the Super King Air.

Ninety minutes later saw them turn final for the short dirt runway on Taman Nasional Takebonerate, although the Kodiak had no problem and used just half of the 610 metres available. There was a rough parking area on the east side where the Kodiak lurched clear of the strip, nearly opposite a sandy track coming in from the west where a battered old flatbed truck sat waiting.

As they got their gear together, Tommy spoke to Bob the pilot. 'You'll be waiting here for us, I hope?'

'Yeah mate. I've got food, drink, music, a good book and a blow-up mattress if you're late. I've slept in this old girl before and I guess I'll be doing it again if I stay with this job.'

Tommy laughed, 'I'm glad you're prepared. We'll be awhile and it'll be well after dark before we're back. Can we fly out of here at night?'

Bob winked, 'Not supposed to, seeing as there are no landing lights, but there just happens to be an old oil drum at each end of the strip and all it takes is some wood and Jet A from the tank drain and I'll have an aim point. The landing and taxi lights on this thing are pretty good as well. We'll be right!'

'Okay, that suits me. Once we're back I'd like to get out of here as soon as.'

'Amen, brother. Good luck with your little excursion.'

'Thanks mate, see ya.'

With a rattle and clatter of worn bearings, the old truck swung to a stop near the aircraft, a small woman at the wheel, a patient look on her face.

'Lintang, I presume?' Tommy ventured, hoping like all hell she spoke English, and happy when she spoke with hardly an accent.

'I'm Lintang and you are Mr Tommy and Miss Sara?'

'Yeah. Thanks for picking us up and organising your husband to make the run. Here, I've got this for you.' He handed over the thick envelope, relieved when she didn't bother to count it.

'Okay, we must go now. You have a long trip ahead and not so comfortable. You have food and water?'

'Yes, we do thank you.'

Without further talk, she competently swung the old truck away from the aircraft, and headed down the narrow track on the west side of the landing strip. It led onto a slightly wider dirt road which ran north, with the sea on the left, until they came to a scattering of houses where Lintang took a left and a right to drive along a street close to the beach. Abruptly, she swung around a patch of scrub onto a well-made jetty that poked out into the shallow water inside the surrounding reef.

Several motorised long canoes were tied up to either side, but she drove out near the end where a somewhat bigger outrigger canoe bobbed quietly, a nuggetty man sitting on an old packing case nearby. Apart for a rudimentary woven-thatch cabin the boat was open, although the large outboard mounted on the stern looked modern enough.

'This is Arief,' Lintang introduced briefly, giving her husband a brief wave before expertly backing the truck back down the jetty.

Arief was equally economical with his speech and briefly shook hands before shooing them on board, starting the engine and casting off the bow line. Without further discussion, he waved them to the little cabin, before heading south parallel with the beach, keeping the speed down in the relatively shallow water, until nearly three kilometres later, they passed out through a gap in the fringing reef and Arief turned left and cranked on some speed.

'Talkative bugger, isn't he?' Sara commented as the wind of their forward motion whistled through the beautifully made woven structure, providing welcome relief from the ever-present, energy-sapping heat and humidity.

There were a couple of bunks in the little shelter where they could sit out of the sun or lie down if they wanted, and Tommy was tempted to say they could pass some time more comfortably and pleasantly, but Sara gave him a look that suggested it wouldn't be a good idea to even suggest it. Arief remained aft, steering the long craft directly from the outboard, perched on another worn packing case and appearing to be perfectly comfortable.

The canoe with its two slender outriggers slid easily over the waves, its 50 or 60 foot length leaving little disturbance in the water and seemed to Tommy's untrained eye to be easily driven. Certainly the big outboard wasn't working hard at what seemed like a modest power setting, the canoe going quite fast with licks of cool spray flicking up as they slid over or through larger waves.

The motion was comfortable and apart from the whistling wind, they could talk easily enough, going over the plan again to make sure that they had covered everything. Finally, Sara lay down on a bunk and soon dozed off. Tommy sat up for a while watching the sea rush past, but then took the other bunk and he too fell sleep, soothed by the gentle motion and the hissing rush of water.

He was woken by Arief shaking his shoulder and launching into another of his lengthy speeches, 'Wakey, wakey. We arrive.'

Tommy sat up with a start, the total absence of sound and movement disconcerting.

'Crap! Where are we?'

'You sleep; we at island.'

'Oh, fuck! I was supposed to make sure we came in on the east side opposite the cove where the boats are parked.'

Their voices finally woke Sara who sat up in alarm and stayed quiet, thankfully not repeating Tommy's questions.

Arief gave Tommy a disgusted look and waved around them, 'We in proper place. You think I know fuck-nothing?'

Tommy finally looked around and noted that Arief, with his smuggling and piracy background, had naturally brought them to the opposite side of the island and must have made a stealthy approach from well out to the east, letting the island shield them.

He'd even tucked them into a tiny little cove which barely fitted the canoe, but did a good job of hiding it from casual surveillance.

'I'm sorry Arief. I shouldn't have been asleep, and you have done a wonderful job to get us here without detection. Thank you!'

The little man huffed, but nodded acceptance of the apology and retreated aft to change fuel tanks and check over his beloved outboard motor.

'Whew,' Tommy said to a wide-eyed Sara, 'just avoided disaster there. Anyway, we'd better get moving. By the look of the sun, there's only about an hour or maybe a bit more before we lose light.'

That galvanised her into action, but suddenly she stopped. 'Uh... I need to pee, like really badly!'

'Can't you wait to go ashore?' Tommy asked. 'Like; it's just there!'

'No! Turn around. I'm going up front a bit.'

So, he did, although he saw that Arief was having a quiet chuckle to himself and hadn't bothered to look away. From the sound of it, she really had needed to go urgently, and it reminded him his own bladder needed draining as well, so he did so in the time-honoured manner of all male boaties, straight over the side. Both relieved, they gathered their gear and had Arief pole the boat in close enough that they could step off the bow, carefully avoiding the fancy jaws arrangement like a gaping marlin mouth which traditionally adorned the extended prow.

Their tiny cove was heavily overgrown with small trees which grew densely down to the water's edge, overhanging the water in places, making a landing awkward, but they carefully pushed through until they gained more open ground. Tommy led the way, moving slowly and trying to minimise the noise he made. To his slight annoyance, Sara moved much more quietly and easily and he thought he heard the occasional muffled giggle when he tripped over a dead branch or exposed root.

'Yeah, yeah. Very funny,' he growled softly. 'I'm better at creeping around buildings rather than this fuckin' mess of scrub and rocks.'

She made no reply, saving her breath as the ground sloped up steadily, then descended slowly. Through the occasional gap in the trees, they caught glimpses of portions of a boat hull, while the mast of the big cat stood up like a black guidepost. Finally, Tommy judged they were as close as he dared and they scouted around for a spot which would give them a fairly open view of the boats.

Naturally, it was Sara who found a small opening where they had a partial view between two trees and over the top of a shorter third one. She immediately started firing off frames, playing with the zoom to get as many shots of the people aboard as possible. There were several figures moving around, both male and female, and seemed to be a bit of a drinking party happening in the cockpit of the big cruiser.

'I've counted ten people so far,' Sara murmured, 'and there's a small cat as well, but nobody seems alarmed, so I guess we haven't been detected.'

'You've seen the photo of Lara. Is she among them?'

'I think so. There's a blonde woman with her back mostly to us who could be her. The bloke next to her looks vaguely familiar, but I can't place him. I'm terrible with faces and names. Hang on... Blondie is turning to speak to the dude beside her. There! That's a good profile shot, but I'd like to get one front on if she'll just stand up for a moment.'

Tommy stood up carefully and looked around. 'I'm getting a bit antsy about staying here any longer than we have to. If you reckon you're got some shots of the blonde woman and good ones of the rest of the crew, I'd like to get out of here. This is starting to give me the creeps.'

'Settle petal! Just a few more minutes. Blondie's starting to have an in-depth conversation with the guy next to her, so I may get a better frontal shot.'

'Well, the daylight's getting dim and I've got a weird feeling we're being watched. C'mon. We're getting out of here with what we've got. Stuff Xavier and his ultimate proof.'

Sara fired off a few last frames, 'Okay. I'm coming. You go Hugo, and I'll be right behind you.'

'Ha, ha! Very funny. I'm gone.'

With that he turned and retraced their steps back uphill, while Sara carefully made sure all the photos were saved to SD card before packing the camera away in her backpack. He was right about the light, because when she turned to follow him, the bush was quite dark.

Tommy sounded like he was about 50 metres or more away as she quietly and carefully started to follow, but he suddenly gave a terrified scream, followed by several more and seemed to be thrashing around making a tremendous noise. There came a loud, unearthly howling sound which didn't come from a human throat and the thrashing noises seemed to be Tommy, suddenly headed off to the north, along the low spine of the island. Another of the weird howling sounds shut all the disturbed birds up instantly, but it seemed to be moving along with what Sara presumed to be Tommy.

Terrified, she could think of no way to help Tommy, and mindful of the expressed requirement that the photos were vital evidence, she decided to move as quietly as possible straight back to the boat. Partway up the slope, her foot slipped on something wet and slippery, and although there wasn't enough light to see clearly, it looked like black oil had spilled over the rocks and dead branches which were strewn over the patch of ground. There was also a large lump of matter covered with more of the black oil-looking stuff that her mind reluctantly accepted as being blood. And most likely, blood which had belonged to Tommy just a few moments earlier.

She refused to speculate as to the nature of the lump of matter, preferring to focus on moving quietly and quickly back to the boat, an objective she gained without further incident.

To her immense relief, she found a rather agitated Arief still there, but ready to immediately depart.

'We have to wait for Tommy,' she protested as he started poling them clear of the shore.

'Mister he 'pinish!' was his simple and direct answer. 'Jungle cat take him. Him no more!'

'But he needs help,' she said as quietly as she could, 'we have to wait!'

'Him past help – no more! We go – now!'

With that final pronouncement, he fired up the engine and idled away as quietly as possible, not increasing power until well clear of the island. Sara retired to the hut after scrubbing her hands clean in the purifying salt water, sitting in the dark, tears leaking from her eyes, trying to come to grips with the idea that Tommy was gone in the most horrible circumstances.

CHAPTER 42

FIREBIRD, KAKABIA ISLAND, FRIDAY

The day had started well and we had settled into a bit of a comfortable and happy routine in our little sheltered cove, despite the thoughts that Xavier and his crew weren't far behind us and a confrontation was on the way. I had an early morning swim and was joined by first Charlie, my usual early morning swim partner, then to my surprise, Lara as well. Despite having all the attention from Gilbert she could handle, Charlie still seemed to take every opportunity to swim naked with me and I wondered how long it would be before she wanted to get really close-up and personal. There had already been a couple of occasions when she had gently and playfully grabbed a handful of my most sensitive bit, and it had felt really nice, but nothing developed past that.

I was saved from having to make a decision yet again, by Lara making an appearance at the top of the steps where she shed her sleeping shirt and carelessly bare, slipped into the warm, limpid water beside us.

'I'm not interrupting anything, am I?' she enquired politely, noting that we were rather close.

Charlie shook her head, 'Nah! All good. We were just quietly chatting. For the moment, anyway.' she added cheekily.

Lara giggled, 'Oh. It's like that, is it?'

I smiled, 'I'm behaving myself!'

They both laughed, but then Lara asked, 'Are we still doing the right or even the best thing by continuing to hide out here? I mean, we can still run south and call up the Navy.'

I mentally sighed, 'I agree it seems silly to just wait for the bad guys to catch up with us, but every time you have these doubts, just think of what would happen should any details leak about what has gone on over the last few months in West Australia and all the mess associated with that. I agree that the Navy could protect Andy from the bad guys, but what happens when he goes ashore? He'd be a target all over again unless these people are exposed for what they are.'

Charlie eyed me speculatively. 'Sounds like you're using us as bait to draw these arse-holes out of hiding.'

I nodded. 'Can't deny that. There seemed no other way. It's a risk, but this whole enterprise has been one giant risk.'

She smiled acceptance and let the subject go, but I knew it would come up again soon. We paddled around just chatting until sounds of life came from the galley and the smell of toast drew us from the water to rinse off, dry and toss some clothes on. Since Charlie and Lara had joined the crew, their modesty standards had suffered a major revision, something quite common on boats in tropical loca-tions, and something they both seemed comfortable with.

We had just finished breakfast and I was doing my daily rounds of the upper deck to check the state of health of all fittings and equipment, when Corrine walked forward on *Seeker's* long foredeck to talk.

She nodded her head slightly upwards. 'If you glance around, then lift your eyes up over my head, you'll see a small aircraft. It looks like a twin turbo-prop, maybe a King Air. I know that this is an air-route to and from some of the major islands, but if it turns or comes back, we'll know for sure.'

Only too aware from the Middle East days, just how effective big lenses on cameras can be, we stood by the bow rails just chatting.

I was the one facing west, when less than ten minutes since our first sighting, I saw the flash of a window catching and reflecting the early morning sun.

'Okay' I said quietly to Corrine. 'There it is again, but offset a couple of miles. I'm not going to believe in that much happenstance or coincidence, so we can assume it's the first piece of enemy action!'

Corrine nodded thoughtfully, 'Yeah, that'd be right. But they still won't move in force straight away, will they?'

'Nope. If that's the first sighting, and I'm sure it is, then they need to get more Intel on us. I'd expect them to make a small probe to check us out, make sure the PM is here and see how many live bodies we have.'

'When could we expect that to happen?' she asked. 'Today or tomorrow?'

'Could be either, I guess, but going by the time, today is quite feasible. I wouldn't want to get here too early; just before sunset would be best so they can escape under cover of darkness.'

'Makes sense. We just have to wait and stay alert.'

'That's the idea. Waiting's never easy, but we've both had a lot of practice over the years.'

'That's for sure. Are you going to put your radar on with target range warning set.? Your antenna is higher than ours.'

'Yes, it's a good early warning system. But we'll keep an eye and ear out for anything unusual. I still think they'll try a ground recce later today just before dark.'

I briefed Sandy and we kept an eye out for any more over-flights, but the skies remained clear, except for the occasional contrail at high altitude, which could be safely ignored.

Over lunch, taken on *Seeker* where Bree and Jill whipped up a varied selection of spicy and tasty finger foods, all washed down with a couple of beers each, I brought the rest of the crew up to date on what we'd worked out.

'There's no need for panic or even concern. If it is just a recce probe, they'll be trying hard not to be seen, so we don't expect any confrontation. Later this afternoon, we'll gather in the cockpit here and have our usual drinks, but I'll be activating the masthead camera on *Firebird* and putting it in motion-detect mode. Likewise, both radars will be on, but a covert approach by sea to the other side of the island won't be seen on radar because the antennas are too low to see over the small hill in the way.'

Nobody looked concerned, so the rest of the day slipped away pleasantly with a refreshing swim an hour after lunch, followed, in the case of Sandy and me, by a lovely romp which made delightful use of the time available. With the fun stuff regretfully over, I chased up Corrine and while we kept watch in *Firebird's* saloon on the masthead camera feed, we refined our plans.

THE RECCE

It was hard to see at first, but the camera motion-detecting and target-tracking software was way ahead of the human eye in this case, and had smoothly locked on to the tiny distant dot coming straight at the island from the east. As it got closer, it resolved into a long, double outrigger canoe with a low woven grass shelter set amidships. Closer still, only one person was visible, the Indonesian driver, sitting in the stern, hand steering the big outboard. It was hard to judge its speed coming straight at us like that, but it seemed to be doing about 25 knots.

The skipper slowed his boat and was careful about crossing the reef, before he eased it in close to the shore. My whiz-bang camera couldn't look around corners unfortunately, so we lost sight as it nosed in close to the shore.

'I bet they're going into that tiny little inlet,' Corrine exclaimed excitedly, 'then they'll come across that slight saddle in the spine of higher ground. It'd be easier than crossing further along.'

'I won't argue with that, Mouse. The only question is; how many will be doing the recce?'

'Two, tops,' she said confidently. 'There's no need for any more. They'd be falling over each other otherwise.'

'Once again, no bet!' I grinned, not taking my eyes off the camera. 'So how about we get going before the eyes are upon us.'

'We definitely want one alive to interrogate?'

'Yes, please. A degree of terror and pain is quite acceptable, but

I'd really like to have a bit of a chat before we need to put the rubbish out.'

'Roger that, boss. But you'd better tell Jasper. He looks hungry!'

I laughed as I looked across at my beautiful and deadly, big black
cat, dozing on the dining seats, flat on his back; all four giant paws
in the air and snoring like a drunken sailor!

'Yeah. He does have the lean and hungry look about him. Pity
about the PAL farts; they give him away every time!'

'Geeze Harry. Didn't anyone tell you PAL is for dogs?'

'Yeah, many times. But he pinched some food off Ray Albert's
dog, Fang one day and now the rotten bugger loves it! It's become
his staple diet so I've been thinking about renting him out to you
guys to fumigate *Seeker* and get rid of all those bugs you breed in
your bilges.'

She bristled and smacked my arm as I knew she would, when
aspersions were cast on her immaculate boat where dinner could
be eaten off the engine room bilge without the slightest fear of
contamination.

'OK, let's go and leave the actors to put on a good show.'

Corrine, Jasper and I dropped off *Firebird's* bow into knee-deep
water and waded ashore, confident it was way too soon for observers
to have made their way across the ankle-breaking obstacle course
which was the pretty little island's limestone legacy. We had taken
the time to decorate our faces and limbs with streaks of black and
green paint and wore black watch caps to conceal hair.

Once ashore, Corrine in particular was in her element, and I
wasn't too proud to admit that she scared the shit out of me! In this
environment, she became an indistinct, soundless shadow, melding
into tree trunks when she paused to listen. Although I considered
myself a good bushman, she put me to shame and roamed on ahead
of my advance, Jasper at her heels, re-appearing from nowhere to
make my heart hiccup.

She'd scouted likely observation places and found a good spot to
wait for our prey to come to us. Naturally, Jasper just padded along

in total silence and was next to invisible in the mottled shadows cast by the heavy vegetation.

The light pressure of her hand on my arm caused me to freeze, although it was several seconds later I heard what she'd picked up from the background chorus of insects.

It sounded like 5 or 6 careless troops were pushing their way through the scrub, but it turned out to be one guy making 98% of the noise through sheer clumsiness. His partner was a slim girl who was far better at moving quietly and was content to let the guy lead the way. As they passed the peak of the island's backbone, the girl took the lead and slipped almost noiselessly down toward the shore overlooking our cove, pausing when she discovered the lookout spot Corrine had already scouted.

I almost chuckled when they set up their surveillance and even though they spoke in murmurs which carried far less than whispers, we heard them clearly. Despite them being within two metres of us, the guy still failed to see us, his eyes sliding right over us, each time he looked around.

Their conversation gave me some new Intel that would be useful, but I still resolved to grab one of these two and the guy was obviously the team leader, so he got elected, provided Jasper left enough to enable him to talk! The comments from the guy about the feeling of being watched at least showed he had some intuition, although as one of Xavier's operatives, I had zero sympathy for him.

When it started to be obvious he would move out shortly, Corrine lightly dragged her fingers across my arm in the uphill direction, and while the camera was busily clicking away, we three faded into the deepening gloom, the man's querulous comments to his female partner fading after a few paces.

I left it to Corrine to set up the ambush and parked myself several metres away, crouched down beside a bush as I had at their observation post, my camo markings blending me into the foliage. Jasper stayed with Mouse as per the plan.

We didn't have to wait long. For some reason, the man blundered uphill by himself, the clicking of the camera telling us the girl, in the manner of all good photographers, wanted a few more shots in case the best one of the shoot was amongst them.

It was Corrine's decision whether to take this clown or not, but it was obvious when she made her move.

The guy had no warning that anyone else was on the island, let alone less than a metre away with a long, gleaming black knife blade held against his throat. An involuntary terrified scream escaped his mouth, before the increased pressure of the razor-sharp knife blade against his throat and a warm trickle of wetness that swiftly ran down his chest, reminded him to keep quiet.

'Walk, bozo!' I heard Corrine murmur. 'Straight ahead for twenty paces, slowly, and I'd advise against moving your head in case my hand slips.'

He started to nod, then seemed to realise the consequences of that polite movement and got on with complying with her directive to step carefully away from the trail. Corinne realised that he was shaking with fear and may even have peed his pants, although minor details like that never swayed her excellent judgment. As he seemed to be a most compliant captive, Corrine made a rare mistake and relaxed the pressure of her blade. If he'd stayed where he was, he probably would have been all right, but he tried to run!

He twisted sideways out of her grasp, and had turned to run north along the spine of the island, when he was nearly knocked flat by what must have felt like a Rugby forward on steroids, but was really only Jasper.

As he fell forward, his back arched as if all his muscles had gone into spasm, and a high-pitched shriek of pain and terror escaped his tortured throat, echoing across the island. It was to be expected, I guessed, since Jasper had delivered his new trademark, a huge wrenching bite on one gluteus maximus, which tore a large chunk of one bum cheek away and must have been a bit painful.

He fell, but seemed to bounce back off the rocky ground and

managed to scramble to his feet, Jasper still on his back, all four sets of razor claws set to maximum gouging mode.

That sent him stumbling forwards, half blind with pain, ricocheting off tree trunks as if he were drunk, with a warm flood of blood cascading down the back of his legs. It was sheer terror at having a mysterious beast on his back which drove his tortured body forward. That involuntary movement was given a helping hand by Jasper letting loose with a deafening, unearthly howl right beside his left ear, although his leg muscles, particularly on the right side, didn't seem to be functioning properly.

With Jasper's weight on his back, accompanied by those razor-sharp claws, he was finally driven, sobbing to his knees, where vice-like jaws promptly clamped around his throat from behind, shutting off most of his air supply and a fair volume of his brain's blood supply as well. That combination seemed to shut him down temporarily, which was a blessing as it kept him quiet while we let Sara make her careful and quiet way back to her ride in the cove below. Shortly after, we heard the outboard start and they departed without him.

CHAPTER 43

'What do we do with him now?' Corrine asked, casually wiping her knife on the dude's shirt.

'I'd like to question him,' I said, 'but that idea's a bit fucked up now. The stupid dick looks like he'll bleed out before we get anything useful out of him!'

'How about we cart him down to the beach,' she suggested. 'It's not far, all downhill and we might get lucky if he does last long enough to pass over some Intel.'

So with Jasper puffing warm, meaty breaths against his ear, we carried him by wrists and ankles, although in the dark and with the uneven terrain surface underfoot, his ripped open backside bumped or dragged on the ground or a rock more often than even I would have liked! We knew he was still alive when he groaned occasionally as we bounced his bulk off a larger rock than usual.

Finally, we staggered to a halt on the beautiful white sandy beach. We laid him down, not worried about getting sand in his horrific wounds since neither of us expected him to last long enough for that to be an issue.

He made a revival of sorts when his torso muscles went into some kind of spasm, arching his body well clear of the ground, with just his head and heels touching the ground. He tried to scream, but his throat was severely damaged and he managed only a croak.

Corrine slapped his face a few times and his eyes reluctantly opened.

'Ah, good. You're awake. Can you hear me all right?'

He nodded, but pointed to his throat and mouth.

'Yes, you can have some water. We'd like you to talk if and

while you can.'

His eyes grew wide at those words, as even with the extreme level of pain he was in, the meaning of that statement was clear.

Corrine dug a small water flask out of a pocket and fed him some that lubricated his throat enough to allow speech. It unfortunately also let him express the level of pain his ruined backside was producing, which required Corrine to slap his face a few times to tell him to shut up. His groans, cries and sobs slowly faded to a more comfortable level and I considered what we could ask that he might just know.

'How many of Xavier's operatives are there here in Indonesia at the moment?'

I could see that he was considering not answering, but then he rasped with obvious pain and difficulty, 'Seven regulars and one local dive charter skipper Juliet has recruited. He's ready to send another twenty operatives if we can prove Lara is aboard one of your boats, especially the big power boat that picked her up in Sumbawa Besar.'

'Where are you based?'

'Sumbawa Besar. Hotel near the airport. Juliet and Mike are in Room 23.'

It always amazed me that once a captive starts talking; it's usually difficult to get them to shut up.

'Was the plan to take the power boat and recover Lara and Andy?'

A frown of lack of understanding crossed his face. 'Who's Andy?'

Suddenly I understood a lot more and cursed Xavier once again for his extreme deviousness by spreading false reasons for chasing the boats and appearing to only want Lara.

'He's with Lara. But what's the big plan to come and get her?'

'If we had confirmed Lara was here, Juliet was intending to send the new operatives here in Mike's boat. They were going to just wipe you out, sink your boats and take the girl.'

'Yeah. That'd be his idea of a plan all right,' I muttered to

Corrine. 'Two can play that game, however, as we have before.' I turned back to the miserable wreck that once was Tommy and who was losing blood at an alarming rate without long to go.

'Was Xavier planning to come here himself?'

'I heard Juliet talking to Mike about it. She was put in charge of this part of the operation because she did the initial scouting run and was first up here, but she doesn't have the experience to run the operation which would finish things off, so Xavier just might do it himself. Since he did prison time, he doesn't trust anybody!'

'So, who's this Mike character? Is he a regular?'

'No. He owns and runs a dive charter boat. Juliet met him when she was trying to find clues to Lara's movements. He seems to be her unofficial lieutenant, seems to be a nice guy and is competent. He doesn't know what's really going on because Juliet told him Lara is her sister and an heiress, who's holding up a massive inheritance settlement by running away. By the way, I might be telling you all this stuff, but it doesn't matter because my partner got away with all the photos and descriptions of the boats.'

I said nothing for a few moments, then cursed in a monotone I hoped Corrine would pick up on, 'Shit! I wished I'd known that earlier. We could have chased her and grabbed the photos back.'

He gave a twisted smile and a breathy chuckle. 'Bingo! I gotcha this time. Way too late. I talk, she gets away. In a few hours' time, first Juliet then Xavier will know that Lara is here. You might as well give up now before Xavier comes.'

That was good information to have, as well as the thought this was the most likely situation to draw Xavier himself to come to organise the snatch himself.

They were his last words as he was losing consciousness quickly and from the volume of blood soaking into the sand; he wasn't going to recover.

'What do we do with him?' asked Corrine. 'We don't want to leave him here.'

'Nah, we can't do that. How about we get one of the RIBs and cart the body out past the reef. The sharks will dispose of the remains and we can shovel the bloody sand into the water here. The next storm or two, probably over the next couple of days from the forecast, will eliminate all other traces after that.'

In the dim moonlight Corrine nodded agreement. 'How about I run back and get it? I wouldn't mind cleaning all this up as quickly as possible rather than wait for you to grope and stumble back. We'd still be here at dawn if I waited for you!'

I laughed, grateful for her suggestion. 'You cheeky little bugger! How dare you speak the truth!'

'Stay put, Harry. Jasper will keep you company and I won't be long.'

She wasn't long, the buzz of the RIB sounding her approach. It was *Firebird's* RIB since it was already in the water. It was the unpleasant work of a few minutes to hoist the bloody body onto the inflatable gunnel of the RIB where I supported it upright until we motored quietly out over the reef. Without ceremony, I allowed it to tip over the side where the residual blood coating the body would attract the ever-present, ever-hungry reef sharks who would efficiently dispose of the carcase.

Corrine had brought two shovels and back on the beach, we shovelled the blood-soaked sand onto a heavy plastic sheet and dragged it the few metres to the water. Six trips removed all traces of mayhem off the beach and I was confident the ants and other small animals would clean up the blood and remnants up on the hill.

As we washed Jasper's head, then scrubbed and washed the plastic and shovels before loading them into the RIB, Corrine remarked quietly, 'You're a cunning prick, Harry. You've really thought this one through, and letting that chicky-babe get away with the photos was a masterstroke. Once Xavier sees the names on the two boats, he'll go ballistic and be on the next flight out of Melbourne to Bali, after he'd ordered the plaque to nail your balls to! If I didn't know better, I'd say you were planning to go get Xavier's team before they get a chance to come gunning for us!'

To hear Corrine spell out the host of ideas which had been whirling around my brain was a revelation. She had just summarised my attack plan, and despite needing some refining, it gave me a real buzz to be able to plan on taking the offensive again, instead of waiting for all these wankers to come and get us. An idea popped unbidden into my head out of the selection awaiting application, so I asked Corrine, 'Remember the set-to we had with the bikies 18-months or so back?'

She grinned, 'How could I forget! Yeah, go on.'

'We had the 10kg sample drug shipment, then the big one we picked up under false pretences. Would I be right in saying that the real contents of the 10kg one actually never did make it back to the Southport coppers?'

She sat on the inflated side of the RIB, and looked at me in the wan moonlight, a cheeky grin on her face. 'Maybe things might have happened the way you say. If they did, the items would therefore be still intact since none of us are users.'

I nodded solemnly, 'That would be the case. Therefore, a kilo or two could be seen as a good investment if it were to be responsible for putting at least six of the opposition team in jail for very long sentences.'

Corrine jumped up and hugged me hard. 'Oh, great stuff, Harry. I knew you were planning something devious! It'll be so good to do something positive for a change.'

'Well, Mouse. I've got to say I'm really pissed off with having this Xavier clown on our tails again. He needs to be taken out of play for good, so we have to lure him out of his Melbourne hidey-hole. You used to work for him so you've got a good idea about how he thinks.

Will the photos bring him up here? Dave will have been visible in some and she got others of the boat names, so he must know who's trying to ruin his snatch and grab raid.'

She nodded, 'Yep. He's a total egomaniac and this will be a like a red rag to a bull. His ego and reputation have been badly hurt, along with his hip pocket, so this will seem to be more like a personal attack. He'll come for sure! Remember what our recently deceased friend said, he doesn't trust anybody anymore.'

'I remember. But let's get back to the others. They'll be busting to know what's happening and we've got some fast planning to do.'

The trip back was a lot easier than the walk across and minutes later we had tied up to *Firebird's* stern and were relating the tale of events to the crew.

First up, Corrine couldn't help but tell everyone we were going on the offensive. 'But Harry's got to do some planning first, so we might have a celebratory drink while he does that.'

Amid the generally high spirits which made me realise the others must have been feeling depressed just waiting for trouble to land on our doorstep, I retired to the chart table office and pulled out my notepad.

Sandy brought me a drink and asked, 'Are you OK?'

I smiled, 'Yeah, thanks hon. It wasn't very pleasant, but necessary. We got some really good Intel and there's a good chance we might be able to turn the tables and nail that megalomaniac Xavier once and for all. But if I can do some fast planning, we might need to move quickly.'

'What are you thinking of doing?'

I roughed out my ideas, which helped settle them in my head and with Sandy playing the part of Devil's Advocate, we quickly made useful changes. I got some hugs and praise for my deviousness, although she didn't enjoy being left out of the lead party.

One good question was, 'Why take the risk of staying at the same hotel? There's bound to be a general shakedown afterwards.'

'True. But I noticed on the internet ad for the hotel, that it has a security post at the entrance. If we stayed elsewhere, we'd either have to sneak in the back way, which would really make us stand out, or try to talk our way through the security. This way, we are just guests, coming and going as we're supposed to. And we'll be squeaky-clean. No drugs, no cigarettes, no booze.

And I need you and Gilbert to look after the boat, as well as

Andy, Lara and Charlie. By having you park a bit further down the coast, you're not associated with *Seeker* just in case of trouble. If Xavier flies in, he won't see *Firebird*, but you and Gilbert are back-up. And Jasper will have to stay with you this time. We can't risk taking him ashore. The locals would freak. Anyway, while I plot and plan, how about you book two rooms at the Samawa Transit Hotel. Better make it for three nights, and make them two doubles in my name as there'll be Corrine and me and I think Alex and Bree to make it look normal.'

She gave me a cheeky grin, 'This rooming with Corrine is getting to be a habit. You're not thinking of doing a swap, are you? Of course, Dave would be a pretty good deal, even though I've become used to older men.'

I laughed with her and felt some tension ebb, 'I'm afraid you're stuck with me, my lovely lady, so get used to it! Anyway, you get onto the hotel and I'll work out more details. Oh, and you might like to touch base with Greg to give him a heads-up, please.'

By the time I'd finished my rum and coke, the plan looked more feasible, so I took it out to present it to the crew, my harshest critics.

When I had their attention, not an easy task as they were several drinks up on me by now, with the PM looking especially relaxed, his face sporting a happy grin.

Finally, I had the chance to have my say. 'As Mouse said earlier, I propose we take this bunfight to the bad guys, rather than sit and wait. If we can take out the crew that's here, it might help spread some confusion and mess up Xavier's last-minute plans, but we have to strike quickly before they have too much time to take in all the information and analyse the photos the young lady escapee lays on them.'

There was a round of clapping to endorse my announcement, so I next addressed Dave. 'Both boats are leaving shortly, but there'll be a change of crews. *Seeker* will be doing a best speed run back to Sumbawa Besar, with *Firebird* following at normal pace. Four of us are going ashore for three days to deal with Xavier's current crew and I'm hoping that if it works as planned, the loss of his operatives will totally mess up his plans.

Dave replied, 'Okay. I presume you and Corrine are going ashore, so who else?'

'I thought that Alex and Bree might like to join the party.'

Dave agreed, but disagreement came from an unexpected source, as Roger and Jill spoke up. 'We just wanted to say; we know you've been sparing us from most of the action, but we are part of this, one way or the other and from what you're saying, there shouldn't be a direct physical confrontation so we'd like to do what we can. I'm also sure Bree and Alex will be of more use on the boat.

Anyway, we aren't rebelling and we'll go with whatever you decide, but we just wanted to have our say.'

I looked at Dave who shrugged and said, 'Roger's right. Bree and Alex will be of more use on *Seeker* just in case Xavier fronts up early. So, if it fits in with you, go for it.'

I smiled, looked back to Roger and Jill and said, 'In that case, welcome to the shore party. Your job is mostly just to act like typical tourists. Corrine and I will do the dirty work, but that shouldn't take long. Then the four of us will have to be seen to be doing touristy-type stuff. You'll just have to avoid bumping into any of them in case they mentally match the photos with your faces, although we'll be in a good position to see when Xavier arrives.'

'We can play that part all right,' Roger smiled, 'and we're willing to help with whatever is necessary. We really aren't non-combatants, just because we're the medical crew.'

'Thanks Roger. Okay, that's sorted, so the only crew change, therefore, will be that I join *Seeker*.'

I looked at Gilbert, sitting quietly. 'Gilbert, I'd like you to bring *Firebird* to Sumbawa Besar at normal motor-sailing speed of 14 knots, just like we did when we came over here from the west. Sandy, Lara and Andy will assist when you need it.

Under these light conditions, that'll probably mean just running on motors only, unless you reckon there's enough breeze to decently assist the motors. You and Sandy have the most experience of the boat, but use Andy and Lara as needed. Jasper will be staying with you, of course.

When we leave, please just follow *Seeker* out over the reef. Dave will have the 3D Sonar going so he'll pick the safest way. There appears to be a high tide so we should be right for depth clearance. The trip is 317 nautical miles and should take you 23 to 24 hours. I've written down the name and co-ordinates of the bay where I'd like you to anchor. It's called Telek Lok, is 6 miles down from Sumbawa, and seems to have a pearl farm there as well. Not exciting, but there is road access if we need help. *Seeker* will be parked up in the cruise ship bay, about a mile south of the city.'

They all nodded understanding, Gilbert looking happy to be given a useful task.

'OK, we need to get going right now, so while I get some gear together, the RIB needs securing, engines started and all the nav gear fired up. I've entered your destination onto the chart plotter so it'll tell you where to go.'

There was a sudden burst of activity as both crews sprang into action, so I went and packed a bag.

Although I couldn't take it to the hotel, I tossed in my Grizzly pistol and a couple of boxes of rounds to suit. I kissed Sandy, spoke to Jasper, thanked the crew, then hopped over onto *Seeker*.

Dave was ready, so we dropped lines and got underway before 22:00, feeling our way out of the little cove with radar going and the 3D Sonar probing ahead for obstacles, but the shallow draft of both boats was wonderful and we slid over the fringing reef without a problem.

Initially, Dave took our speed up to 25 knots to see how the ride would be, but because there was a low swell and almost no breeze, he soon upped the pace to 50 knots, a speed the big boat was comfortable with.

Dave pointed to the chart plotter, 'About 6.4 hours, according to the magic box.'

'There's no real gain to getting there too early, so you could save some fuel and slow down a bit. Arriving closer to dawn will be better and less obvious.'

'Yep. That'll suit me.' Accordingly, he pulled the throttles back slightly until the water speed indicator showed a steady 40 knots and our new arrival time was after 04:00. In that happy state, we thundered on into the blackness, all electronic senses working full time to keep us from un-scheduled encounters with any hard lumps.

CHAPTER 44

SEEKER, SUMBAWA BESAR, SATURDAY

With the trip time expected to be around eight hours, I stayed up for a while, but as Dave and Corrine already had watches organised, when the off-watch crew went to bed, I grabbed a couple of cushions and stretched out on one of the saloon lounges and went to sleep. I woke naturally at 03:00 to see Alex and Bree had the watch, the red night lighting casting an eerie glow, the engines comforting thunder hardly noticeable any more.

Seeing that I was awake, Bree smiled and slipped below to the galley while I freshened up in the crew bathroom. The motion at 40 knots was a bit much for a shower, but I settled for an all-over wash.

Much refreshed, I joined Alex at the wheel and checked progress, seeing from the chart plotter we were passing down the coast of Pulau Mojo, the big island just north of Sumbawa. As we entered the final stretch across Sumbawa Bay, Alex throttled back to what seemed like a crawl at 25 knots, which roused Dave who appeared, yawning, a mug of tea in each hand, to take over from Alex.

Bree was right behind him with a large plate of toast and honey for a welcome pre-breakfast snack.

Our destination was the small bay just south of the city where the freighters and cruise ships docked. There was plenty of room in by the ship docks, as well as a jetty on the city side of the bay which gave access to a road and therefore land transport. With all electronic aids and several sets of Mk 1 human eyeballs and ears working flat out, we slowed further and entered the bay. Leaving the big commercial docks to starboard, we idled quietly over to the left side of the bay where there was one boat already tied up at the jetty, but we eased up on the other side of him and shut down the engines.

At 100 feet long, *Seeker* dwarfed the other local boat, but at first, nobody came out to see what all the fuss was about, so with Bree back in the galley brewing up something which smelt really good, we settled down to wait until such time as we could unobtrusively move around town and check in to the hotel.

After an hour, some dude wandered down to see who we were, but he didn't know much English and unfortunately, we didn't have any of the local Sumbawan language, so after chatting quietly with him for a few minutes with neither really knowing what the other was saying, I handed him a twenty dollar note and he went away happy, pointing to the boat, then the jetty and giving us a 'thumbs-up'.

We took that to mean either he liked the boat, or it was okay to stay where we were. We sat it out until about 09:30, then Corrine did some complicated things on the Internet and found a number for a taxi or hire car company and told them roughly where we were.

Remarkably, ten minutes later, a slightly battered minibus nosed down the narrow track that apparently led to the main coastal road.

Jill, Roger, Corrine and I grabbed our gear and jumped in the taxi, leaving Dave, Alex and Bree to look after *Seeker*. I'd also suggested to Dave it might be more secure to move out and anchor. After looking at a map, we saw that the hotel wasn't even close to the city centre, being opposite the airport, so I had another cunning idea.

'Let's have the driver take us to the hotel so we can dump our gear, then we can do what everybody else seems to do and hire a scooter!'

The driver caught some of that conversation and enthusiastically said, 'You hire scooter at hotel. Him good. I help best price!'

'Well, that's decided that,' Corrine laughed, 'and at least it'll make us mobile.'

Five minutes later, we were deposited at the Samawa Transit Hotel, having passed through a guard post with a pole barrier which opened into a courtyard where an attractive and tidy two-story building welcomed us. Inside was clean and modern and the staff polite, helpful and spoke English. I asked about the security guard at the gate and had the receptionist come to the front doors to point something out to me.

Despite the official check-in time being 14:00, they let us into the rooms which were also spotless and modern with a small balcony overlooking the courtyard. Interestingly, we were in Room #21 with Roger and Jill next door in #20. That put Juliet in #23, just two doors along.

Corrine and I didn't bother unpacking our small bags, although she flashed her trademark cheeky grin as she eyed the king-size bed dominating the room, 'Well, here we are again, sharing a bed. I know we should behave, but the rule is still "what happens in Sumbawa Besar....." isn't it?'

I chuckled, 'Well, we did break our duck in Bali, even though we are here to work.'

'That's my good boss. Well said.'

'Righto,' I said, 'first item of business; a council of war here with Roger and Jill. Bang on that connecting door would you please?'

She did and moments later it opened. 'Like your room?' I asked politely,

'Oh yes,' Jill enthused, 'it's a lot better than I expected. We could be at an upmarket hotel anywhere in Australia if you just looked at the room.'

'Good, but now we've seen the layout, we need a plan of action, so let's head down to the coffee shop and see if we can persuade them to make us something.'

'You want us to be seen, is that right?' Jill asked.

'Yes. I'd like to eyeball this Juliet person, as well as Mike the dive boat owner. Our late and un-lamented friend from last night told us Mike has moved in with her for the duration, so we need to know when they go out. My young lady here needs to go to work.'

'I understand your plan to plant drugs,' Roger said, 'but you'll need access to all their rooms to do it properly.'

I waved his objection away. 'Already got them. Rooms 24, 25, 26, 27, 28 and 29. We need them all out for a short time to do the plant.'

'Hang on,' Roger exclaimed, 'when and how did you get those?'

I nodded at Corrine, 'My lovely new wife whipped behind the reception desk when I was blathering on about the security guy. It only took a second.'

Roger laughed and followed us down to the coffee shop which wasn't officially open, but the obliging couple who ran the place were easily persuaded to fire up the big coffee machine. Corrine disappeared for a couple of minutes, before re-appearing with a grin on her face.

'The occupants of room # 23 are out of the Hotel for now and aren't expected back until after midday. They told reception that so their room can be serviced while they were out.'

'Great work, Mouse. I wonder if the other six will be out as well?'

She gave a cheeky grin, 'I'll check on that, but if you see someone who looks like Juliet or similar to Lara, come back, call my mobile.'

She was gone for about twenty anxious minutes, while we ordered back-to-back coffees, teas and toasted sandwiches. Finally, she came skipping lightly back down the stairs, a silk scarf tied around her neck and a grin on her face.

'You look pleased with yourself,' I commented. 'I presume it went well?'

'I should be pleased with myself,' she retorted, 'and so should you, dear husband! Job done and dusted.'

'Excellent! But what's with the scarf?'

'Because we weren't sure if the other six were all out, I pulled this over my head to hide my hair colour and wore a mask over my lower face. With my solid tan, slight build and a put-on accent, I can easily pass for an Indonesian Housekeeper Supervisor. And just as well I did, since one room was occupied by a girl. She was still in bed, reading, so I told her I was checking all her supplies in the bathroom were okay and asked her if she was crook. She said she wasn't feeling well, having had a nasty experience the evening before and didn't feel like joining the others when they went out to the markets.'

'You were lucky to get away with that!' I remarked incautiously.

That earned me a smack on the arm as she fired back, 'No bloody luck about it, boyo! That was pure acting talent! She even asked for a glass of water and two aspirin from the bathroom, which I was happy to get since it gave me a chance to plant a stash. The others were easy.'

I dared to ask, 'I don't suppose you thought to plant the stuff in different places?'

Another smack and, 'Yes, Dad, I remembered! They're all different and I opened some for good measure.'

'Thanks Mouse. Top job again! I might give Greg a call and start that particular ball rolling in case someone finds their stash accidentally.'

Corrine raised her eyebrows, 'Possible, but unlikely.'

I had a thought. 'Would Juliet recognise you from your time with Steel Associates?'

She shook her head, 'No. She wasn't there when I was, so she might be a new hire when Xavier started up business again.'

'That's good, because I think this is them coming back now! Please don't look around, just talk about diving stuff.'

So we launched into a lively discussion about dive tables, the virtues of the new full-face masks and the little pony air bottles for emergency use. We were nicely into some back-and -forth when seven people walked in, led by a tall, striking blonde having a passing resemblance to Lara. That attribute would make her Juliet and I had to admit that she wore an easy air of competence.

She was closely followed by a tall, well-built fellow with a friendly, open face who I took to be Mike, the dive boat owner. On first glance, he seemed an unlikely guy to be involved in Xavier's brand of thuggery.

The other five were a nondescript, silent group of three men and one woman, all in their late 20's to early 30's and looking rather grim-faced. Juliet detoured via the reception counter where she spoke briefly with the duty manager while the others filed upstairs, presumably to their rooms.

As soon as Juliet had followed them, I dug the Satphone out of my backpack and stepped outside onto the inner terrace where I couldn't be overheard.

'*Gidday Harry. I was wondering where you'd got to. I haven't heard from you for ages. How's it all going?*'

'Hi Greg. Going well so far. We decided to take the offensive instead of sitting back scratching our collective arses.' I brought him up-to-date with the short version of what had happened with the surveillance run.

'*Bloody hell, mate. Be careful what you're stirring up. Our inside man called in to say that Xavier is frothing at the mouth about losing one of his main operatives, although he was pleased the sighting of Lara is confirmed. Anyway, he's on his way! He should be in Bali tomorrow, but will either have to wait until the Wednesday flight to Sumbawa Besar or organise a charter flight.*

According to our man, he's on the point of tipping over the psychotic edge and all the office staff are getting ready to bail. The millions paid for the search and recover contract don't even look like covering expenses, plus he's only been getting the money in instalments, so he's getting extra cash from somewhere else.

Oh, and speaking of that, our financial bloodhounds are extremely close to having admissible proof the whole West Australia thing with EarthCare, was started by a prominent industrialist magnate who felt that he wasn't getting a fair deal from the Government. Several others jumped on his coat-tails for the ride, but apparently they're getting nervous that Xavier is dropping the ball while at the same time, they can see our financial investigators getting close to the truth.'

'Great! That's really good to know because we need this thing wrapped up soonest. I don't like playing games in someone else's country. There are too many things to go wrong and I feel there's about to be some major mayhem happening.

Which leads to my next question. How would you like to get the Commissioner to place an urgent call to his opposite number in Jakarta, or Bali if that works better? He's to say he has positive information that a group of seven Australians staying at the Samawa Transit Hotel in Sumbawa Besar, rooms #23 through to #29, are in possession of a significant quantity of the Korean Super MDMA drug the bikies were frigging around with last year. He also should say he has it on good authority, that the group are planning to set up a distribution network out of Sumbawa Besar targeting dive groups from overseas countries to act as couriers.

Have him say that while this group is wanted for questioning by the Australian authorities, if the Indonesians grab them, there won't be any effort wasted on extradition proceedings. And add that this is happening right now.'

'Do I smell a set-up?'

'Maybe yes? Maybe no. But the coppers will find drugs if they don't shag around too much, so call whoever you think is appropriate and get it underway immediately if you can. I'd call my people except I'm not really here.'

'Yeah, righto mate. I'll call somebody. In fact it might be best if Bob calls the Commissioner and lets him pass the message. That's about all that's going on here, so good luck with Xavier, and remember, he's not the semi-rational egomaniac he was. He's much worse!

'Yes, Mum. I'll remember.'

'Smart arse. See ya Harry and be careful.'

I re-joined the others on the coffee shop terrace, noticing the reception area was now empty except for two staff pushing bits of paper around and tapping on the reservation's computer. Corrine raised her eyebrows at me.

'All OK?'

I smiled grimly, 'Wheels are in motion, but the timeframe is uncertain. I don't know how quickly the police can get motivated over something which is being reported like this.'

Roger and Jill looked pleased at the final part of the cunning plan being put into motion, not having anything in the way of pity for these knowing pawns of Xavier.

'So what now, Harry?' Roger asked. 'Thanks to you and Corrine, our work seems to be complete.'

'The work is complete, but for appearances, we have to hang around for the next two days, otherwise it might arouse comment. Of course, if the raid does occur as we hope, we can perhaps bung on the outraged act at being surrounded by drug traffickers and check-out sooner. We'll see, but perhaps we should go out for a while, so long as we get back within say, three hours, to see if the cops are on the ball.'

'Let's do that,' Corrine said enthusiastically, 'the markets aren't far now we've got those scooters. Two hours poking around and then back here for late lunch. How about that?'

It was a plan and we were keen to do something, so in a rather festive mood, we sorted out scooter colours, found helmets that fitted and armed with directions, roared off in a cloud of blue two-stroke smoke and the mighty buzz of seven horsepower. It'd been years since I'd been on two wheels and reminded me again of how much fun it was. Thoughts of a Harley Fat Bob sprang to mind and I resolved to look at getting one when we returned to the Gold Coast.

The markets were a seething mass of people all chattering, bartering and laughing, making the visit truly memorable. Corrine and Jill picked out some pretty headscarves and wraps for what seemed like a ridiculous number of Indonesian rupiah, until it was pointed out in no uncertain terms by Corrine's elbow, that 20 Aussie dollars bought something like 120,000 rupiah! They wandered away, came back with more parcels, then it was time for home – or hotel as it was.

We managed to find our scooters again in a parking lot full of thousands of near-identical ones and puttered happily back to the hotel.

We were rather late for lunch, but the coffee shop owner was happy to make allowances for the 'crazy Aussies' and whipped up a delicious batch of spicy finger food of various persuasions, chased down with teas and coffees. We had barely finished polishing off the lot, when there was a loud commotion out in the car-park, with vehicles pulling up, orders being barked, the pounding of booted feet and the slamming of doors. A Senior Police Officer in a subdued dark uniform strode into the reception area, followed by ten or twelve constables or whatever was the equivalent, and barked a series of questions at the startled staff.

While they looked at records, he glanced around and spotted our group of four.

Trotting over he asked politely, 'Are you Australian tourists?'

'Yes, we are,' I replied, 'we just checked in this morning. Is there a problem?'

'May I see your room keys, please?'

Corrine had ours and Roger handed over theirs. He took one glance, returned them, bowed his head slightly and said, 'No problem for you, thank you. Please enjoy your stay on our beautiful island.'

'Thank you Sir,' I replied, as one of the non-coms hastened over and whispered rapidly in his ear.

'Excuse me, please. We have urgent business to attend to.' He and the deputy hurried back to the reception counter, conferred with the staff, then rather more quietly than their arrival, the whole troop headed upstairs.

I looked around our table, 'It seems I owe the Indonesian Police Force an apology.'

Within moments, a series of shouts and mixed cries of alarm and outrage rang out from the rooms above us and continued for some time, until the same group who we last saw going upstairs, were escorted back down in handcuffs by a grim-faced bunch of police officers. Juliet looked very upset, while the guys either looked bewildered or angry, and the other two girls were in tears. The senior officer marched triumphantly behind them, several plastic bags clutched in one hand.

By the continuing noise upstairs, the other officers must have remained behind and it sounded like they were taking the rooms apart, much to the distress of the management.

Outside in the carpark, there was more shouting and banging of doors, until most of the convoy of police vehicles roared out the gate, just as another convoy roared in, disgorging a bunch of uniformed police and technicians who streamed upstairs with a collection of cases and bags in hand.

'Well,' I commented to Roger and Jill who looked rather stunned at the results of Corrine's handiwork, 'that seems to have worked rather well. I imagine Xavier will go off his tits when he hears about this little setback to his plans.'

'Does Greg know where Xavier is at the moment?' Corrine asked.

'Good question. How about I call him right now?' I looked around to make sure that no one else could overhear us, fired up the Sat-Phone and he answered almost immediately.

'Hi Harry. What's going on up there?'

'Just a quick report that the cunning plan has worked well, with all of Xavier's on-site crew currently in police custody for suspected drug smuggling, possession and possibly dealing. We're going to keep our heads down and not ask too many questions, apart from those expected from genuine tourists, but we will ask the management what it was all about and see what their response is.'

'That was certainly a fast response from the police. I know the Commissioner has got some very good connections with senior police up there, but it's only been a few hours since Bob talked to him!'

'Well, we know they have a tough attitude to drugs, so it's good to see it translates to real action. However, there's one other question. Do you have any Intel to say where Xavier is at this moment?'

'Yeah, we do. Just let me get my notes...okay, here we are. He and a female assistant called Dell Petrie, caught a commercial flight out of Melbourne this morning, so should be in Bali this afternoon, your time. I'm guessing he won't be able to get to you before tomorrow afternoon, unless he charters an aircraft.'

'Yeah. There aren't many commercial flights into here, but there are several air charter companies in Bali, so knowing his mood, he probably won't shag around. What time was his flight supposed to land in Bali?'

'*Looking, looking......Here it is. They flew Jetstar and that left at 09:15 and should have landed in Bali at 13:15 local time, so if he chartered something from there, he could be landing on your door step anytime from 15:00 onwards. Be careful, Harry. Even though he doesn't know you, you'd better get out of there right now and get Corrine out of sight. You've done all you can by taking out his crew.*'

As I'd had the phone on speaker, the others heard Greg's comments and I noted Jill and Corrine got up and left.

'Good point, mate. Although I must admit I would like to stick around to see what this character does. Can you keep feeding us any Intel you pick up from your inside man as soon as you get it, please? If there's a chance to take this bloke down without upsetting the local authorities, we might grab it. I feel he's in need of terminal attention.

Meanwhile, we're doing something about Corrine's appearance in case he's nearly here, so we'll talk later. Thanks Greg.'

'*Hang on a minute, Harry. You're taking a big chance doing that. Why not bail out while you can?*'

I thought a moment, watching Roger across the table nodding enthusiastic agreement with the 'bail out' idea.

'Yeah, we could, but this guy has got up my nose a bit. Last time his goon squad chased us all over Bass Strait with orders to inflict serious harm, and now he's doing it all over again. It seems he can't be stopped by normal legal processes, so someone has to do the dirty work.'

'*Aww! C'mon mate. It doesn't have to be you all the time. Just kick the ball upstairs and let those on the higher pay scales take care of it.*'

'I appreciate the thought, but we both know nothing will be done. He's too well connected and somehow, still very well funded. We really need to trace the source of his funding since it appears to be almost limitless.'

'*The best we have so far is apart from the lucrative contract fee to find your VIP, he's funding this operation from his own resources.*'

'But we grabbed his stash! Or at least Dave and Corrine did. Are you saying that he's got another one?'

'*Looks like it, I'm afraid. He's apparently got some sort of deep-seated personal issue with you and your passenger, and has become totally obsessed with this project. He's determined he'll succeed regardless of the cost.*'

'Terrific!' I commented a trifle sourly. 'He runs around causing trouble without any intervention, while we're expected to duck for cover!'

'*Yep! That's what you need to do, please Harry.*'

'Bullshit! Sorry Greg; not your fault, but I'll not be hamstrung at this point of the operation with this bloke and his crew gunning for us. We're staying here and I'm working on a few ideas to make our Mr Xavier wish he'd never heard of Australia!'

CHAPTER 45

Twenty minutes later, the girls were back at our table on the courtyard terrace, a fresh mug of tea and coffee in front of each. Corrine's lovely long, red hair was now a deep brown shade and tied in a ponytail. A dopey-looking sun hat and some subtle make-up shading by Jill gave her a gaunt, slightly haunted look which aged her ten years or more. It really was a case of 'less is more' as I studied her new look carefully.

'Nice work ladies. I really think that even someone who knows you well would think twice before they challenged you.'

Both girls beamed. 'Thanks Harry,' said Jill, 'we didn't have much to work with, so we made do with what we had, although it seems to have worked out alright.'

'Bloody brilliant!' I commented, before looking at Corrine. 'But I need to know how well Xavier knew you. I mean would he recognise you from say mannerisms, or particular words or phrases you normally use?'

Corrine shook her head. 'No way! I met him at the initial interview, but that was about three years ago or more, although I did stand out to a certain extent because I was the only female sniper and wet-work specialist he'd ever come across. After that it's always been phone contact so there's a low probability he'd recognise me, especially since I had short hair then, but we thought we'd change my looks a little bit to be sure.'

'Good thinking, 99! But I'd really like to know anything about Xavier which might help us bring him undone. In particular; what does he hate or love most of all, or is there anything he's afraid of?'

She started to shake her head, but then said, 'Apart from loving himself and money, there wasn't much talk about that, but there was something I heard from one of his executive assistants. She was tired of being at his beck and call 24/7, and was trying to get out. For some reason she asked my advice, but since I was new, I didn't have anything special to tell her except to just disappear and stay gone.

I must have looked exasperated at this rare bit of waffle from my former Sergeant, so she apologised before getting to the point. 'Sorry Harry. I was just remembering what she said and at the time, how I thought it was a bit bizarre. She said Xavier is afraid of cats to the point of becoming physically ill if he comes into contact with one!'

We stared at her a few moments, before Roger spoke. 'If that's the case, then his fear has developed to being a full-blown phobia, it's called ailurophobia and it's a very real and debilitating thing.'

'Is that what Xavier's got?' I asked Corrine.

'No, nothing like that. I'm sure she said he had something called gates.'

Roger chuckled, 'That's another name for the phobia. It's also called Gatophobia or Felinophobia.'

'OK. But how would it affect him? I mean, what would be the symptoms?'

Roger spoke again. 'Depending on how badly he has the phobia, he could become very anxious and incapable of normal function. He'd be mentally confused, and physically, he'd be sweating, have a bad case of the shakes, even vomiting and a bad case of the trots.'

I looked at Corrine. 'Did your friend mention anything like this with Xavier?'

'I don't remember her saying anything like that, although she said that once he took her with him when he visited a woman who had cats and even though there were none present, he quickly seemed to have trouble breathing and they had to leave. She had to drive him back to his house so he could get an adrenalin shot. He usually carried an EpiPen with him all the time.'

Roger nodded and added, 'That means his phobia is so strong it can push him into anaphylactic shock which can be fatal.'

About then, a few delightfully nasty ideas popped into my head and while I let them shuffle around slowly making sense, Corrine noticed I had temporarily zoned out. 'Oh dear,' she told Roger and Jill, 'I'm afraid Harry is thinking up a cunning plan. He's got the 'thousand-yard stare' going!'

Shortly, a plan had half-gelled in my mind, but before I could share my diabolical thoughts, a taxi pulled up in the courtyard, decanting a slightly portly man of nondescript looks and of medium height. Barking a few words over his shoulder toward the taxi, he marched into the reception area, yelling for service and leaving an attractive woman to struggle out of the vehicle in his wake, retrieve several bags, then pay off the driver.

In the reception area behind us, the yelling continued as the staff tried to placate the man, but with little success as he seemed determined to misunderstand them. As stress levels rose along with the voice levels, the thought 'opportunity' popped into my mind.

Leaving our table, I stepped quickly inside and approached the desk where the vocal visitor was turning red in the face and appeared ready to lunge across the desk at the duty manager.

Adopting my best British accent with a touch of James Bond shaken into the mix for good luck, I announced loudly enough to break into the verbal squabble, 'Good afternoon. There seems to be a communication problem. May I be of assistance?'

The man turned to me briefly, looked me up and down and snarled, 'Who the fuck are you?'

'I'm a guest here and your altercation is disturbing my wife and our friends just over there on the terrace. Either let me help sort this problem out or leave these people alone. They obviously cannot understand you when you scream at them like you have been!'

'Don't you try to tell me what to do, you stupid prick!' was his belligerent reply, adopting the typical bully attitude with hands on hips and his head thrust forward.

I sighed theatrically. 'What are you trying to find out? Along with half the neighbourhood, I heard something about missing colleagues.'

'Smart arse aren't you? Yeah well! I was to meet six or seven of my staff who were staying here, but this moron behind the desk keeps rabbiting on about *Polda!* What the fuck's a *Polda?* If you want to help, tell me that!'

I smiled grimly. 'He's been trying to tell you, should you care to listen for a change, that your associates have run foul of the local police. I believe it had something to do with a large quantity of drugs. Something the local and national authorities take a very dim view of, and will most likely result in them all being executed. There's no messing about here with slap-on-the-wrist drug laws. One slip and you're shot!'

His eyes bugged out and his face became even redder at that news. 'Drugs? My people don't frig around with drugs! This is bullshit! I've got to go and bail them out. Nobody executes my people!'

I smiled again, 'I don't think you'll be bailing anybody out, and your ranting and raving counts for nothing in this country! Didn't you just hear me say they impose and carry out the death sentence for most drug-related offences. You really need to close your mouth more often and open your ears instead. Better for everybody that way.'

He actually spluttered, at a loss for words, so I took the opportunity to say, 'I'll leave you with those thoughts while I re-join my friends. Pity about your people, but as they say in the classics, "don't do the crime if you can't do the time!" Or in this case, there probably won't be too much time. The courts move quickly in big drug cases like this.'

With that parting shot, I moved away, taking a moment to lay a smile on his female companion who had joined us in time to hear the last half of the conversation. She really was very pretty, with a lovely curvy body and the worried, polite smile she returned was still worth the effort.

Outwardly composed, but inwardly gleefully chortling, I sat back down at our table and gave the others a short version of the exchange. With the subject of my mental scheming close at hand, I withheld my thoughts on taking him down until we had some privacy.

'Well, that was highly useful,' Corrine commented dryly, 'you've pissed him off no end! And since your deviously cunning plan is bound to involve me doing something illegal and dangerous, you always make my job harder.'

I smiled at her. 'You love the challenge and always rise to the occasion, my darling Mouse. Anyway, maybe my plan involves Roger.'

The look on Roger's face was priceless, so I hastily added, 'Well, maybe it does involve you, Mouse, but we'll talk more later.'

They all nodded, until Corrine said softly, 'Incoming.'

Xavier stood behind Corrine's chair, resting his pale hands lightly on its back, coughed twice, cleared his throat once, then looked at me.

'Ahh...Look. Sorry about what I said in there. This has all been a bit of a shock; I mean I fly up here to talk to my crew, only to find that they've just been carted away by the coppers on trumped-up drug charges. Anyway, I thought I'd apologise and introduce myself; I'm Xavier Johnson from Melbourne.'

I looked at him, taking a moment to consider how to respond, before standing up and holding out my hand. 'In that case, I'm pleased to meet you, Xavier. I'm Gordon James, and this is Jill, Roger and Muriel. But tell me, how can you be so sure the drug charges were trumped up?'

'They weren't drug users. Not any of them. I don't know who might be behind this put-up job, or why, but I'll find out. You haven't seen any other groups hanging around, have you?'

I shook my head. 'No. No other groups. Just a few couples passing through on dive trips like us. We were talked into coming here for the diving by some mates who said the water was the clearest and the reefs superb for photography which is what we're interested in. We'll probably go to a dive resort tomorrow now that we've sussed out what's good.

What business did you say you're in?'

He looked wary. 'I didn't. Why do you want to know?'

I bunged on a casual look. 'No particular reason, except if all those people we saw the coppers take away were your crew, I was curious about what such a large group was doing in this backwater area if they weren't diving. That's probably the question the coppers will be asking as well.'

Xavier didn't bat an eyelid as he replied, 'We have a contract with a movie production company to scout for deserted island locations. We do the preliminary search by air, then go in by boat to do the final check-out.'

I successfully feigned interest. 'That sounds like fun! Have you found many?'

He seemed to accept my explanation of casual interest and the dopey playboy act, and replied, 'Only a few, unfortunately. Even though there are 18,307 islands in the entire Archipelago, nearly all are inhabited to some extent. We were asked to look for totally un-inhabited ones in this south-eastern part of the Archipelago and have found a few the customer might want to use.

We were supposed to go out there on a dive charter boat my main operative had located, but that's buggered up now until I can get them out on bail.'

I nodded, trying to look thoughtful and impressed. 'As I said before, bail might be a problem in a drug case, but good luck with your efforts. Anyway, we mustn't keep you from finding out about your crew any longer, and thanks for coming over to introduce yourself.'

Xavier gave a strained smile, 'Maybe we can catch up later for a drink. I need to go and find out what happened first, but I'd really appreciate hearing what you saw, plus I feel I owe you a couple of rounds for being so rude earlier. Will you still be here in a couple of hours?'

I said casually, 'Oh sure. We're free this afternoon, so an extra drink or two certainly would be welcome. We'll be propping up the bar by then for certain, so look for us there.'

With that, he and his lissom companion checked in, disappeared upstairs to dump bags, then bustled back down to be met by a private taxi, the transport of choice in Sumbawa Besar.

As soon as they left, I strolled over to reception where the manager spoke perfect English.

'Yes sir. May I assist you in some way?'

'Yes, I hope so. My friends and I are keen to see some Komodo dragons in the wild. I believe they are on some islands not far from here. Can you recommend the best place to see them?'

'Yes, I can do that, although they are on a group of islands several hundred kilometres from here and only accessible by boat.

'Oh, that's no problem. We were either going to charter a boat or wait until some friends arrive with theirs.'

'Very well. There are just five islands where the dragons live and they are known as the Lesser Sunda Islands located on the western end of Flores Island. The islands are; Komodo, Rinca, Gili Montang, Gili Dasami and Flores itself.'

He dragged out a map of the area and pinpointed the islands concerned. 'These are the islands where the dragons live, but all are inhabited except for Gili Montang. Because no one lives there, the dragons are more aggressive than on the other islands. Maybe it's also because the island is much smaller than the others, but as they can be extremely dangerous to humans, few humans visit the island and you must not either. Their saliva is very toxic and has been known to kill a man, painfully in just a few hours.'

He didn't know it, but the information was perfect and as the map had good detail, I asked if I could buy it.

'Please have the map with my compliments for assisting with the unpleasant gentleman. He frightened my staff, unfortunately.'

'That is a shame and thank you for the map.'

I returned to our table in time to hear Roger say, 'So that's the dreaded Xavier. He doesn't seem so bad.'

Jill shook her head. 'Sorry, hon. Regardless of how he sounds or what he says, that man is pure evil. I could feel it pouring off him!'

I raised my eyebrows and Roger hastened to explain. 'Jill's a "sensitive", as in, she can feel what people are really like, despite what they might pretend to be.'

'That's a very useful talent,' I remarked, 'I didn't know you could do that.'

She smiled, 'I didn't mention it because I haven't felt any anomalies with anybody up to now. Everyone's been straight.'

We all had a good laugh at that. 'Good call and glad to hear it!' I replied. 'In which case, now might be a good time to tell you my cunning plan to deal with Xavier, although I'm not sure what to do about his companion, the delectable Miss Dell Petrie. It probably depends on her attitude and whether she thinks the same as her employer. Maybe you can help with that if we get to socialising.'

'I need to get physically fairly close to get a reading, so I can't help for now,' Jill replied.

I grinned at her concern, 'No problem. You should get your chance if Xavier comes good with his offer of drinks later. Anyway, we'll sort out Miss Petrie after we deal with Xavier, but let's go up to our room for a bit of privacy and I'll tell you my plan.'

CHAPTER 46

HARRY, SUMBAWA BESAR, LATER SATURDAY AFTERNOON

'I've got to say in my professional medical opinion, it's a bloody dangerous plan, Harry. I mean, you'll be messing around with a condition which could kill and I certainly can't tell you in advance what adverse mental effects it might have.'

I nodded, 'Point taken, mate. But what if we take the other viewpoint that I really don't give a fuck! Jill has already given us her read on his character and Corrine, Sandy and I all know what he's tried to do to us and a lot of others in the past, as well as what he's capable of. From what Greg says, he seems to have tipped over a mental edge with this obsession with finding Andy, and who knows what he'll do with him and Lara if he gets his hands on them. So, based on that, I don't really care!'

Roger shrugged, 'Yeah, understood. But I may not be able to help much if it all goes wrong. I don't mean I would bung on the outraged Doctor routine. I was speaking practically in that it all depends on how he reacts.'

I smiled grimly, 'There won't be any such thing as 'going wrong' with this prick, unless we accidently give him a break, and that's not going to happen.'

I looked at Corrine, 'What do you reckon, Mouse? Is your part feasible?'

She shrugged, although a glint of excitement showed in her eyes. 'Practically, there's no problem. I just need you to let me know when it's the right time and I'll move from there. That woman, Dell Petrie, complicates things a bit. We need to decide is she a good girl or a bad girl?'

'Yeah, she's a bit of a dark horse. I'd like to know a bit more

404

before we have any more talks with Mr Xavier. I wonder if Greg can help?'

Answering my own question, I dug out the Sat-Phone and dialled, catching him on the way out of the Station at the end of a working day.

'Dell Petrie? I hadn't heard of her before our mole reported she was travelling with Xavier. If it's important, I'll have to go back inside and make some calls.'

'Yeah mate. It's important, sorry.'

'Ok. I'll get back in fifteen or twenty minutes. Don't go away.'

We kicked things around for a while, not too concerned about the time lost, since I was sure Xavier wouldn't be back from the police station for another hour or so. Finally, the Sat-Phone trilled and Greg sounded excited.

'OK. Finally got a line on the young lady. She's a recent hire by Xavier, taken on when his last PA left in a hurry under mysterious circumstances. Some close friend recommended her, so Xavier didn't vet her too closely, which was a major breach of his own protocol and a major blunder as it turns out. Remember I told you there were two teams chasing your VIP?'

'Yes, Mum. We remember!'

'Well, one team represents the billionaire industrialist who wanted to create an Australian Republic overnight with himself as the President and they are the ones who put out the $20 million contract.

The other team are rather more shadowy but have been revealed as set up by the previously-unheard of, "Australian Consortium of Union Superannuation Funds" who are effectively the Union Super Fund Managers who were looking for the disruption of the oil and gas industry to create a chaotic situation which would have suited the aspirations of our industrialist.'

'OK, so the two groups were loosely working together?'

'Yeah, but extremely loosely. They each had their own agendas and just overlapped on this issue.'

'OK. We get that now. That confirmation of information has

made a few more things drop into place, thanks mate. Where does the lovely Miss Petrie fit in?'

'*She just happens to be the Chief Investigator for the boss of the biggest Union Fund in Australia. She's an undercover plant and silly bloody Xavier was so focused on chasing Lara and Andy, he didn't research her background!*'

'So, to summarise, she's definitely not on Xavier's side. Can I classify her as a player, but neither assisting nor hindering Xavier?'

'*That would be a fair call. Whether she would actively fight you is harder to say. Probably if her arse was in danger, she would, but otherwise she'd probably sit on the fence and stay neutral. It'd be nice to get her to spill her guts, metaphorically speaking only please, on what she knows of the ACUSF. That would wrap up half of this massive investigation immediately!*'

'OK, got that. Thanks mate. We'll definitely get what we can from her and might even let her walk away if she co-operates. Otherwise, she might have a nasty accident alongside Xavier.'

'*Ah...shit, Harry! Are you still going ahead with that?*'

'Hell, yes! I said someone had to shut this clown down once and for all. You guys can't do it officially, so we have to do it under the radar.'

'*OK. I don't need the details. Is that all you need for the moment? I have a dinner date with a very pleasant young lady, I really don't want to miss.*'

'Yeah that's all for now, thanks heaps Greg. I'll keep you informed as things happen. Cheers mate.'

'*Tread carefully Harry! Talk to me soon.*'

I disconnected from Greg, conscious of the wide-eyed gaze of my three companions, but held up a hand to forestall any questions as I dialled another number immediately.

'*Gidday Harry. How're things going?*'

'Developing quickly, thanks Dave. To the extent that I'd like you to be ready to take on passengers this evening. If you could be at the jetty where we got off, we might join you with some extra guests, but it won't be until well after dark. The timing depends of the guests and I'm uncertain of their movements at the moment. There will be three of them and we'll need the bow cabins as lockups.'

He chuckled. '*This sounds like old times and should be fun. By the way, Sandy and crew have arrived safely.*'

'Great! That was my next question. I'll get you to let her know we're all okay and I'll need Jasper and Krazy on *Seeker* when we arrive.'

'*No problem there, mate. They're rafted up alongside as we speak. Are the passengers going to be active and/or hostile?*'

'Nah. If the plan works out, they'll probably be semi-mobile but will seem to be in a drunken stupor, courtesy of Corrine's little pills, so there'll be no problem with them being aggressive. Just do what you have to do to convert the crew cabins to cells again, but it'll only be for a short time. I expect two of them will be leaving us within 24 hours, while the other one will be dropped off at an island 170 miles away. Will you be all set to make the run?'

'*Yep. No problem. You remember the caretaker or whatever he was who came down to see us when we arrived?*'

'Yep.'

'*Well, he was so impressed with the boat and Jasper, he helped organise fuel for us, and good quality stuff at that; I've completely filled Seeker and Firebird including the auxiliary tanks. I thought we might be moving into the endgame soon and wanted to be prepared, because there aren't too many refuelling places out this end of the island group.*'

'Brilliant work, and thanks for that. That'll work out beautifully. Hopefully, we'll see you this evening.'

'*Take care Harry. See you then.*'

I disconnected and looked at my companions. 'OK. That's our getaway organised; now we just have to wait to see if Mr Xavier and crew will fall into line with our plans.

'Bloody hell, Harry,' Corrine said, shaking her head in amazement. 'Could Xavier really have been so dumb as to hire a spy as his PA?'

'Apparently,' I replied mildly, 'and it could make our job a lot easier if she's already got a lot of the info we want. We just have to persuade her to tell us all about it!'

Corrine got that shit-eating grin on her face that I'd first seen in the Middle-Eastern desert, just before a nasty covert operation. 'I guess I'd better dig out my first-aid kit.'

I shared her grin as Roger and Jill just looked worried. 'Yes please, Mouse. And at the appropriate time, I think it should go like this...'

After laying out a loose plan, applying the sage advice of Field Marshall, Helmuth von Moltke, who said, "no plan survives first contact with the enemy", we waited for Corrine to get a few items from her 'first-aid' kit, before returning downstairs to the bar where our friend, Rizky from the coffee shop, was pleased to open the bar and serve us some rather more fortifying beverages.

'I must thank you again, my friend, for your timely intervention earlier this afternoon with the unpleasant man and his abusive comments,' he said in his perfect English. 'Unfortunately, my colleagues are not so comfortable with your language and were quite upset by his attitude and bad words.'

I bowed my head in acknowledgement of his gratitude. 'Yes. He was being obnoxious and I'm afraid he will be coming back soon and may have cause to be extremely upset again, so be prepared. I will, however, do what I can to deflect some of his anger. Unfortunately, my friends and I may have to checkout tonight. The events of the day with the police arresting the drug smugglers has upset us so we may move to a dive resort on the coast.'

'That is very unfortunate and I do apologise for the disruption to your stay with us, but I completely understand your desire to re-locate. When do you wish to check-out?'

'Not immediately, thank you. It will probably be after dinner, as we actually have a meeting organised with the unpleasant man when he returns, so we'll have some drinks and perhaps some more of that lovely finger food you produced earlier.'

He beamed, 'It will be excellent to have you here when the man returns. My alternative would be to call the police again, which I fear would create even more disruption. When you are ready, please allow me to supply the meal at no cost to you.'

I nodded my thanks as he made up a round of drinks and we settled in to wait for Xavier's return.

The day was advancing rapidly and, at least for us, painlessly into evening, with the semi-outdoor bar surrounded by the ubiquitous and fascinating little house geckos making their distinctive chirping sounds as they scurried around chasing spiders and other insects which comprised their normal diet. We had reached the stage of happy intoxication where we were placing bets on which gecko would catch a particular juicy insect first, when a raised voice from the carpark heralded the arrival of the outspokenly unpleasant Xavier Johnson and the return of less-pleasant reality.

Moments later he strode through reception, barking a brief stream of abuse at the hapless staff, before entering the bar. He acknowledged our presence with a flap of one hand and was accompanied by a harried-looking Dell Petrie, and a tall, rugged and shaggy-haired blonde man who I guessed was the dive boat owner, Mike.

He rudely demanded a round of drinks from the gentle and polite Andi, waved Dell and Mike, if that's who he was, toward an outside table, before looking over at our table with its bunch of cheery drunks. He glared at our happy faces and growled, 'I need to talk with you shortly, Mr James, when I've finished having a chat with Mike here.'

I smiled vacantly, waved a hand back and said, 'No problem, old stick. We'll be here as long as the drinks keep coming.'

He muttered something under his breath about pissed Pommies, which was good coming from an ex-Pom who still had a Cockney accent, but given what was in store for the unpleasant Mr Xavier, I was happy to let it slide. Corrine was less charitable and looked as if she'd cheerfully strangle the prick then and there, but I played the part of an affectionate husband and patted her knee until she settled.

Without being too obvious, we kept an ear or two on Xavier's little 'discussion' with Mike. It was fairly amicable at first, but quickly became heated and we gathered the police had released Mike only after a huge amount of cash greased the correct palms. They noted he was merely employed as a contractor by Xavier's group, and was a local businessman well known to the police as being totally intolerant of drugs. His only crime was to be actually in the company of the others when they were found with the drugs in their rooms.

Xavier, however, seemed to have other ideas and tried to blame Mike for the tip-off to the police that sparked the whole debacle. That line of thought was quickly shut down when Mike stood, his green eyes blazing and fists clenched. Like most bullies, Xavier folded like a house of cards when faced with the threat of imminent and personal violence, and didn't make it even halfway out of his chair before subsiding. At that point, with several early diners looking alarmed by the fuss outside, I rose and made my way over to their table.

Speaking quietly in my neutral accent, I said to Xavier, 'Look sport. You're doing it again. You've abused the staff, upset the residents in the dining room and are on the verge of receiving a visit from the local police for disturbing the peace and being a public fucking nuisance. Now, how about you moderate the tone and the words, or if you think that's not possible, then come over with me and have a quiet, friendly chat with us, while you buy us all those drinks you promised.'

For a moment, he looked as though he'd protest in the only way he knew, by being loud and obnoxious. However, faced with me towering beside him and a snarling Mike across the table with Dell hanging onto his arm rather more closely than necessary, sanity prevailed. Grumbling under his breath, he pushed his chair back and stood, to the obvious relief of staff and patrons, while Dell and Mike laid beaming smiles on me. Back at our table, I let Xavier order drinks for us all and when he was seated, proceeded to gently extract what information I could about current activities.

For a short time, he was surprisingly forthcoming about much of what we wanted to know, although when it came to his employers he clammed up. I could see he was also starting to burr up about being asked such leading questions about his work by a bunch of what he'd thought were pissed, layabout diving types, so I made the decision to pull the pin on the trio and gave Corrine a nod, before interrupting Xavier's latest tirade, and in a slightly slurred voice said, 'I think it's time I bought you and your associates a drink and how about some food. Rizky here has an excellent chef and has the food ready.'

Xavier must have been at least a little bit off balance, since without argument he replied, 'Well, I suppose another drink would be pleasant after this shitful day I've had and a good feed won't go astray either.'

He waved the other two over and they reluctantly dragged chairs up to join us. I went to the bar to get more drinks and asked Rizky if he could get the food out ASAP before any more unpleasantness happened.

'I'll make sure there is no problem after this, I assure you.' I suggested.

'No problem, Mr Harry. I have complete faith you will keep our bar and dining area clear of nastiness tonight.'

With that endorsement spurring me on, we had to succeed with the night's activities. Corrine came to the bar to help collect the drinks, and specifically took those for Dell, Mike and Xavier. Really, the girl should have been on the stage doing sleight-of-hand tricks she was so slick!

With everyone settled and chatting harmlessly, Rizky nervously brought over the platters of super-tasty finger food, steaming hot from the kitchen and thankfully hunger immediately overcame chatter. It was difficult to see if Corrine managed to wave her hand over the right bits of food as well, but I had faith she had done the job.

As everyone ate, she managed to make a slight nod in my direction which I took to mean that whatever she'd managed to do, would soon be effective. The first indications of her handiwork were that Dell and Mike, showing signs of a blossoming mutual attraction, started chattering about non-sensical things that had no bearing on the current situation. Within ten minutes they were behaving as if quite drunk, and when Xavier started talking braille, it showed he was close behind them.

Dell and Mike didn't suspect anything, but Xavier became a bit agitated when he saw Dell and Mike starting to pass out. He tried to bellow in protest, but was too far gone to do much more than mutter a string of curses which became more incoherent by the second. Soon, all three had their heads down on the table and were snoring softly.

We four finished our drinks and the lovely food, before I went over to speak with Andi.

'It would appear our new associates have had too much to drink and have passed out. If you would be so kind to organise a private taxi, like a mini-van, we'll take responsibility for removing them from the premises.'

He bowed his head in appreciation.

'Thank you, Mr Harry. That will be good, since I don't think the unpleasant man will be very co-operative when he awakes.'

I chuckled, 'You're right there. We'll take them to a friend's home to sober up, but the main thing is to get them out of here. We might even take their luggage with us and I'll settle the account.'

'That's very generous of you, Mr Harry and greatly appreciated. I'll have the housekeeper collect their baggage and bring it down and the taxi is on the way. Will there be a forwarding address?'

I had a chuckle to myself, but outwardly I said, 'No. The gentleman and his companion are already booked on the return flight to Bali, then back to Melbourne on the first available service.'

'Excellent, sir. I can see they are very lucky to be in such safe hands.' Andi's tone was slightly ironic as if he guessed something untoward was planned, but as long as the trouble moved on, he was happy.

We collected our bags from our rooms and while the house-keeper rounded up Xavier's and Dell's stuff, I settled all the accounts, counting the total a cheap way to be rid of most of Xavier's crew and to get our hands on what would hopefully prove to be good intelligence.

The taxi arrived and we pitched in to help walk, firstly Dell, then Mike, and lastly Xavier out to the mini-bus, where I propped them up in the rear corners of the back seats. Roger, Jill and Corrine jumped in to hold them in position and to re-assure the driver they were only drunk and not dying. Yet!

Rizky helped bring out the collection of suitcases, including a large handbag obviously belonging to Dell and an expensive tooled leather briefcase which had to belong to Xavier.

I said to Corrine, 'First thing back aboard, go through both of those and see what papers and notes might help us.'

'No problem. I have a feeling that Dell's might be as productive as Xavier's, and I'll go through their suitcases very carefully as well.'

Farewelled by a beaming Rizky, we lurched into motion and waved at the sleepy guard at the gate as I pointed the driver in the direction of the coast road that led to the bay where the boats and my dear Sandy were ready and waiting.

CHAPTER 47

SEEKER/FIREBIRD, SUMBAWA BESAR, SATURDAY NIGHT

It was getting on for 21:00 by the time we loaded luggage and semi-conscious bodies aboard *Seeker*. I was delighted to hug my lovely Sandy again and Jasper and Krazy gave us all a big welcome. I told Jasper that Xavier was a very bad man and he should be watched carefully. A deep growl was his reply, after sniffing him over carefully. I also told him Mike was a good guy and Dell was maybe not so good and should also be watched carefully. He huffed at the advice about Dell, so I thought it meant he probably wouldn't bite her if she blinked too often or at least not too hard.

When everything was settled, I called a round-table conference in *Seeker's* big saloon and explained to the boat crews the essence of my cunning plans. Corrine had already gone through Xavier and Dell's luggage looking for papers or other clues and was starting on the handbag and briefcase.

'So that's the plan,' I finished up with, 'we need to extract as much info as we can, but I believe Mike is fairly innocent and won't have a lot to say, although that depends on how much Juliet confided in him. I thought we might soften up Xavier with Jasper and Krazy first. Does anyone have thoughts on that?'

'Better tie the prick's hands and feet first if he's not going to be drugged,' was Dave's good suggestion.

'Good idea. Anything else?'

'How about we ask Mike a few questions first when he's coming out of the sleepy drug,' Roger suggested. 'Is there an antidote to what you gave them earlier?' he asked Corrine.

Without lifting her head from the piles of papers she was carefully going through, she said, 'Yeah. It's a 0.2ml injectable that'll bring him completely awake with no memory at all of the last few hours. He'll be a bit disoriented to be in a different environment, but there is one odd side effect. He'll be very horny!'

That raised a general laugh and Bree suggested he and Dell should be put in the other cabin together to work off the side effects.

'But perhaps she should be interrogated first?'

'I think she'll be far more relaxed after an extended session with Mike,' Sandy added with a cheeky grin.

I grinned back at her, 'Great idea, dear lady. Let's do it. Corrine!'

'Yeah, yeah. On it, Harry. Give me a moment.'

She had her first-aid kit handy, sterile wipes for good needle hygiene at the ready and in moments, had injected both snoring guests.

'How long does that take to work?' asked Roger, always the medical professional and mildly disapproving of military medics doing stuff off the battlefield.

'Just about long enough to get them for'rard to their cabin and stripped off. I'd like to search their clothes for any info that might be inadvertently tucked away.'

'Oh dear. They will have a lot of fun when they get over the initial shock!' Sandy commented with a giggle.

Minutes later, two naked bodies were laid out on the two bunk beds and their clothes bundled up by Corrine. I noted that a naked Dell was even better built than I'd thought with her clothes on.

'Monitoring and recording on?' Dave asked.

'Absolutely!' I replied. 'They might drop some good stuff as they wake and sort out where they are.'

We took the opportunity to place Xavier in the adjacent little bow cabin and I told Jasper to guard him, but not to touch him. At the last minute, I decided not to put little Krazy in there as well, figuring Jasper's size would be quite sufficient to trigger Xavier's allergy. His wrists and ankles were strapped with cable ties and his clothes also removed for careful inspection by Corrine. He wasn't given the antidote, as we wanted to see if his allergic reaction would overcome it naturally. His cabin audio was also put through to the intercom and recorded, although Roger insisted on listening for any signs of extreme respiratory distress.

With our guests set up, we waited to see what happened, watching Corrine still sorting through papers.

'Anything interesting so far?' I asked her.

'Yeah, lots of stuff,' she answered distractedly, 'but I'm not sure how it all ties together yet. There are a lot of references to Lord Howe Island, of all places. It seems Xavier has a property there, but nothing about what it is. I'll keep looking, although there is some evidence that the $20 mil contract money from the industrialist dude is long gone and that Xavier is spending his own funds.'

I gave a short laugh, 'That's probably why he's so shitty all the time. But I'd really like to find out where his funds are located. Is it a stash like you and Dave found, or is it more legal?'

'Dunno! But I'll keep looking. We may have to wait until dear Dell has finished playing with Mike and is willing to talk.'

'Yeah, that's true. Anyway, you've found a good lead with the Lord Howe stuff.'

It wasn't long after, when the sensitive mikes in both cabins started picking up noises. Xavier's recorded loud and laboured breathing which concerned Roger to the extent he told me he needed to check on the patient. I went forward with him, Alex coming along for extra security and we noted murmurs coming from the shared cabin next door.

Opening Xavier's door, we found Jasper at rest, watching the prisoner carefully. Xavier was on the lower bunk, on his back, partly conscious and with laboured breathing and moaning softly.

Roger examined him and I could see that his face was indeed swollen, as was his neck.

'I'm not happy with this reaction, Harry. I think we should remove Jasper for now and give him an adrenaline shot. If he comes out of that alright, then we might try one of Corrine's scopolamine injections.'

Jasper was temporarily relieved of duty and with the sound level next door rising considerably in a manner which left no doubt that Dell and Mike were becoming very closely acquainted, Roger went to get his kit.

He quickly returned and Corrine was with him. The adrenaline injection worked quickly and Xavier's breathing eased markedly. Unfortunately, as subsided, his consciousness increased along with his bad attitude.

'Where the fuck am I?' was his first demand. 'And why am I tied up and naked. I can smell a cat. I have to tell you I'm severely allergic to cats. I've been told without treatment, my allergy could kill me.'

'Point noted, Mr Johnson,' I said, 'this gentleman is a Doctor and is monitoring your condition. Unfortunately for you, he's not very sympathetic to your suffering and is prepared to keep you alive as long as you answer my questions. If you don't feel like talking, he'll go away and the very large cat who was keeping you company will return.'

'You can't bring a cat in here! I've been told I can go into anaphylactic shock if I get too close to a cat! You don't want my death on your conscience.'

I gave an unpleasant laugh. 'In fact, Mr Johnson, I'd like nothing better than the have your death on my conscience. It would be a perfect end to a long chase.'

For the first time, some of Xavier's bluster left him and with his pathetic, pale, naked body stretched out on the bunk, he looked and apparently felt, very vulnerable.

'Who are you people? What am I to you?'

For answer, I stepped out of the cabin and called back aft, 'Andy. Lara. Could you come here please?'

Shortly, both were at the door and Roger stepped outside to give them room. They stepped into the small cabin and with an appropriate degree of drama, I said, 'Mr Terry Xavier Johnson, may I present the persons you've been spending several small fortunes trying to find. I'm pleased to be able to say you've finally found them, but it's not going to do you any good whatsoever. On my left is Miss Lara Bishop whose look-alike distracted your men so easily on the Gold Coast. You may like to know that her stand-in was a serving Queensland Police officer.'

I was glad Roger wasn't in the cabin at that moment as Xavier's face went bright red and a large vein stood out on his forehead. Despite this, I moved aside slightly to show him the man standing just behind my right shoulder.

'On my right is the main subject of your search, Mr Andy Friar, the Prime Minister of Australia.'

Andy stepped forward a pace and gazed impassively down on Xavier's naked form. After a moment, he snorted. 'Utterly pathetic little worm,' before turning on his heel and leaving with Lara who was still giggling from her very obvious inspection of Xavier's shrunken genitals.

I viewed the results of the last revelation, noting with interest the suffused red on his face had gone purple and he seemed incapable of speech. Roger came back, checked his pulse, shook his head and motioned me outside with a toss of his head.

'He's borderline cardiac arrest at the moment, so I wouldn't recommend any more drugs until he settles down from those shocks. They must have really got to him to have that level of reaction.'

'Well, he has just spent a fortune chasing the PM and to come face-to-face with him under these circumstances is a very severe shock. But while I'll take your advice for the moment, before long we need to get some information out of him. And that's going to take an injection.'

'Yeah, okay. But let me have a look at him first before you start. He'll be no use if he falls off the perch before he can talk.'

I nodded as we left the hapless Xavier and locked the door, smiling at the sounds still issuing from the next cabin.

On impulse, I turned back suddenly, 'I think we might drag Mike out of there for a bit of a chat. He's had enough fun for one day!'

I unlocked the door to be met with a wave of musky odour, and the sight of Mike still firmly implanted in Dell, which was a feat of impressive endurance. It took a few seconds for our presence to register and even then, he just looked over his shoulder to see what the noise was.

'Who's that? Can't a bloke have some privacy? What do you want?'

I suppressed a chuckle, 'You, as it happens. How about you extract yourself from that rather delectable young lady and come with us, excuse the pun. Without wishing to sound too dramatic, your answers to our questions may determine your fate!'

Dell had a decidedly unhappy expression on her face as he reluctantly performed the necessary extraction, and tried to compose herself as best she could under the circumstances. Mike looked around for clothes, although nothing was going to hide him properly for a while, so he settled for a totally inadequate towel from the bathroom draped around his slim hips.

As we turned to leave, I said to Dell, 'I'll be back to have a chat with you too, young lady. While we're gone you may care to consider your position in this business, given that the man you've been spying on, is in the next cabin in the process of losing his mind. We know who you are and would appreciate learning all you've found out from your time with him. Not voluntarily speaking will result in us having to use more unpleasant means to extract the information we require. Please consider.'

She started to say something as I closed and bolted the door, but I kept moving, while Roger escorted a more subdued Mike ahead of him, with the menacing black shape of Jasper pacing silently alongside, a sight which always tends to subdue the ungodly.

Corrine came down and tossed him a pair of pants and a shirt. His mind must have been really fuzzy, for he suddenly said, 'Hey! You're the guys from the motel. What's going on?'

Corrine silently led the way to the upper level and pointed to a chair at the head of the dining table. He took the hint without protest and Jasper sat within lunging distance, his big eyes fixed unwaveringly on Mike's, his mouth agape slightly to show his gleaming white teeth.

'What the hell's that thing? It looks like a cat but it's bigger than most dogs. I don't like the way it's looking at me!'

I sat on the next chair. 'He's a jungle cat and has and will happily rip arms or legs off people he doesn't like. At the moment, he doesn't like you or the two with you. Whether his attitude changes is up to you and the answers to my questions.'

'But who are you people?'

'Sorry, I'm the one asking; you're the one answering. Make me happy and I might do you a favour. You've associated yourself with the wrong bunch this time, and you need to decide if you owe them anything. One word from us, and the police will have you locked up with your other girlfriend, Juliet, and this time there won't be any bail. It'll be the firing squad alongside the others.'

'Whoa! Hang on now. I had nothing to do with any of that drug stuff. I didn't even know it was there! We were just having a meeting to decide when to use my boat to visit an island they'd found from the air. They told me they were looking for some runaway heiress who was Juliet's sister. I saw her photo and she looked like Juliet.'

I glanced at Corrine and she nodded slightly, so I raised my voice slightly and called, 'Lara. Would you mind stepping in here please?'

Moments later, she stepped around the dining area partition and stood in front of a slightly gob-smacked Mike.

'Is this the lady whose photo you were shown?' I asked.

He looked carefully at Lara who obligingly turned left and right to show her profile.

'Yeah. That's her. She matches the photos I was shown. But what's going on? If she's supposed to be missing, what's she doing here with you guys? Fuck it! I don't know what's happening!'

I smiled at Lara, 'Thanks Lara. That'll do for now.'

'Now Mike. It would appear you've been sadly misled. You've had a lovely time getting into Juliet's pants, and no doubt you were promised a fat charter fee for the use of your boat, but what you weren't told was that this wasn't a search to find a missing heir-ess, but was a kidnap plot to abduct Lara, which is her real name, for reasons you don't need to know about. She happens to be the long-term lady-friend of a very prominent Australian person who would rather she stays free and not in the clutches of Xavier and the people he represents.

I'd prefer not to say anymore, as that would involve you in the shit far deeper than you are already. It's up to you as to whether you choose to accept my statement or not.'

He was clearly conflicted and showed his agitation by rubbing his temples with both hands. He finally asked. 'There won't be any long-term charter, will there?'

I smiled gently, 'No. There's no charter because the customers are probably going to be shot or at least locked up for life; there's no pay for the time you've already spent advising these idiots and running them around; the girl you've been bonking will soon be stood up against a wall and shot for heavy drug possession, and it's only your clean reputation with the coppers that's let you walk free today. Just one squawk of protest from you and the police will lock you up again so fast your head will spin. One word from us will have the same effect, I might add. The only upside from your perspective is you got to bonk two attractive ladies of very dubious backgrounds.

Now, which way are we going? Jail and maybe a firing squad, or talk to us and maybe, just maybe, you get to have your old life back?'

He looked at Corrine and me with stricken eyes. 'There's no choice is there? So, what do I have to do to turn the clock back?'

'OK, that's what we like to hear; some co-operation at last. Now, start talking about how this whole thing started. Right from the beginning and pretend we know nothing. Don't leave anything out, because we'll be checking.'

As is fairly usual, once he decided to save his hide and talk, there was no stopping him, so we got the whole story and it made sense. We knew some details, but there was a lot of additional information gained from the briefing sessions with Juliet's group and a certain amount of pillow talk which filled in a lot of gaps.

Corrine took notes for all the important points and at that stage I left them to visit Dell. Behind me I heard Corrine say in her quiet, serious voice, 'I think I'll have you go over all that again, if you don't mind. There's a few points I'm still not clear on.'

On the way down below, I grabbed a pair of panties off a pile of female clothing with all the seams unpicked and ruthlessly pulled apart. I probably could have started a new fashion trend among the hip younger set with that look. I unlocked Dell's door and found her in much the same position as before

'Okay missy. Your turn, but put these on please.'

'Fuck you, smart arse! I'm not going anywhere with you. And what was all that bullshit you spouted before? How come you know anything about me?'

I smiled patiently. 'All will be revealed. Please put those panties on and behave yourself. Any attempt to get away or do harm to anybody here will result in a world of hurt, the likes of which you've never imagined.'

She sneered even as she snatched the panties off my outstretched hand and pulled them on. 'Big words tough man. But do you really know who you're messing with?'

I grinned at her, trying to cover her bare breasts with crossed arms, a gesture that always managed to look faintly ridiculous. 'Hmmm. Let's see now. I think the police officer who told me all about you said that you were, 'the Chief Investigator for the boss of the biggest Union Fund in Australia.' Did I get that right? It sounds terribly impressive!'

She'd gone white around the mouth with supressed rage and was almost dancing from foot to foot in her agitation. 'I don't know how you found that out, but do you really think you can fight against the power of the Unions. What are you, some private investigator who's stumbled across a little bit of information?'

I smiled, 'No. I'm not some private investigator. In this instance, you will have to accept that I happen to represent the law enforcement arm of the Australian Government. That means I really can lead the fight against the power of the Unions and win. You see, in this case, the Unions have really stepped on their own dicks by being conned into buying into a dirty little scheme which was better left alone. All that money and power have done a great job of corrupting some otherwise good people. Getting involved in politics is always a bad move when you claim to represent the welfare of the worker masses. If those masses find out that their precious fees have been used in a failed attempt to overthrow the Australian Government, do you really think they will just shrug and continue to toss a chunk of their weekly pay packet into your bulging coffers?'

Her rage had subsided with my words and she just looked deeply concerned. 'How the fuck do you know all this? Only five or six people know those details.'

I shook my head. 'Sorry sweetheart. A great many more know those details, and they are mostly in law enforcement like me. But I'm going to make it simple for you. Tell me everything you've learned from your time with Xavier, plus whatever we want to know about how your Union boss stuck his nose into the political arena, and I'll let you apply for immunity as a Crown witness. I may even put in a good word for you.'

She shook her head in wonder. 'You have got to be kidding me! Do you know how long I'd last if I did that? Zero!'

'No, that's not quite right. You would find yourself well protected and looked after in the Commonwealth Witness Protection Program and they've never lost a client. But if you're going to be difficult, as much as I'd love to hear your story because it would really help unravel this mess, I can get the information by other means. Therefore you become redundant and can't be allowed to go flapping your gums to whoever will listen. That, in turn, means you simply won't return from this little gig. And the terms of your passing will be nasty indeed, since you will be sharing your demise with your most recent boss. I don't like to see lovely ladies suffer, but that's how it'll be.'

She tried, but failed to strike an aggressive pose. 'So what are you now, judge, jury and executioner? I thought you said you represent the law.'

'Yes, and yes. In capital cases like this, and unfortunately for you, I'm the one who makes sure the bad guys don't get to hide behind a team of high-priced lawyers and get away with anything they want – again. Therefore your choice is simple. Co-operate or you won't leave these islands.'

'You really think you can do that, do you?'

I looked back at her with my pissed-off Major stare, 'No, I don't think it; I know it. Although unlike my female colleague, I don't like it, but I've done it before and I'll be doing it again. So whether it's you as the next target or some other fool who tried to be too clever, is entirely up to you. Because I'm basically a nice guy, I'm going to let you consider my remarks and the offer which is on the table for just sixty minutes. After that; well, we've been over it too often already! As I said earlier, please consider.'

With that, I closed and dropped the locking bar across the door to really secure it, and thought that I heard a soft sob as I walked away.

CHAPTER 48

SEEKER/FIREBIRD, SUMBAWA BESAR, SATURDAY NIGHT

All was quiet up in the dining area, as the rest of the crew had all taken to their beds, except for Dave and Alex sitting out in the cockpit. Corrine had obviously finished the second iteration of Mike's story and gave me a nod when I came in. 'It tallies, boss. There's some good information he picked up from sitting in on briefings, and will tie up some loose ends for us, but otherwise, he's probably innocent of doing anything bad. They really did offer him a good charter, but otherwise, he just got dragged in by some slick talk and willing pussy.'

The object of her analysis was sitting on the lounge at the rear of the saloon, staring out at the water, apparently contemplating his stupidity, with Jasper in close attendance.

'Do we let him go?' I asked.

'Yeah. Scare the shit out of him, although what you said earlier was probably enough, then cut him loose. I'd warn him again about trying to talk to the police. If he just keeps his head down, he should escape any fallout from the drug arrests.'

'OK. Sounds good. I'll do it now unless you think we should keep him here a bit longer.'

'Nah. I've got all he knows, although you might like to let him know we can always chase him down again if necessary.'

'Good thinking, Mouse. Consider it done.'

I walked aft to where Mike was sitting.

'Happy now?' he said a trifle bitterly.

'Yes, as a matter of fact, I am. Which is good for you.'

He finally raised his eyes to meet mine. 'How so?'

'Do you remember everything I said earlier?'

'Of course. I'm not always an idiot!'

I smiled gently, 'OK. If you give me a guarantee you'll remember those words from this point on and abide by them, I'm prepared to let you resume your former life as a dive boat operator. The only condition is, you do not speak of any of this to anybody, anywhere and for any reason. If someone is holding a blunt knife to your nuts, just remind yourself, I can and will do a great deal worse. My big cat here will be just the start of your worst set of nightmares. He specialises in ripping body parts off bad people and that's while they're still alive! And please don't make the mistake of thinking I'm kidding.

I have the resources to find you at any time, anywhere, should I even think you've flapped your gums about any of this crap! So, as they say in the classics, 'go forth and sin no more'.'

He looked disbelievingly at me. 'So that's it? If I don't make waves; don't talk about this to anyone, and just go about my business, I can go with no further trouble from you or anyone else?'

I made a show of considering his words, 'Yep. That's about it! We'll take care of any loose ends here which might cause you trouble in the future, so you could say thanks. But otherwise, go in peace, think good thoughts and do good deeds.'

He stood, eyeing Jasper carefully. 'So I can just walk off the boat. No further trouble?'

I smiled patiently, 'Yes Mike. You can just walk off onto the jetty. You can even call for a taxi using our phone if you want.'

'Really? That'd be awesome, thanks.'

I showed him the boat's mobile which was on international roaming and he made a quick call, but I suspect it was to a friend and not a taxi.

Moments later, he was over the side and disappeared into the darkness. I sat with Dave, Alex and Corrine in the cockpit for a quick briefing.

'I think we should get going right now. I don't totally trust Mike and it would be best if we were well away by daybreak.'

'Yep. I agree, and no problem leaving. Our guard friend said there's no strict port control on private boats as long as they have their inbound clearance still current.'

'Good. Now I suggest we put Jasper in with Xavier for a short time, like maybe ten to fifteen minutes, which should shut him up for a while. I told Dell she had one hour to decide whether to co-operate or not. If she doesn't, I propose to land her and Xavier on Gili Montang tomorrow. It's a 12-hour run at 14 knots so getting there around midday should work out well. If she's willing to reveal all, I think I'll continue the interrogation on *Firebird*. Corrine, are you happy to sit in and take notes?'

'Yeah, no trouble. Are you going to get her decision first?'

'Yeah, I'll go get it now, and if she'll talk, I'll blindfold her and walk her over to *Firebird*.'

Corrine suggested, 'Just another thought. If she's going to talk, I can either inject her with scopolamine or Jill can sit in and say if she lies.'

I thought a few moments. 'It might be best to stick her with your you-beaut truth serum. We'll leave Jill out of this one, but I'll see if she's made the right decision first.'

'Amen to that, brother.'

I went for'rard with Alex, Corrine and Jasper in attendance. Firstly, we unbarred Xavier's cell and found him in a foul mood although still slightly affected by Jasper's earlier presence. He launched into a tirade of abuse, but cut off immediately Jasper padded into the cell. 'No, no! You can't. That's a fuckin' big cat! Oh shit!'

'He's here for a short time, so shut up and behave. He won't come near you and you'll be better off if you don't move or get too excited. I'll be back shortly.'

Having told Jasper to stay by the door unless the bad man tried to attack him, we left to a stream of Xavier's pathetic pleas. It was hardly necessary to bar the door, so I just locked it, before we unbarred and unlocked the next cell.

Opening the door carefully, I let Dell get a look at the menacing bulk of Alex. She was standing in the middle of the small space, poised as if to charge me down, but relaxed when she saw who was blocking the doorway.

'Sit on the bunk and give me your decision.' I said as I stepped around Alex.

'Not so fast, big fella. Tell me the deal if I do tell all.'

'Like I said before, with a guarantee of immunity from prosecution for previous sins, you enter the witness protection program where you are initially under guard 24/7 by Commonwealth officers. You disappear from your former life completely. After you've done what is necessary to secure prosecutions against all those involved in this mess, including anonymous testimony in court, you'll be given a new identity, a modest place to live and a decent job.'

'Is that it?'

'Not quite. You have to tell the whole story to me first, including everything you've discovered from Xavier, however inconsequential it might seem. That will include notes you might have hidden somewhere. You also have to tell the truth completely, as we don't have time to fuck around double-checking everything. In fact, the clock's ticking as we speak and the pathetic piece of shit known as Xavier Johnson is scheduled for disposal in around 13 to 14 hours time. The first hint that you're lying or not revealing everything, and my offer is cancelled and you're sharing his fate in 13 hours' time.'

'How can I convince you that I'm not lying?'

'My colleague is well practiced in the art of interrogation and will administer an injection of scopolamine which you may or may not know, is widely used for assisting people tell the truth. It has no adverse side effects and you will sleep it off afterwards. Co-operation places you under protection immediately.'

'I don't like needles and how can I trust you?'

'The same way we can't fully trust you except by demonstrating we can do as we say. You can't lie under this drug, so it removes any doubt on our part. Remember, we already have a certain amount of information and if just one thing doesn't fit, you'll be joining your new boss Xavier about this time tomorrow.'

Stiffly she nodded. 'All right, get it over with. I'll co-operate on the terms you've just spelled out in front of witnesses, for what that matters. Perhaps at some stage you'll tell me who and what you are. I'm taking a lot on faith here.'

I smiled at her for the first time since at the motel. 'Everything I have said is the truth, including the threats. Maybe someday you will learn more about us, but for now, small steps.'

I beckoned Corrine forward as a faint rumble sounded and a slight vibration signalled that Dave had fired up the big diesels.

'What's that?' Dell asked, hardly wincing as Corrine expertly slid the needle into her arm.

'That's us getting out of here. In case you hadn't noticed, you're on a boat and in a moment, we're going to transfer you to another one. We have to blindfold you for now, so be cool. You're in good hands and will be kept safe so long as you behave.'

'Ok. I get it. I'll be good. I promise, but you might have some fun with Xavier. He hates boats and being on the water. How long before this stuff kicks in?'

Corrine answered, 'Oh, about another five minutes or maybe less. You'll feel comfortable and relaxed, so just go with the flow and all will be well.'

I produced a large cleaning cloth I'd pinched from the galley and tied it around Dell's eyes as she asked,

'Can I have some more clothes on, please?'

'Not yet, I prefer you as you are for now, but maybe later. It's not cold. I want you to place your left hand on Corrine's shoulder and follow her instructions very carefully. Do not remove the blindfold at anytime unless told. You are being guarded by several different guards who will be intolerant of any deviation from instructions.'

'Fuckin' hell. You guys don't let up for a minute, do you?'

'That's why we win and the bad guys lose!' was my short answer and Corrine led her slowly out of the cell while Alex and I went to open Xavier's door to retrieve Jasper. A quick look showed he was in poor shape with breathing difficulties, swollen face and neck. I locked the door, barred it and followed Corrine and Dell up to the saloon.

'Can you get Roger to look in on Xavier soon, please mate. He doesn't look the best at the moment after fifteen minutes with Jasper.'

He grinned, 'No problem. I'll let you lead the way out. There are no particular obstacles and the nav beacons all seem to be working.'

'Thanks. After we get what we want from Dell, we'll transfer back as I want to have a final shot at getting some Intel from Xavier before we dump him on Gili Montang.'

'No problem.'

By the time I reached the railing, Corrine and Alex had successfully transferred Dell to *Firebird* and Sandy was waiting with our engines warming up, having been alerted by the sound of *Seeker* coming to life. I thanked Alex for his help and let him re-join *Seeker*.

'I told the others to stay out of sight for now,' Sandy said, 'but maybe Gilbert will help in getting *Firebird* out of here, since he did such a good job coming in.'

'Good idea. I want to start in on Dell as soon as we can. If she tries to stuff us around, she's joining Xavier on Dragon Island.'

In short order, we cast off lines linking us to *Seeker* and motored quietly away, red lighting throughout and all electronic devices functioning. The radar, chart plotter and depth sounder were most useful to help grope our way out of the anchorage and ensured we had a clear, uneventful run. Once clear of the mudflats at the mouth of the harbour, we turned northeast for the run up past Pulau Mojo, then curved east to seaward of the small island of Pulau Satonde. It was a clear run, curving further south-east to pass between Pulau Sangeang and the main island of Sumbawa. A further curve to the south, southeast put the big island of Komodo on the bows. But we wouldn't be reaching it until late morning and in the meantime, there was a lot of interrogating to do.

We all wanted sleep badly, but I needed to hear what Dell had to say and decide if she was speaking the truth, so with Gilbert and Sandy on watch, I had Corrine brew up a rare coffee for the three of us and we settled in the dimly-lit saloon to hear the tale.

The tell-all cocktail Corrine administered was very effective and I let her take the lead to establish how open Dell was going to be. I was mindful that a well-trained operative can fool most of the so-called 'truth serums', but I suspected Corrine's brew went a lot further than most. Even some embarrassingly personal questions were answered without hesitation, so finally Corrine was satisfied the brew was working properly and that Dell wasn't fooling it, so I took over, a mobile phone in recorder mode on the table between us.

I followed on from where I had been in the cabin on *Seeker* and her answers came straight and sounded truthful. She painted a detailed picture of her Union boss and his part in the plan to disrupt the oil and gas industry as part of the overall plan to bring the Australian Government into disrepute so the head of a very minor political party could take over. She'd come to realise things weren't going to work out, when she discovered that promises of huge sums of Union funds had been made to all in the Party who assisted. To cover her own little backside, she copied a number of documents linking the Union payments to the political party principals.

By now I realised, she wasn't so dedicated to the Union movement as she had suggested and my offer of immunity was just what she was looking for. She told of a stash of papers which would blow the lid off the whole deal if we could get to them first.

The whole story-telling took over an hour, and at the end of it, I took Corrine out into the cockpit to get her final opinion.

'She's telling the truth, Harry, I'm sure. My vote is to keep her. She knows more than we'll get from Xavier about the Union business, simply because she was on the inside. We should inject Xavier though, and ask questions about Lord Howe and what's going on.'

'Yeah. Good idea, but that can wait until we have some sleep. He's going ashore with the dragons regardless, so anytime before then will do to get those questions answered if he will.'

'Sounds good. I'll just kip on the lounge for now, but where are you going to put missy?'

'I'll put her in our dressing room right for'rard. I can lock the hatch from outside, the porthole is too small to get through and I won't need to lock the escape hatch with Jasper camped on the floor beside the bunk all night.'

She laughed, 'That'll do it, all right. She'll be safe.'

'I might get you to supervise her going to the toilet first though, if you wouldn't mind.'

'No problem. I can leave her blindfold on for that and she can take it off in the cabin.'

We got Dell toileted, washed and escorted to our dressing room where I cleared the bunk of discarded clothes. I told her about Jasper and explained to him she was to be confined to the bunk for the rest of the night. Any attempt to leave the cabin was to invite an attack.

Finally, I took the blindfold off and she gave a shriek when she saw his sleek, black form sitting quietly near her feet.

'Show the lady your teeth, please Jasper,' I asked, getting a strange look from Dell. I got an even stranger one when he did it, giving her a good look at his sharp, gleaming white fangs.

'OK. I'm convinced,' she said in a shaky voice. 'I love cats, but he's something else.'

'Yes, he is and please remember you're on probation for now and Jasper is your permanent guard. He'll be sitting in the doorway all night and has instructions to restrain you forcibly if you move away from the bunk or try the hatches. I'll be sleeping in the next cabin so please be careful. If he growls, that's the signal to stop what you were doing and get back into bed or he'll bite you and that will really hurt! He's ripped arms off bad people before today!'

'But,' I continued on a lighter note, 'if all goes well in the next

12-hours or so, I'll give you a lot more freedom, but take what you get for now and be grateful.'

She tried to look happy with that arrangement, but it fell a bit flat. 'Tell me this, please. If I'm on probation, that means you trust me a little bit. Yes?'

I nodded, 'Yep, that's right. I'm just not offering you too much temptation for now.'

'OK. But I have two questions I'd really like answered. What do I call you and how the fuck can you give complex verbal instructions to an overgrown cat, and have him apparently understand and obey you?'

I laughed easily for the first time in days. 'My name is Harry and the full Jasper story will have to wait for another time, but he's actually a jungle cat from the west side of the Archipelago. His genes were supposed to have been diluted by several crossings with domestic cats, but somehow the process was reversed and he went back to almost pure jungle cat. Happily, he's ended up with most of a house cat's domestic traits. The jungle cat side of him shows when he defends the boat, my friends or me. That's the side you don't want to see. He's killed several people already in the defending role and it wasn't pretty.

Anyway, try to get some sleep and we can talk more later this morning. We have a busy day ahead.'

At that, I closed the door most of the way after patting Jasper and telling him that Dell wasn't a bad person any more, but she still had to stay in the cabin for now. He huffed as usual to signify understanding and settled into his sphinx position on the floor, most of his attention on Dell perched on the bunk.

'Hey, Harry. Are you married or got a girlfriend or anything?' Dell called.

'Yeah, I have got a girlfriend and she's called Sandy. She's on watch at the moment. Why?'

'Oh, nothing. Just curious.'

I shook my head as I climbed into bed, but was asleep before I could even start to wonder what that question was about. Which showed once again how little I knew about females.

CHAPTER 49

M y darling girl let me get a solid six hours sleep, so it wasn't until 09:30 I woke naturally and refreshed, driven by the need to empty a full bladder. After cleaning up, I dressed, and made a critical phone call to my people to appraise them of the latest situation.

Their response was slightly disturbing, but made some sense. I mulled it over when I went to Dell's cabin and opened the dressing room door to find her still asleep, snoring softly, so I left her like that. I sent Jasper to pee or poop or whatever he needed to do and left the door open, confident her furry guard would return to guard duty soon.

Corrine was awake on the lounge when I relieved Sandy and Gilbert on watch and sent them to bed, although the lovely girl made me a mug of tea and a pile of toast before she went. The other three were still asleep after the disturbed night.

I checked our position and saw that we still had another 3.5 to 4 hours travelling before we would be pulling into a small bay on the northwest corner of the small island of Gili Montang, where it tucks into a notch in the southern coastline of the much bigger island of Rinca. On the maps, the island looked hilly, being mostly the remains of a small, extinct volcano and quite desolate. I could easily understand why it was uninhabited.

The breeze was up and Sandy and Gilbert had the sails set nicely, so that only one engine was kept running to make sure we maintained a steady 14 knots, with *Seeker* keeping pace, 50 metres off our port quarter.

With some reviving coffee pumping caffeine through her veins,

Corrine was functioning again, so we talked over the information we'd got from Dell earlier, including the papers she claimed would link the Union bosses and Super Fund managers. The link would tie them into the same mismanagement of public monies charges and we decided there wasn't much more Xavier could tell us. Nevertheless, it made sense to take the opportunity to transfer Corrine back to *Seeker* where she could inject Xavier with her tongue-loosening drug just in case he did let something slip.

Consequently, I called Dave on the radio and we decided it would save time overall if we cleared out of Indonesia by dropping into Bima first, to save having to either backtrack, or find another clearance port further east. We wouldn't mention the brief stop at Gili Montang where we wouldn't be setting foot on land anyway.

Or to be exact, one of the current 'crew' would, but he wouldn't be getting back aboard.

Dave was good with the idea, so he eased smoothly alongside, the quiet seas with a low swell helping to get Corrine over the rail and back onto the big, blue boat. She knew what questions to ask and also that I was more focused on what was happening on Lord Howe Island and what Xavier had been up to there.

Engaging George the autopilot, I went below to see if Dell was awake and she was, sitting up on the bunk, busting for a pee, but too scared to move with Jasper glaring at her from the door.

'Thank Christ you're back!' she announced. 'I've been a really good girl and not tried anything, but I'm busting for a pee, so can I? Please?'

I smiled, 'Of course. Jasper, Dell can move anywhere around the boat now, so just keep a loose watch on her, OK?'

My beautiful, big cat blinked lazily at me, then rose and quietly padded aft to pee himself, wake up his little mate Krazy and to get some breakfast.

'He is one super-scary cat,' Dell said, sliding her neat little panty-covered bum down off the bunk. The view of her bare breasts was pleasant as well and she was well aware of the effect her nearly naked body was having.

'As well as needing to pee, I'm starving. Can I go to the kitchen after I've peed and get some food?'

'Galley.' I replied.

'What? What's galley?'

'The galley is what the kitchen is called on a boat. You have to call things by their right name on a boat.'

'Oh. OK, sorry. I'll try if you tell me what they are.'

'OK.'

'Oh, and can I have some clothes. I'm really not used to running around nearly naked.'

'Not for the moment. We prefer you like that and you're less inclined to go walkabout with no clothes on.'

'Oh. But how many others are there here?'

'Five. Sandy's asleep in the next cabin, so try not to wake her. Then there's Gilbert, who's a mute and shares with Charlie in the stern cabin, then Andy and Lara in the cabin over the other side from here.'

'Oh, so Gilbert and Charlie are a gay couple. Are Andy and Lara straight, or are they gay too?'

I had to laugh. 'No, Charlie is a girl and Gilbert is an outcast, highly educated Eurasian Islander. Andy and Lara are.....well, you'll find out when they get up. They're all asleep at the moment'

Just then a sleepy voice sounded from the cabin next door, so I stepped through. 'All of them are asleep except for the crew who drove this barge all fucking night, and then gets woken by my man chatting up a new female and naturally she's nearly naked as well. Good on ya, Harry. I'm glad to see you haven't lost your touch. I guess you must be Dell. I'm Sandy and welcome aboard.'

Sandy sat up, the sheet spilling down and showing her own bare breasts, both ladies eyeing each other off appraisingly.

'I must say, Harry, you do pick the nicest sort of prisoner to drag home. Has she got free run of the boat?'

I nodded, 'Yep. All good and she's promised to be a good girl, haven't you Dell?'

'I did say I'd try,' Dell said with a grin, happy to be able to join in a bit of light-hearted banter for a change.

'Geeze. Not too good I hope,' was Sandy's response. 'A girl's gotta have some fun occasionally. I'm not getting much joy from old grumpy-bum here at the moment.'

Dell giggled. 'You two are funny. Good to meet you too, Sandy. I guess you've been boat-sitting the last few days?'

'Yep, that's me. Resident boat-sitter. Which reminds me, I've got to pee as well so I'll go first seeing as you too have been flapping your gums for so long, you can't be busting as much as I am.'

With that pronouncement, Sandy slid decorously out of bed, smiled at Dell and padded aft, unconcernedly naked which is normal for Sandy and me on our side of the boat.

I mentioned this fact to Dell who was still eyeing off Sandy's firm bum as she walked away.

'That's one of the reasons why I suggested you stay as you are. It's normal on board and much more comfortable in the heat. Anyway, when Sandy's finished, go do what you need to, then come up to the saloon where the galley is and I'll show you where stuff is.'

She nodded and made to go, but then asked, 'If everyone's asleep, who's driving the boat?'

I laughed, 'Oh, that's George the Autopilot. He never argues, never strikes for better conditions, never complains and never gets sleepy. And doesn't belong to a Union either,' I added cheekily.

'Ha, ha! But what if something gets in the way?'

'Ah. That's when his mate, the radar, will tell him to change course to miss it.'

'Clever stuff. I can't wait to see more.'

Sandy came back, the two girls passing in the narrow corridor, where Sandy gave Dell a pat of encouragement or something, although the place she patted her wasn't the usual place for a casual pat and would have earned me a smack if I'd tried it, but Dell seemed to thoroughly enjoy it. It occurred to me that Sandy was proving to be a real magnet for ladies who seem to like to have a bit of a play both ways.

With Sandy back in bed, waiting for her mug of tea, I showed Dell around the galley and she proved quite competent, whipping up a beautiful omelette in minutes without messing up every pan in the galley like I would have. She made one for me as well and I ripped in, as soon as I'd delivered the necessary mug of tea to my lady below.

We ate out in the cockpit and Dell was fascinated with the vast spread of sail we had set to assist the one engine, and which were pulling nicely in the light breeze. She also was taken with the layout of what she could see of *Firebird* and the green-clothed, rugged high ground in the misty distance off our starboard side.

'Where are we?' she asked, finishing off the last crumbs of omelette.

'That's Bima over there in general, and the rough stuff poking up is the remains of a large volcano. There are lots of them around here and not all are extinct!'

She changed tack with her questions, and I was to find out in the coming days that her mind worked quickly and was capable of processing a prodigious amount of information all at once.

'So it looks like you live on this boat full-time? Does Sandy as well?'

'Yep. And my two cats. You've met Jasper, but there's also a black kitten called Krazy. She's probably in bed with one of the other couples.'

'Ok. That's good. I actually do like cats, but it'd be nice if Jasper wasn't actually guarding me all the time. It'd be nice if he and I could be friends. Is that possible?'

I tried to look as though I was thinking deep and meaningful thoughts. 'Hmm...maybe. Behave yourself today and maybe I'll introduce you properly. But if I do, be warned Jasper will be told the limits of your freedom.'

She frowned at that, but then said, 'Oh well. At least it'll be an improvement on my current situation, but you told me there were four more people aboard. Will I sleep in the same cabin that I was in earlier?'

I smiled. 'Yes, you'll sleep there and we'll just have to live with the privacy thing. We've had both males and females up there before and it seems to work out all right, so long as modesty is largely ignored for the duration.'

She grinned. 'After chatting with Sandy, I can live with it if you guys can.'

I smiled cryptically, 'Sandy usually makes sure we do.'

As a distraction, Lara appeared, Krazy dancing about her feet demanding food. She was fetchingly dressed in sleeping attire consisting of a short T-shirt and panties.

'Oh, hello,' she said brightly, 'a fresh face. I'm Lara.'

Dell's eyes widened as she stood and shook hands with the older woman, 'Oh, crap! You're the lady Xavier's men have been chasing all over the Gold Coast. How come you're here? Teleportation?'

Lara laughed easily, 'No, silly. The whole thing was a set-up from the start when we knew what Xavier was up to, so I had a stand-in. A Queensland Policewoman who looked enough like me to fool someone who'd only seen me at a distance. A long wig on her and 'voila' — an instant double for the stumblebums to chase.'

'Bloody hell! Xavier will have a cardiac arrest when he finds out. He spent a fortune organising the surveillance thing, waiting for..... hang on. If you're here, where's...'

With the perfect timing which the best actors and pollies seem to be born with, Andy stepped into view, wearing just a pair of ragged shorts and a three-day-old beard.

'I presume that'd be me you're about to refer to, and I'm right here where I've been for some time!'

Dell stared silently for a few moments and then broke out into helpless laughter. When she recovered a bit, she gasped, 'Have you any idea how many people and how much money has been spent looking for you? They've been going nuts running around in circles and still are. I'm so glad I'm out of all that bullshit.'

She stepped forward, hand outstretched, 'I'm happy to say I'm very pleased to meet you, sir, and very glad you're safe and well. I can see Xavier and his crew have grossly underestimated you.'

Andy grinned and shook her hand. 'Pleased to meet you too, Dell, but do drop the sir. I'm just Andy, especially in such close quarters and with your delightful dress style. It's even more informal than mine!'

He copped a friendly smack on his arm from a grinning Lara for the comment, but continued, 'I believe you've been helping Harry sort out this mess and I thank you for that. But I have to say, all the credit is due to Harry for planning and arranging this highly entertaining way to hide me away from public scrutiny for a while.'

Dell giggled at his cheerful byplay, 'Thanks Andy. Harry convinced me to dress down and I'm glad to see that I fit in.'

In short order, first Charlie, then Gilbert appeared and joined the party after making mugs of coffee, their preference, and were introduced to Dell. Her eyes went wide again at the sight of Gilbert and she was obviously interested in him, much to Charlie's amusement.

Dell broke off that scrutiny and looked at me, 'I have to ask. What's happened to Xavier? If he knew Andy and Lara were here, he'd go nuts.'

I grinned and Andy spoke for me. 'He's right over there on *Seeker* and you're right, he did go nuts when Lara and I walked in on him. So much so, our highly-competent Doctor thought he was on the verge of a coronary, but I think he's settled down now.'

She looked at me again. 'Did he manage to add much to what I told you?'

'Up to the time we left, he hadn't, but Corrine was due to have another session with him this morning. There had been several references to Lord Howe Island and the house there. If there's anything else you might remember about it, it would help a lot. It seems there's something strange going on there, and we might have to make a visit to find out.'

'Okay, I'll certainly try to remember something. But what's going to happen to me?' She asked. Her upbeat mood slipping as she contemplated a bleak future in the Witness Protection Program, after a dangerous period while the court case against the Union heavyweights was happening.

'Well, I can finally tell you something about that. You were supposed to be sent back to Canberra under ACP Protective Custody along with Andy, Lara, Charlie and Gilbert when they fly out from Darwin on a RAAF VIP flight.'

Her face fell at the thought of being back in the clutches of civilisation and the attendant hazards of the union people she'd betrayed to the authorities.

I saw the change to her expression and hastily added, 'But! My people in the ACP have suggested that for now, you would be much safer if kept as isolated as possible until your testimony is needed. Therefore, they've asked me to keep you aboard until the formal charges have been laid on the various bad guys and the legal processes have ground into gear. They have a lot to go on with, but will need further statements and even depositions from you, but we have all the facilities on board to take care of those remotely, and it helps that Sandy is a serving Queensland Police Inspector.

So there you are, like it or not, you're staying aboard for a fair while longer.'

I was expecting a howl of protest and was therefore totally unprepared for the flood of tears, her warm body pressed firmly against mine, arms wrapped around my neck and tears running down my face and chest.

'Oh, thank you Harry. I don't know how you did it, but I've been so worried about being sent back to Australia where I know how easily the union guys can grab people and make them disappear. This has just relieved my mind so much it's like having a nightmare turn into a good dream!'

There was a chuckle behind me as Sandy arrived. 'Bloody hell, Harry. You really can't stop molesting the prisoner, can you? I'm sure there's a police regulation I've read which covers it, so perhaps you should disengage yourself from that naked young lady and re-arrange that tail-on-backwards which is interfering with the shape of your shorts.'

I laughed and gently pried a reluctant Dell off me, whereupon she transferred herself to Sandy. I wouldn't have thought the news warranted such a response, but who can tell.

'The other thing I hadn't passed on is; we're going into Bima City to clear outbound Customs. Just Dave and I will go ashore to take care of the formalities, but I'll need your passports and some extra photos from each of you. We'll be there in an hour or so, and there'll be no mention about calling in at Gili Montang or Komodo Dragons.

After we've put Xavier ashore, we'll be heading straight past the west tip of Timor and then to Darwin. It'll take two or three days for that run.'

Everyone was happy with that arrangement, and drifted off to collect their documents.

CHAPTER 50

The new clearance procedures for yachts entering and departing Indonesian waters made the process for us much easier. Forewarned about having multiple copies of everything including photos of all crew and a good supply of currency, overcame any possible problem and the surprisingly genial Port Captain and Customs Official processed our papers in an efficient manner.

We made a show of wanting to contribute to their retirement fund and this helped to restrict the number of questions about our movements to a minimum. We were able to honestly show our course south east past Komodo Island and just west of Timor to exit Indonesian jurisdiction as quickly as possible, and in answer to the question, 'Do you intend to make any stops on the way?' we both lied with straight faces. We happily praised the quality of the diving and the hospitality of the people and left the offices with our clearance papers all in order and the best wishes of the officials ringing in our ears.

I commented to Dave how they should be happy, having each just received about six months' extra pay!

Back aboard, we exited the well-protected harbour surrounded by rugged hills with almost indecent haste. In truth, we were all keen to finish up this less-pleasant side of the last few days and put sea-miles behind us, heading for the familiar and comforting territory of Australia. As there were still 83 nautical miles to go to Gili Montang where we'd be finally rid of Xavier, we wouldn't be there until late afternoon. So before we left, I crossed over to *Seeker* for the first part of the trip, leaving *Firebird* in the capable hands of Gilbert and Sandy.

I sat down with Corrine and asked, 'How's it gone with Xavier?'

'Ha!' she barked a short laugh. 'It took Alex to hold the slimy bugger down while I shot him up with my jungle juice, but he gave up very little extra. Mostly because he knows something unpleasant is going to happen, but also he's had training to resist the urge to talk which is the basic way this drug functions. So, he's pretty much a shot duck as far as I'm concerned.'

'Bugger! What about his papers? Have you had a chance to go through them yet?'

She smiled, 'Yeah! That's been a much more productive exercise! But to summarise for you, there's evidence to suggest maybe Lord Howe Island is part of a rare, precious gem smuggling operation. The rocks are taken to the mainland, then on-sold world-wide.

Xavier's house on Lord Howe is the collection point and it looks like the caretakers Dell mentioned are active guards as well.'

'Was there mention of where the rocks come from?'

'Nah. As they're stolen from the mines by individual miners, there's no paper trail. Maybe an expert can say what area or even what mine a particular stone comes from, but there's nothing in the files to say that. The delivery method is they're dropped over the side of a cargo ship at night a few miles off the coast with a radio beacon fitted and are picked up by a couple of bent fishermen. There's a drop roughly every month.'

'How have they managed to keep an operation like that quiet? It's only a small population on the island, so someone must have noticed odd goings on.'

Corrine shrugged, 'Dunno, boss. Maybe Xavier and his thugs used their special brand of diplomacy and scared the shit out of everyone who looked like they were going to protest.'

I thought a moment. 'Yeah. That'd fit his style, wouldn't it? Anyway, so you reckon he's been wrung out as much as possible?'

'Yep! Nothing more to get there. I've got more papers to go through, so there may be some gems still to come, excuse the pun, but certainly not from Mr Johnson.'

'OK. I'll pass the information about the rare gems onto my people, if you'll keep looking at his papers. We should be at Montang Island by 16:30 or 17:00. I can't wait to get rid of the prick.'

'Amen, boss. With you on that!'

I thought a moment about what she'd said. 'How about I bung in a call to Mr Jacobs, asking why someone would try to smuggle precious stones into Australia when there are no particular restrictions on legal imports.'

'Yeah. Good idea. Might save us some time and a lot of speculation, so that'll make it worth it.'

Jacobs' Fine Jewellery, good afternoon, this is Miriam.'

'Hi Miriam. This is Harry Stevens. We met you on our visit a few weeks ago.'

'Of course, Mr Stevens. Delighted to hear from you again. I'm afraid I've nothing more to report about your amazing stones, except that they are in the hands of the auction house assessors, who are more excited about them than we've seen before. They keep calling them, "the find of the century!" Which bodes well for the auction and the eventual sale price. Oh, and there have been some officially, unofficial leaks to the industry about a fantastic new find as well as hints about the "cursed double triplets"! Already, collectors, as well as several major museums are showing strong interest in bidding.

The auction house, the same one as last time, are holding off printing the catalogue until the very last moment to keep everyone guessing, since the printers are the worst people to keep a secret! But that's all I can tell you for now, I'm sorry.'

'No problem, Miriam. That's welcome news. But the main reason for my call was to ask you and your grandfather about smuggling rare gems into Australia. As in, why would anyone bother to do it?'

She laughed. *'My Grandfather is not here at the moment, Mr Stevens, but perhaps I can answer the question if you don't mind, since it is a topic which comes up from time to time. The answer is, as you say, there isn't much incentive to smuggle gems into Australia apart from saving some customs duty, but it's generally not much anyway.*'

Mentally, I groaned to hear that, because it left the reason for Xavier's interest in Lord Howe Island still a mystery. But then she went on.

'Of course, there is an exception to the rule. If a quantity of special rare gems were to be smuggled directly out of the mines, without being processed through the cartel system, that would be a different matter. It's the cartel which regulates the movement and sales of all gemstones to keep demand high and prices stable. Rogue gems are being circulated all the time, but tight security at the mines minimises the number getting away.

In the industry, we hate rogue gems as they mess with the stability of prices, and in a worst-case scenario, could slash a lot of the value off precious gems overnight if a large quantity of gems were dumped onto the market all at once.'

'Yes, I can understand that. But you're saying, if there were enough of these 'rogue gems' available, then it would be worthwhile setting up a pipeline, so to speak, to move the gems far from their source.'

'Yes. That sums up the situation quite well. If there is a smuggling operation happening right now, then there must be not just a good collection of rare gemstones available to move, but the ways and means to extract them on a regular basis from the mines without tripping over security. Is this just an idle question, Mr Stevens, or do you have knowledge of such an operation?'.

'We've uncovered some hints and references to such an operation, but nothing confirmed so far, I'm afraid, so we're investigating further.'

'Ah...May I ask if this would be an official investigation?'

I laughed, 'It is actually semi-official, in that the relevant authorities have asked us to quietly look into a possible smuggling operation.'

'My goodness, Mr Stevens. You do lead an exciting life. I suppose it's a waste of breath asking you to be careful?'

'Yeah. I'm afraid so. We just do what we have to do and try to plan better than the other guys.'

On that cheerful note, we parted verbal company, with Miriam promising to pass all my information onto her grandfather as soon as he came back and to have him call if he came up with anything useful.

I stayed on *Seeker* for the rest of the run to Montang and when we came close, had Dave take the lead while I directed him to a pretty little bay, with a white sandy beach on the north eastern tip of the small island which was roughly 4 kilometres by 3 kilometres in size. The shallow, sandy bottom was clear of rocks, so I had Dave nose *Seeker* gently in until the bow grounded softly within a few metres of the water's edge.

I asked Bree bring up a few large pieces of casserole beef she'd been thawing ready for the evening meal, and with a grenade-throwing action, I threw the meat chunks as far as I could in amongst a collection of green bushes which grew on the beach itself.

The results were fast and frighteningly effective as two huge lizards scooted out from shelter and snatched up the meat, swallowing it all in seconds.

'Crap!' exclaimed Corrine who was with me. 'Look at the size of those buggers. That one on the left is an absolute monster. He'd have to be 3-metres long!'

There were similar expressions of amazement from the open doors to the wheelhouse where the rest of the crew were gathered. On the beach, the two huge dragons sniffed at the bloody sand for a few more minutes, then turned and waddled back to the shelter of the bushes.

'OK,' I said to Corrine, 'let's get shit-for-brains up here and get it over with. We'd better blindfold him very tightly, but free his ankles. Oh, and perhaps a few discrete cuts and scratches will speed the process.'

She grinned tightly and went below, Alex in tow. Moments later, there was a minor eruption of yelling and abuse from the forepeak cabin, before the still-naked figure of the once dreaded Xavier Johnson was half-dragged on deck, a blindfold tied tightly around his head, his wrists now tied in front.

Alex led him over to where I was standing in the bow. 'Good afternoon, Xavier. I trust you've had a restful time contemplating your many sins over the last 24-hours?'

'You! You can't do this to me! Who are you anyway?'

'I can tell you now, because I'm about to let you go ashore and I won't see you again. I'm Harry Stevens and I'm the guy you were chasing around Bass Strait while I was looking after two girls and a lady. You remember — you were trying to kidnap them at the time. That makes me the guy who consistently outsmarted you and took out your operatives, including that Cessna floatplane.'

'You arsehole! I'll get free of this place and track you down again. And this time I'll make it permanent.'

'No, I'm afraid not, old mate. But at least I am letting you go.'

'What about some clothes?'

I laughed, 'Not necessary. The place is deserted and there's a lovely sandy beach for you to work on your tan. You'll be right.'

I stepped him up to the railing and opened the hinged section that allowed the anchors to be easily swapped over. I waved my hand behind me and Corrine darted forward, her favourite double-edged flick knife appearing like a black finger in her hand. Almost too fast to follow, her hand flashed and a series of red lines appeared on Xavier's white legs and sagging backside, that rapidly thickened as blood flowed.

He shrieked more in fright than pain, since Corrine's knife was so sharp, it would have felt like he was being tickled.

I spoke quietly into his ear as I held him poised on the edge of the bow. 'There's a short drop into shallow water in front of you, so when I say so, just take a small jump.'

Naturally, before he had time to protest, I pushed him in the back when I said 'Jump' and he let out a howl of fright as he dropped the two metres into the knee-deep water, but as he fell over on landing, there was no risk of broken leg bones.

His first action was to rip the blindfold off, but that took a few fumbles and Dave had *Seeker* smoothly reversing off the beach by the time Xavier had regained his vision and oriented himself. We backed up 50 metres or so, then hung there, morbidly awaiting the situation to resolve itself.

After a stream of screamed abuse which had seagulls flying away in fright, Xavier dragged his naked white and red streaked body out of the water where he collapsed on the glaring white sand. He looked around a few times, taking in the steep, scrubby hills surrounding the beach, before focussing his attention and frustrated anger on the boat and his tormentors who had gathered in the bow to gaze at the deadly action about to unfold.

All his yelling was also helping to attract the attention of the dragons and we knew, with at least two in the bushes, the scent of blood would be driving them crazy.

Within two minutes, the first head appeared, its forked tongue flickering out to taste the air, and although wary of the endless yelling, it was driven by the smell of the blood dripping off Xavier's legs and backside to soak into the pristine sand. It was a big male who was the first to slowly and silently commence to stalk his prey, with what looked like a slightly smaller female following close behind. Two more appeared from the bushes further along and all four slowly converged on their hapless prey who was still sounding off.

At the urging of most of the crew, we didn't stay to see the inevitable, gory result. As the first terrified, agonised howl drifted across the otherwise peaceful bay, I was content that Xavier wouldn't be able to escape the attentions of four dragons and that he was receiving back some of the agony and terror he'd enjoyed inflicting on so many of his victims for so long.

We all resolutely turned our backs on the violent, bloody scene on the beautiful white sand beach, confident that within hours, nothing would remain which could be identified as human. It was therefore, once we were clear of the small island, spirits lifted and passengers were shuffled between the boats based on who had to go to Darwin by the fastest means. *Firebird* ended up with Sandy and I, Bree, Alex and Dell taking our time to track for Darwin for re-fuelling, some 700 nautical miles and 2.5 days away. *Seeker* took Andy, Lara, Charlie and Gilbert to make a high speed to Darwin, to catch their flight south, while Jill and Roger crewed for Dave and Corrine on the run back to the Gold Coast with all the treasure.

EPILOGUE

1

No longer held back to *Firebird's* slow cruising speed, and after dropping her grateful and healthy passengers, *Seeker* made a fast return to the Gold Coast. On the second day after its return, a medium-size furniture removals truck with a crew-cab appeared in the Yacht Club carpark and disgorged five large young men. They used a number of sturdy hand carts to move a series of oddly-shaped wooden boxes, some small and obviously very heavy, while others were quite large and also heavy, from *Seeker's* marina berth to the truck.

Once loaded, and if any of the endlessly speculating patrons of the Yacht Club bar was observant enough, they would have seen the truck appeared to be sitting considerably lower on its suspension than when it arrived. The diminutive, red-headed girl and her tall, well-built blonde male companion who drove out of the carpark in an old Falcon sedan, were not obviously connected to the activity around the truck.

The same two persons entered the jewellery shop in the Southport Mall ten minutes later, to be greeted with old-world courtesy by an attractive, dark-haired young woman. When they produced a letter bearing a familiar signature, she read it swiftly, then excused herself to go to the back of the store, returning moments later with her Grandfather who she introduced as Mr Jacobs, and herself as Miriam.

On being told of the imminent arrival of a truckload of precious goods, the front door was promptly locked and Dave and Corrine ushered out the back, where they discovered there were a series of rooms, the last of which opened onto a rear lane. Dave called the truck driver and told him where to come for the drop-off as the rear entrance was conveniently not marked as belonging to the jewellery store.

Thirty minutes later, the muscular moving crew had placed all the boxes to Mr Jacobs' satisfaction, where he and Miriam could access them without needing to lift anything. Dave paid off the crew in cash, including a healthy bonus, for which they were most grateful.

As they had the master inventory list, Dave and Corrine stayed to assist in opening all the crates and boxes, and making sure their list matched the one generated by the efficient Miriam. Finally, with the sun settling low on the western horizon and the warm, salt-scented Gold Coast evening drawing in, four weary people sat around one of the back rooms surrounded by piles of wood, packing materials and a genuine pirate's cave of treasure. Two of them, the oldest and the youngest, wore bemused expressions as they gazed at the glittering piles of gold, jewellery and normally mundane items items like plates, cups, candelabra, except they were nearly pure gold and in many cases, heavily encrusted with precious jewels. Mr Jacobs had already determined the gems were all genuine precious gems, not just coloured quartz.

Although the entire load of treasure had been brought to Mr Jacobs' shop, he advised the gold ingots would be passed on that evening to Gold Bullion Australia, who had a high security facility located on the Gold Coast, specifically designed for storing large quantities of precious metals. A phone call mentioning the sheer quantity of bullion, secured the promise of a discrete, un-marked armoured truck which would be at the back door in thirty minutes to make the collection.

At the same time, an appointment was made for Dave and Corrine to visit the Miami secure repository the next morning, for a valuation of the hoard. The armoured truck was prompt to the minute and the crew very professional in their method of dealing with large quantities of gold. With photographs taken and inventories signed before the crew departed, it still left many precious items scattered around several rooms.

Now he'd had a chance to view the items first hand, Mr Jacobs swiftly revised his rough estimate of the value of the collection steeply upwards, although he refrained from actually naming a price. He did say that the origins of the collection would attract a much wider range of potential buyers and that in turn, would push the end price much higher. Finally, they had receipts and photos of every individual item and the elated, but weary pair, left Mr Jacobs and Miriam to tidy up and begin the long task of preparing the presentation to the auction house.

Promptly at 10:00 the next morning, Dave and Corrine presented themselves at the discrete and plain frontage of the local branch of Gold Bullion Australia in the suburb of Miami, where they were met by polite and professional staff who discussed the collection of ingots they had retrieved the previous evening. On being told, that at the current spot value of the metal made the hoard worth US$7.12 million, they were delighted and asked if the funds could be split between two accounts at the Bank of Vanuatu. Nothing was a problem and the necessary paperwork was swiftly completed. With business completed, the pair headed north. Dave held off notifying Harry and crew until they were safely back aboard *Seeker* and clear of inquisitive ears!

With nothing else to do until Harry returned, Dave and Corrine slowly went back to their moored routine, getting the big boat back to pristine condition after its long run over to the West Coast, up to Indonesia and back home.

2

Based on the information Corrine had been able to glean from Xavier's papers and notes, Harry and Corrine discussed their findings with Dell and concluded that Corrine's initial assessment of the gem smuggling operation was most likely the truth behind the Lord Howe operation.

Dell added more thoughts about the rushed trip to the island just before she and Xavier went to Indonesia. She had been dragged along as an afterthought by a upset and distracted Xavier and confirmed there was a 3-bedroom house on Lord Howe with two caretakers, male and female, who were very tough. Xavier had a locked room she wasn't allowed to see inside of, but he collected something from the room, before they flew back to the mainland on the next flight. Xavier had several meetings with his caretakers which Dell wasn't supposed to hear, but she caught a few words which indicated a shipment of some description arriving soon. Before they left, a couple of men who looked and smelled like fishermen had come to the house to speak with Xavier, but she didn't hear what they said.

At the time, Dell had thought there might be some sort of smuggling operation happening.

Harry reported their conclusions to his Controller in Canberra and was ordered to make his way to Lord Howe Island with all haste, to discretely investigate what Terry Xavier Johnson might have set up in the way of a rare precious-gem smuggling operation.

He was also instructed to keep Dell Petrie safe, on board and under close scrutiny until her testimony was needed.

Being officially on a new case, Harry decided to take Sandy, Alex and Bree in *Firebird* to Lord Howe Island since he was still looking for Xavier's source of funds and suspected it had been concealed in the house. The presence of the two tough caretakers would hopefully be a relatively minor problem the presence of big Alex could help resolve.

3

Andy and Lara, along with Charlie and Gilbert, left *Seeker* in Darwin and returned to Canberra via an RAAF VIP Challenger jet.

4

Roger and Jill stayed with *Seeker* for the run back to the Gold Coast where they intended to set up the 'Green Gold Herbal Pain Relief Clinic' going 50/50 financially with Corrine and Dave.

5

Charlie and Gilbert stayed in Canberra since Charlie still had her job as the Boss's PA. She introduced Gilbert around Canberra society where he was a huge success, especially with the ladies. After a while, however, he moved to the Gold Coast to assist with the Green Gold Clinic, advising on refining batch strengths and liaising with Mikhail on Herba Island where he made the occasional trip to collect supplies and check on production standards and methods.

6

The only fallout from Xavier's demise was his possible legacy smuggling operation on Lord Howe Island. There were very few Stainless Associates operatives left in Australia and those few quietly faded into the landscape once word filtered down that the boss was dead.

7

In the Honours List at the next Australia Day, Harry was surprised to be told he had been made an 'Officer of the Order of Australia' for 'Distinguished service of a high degree to Australia or to humanity at large', with the specifics of the service rendered left unspecified.

ALSO BY THE AUTHOR
IN THE FIREBIRD SERIES

Harry Stevens, the Middle-Eastern war hero from Hitch-Hikers, the first book in the *Firebird* series, thought that having dinner at the pub and chatting up the waitress was a safe and pleasant way to pass an evening, but circumstances conspire to dump the delivery of a new super-drug as well as a large bag of bikie gang cash in his lap. Assumptions are made, confusions are leapt to, shots are fired, people are dead and Harry finds himself in the middle of a bikie gang war with both sides looking to take him out. And that's not to dinner!

Being on the hit lists of all the Outlaw Motorcycle Clubs in SE Queensland, Harry is forced to run for his life, but not before stocking up on lovely girls, rum and a few select close friends. Harry's mystical giant cat, Jasper once again proves that he's more than worth any two humans in a fight.

Harry, the floating trouble magnet, discovers that being shot in Afghanistan was nothing like being the focus of attention of all the OMC's in South East Queensland. His inventiveness gets the workout of a lifetime as he tries to stay one jump ahead of the bad guys as they form strange alliances to find him.

"This is Book 2 in the Firebird Series, and *Backpackers* leads us on another adventure with a maritime background. All the drama and action we have come to expect from Ian, we are left with just one question... when can we expect book three?"
—Alison Lewis, author of "Missing"

Praise for *Hitchhikers* (Book 1 of the Firebird Series)

"The hero, Harry, when asked what he has been doing lately, answers "Boats, bad guys, bullets and old friends." What he fails to add is — beautiful women, sex, a bad-ass black cat, and Bond type cunning to overcome the bad guys. Piqued your interest? This is a great fast paced read and I am looking forward to the next phase of Harry's life as promised by the author.
—Judith Flitcroft, Author of *Walk Back in Time*.

ALSO BY THE AUTHOR
IN THE FIREBIRD SERIES

Harry Stevens, a Middle Eastern war hero, thought that recovering in Eden with his huge and mystical cat, Jasper, after his catamaran is bashed around by a storm, would be a delightful break from his sailing voyage around Australia. However, the finger of fate in the very pleasant form of an abused, runaway wife and her two lively, wilful and beautiful teenage daughters lands Harry in more trouble than he could ever imagine.

Harry's hopes for a quiet time in this beautiful and peaceful town are shattered as he learns that the psychotic, vengeful husband is pulling out all stops in an effort to locate, not just his wife, but even more so the girls for his own, much darker purposes. Suddenly on the run, Harry is forced to fall back on his natural inventiveness and SAS training to combat an increasingly resourceful foe who shows that there is truly no limit to human lust, greed, depravity and treachery.

Barely staying one step ahead of his pursuers, Harry forms some most unlikely alliances to try to defeat his many opponents with their limitless resources.

"It is always a pleasure to read a new and entertaining series from a first-time Australian author. This novel will take you on one hell of a ride where the goodies are okay and the baddies are really BAD."
—John Morrow's *Pick of the Week*

"The hero, Harry, when asked what he has been doing lately, answers "Boats, bad guys, bullets and old friends." What he fails to add is — beautiful women, sex, a bad-ass black cat, and Bond type cunning to overcome the bad guys. Piqued your interest? This is a great fast paced read and I am looking forward to the next phase of Harry's life as promised by the author.
—Judith Flitcroft, Author of *Walk Back in Time*.

ALSO BY THE AUTHOR
IN THE FIREBIRD SERIES

An Eco-terrorist organisation formed with lofty ideals...a ratbag wealthy industrialist egomaniac...a plot to overturn the entire Australian political process...a major natural gas processing plant at risk...a giant crocodile...RAN patrol boats...an assassination contract targeting the PM. All the ingredients for a Firebird cocktail...definitely shaken, not stirred!

Book 3 in the Firebird series sees the Special Marine Strike Force (SMSF) head for the Pilbara to deliver their own special brand of mayhem and retribution on the bad guys.